# FAMILY RECIPES:

A Novel about Italian Culture, Catholic
Guilt and the Culinary Crime of the Century

## MIKE CONSOL

The following is a work of fiction. Though it includes the names of actual people, businesses, organizations, institutions and locations, the stories told are purely the product of the author's imagination. Any resemblance to actual events is accidental.

Copyright © 2022 Mike Consol All rights reserved. No part of this publication may be reproduced, distributed, or transmitted in any form or by any means, including photocopying, recording, or other electronic or mechanical methods, without the prior written permission of the publisher, except in the case of brief quotations embodied in critical reviews and certain other noncommercial uses permitted by copyright law.

ISBN: 978-1-66784-056-7
eBook ISBN: 978-1-66784-057-4

*To my big Italian family for filling my life with
so many colorful and dramatic experiences it was
impossible not to write this book.*

The following is a work of fiction. Though it includes the names of actual people, businesses, organizations, institutions and locations, the stories told are purely the product of the author's imagination. Any resemblance to actual events is accidental.

# THE OBSESSION

Food is an American phenomenon. It has replaced sex as the nation's chief form of intimacy. We take it in our mouths, masticate it with our teeth, maul it with our tongues and swallow it into our bodies. It's second only to the weather as a topic of conversation between strangers and casual acquaintances.

A fine meal is a mandatory accompaniment to any romantic encounter. An aptitude for cooking and food preparation is the most essential talent a spouse can bring to marriage. It's often used to spice up our sex lives. Frank Sinatra famously ate a ham-and-egg breakfast off the chest of a Las Vegas call girl. Less famous lovers dip and smear genitalia with flavored oils, lotions and syrups. I once gnawed a pair of edible panties off my wife's pelvis.

Friends wouldn't think of sharing significant moments without breaking bread. Food is so abundant in post-industrial societies that eating isn't strictly about subsistence anymore, it has become recreation. Most of us cannot fathom missing a meal. Doing so creates the illusion that we have entered a state of starvation. Being deprived of food is a popular form of torture. Trying to lose weight by restricting calories is a page straight out of the *Masochist's Handbook*.

Nothing provides more abiding enjoyment than eating. We can dine repeatedly without diminished pleasure. We indulge several times a day without having to think about it. Food is something even the most disciplined among us simply cannot resist. Our favorite meals are more addicting than tobacco, alcohol and firearms, as well as controlled and illegal drugs.

Food gives us comfort. Light, chilled dishes cool our bodies in the summer. Hot, dense entrees warm us during winter.

The variety of ethnic cuisines and their styles of preparation stagger the palate. We bake, barbecue, broil, fry, grill, roast, sauté, sear, steam, microwave, fondue and flambé them. Certain foods are even given magical qualities, such a chocolate, garlic, truffles and red hot chili peppers. Just thinking about food makes mouths water and stomachs growl in the language of visceral desire. No aroma is more heavenly than a meal in preparation.

There's no stopping America's all-you-can eat gluttony. Breakfast, lunch, dinner, desserts and in-between-meal snacks are so prevalent that 30 percent of us have eaten and waddled our way into obesity. Another 30 percent of us are clinically overweight and well on our way to joining the rotund ranks of the obese.

Food is a matter of life and death.

I should know. My name is Mickey Marciano, and food is my life. I cook and tend bar at my brother Vinny's restaurant. It's called Marciano's Mangia House and it is, without a doubt, the most successful Italian restaurant in all of upstate New York. The restaurant's sterling reputation spans the state and brings diners from Buffalo and Niagra Falls, Syracuse and Rochester, Albany and Poughkeepsie — and even from the Big Apple itself, the world's supreme restaurant market. Our menu and monumental success is built upon two dozen secret family recipes brought from Italy to the New World by our immigrant grandparents. We pack the joint nightly and rake in a cash flow that would make an old-fashioned Latin American drug cartel proud. This is a family-run operation in the truest sense of the term. Marciano's belongs to Vinny lock, stock and barrel, and every key position is filled by a family member. Our parents and siblings all work here. We all draw fat salaries that keep us in living in big homes and driving late-model automobiles.

While I uncork bottles of wine, draw beers and polish down the bar, my sister Ginger plays hostess, escorting famished diners a group at a time into the enormous dining room, made to feel even more spacious by its 25-foot high ceiling and crown molding. Sister Maria runs the dining room as head waitress, and sister Angie keeps the books and manages inventory. Brother Ringo stretches and dresses the dough for our legendary pizzas. Mother Margherita and father Albie are on the cooking line, slaving over hot stoves, boiling kettles and sizzling sauté pans. Vinny is the floater. He jumps in whenever and wherever needed. Mostly, though, he has a good time playing master of ceremonies with our many regular customers, and telling everyone to *Mangia! Mangia!* — butchered Italian for *Eat! Eat!*

He visits me at the bar often so I can blend his favorite drinks and light his cigars.

Then there is the most important Marciano of them all, Uncle Nunzio, the founder of Marciano's Mangia House and the final word on all matters pertaining to food, beverage and Italian pride and culture. He is the family's undisputed leader and vanguard of the secret recipes, upon which the business has flourished for more than half a century. They are the family's secret covenant, and he is Grand Master of their clandestine preparation.

# THE FAMILY

One couldn't help but have concluded that Uncle Nunzio was predestined to play a lifelong role as culinary wizard and restaurateur. From his early teens he was standing next to the stove, at his mother's elbow, getting splattered with hot grease, asking questions, helping her cook and being called a "femme" by his jeering brothers. Nunzio would not be deterred. He was fascinated by food's plant, animal and mineral origins, and how they could be paired and fused in ways that electrified the taste buds. The universality of food was remarkable to him. It was the most significant thing all living entities had in common — the need to consume nutrition.

The old woman never tired of giving her protégé detailed explanations of food combinations, cooking temperatures, culinary styles and the proper use of kitchen utensils. She taught her son the treasured family recipes hailing from a mountainous Abruzzo Province east of Rome and dating back numerous generations. Nunzio started with simple sauces and salads. But soon he was grilling fish and making layered dishes such as lasagna and various parmagianas. Then he was sculpting and frying meatballs and mixing and squeezing dough for homemade pasta. As his skills and confidence with cookery improved, Nunzio eventually prepared complete family dinners on his own.

World War II took Nunzio off to the military and a U.S. Army post in New Guinea, where he played a starring role in the mess hall. He proved himself a crackerjack chef and baker. Nunzio became more addicted than ever to the power of food and the outpouring of attention it could earn its purveyor. What could be more fulfilling than earning your keep making people plump and happy, he decided. What could be a more basic and noble endeavor than providing life-giving nourishment to mankind?

"An Army runs on its stomach," the post's commanding officer continually reminded Nunzio.

When the war ended he returned home and announced his intention to open a restaurant bearing the Marciano appellation and family crest. Parents and siblings rallied around the idea, pulling together the modest sums of money at their disposal to put Nunzio into business. The largest portion of the venture's startup capital was provided by his parents. Just prior to handing over the bankroll that was the realization of Nunzio's dream, Grandma Marciano swore her son to eternal secrecy about the family recipes. Generations of family member had protected them for posterity's benefit, Grandma Marciano told her son in harshly accented English, and the recipes were never to escape the family circle.

Nunzio kissed his mother's hand and said, "I'm a good Italian boy, mama. You know I would never betray the family. Besides, you would slaughter me like a fatted calf if I ever shot my mouth off."

And with that, Grandma Marciano rolled the tightly wound wheel of money across the table and into Nunzio's dough-encrusted hands.

He leased a building picturesquely situated on the northern bank of the Susquehanna River. The year was 1946. The place filled quickly and the dishes it served were greeted with gluttony and superlatives. The Mangia House's reputation fanned out across the region. Word eventually reached the food connoisseurs of Manhattan. Even members of the snobbish New York City restaurant scene made pilgrimages to get a grasp on how an upstate restaurant located 200 miles northwest of the center of the food universe could be causing such a stir.

Uncle Nunzio's stature grew. Despite the grinding six-day-a-week work schedule, it seemed the Great Man would go forever.

Then along came a 2,000-year-old malady known as gout.

Albie and Margharita Marciano took too seriously the biblical decree to be fruitful and multiply. No sooner were the nuptials completed than they got busy procreating. The fruits of their furious efforts sprang forth a mere nine months after their wedding date in the form a daughter they named Fiona, who later renamed herself Ginger after the ship-wrecked and breathy glamor-girl played by Tina Louise on the television series *Gilligan's Island*.

Albie was a science teacher at the local middle school, during an era when it was still legally defensible to physically assault students who didn't do what they were told. Father accumulated a well-worn reputation for strong-arming and bitch-slapping errant pupils. Margherita was a frazzled mother and housewife. She escaped the pressures of child rearing by watching soap operas and Downy commercials.

Both parents came of age during the Great Depression. The lessons of those days seared my parents in different ways. For Albie, it left the indelible impression that the world was hampered by two critical shortages: food and money. He would spend the rest of his life stockpiling and consuming as much of those items as humanly possible.

For Margherita, it meant agonizing over all decisions, big and small, because one never knew what kind of disaster a wrong choice could trigger. She instilled the same indecisiveness and fear of change in her children.

Albie and Margherita became a couple after mutual friends hooked them up for a blind date. Having just returned from his tour of duty as a communications specialist in World War II, Albie wore his Army uniform for the occasion. Margherita was in a bright summer dress. She thought Albie looked manly and intelligent in his crisp uniform and wire-framed glasses.

Albie found Margherita's puckered little mouth a source of lust.

"What do you like to do for fun?" Albie asked

"Oh, I don't know," Margherita said. "Just about anything."

As droll as their exchanges were, a blue spark of intimacy was taking shape between them.

Soon they were wrapped in the bonds of holy matrimony. The nuptials were subdued and auspicious. The marriage stood a high probability of success, based on Albie's industrious and self-disciplined nature, and Margherita's aversion to change.

Fiona "Ginger" Marciano, the first conceived of their six children, was born with the glamour gene. From her earliest day Ginger sought the limelight and yearned to be rich and famous beyond definition. It was part of a syndrome common to first-born children who are showered with unprecedented quantities of attention. It created an emotional addiction that required constant feeding, yet could never be satiated.

She became a devotee of the *fake-it-until-you-make-it* motivational movement. She felt perfectly natural pretending to be something she was not.

"Don't be who you are," she told her younger sisters, "be who you want to be."

Ginger did exactly that, carrying herself like a Hollywood starlet, believing life wasn't really worth living unless it was done in the limelight. Her every stride, her every glance, facial expression and movement was done under the gaze of imaginary motion picture cameras. Ginger fancied herself being watched by millions.

She patterned herself after Twiggy and Cher. Twiggy because of the fame and glamour she achieved as a British supermodel; Cher because she was a multi-talented screen and music star who, like Ginger, wore her black hair very long and ramrod straight. Wistfully, she watched the *Sonny & Cher Comedy Hour* every week.

Good posture was practiced by walking around the house with an algebra textbook balanced on the crown of her head.

On the advice of a bestselling self-help book, Ginger sat down one day and wrote her own obituary that summed up the life she was convinced she would live. It was a lavish treatment of a career celebrated by fans the world over. There was a modeling career, movie roles, product endorsements, television commercials, magazine covers, a ride on a Rose Parade float, semi-nude spreads in Playboy and Penthouse, USO shows for the troops overseas, high-profile affairs with Paul McCartney and a U.S. president, coffee table picture books of her life, and a widely reported meeting with the Queen Elizabeth of England and her Royal Family. In time, marriage to one of Hollywood's leading men came along. They sired three daughters blessed with special talents that seemed certain to carry on Ginger's legacy. There was even speculation of a family dynasty in the making. She died peacefully in her sleep, while taking a mid-day nap on a chaise lounge in her sumptuously appointed home in Pacific Palisades, California. She was 100 years old and still so picturesque in her death scene — clad in a lacy Victorian blouse and Versace wool skirt — that snapshots of her final resting place were released to the media. A quote from the *New York Times* read: "Ginger Marciano established herself as the century's undisputed archetype of female class and beauty."

Unabashed by the grandeur of her dreams, Ginger handed the mock obit to her high school English teacher and said, "Well … what do you think?"

After carefully regarding the typewritten treatise, the instructor replied, "You forgot to credit yourself with eradicating world hunger."

"Let's not go overboard," Ginger said, taking back the sheet of paper. "It's important that I be modest."

All this carrying on led her high school classmates to conclude that Ginger Marciano was hopelessly stuck up and delusional. Sisters Angie and Maria had theories about adoption.

Though many boys were attracted to Ginger, she condescended to date a very few. None of the boys at her Catholic high school measured up; not for a girl was fantasized about having *Casablanca*'s Humphrey Bogart or *Star Trek*'s Captain Kirk riding roughshod atop her. The boys she did date were strictly props, and she certainly didn't sleep with any of them. It was all part of her attempt to create an aura of unattainability. Just like real divas of the Silver Screen, Ginger wanted to be a fantasy that was beyond the reach of the men who desired her.

By time she donned her cap and gown and was handed her high school diploma, Ginger had decided that fashion modeling would be her first act, the wedge that pried open the door to the entire entertainment industry. By Ginger's estimation she possessed three of the four requisites for being a supermodel — a thin figure, small breasts and poise. The missing characteristic was height, which she figured could be overcome with a very steep pair of stiletto heels. An "education" loan was secured and she headed to a Chicago-based school named after a once-popular model who had gotten too varicose to keep strutting runways. Midway through Ginger's second semester the school went bankrupt and closed its doors.

So Ginger exited modeling as fast as she had entered it. Still, she never lost that sense that life was being lived under the unblinking eye of the motion picture camera. She continued to be supremely self-conscious, dressing and behaving as though her life was being viewed by the multitudes.

Before long, Ginger was in her thirties and fixated on staving off the ravages of aging. There was a stubborn refusal to look her age. She wore revealing fashions, moisturized twice daily, ate plant-based vegetarian foods, avoided sunlight, quit smoking, limited herself to just a few drinks a week, exercised daily on her Nordic Track, drove a sporty car, took vitamins, laughed often, listened to subliminal tapes and treated all ailments with herbal remedies.

Ringo was a problem child from the time adoring faces peered into his incubated crib on the day of his birth and prophesized that he would one day become President of the United States. Not only did he lack any interest in the nation's top job, Ringo didn't want to be employed at all. He was flat-out allergic to work. When, later in life, he discovered that a disease known as chronic fatigue syndrome existed, he immediately claimed that as his affliction. Subsequent medical tests for auto-immune disease proved that was not the case, leading us to conclude what we had assumed all along — that our brother was simply lazy. Exertions of all kinds were avoided so fervently that he expended more energy evading work assignments than would have been required to actually complete the task.

Happiness would have been to spending his life sitting in front of the TV set watching sports programming and sponging off the Marciano family welfare system. Alas, parents and siblings organized several career interventions that consisted of hounding and shaming Ringo into eventually agreeing to work in the safe and forgiving bosom of the family business.

Oddly enough, Ringo was Ginger's polar opposite. While his older sister sought public attention and eternal youth, Ringo was an artless and tortured soul who made no bones about the fact that he didn't like his fellow man, preferred anonymity and wanted to die young. It annoyed him that our family had good genes. Heredity suggested Ringo's expiration date wouldn't come due until his early-80's, not accounting for advances in medical technology. Measures were taken to counteract that by pursuing a lifestyle designed to precipitate his demise. He ate to excess, overslept, didn't exercise, never visited doctors and prayed for the Grim Reaper to pay him a silent and painless visitation.

Ringo's philosophy was simple: Life on planet Earth was the fire and brimstone of biblical lore, and he was fully engulfed in the conflagration. He found comfort in the Catholic religion's promise of heavenly rewards heaped upon the deceased. With such bliss awaiting us in the afterlife, he reasoned, why prolong the journey? Suicide was contemplated and threatened when he wanted the family's undivided attention and solace. We called upon wisdom of Father Benito Saragusa, head priest at Our Lady of the Immaculate Conception. The preacher read grave scriptural passages to Ringo that warned of the seriousness and eternal consequences of taking one's own life.

Such revelations didn't do much for Ringo's mood. Frowned upon by the Almighty, Ringo dropped suicide as a viable option (though he continued to play the topic as a conversational trump card).

In a family rife with hot tempers, Ringo had the most volcanic temper of us all. Having to work or disruptions to his clockwork-like daily routines were two excellent reasons to go ballistic. Nothing sent Ringo into intergalactic orbit more readily than disagreeing with his premise that he was "different" than the rest of humanity. Ringo insisted he was abnormal — handicapped, in fact, the victim of a chemical imbalance that severely limited his capacity for happiness. He often made mention of his "handicap" in hopes of provoking us into disagreement so he could let loose with one of his King Kong-like shouting fits and then storm off for a nap or communion with his television set. Whatever Ringo lacked in happiness hormones was more than made up for in vocal chords. He had a yell that could tear roof off most wood-frame structures. We avoided hearing loss by learning to ignore or simply humor him by wholeheartedly agreeing with his hypotheses.

One of the most controversial events of Marciano family life was sister Maria's decision to marry. It wasn't the act of marriage itself, but who she married that caused a family crisis.

Maria's attraction to men the size and strength of Hercules sent her hurtling towards the altar with a sizable Sicilian named Shekko Lombardi. My brother-in-law's style with everyone he brushed up against was purely confrontational. That didn't matter to Maria, who liked her men big, strong, bellicose and chauvinistic. Nothing refreshed my sister's sexual passions more urgently than being physically dominated by the male of the species. That domination took forms ranging from general manhandling to being forced to participate in unusual bedroom acts still outlawed in several southern U.S. states.

Despite its fetishes, the marriage sailed along, both partners getting what they wanted. It tripped over just one crisis, a suspected affair. Shekko was making a routine rummage through Maria's purse when he intercepted a light-blue square of folded paper that contained, in Maria's handwriting, one three-letter word: *Wet*. It was the very word Maria once used at the start of their relationship, in writing, on a slip of paper, to shyly communicate her state of arousal. Shekko naturally took this repeat performance to mean the same — but *who* was this salacious missive destined for? Certainly not him; Maria was long past using indirect communication with her husband. There was an interloper among them, he surmised.

A rage ensued. Several pieces of furniture were busted as he demanded to know the intended recipient of her scandalous note. Maria, hyperventilating for her life, insisted the word was the start of a brief shopping list. Wet, she cried, was shorthand for Wet Wipes, which she used to clean kitchen and bathroom fixtures. But Shekko had already come completely unhinged and would not be that easily appeased. He demanded again and again to know who the note was earmarked for. Maria barely managed to stand by her story.

Shekko wasn't buying it. Over the next few days he conducted an investigation that included a review of the household's phone records. A pattern emerged, a repeating number with a prefix corresponding to the local junior high school where two of the Lombardi's four children were currently being educated. It was the same school where Maria seemed to be participating in unusually frequent parent/teacher conferences. He called the number. A voicemail system answered with the recorded message of a man identifying himself as vice principal Jeremiah Croft. This was the same name Shekko had once heard his wife swoon over while chatting with a girlfriend. The same guy she had met with several times this school year, ostensibly to discuss disciplinary problems with their eldest daughter. Slamming down the phone, Shekko Lombardi dashed to the school. With spittle flying in all directions, he made the acquaintance of the trembling vice principal. Doing his best John Gotti imitation, the madman described several pieces of the educator's anatomy that would be severed from his torso if he ever so much as came within one square acre of his wife.

As a visual demonstration of his promise, Shekko tore a leg off Jeremiah Croft's 300-pound oak desk and waved it maniacally across the air. Anticipating the imminence of death, Croft's eyes starting rolling toward the back of his skull. Shekko departed school grounds moments before two police department squad cars came blaring to the scene.

Jeremiah Croft, standing haplessly behind his busted and slanted desk, told two disbelieving police officers that he had been involved in nothing more than a mild misunderstanding and had no interest in pressing charges.

Angela "Angie" Marciano emerged from the womb on a sub-zero February evening and immediately set the medical community around her into a panic. For reasons still considered a medical mystery, Angie came struggling out of the birth canal with the umbilical cord tightly wound around her neck. The doctor quickly and unceremoniously clipped the cord and unraveled the hang-man's noose off her throat to bring Angie gasping to earthly life.

Whatever the true cause of the shocking condition, it got sister number three off to a bad start in life. Angie has been angry ever since. Indeed, anger was not only my sister's dominant mood it was her constant mood, overriding all other emotions. Though other emotions — such as mirth, melancholy and delirium — could be superimposed over her anger, the anger was always present, like the backdrop of a stage production, impervious to the goings on to the foreground. A particularly keen hostility was directed towards her mother, whom she blamed for tying the hang-man's noose around her infant neck. Margherita denied having committed this supernatural act and instead accused Angie of recklessly goofing around with the umbilical cord during her gestation and inadvertently strapping it around her throat. Daughter would eventually try to have mother charged with attempted murder.

Determined to resolve the post-traumatic stress issues created by her strangulated birth, Angie started aggressively reading the works of legendary psychologists such as Freud, Jung and Pavlov en route to becoming the family's pop psychologist. Her diagnosis was grim: The Marciano family was seriously dysfunctional and sorely in need of individual and group therapy. If this was true, Angie certainly made her contributions to familial disturbance. She was a constant source of worry for my parents, who agonized over her increasing isolation and lack of social life. Angie spent evenings holed up in her apartment crunching down bowls of popcorn and sipping glasses of blood-red merlot while reading books authored by Dr. Arthur Janov. Of particular fascination was his seminal work *The Primal Scream*. She became especially enamored of Dr. Janov, who hypothesized that childhood traumas, including the birthing process, tormented us the remainder of our mortal lives, and that these traumas could be purged from our system. He taught methods for accessing past and forgotten traumas, re-experiencing their horror, then screaming at the top of one's lungs to eradicate them from the nervous system, never to be bothered by them again.

A primal scream, when properly executed, would make the protoplasm in an observer's bloodstream turn to curds and waves. Angie quickly became a Janoff acolyte, embracing his teachings and becoming a serial primal screamer. After the police had twice been called to her place because fellow apartment dwellers thought a homicide was being committed in her unit, Angie started screaming into her pillow. She even made a couple pilgrimages to New York City to meet with the great Dr. Janoff himself and let out a few screams under his watchful supervision. She was led through a regression technique to re-experience coming out of the womb, choking on her own umbilical cord and screaming for her bloody life and psychological well-being.

Despite her most diligent efforts, Angie never managed to cleanse herself of childhood demons. She just kept screaming over the years, convinced she was in a steady state of recovery.

Mother became convinced that what Angie really needed was a man, someone outside herself to focus on and help alleviate the self-obsession. The problem was that Angie wasn't dating. Mother implored Ginger and Maria to intervene by introducing her to a man of her nationality she might wish to settle down with.

It took several years, but Angie did eventually meet someone, though he was an engineer of German extraction named Hans Sprink. Hans worked for a toy company where he was charged with coming up with better, safer and more exciting designs for captivating children.

They ran off to Germany together for Octoberfest. They ate dozens of sausage links and drank gallons of beer. When they returned home they sent mother spiraling into a month of sleepless nights when she announced at a Sunday family dinner that she and Hans had tied the knot the day before at a private ceremony conducted by a Justice of the Peace. One of Hans's college buddies served as witness.

Mother's head started lolling on her neck. "Holy Mary Mother of God," she wailed. "No church. No family. No reception. What the hell kind of ceremony did you have?"

The assignment Ginger and Maria had been entrusted with had been botched in the worst kind of way, mother angrily concluded.

Then she turned to her youngest and most troubled daughter and said: "What's that scream thing you do, Angie, I think I need to try it."

Before mother could swim anymore deeply into the abyss, Angie promised that she and Hans had planned all along to get married again — this time in a big Catholic ceremony followed by a lavish reception and a honeymoon at the Vatican. All but mother knew those plans would never come to pass; they were solely designed to pacify the stricken Margherita.

Angie loved Hans, even though she detested his surname, so she kept the Marciano name as her own. When Hans wasn't around Angie would say, "I can't be a Sprink. That sounds like something you do in the bathroom."

By the time I came along my Italian family was in full chaotic bloom. The household was loud and loving and antagonistic. The air always smelled of garlic sizzling in hot olive oil.

The whirlwind of ethnic living had humiliating consequences. I was an incorrigible bed-wetter. The leakages carried on for years and got so troublesome that father turned to a technical solution. A small gangly salesman toting a large black case paid the house a visit one day. He sat down with my parents and me, and asked us to call him Desmond.

"I understand we have a moisture problem," he said.

"Our son is nine years old and he still wets the bed," my father somberly reported.

I shrank into the sofa cushions.

Desmond looked my way and placed a consoling hand on my knee. "You're not alone little fella. Millions of children have this problem. Some of your friends probably wet the bed and you don't even know it."

Then he mustered a pained expression and confessed, "I used to wet the bed too. That's why I got into this business. I know the agony and the embarrassment of this affliction, and I want to help other young people, like you, to avoid that. I know what it's like to have to skip slumber parties and camping trips for fear this very personal condition could go public. Friends might take notice. Jokes might be told."

Desmond finally removed his hand from my knee and popped the latches on his black case.

"What's your son's name?" he asked my parents, as though I weren't in the room.

"His name is Mickey," mother said.

"Why do you think you urinate in your bed, Mickey?"

Shrinking more deeply in the crevice between the sofa cushions, I shrugged. "I don't know. I have a lot of scary dreams. Maybe they're upsetting me."

Desmond assured me that nightmares were not scaring the piss out of me.

"There are three possible causes of this problem," he said, "a small bladder, deep sleep or a shortage of an anti-diuretic hormone whose name escapes me."

Desmond pulled a set of flash-card diagrams out of his case to assist him in elaborating on the causes of bed wetting. When he finished with the cards he added, "Whatever the case may be, when your bladder fills during the night it should be alerting your 'reticular activating system' and awakening you to go to the bathroom. Your brain is apparently not getting the message. Your signaling mechanism hasn't properly developed. As of now, it's broken."

My father remained his usual stoic self while mother appeared dazed by the salesman's torrent of physiological references.

"Having said all that, let me add there's nothing to worry about because with proper therapy most children can overcome this problem — and fast."

Desmond reached into his bag again and pulled out an electrical box in a rectangular white plastic casing. It had a small light and a black dial on the front. Two wires came out the back, each with an alligator clip on the end. He also took out two flexible metallic sheets about the size of welcome mats. One of the two sheets was perforated with dozens of small, perfectly round holes. The last thing to come out of the bag was a larger white cotton sheet that he slipped in between the two metallic sheets and laid them on the coffee table.

"You are looking at the Bed Wetting Alarm Activation System. It is, without a doubt, the safest and most effective approach to eliminating the predicament we're discussing. In simple terms, this is a bed-wetting alarm. This electrical device will set off an audible buzzer and wake your child up as soon as he begins to pass urine. This is what you call 'negative reinforcement' because it will force Mickey's stubborn little brain to associate releasing his urine with the unpleasant event of being jolted awake."

Desmond leaned back and gave us a *what-do-ya-think-of-them-apples* expression.

"Allow me to demonstrate." Using the alligator clips, he fastened a wire to each metallic sheet. Then he went to his hands and knees to find an electric outlet and plugged in the unit.

"Now," he said, returning to his seat and brushing off the knees of his slacks, "could I trouble the misses for a glass of water without ice?"

Mother hustled off to the kitchen.

Father fingered the metallic and cotton sheets, curious about their consistency. Desmond nodded approvingly. When mother handed the salesman the glass of water, he reached over and turned on the alarm box to full volume. Then he started dipping his fingertips in the water and sprinkling it on the top metallic sheet, the one shot full of holes.

"This is Mickey urinating in the middle of the night," he said. "What you will see is the water making its way through the holes, dampening the cotton sheet in between and creating a harmless electrical connection between the top and bottom sheets."

*Bzzzzzzzzz!*

"Which sets off the alarm!" he shouted to be heard above the din.

*Bzzzzzzzz!*

Desmond looked at me and smiled. "Do you think that will wake you up, Mickey?"

*Bzzzzzzzz!*

My head started bobbing.

"Ha! Ha! Haaa! You *betcha* it will!"

*Bzzzzzzzz!*

Desmond finally switched off the alarm and leaned towards me. "Every time you start to pee, Mickey, this alarm will wake you up before you get more than a few drops out. Then you can finish urinating in the bathroom. Use this system every night and it will train your mind to recognize the sensation you feel just before urination. And your mind, being the amazing organ that it is, will learn to automatically wake you up before you leak and set the alarm off."

"Let's get down to brass tacks," father said. "What are you charging for these gadgets?"

"From our economy to deluxe models, they range in price from thirty-five to sixty dollars."

"Christ almighty," father gurgled, "you're charging a fortune."

Father's outburst caused Desmond to tilt on his sofa cushion.

"*Albie*," mother cried, "you know not to use the Lord's name in vain." The sunlight slanting through an adjacent the window flared off the silver crucifix dangling around mother's neck, as if to add mystical clout to her statement.

"We're a middle-class family," father continued. "I've got eight people to feed and clothe. I can't afford to be squandering money on a simple alarm system. What time of year do these doohickeys go on sale?"

"I'm afraid, sir, that this isn't a retail item that you find at the local department store. We don't have any Labor Day or after-Christmas sales."

"Well, I've got to think about this," father blurted, looking out the window.

Desmond sat back in his chair, crossed his legs and attempted to regroup. "Sir, I understand you're having some price sensitivity, but I would encourage you not to think about this purchase as plastic box wires. Think instead about the problem it solves. What's it worth to you — not to mention your precious son — to have this problem disappear forever from your lives?"

Father kept staring implacably out the window. Desmond started looking dyspeptic at the prospects of losing this sale.

"Albie," mother said, "don't be rude. Answer the man."

"I'm thinking."

"Take your time," Desmond said, as he reached into his case one last time to retrieve a purchase agreement. He set the document on the coffee table in front of my father along with a pen that he pulled from a plastic pocket protector. "Just thirty-five dollars will get you our economy model." Careful not to disturb father's thought process, the salesman spoke in the hushed tone of a sports announcer broadcasting a key putt at a golf tournament. "More importantly it will give your boy back his self-esteem."

In time, father caved and the electrification of my bed was complete. Unfortunately, the Bed Wetting Alarm Activation System never worked for me. The alarm did go off when I urinated, but it also went off a few times a night while I tossed and turned, an act that displaced the cotton sheet separating the two metallic pads. My mind, confused about what lesson the alarm was trying to impart, never got the hang of it. So I continued to wet the bed and, in time, dispensed with the alarm system altogether.

"What a waste of money *that* was," father would remind me from time to time.

By the time I entered seventh grade the bed wetting had finally ceased of its own accord, though my disconcerting dreams persisted. I headed off to college, earning a sociology degree from Buffalo State. I learned too late that a sociology degree doesn't impress many employers. After bouncing around a few years it occurred to me that a more practical degree from an august institution of higher learner would add gravitas to the resume. My choice was the redoubtable Northwestern University in windy Chicago. This time it was an MBA with an emphasis in marketing. I inauspiciously graduated right in the teeth of a dreadful recession, meaning even America's most successful companies were slashing or eliminating their marketing budgets and putting a deep freeze on hiring. A young man without any other options, I put my newly minted marketing skills to work in the family business, determined to make the recession-proof Marciano's Mangia House even more successful and renowned. I rationalized that it would be a good place to wait-out the economic downturn while adding some sterling achievements to my curriculum vitae.

Over time I realized that once you climbed back into the maw of the family business and all its obligations and entanglements, you never climbed back out.

Vinny was the last born of the Marciano clan, and felt the sense of anonymity that comes with being the final member of any group. He might have gone through life with a flaccid self-image if not for having been endowed in a way all men and boys desire. It was nothing more than a bragging right in the boys' locker room, until that day Rachel Spring, the class nymph, approached him at an outdoor summer beer and pot party attended by 27 members of the high school's student body on the riverside bank of the Susquehanna River flood wall.

The students drank beer, smoked dope and spoke in profane tongues. The boys demonstrated feats of weakness and strength by occasionally wrestling one another to the ground; the girls gossiped about one another's attired and social status.

Vinny was a quiet sophomore, utterly without repute, attending his first flood-wall party; she was a senior with a reputation who had noticed for months the usually pronounced bulge at the intersection of Vinny's dungarees. Convinced she would find a rolled pair of athletic socks stuffed in his Fruit of the Looms, Rachel Spring used hand motions to separate Vinny from the crowd for a rendezvous behind some wild chokecherry bushes for camouflage. She put her lips to his mouth. It perplexed Vinny that this young lady on the verge of full-fledged womanhood, one whose notoriety was so widespread that even middle school students were well acquainted with her sexual resume, was showing interest in an ninth-grade boy. Still, he was ready to comply, sensing he was on the cusp of forever losing his virginity and taking those first tentative steps toward manhood.

Things progressed and Rachel Spring offered the lad her sprouting breasts. Vinny suckled while the girl opened the front of his trousers, reached inside and pulled free the largest of the many penises she had ever encountered. Amazed, she stroked it to full length before slipping her panties out from under her skirt. She pushed Vinny onto his back and spread herself across his lap. It was all she could do to bring him fully within. Carefully she rocked to and fro, whispering dirty incantations, most of which had to do with the sheer size of this evening's offering. Vinny gasped for air and tried coming to terms with the remarkable spasms he was experiencing. Rachel Spring let out a rebel yell and crumpled atop him.

As was habit for teenage girls, Rachel spent the next day tattling to friends about the discovery. She arranged another tryst with Vinny. He accepted with great adulation. This time Rachel Spring was carrying a tape measure in her purse. After teasing Vinny to full inflation, she measured its complete longitude, registering it at an indisputable ten inches.

Word of Vinny's freakish anatomy spread like an infectious disease among the school's girl population. Suddenly he was one of the most sought-after boys. Girl after girl invited Vinny to parties, forest rendezvouses, driven-in theaters or car rides to any number off-road make-out scenes. Most were too timid to do anything more than handle it. New rounds of bragging ensued and the girls continued to line up and await their turn to sample this object of widespread fascination. Vinny was anxious to oblige.

Confidence soaring, Vinny decided in his sophomore year to learn the bass guitar as his ticket for becoming an international rock star. He pulled together three other high school mates with shared ambitions and they formed a band named Roadblock. After growing his hair long, Vinny used toxic amounts of Aquanet hairspray and a hair pick to tease out his mane until it resembled a great cumulus following his head around the stage as he stalked and agitated the crowds.

The band went on the road, playing cities such as Albany, Courtland, Ithaca, Rochester and Syracuse. There were even a few gigs in New York City. Years passed and audiences — tiring of the band's Aerosmith, Black Sabbath and Led Zeppelin covers, and unmoved by Roadblock's few original compositions — became scant. Record deals and national concert tours receded to more distant galaxies, and the income became lousier with age.

When the band reached its seventh anniversary, Roadblock lived up to its name and was declared to have hit a dead end. The band was dissolved. Travel weary and nearly broke, Vinny abandoned his dream of being enshrined in the Rock 'n' Roll Hall of Fame. He moved back into his parents' home, a man of crushed ambition and emotional nudity.

The search for gainful employment turned out to be brief stints as a clothing salesman at a local haberdasher, a foreman at a tiny printing press and a desk clerk at a rental car agency. None offered him the status, earnings potential or the female attention he so ardently craved. He toyed with the notion of resuscitating his music career, with a new and more serious set of bandmates, then quickly disposed of the idea, remembering the depredations of life on the road, the sleepless motel rooms, bad food and tightwad nightclub proprietors. With the onset of depression clouding his consciousness, Vinny began to drink spirits in earnest. One inebriated night he missed his turn and found his car weaving down Loder Avenue, then he made hard left onto Valley Street and went cruising past Mersereau Park where his Little League team, sponsored by Marine Midland Bank, used to practice on weekends, and suddenly the car was bearing right and onto East Edward Street, moving rapidly toward the shuttered riverside restaurant that was Marciano's Mangia House. He skidded to a stop in the front parking lot. He had not been by the place in a couple of years. Lording above the building was a stand of giant elm trees, and rollicking below them was the rambunctious water flow of the Susquehanna River, swollen from the recent spate of rains.

The restaurant's sign was still there, though its colors had faded and were no longer illuminated by artificial lighting. A phantasm of memories rushed through the young man's head, carrying him from childhood through young adulthood of surging crowds, raucous tables of families and friends, sing-alongs at the bar, merriment and revelry. Every night was a party, and at the center of it all was an ebullient Uncle Nunzio, the most famous man in town, the biggest fish in the small pond that was Endicott, New York.

It would have gone on forever, except for the chronic and painful attacks of gout that forced him to contemplate retirement. By this time he had amassed a personal fortune, and scoring a few extra million by selling his enterprise didn't interest him nearly as much as preserving his legacy. The Great Man was ready to bequeath his business to a young family member. Yet, there was no heir apparent ready to step forward, given that Uncle Nunzio never married and sired offspring. Keeping it in the Marciano tribe still should have been a simple matter because Nunzio had a big extended family that included seventeen nieces and nephews. Though he offered the keys to his culinary kingdom — *gratis* — to any one of them who wanted to inherit the stupendously heralded Marciano's Mangia House, nada one expressed interest. Uncle Nunzio was stunned and crestfallen. The restaurant business simply wasn't glamorous enough for youngsters heading off to college in hopes of pursuing careers as history teachers, nurses, cops, city planners, marketers, insurance brokers and, of course, rock stars. For all the guaranteed success and income that would be part and parcel of being the new operator of the Mangia House, it still wasn't all that appetizing, having watched our

Uncle Nunzio work like a mule, day and night, six days a week for endless years, taking just two weeks off per year to fly to the same place every January with friends, the gambling capital of Las Vegas.

Vinny recalled overhearing Uncle Nunzio's lament to Father Albie. "I can't believe my ears. Sometimes I think there isn't a single drop of Italian blood in these kids. I'm offering to hand them a goldmine. They're all college boys and girls now, and all I get from them is big words."

Selling the restaurant to an outsider was unthinkable because its success was banked on the secret family recipes that couldn't be sold or transferred to outsiders in any way without breaking age-old family vows. The irony of the situation pained Uncle Nunzio. Even as a new generation of Marcianos turned up their snotty noses at his life's work, there were businessmen begging and bribing him to reconsider their outlandishly expensive offers to buy the business. Though tempted to violate his vow of secrecy in return for a titanic payday, Nunzio quickly quashed the notion, knowing that his mother would find a way to return from the dead and seek retribution by using one of his thigh bones to boil broth for soup.

In the end, Uncle Nunzio regretfully shuttered Marciano's and paid his annual property tax, refusing to even rent the property for any purpose. It would stand as he left it, a historical monument and a reminder of what was and what could have been.

Suddenly, Vinny was sober, the spirits overridden by a piercing insight that his destiny was now fully in view, a manifest destiny that had long been sitting invisibly right under the stubble on his chin. It was all so blatantly obvious now.

It was a smidgen past 3 a.m. when Vinny finally negotiated his way home. All the windows were dark and mother and father were fast asleep. The young man to make a wobbly and noisy arrival. He kicked his boots off, hitting the floor with a couple of bangs, and turned on the television at a volume usually reserved for the hearing impaired. Soon, father was at the top of the staircase.

"Hold that racket down. It's the middle of the night."

Vinny killed the TV. "Dad, come down here. I need to talk to you."

A plaid-blue flannel bathrobe came creaking down the stairway. Father was wrapped inside it squinting at the light, varicose veins bulging from his over-burdened calves. "Christ almighty, what it is?"

Vinny wasted no words. "Do you think Uncle Nunzio would be willing to teach me his recipes and help me get started in the restaurant business?"

Father's eyebrows jumped at the thought of his son reviving the family business, not to mention raking in the treasure it would produce.

"Sure he would." A cherubic smile spread across father's mug. "He wanted to hand down the business a long time ago. Nothing has changed."

Vinny sat in the living room recliner and levered it into a semi-recumbent position. The room slowly started rotating around him.

"I think I can do it," Vinny said through a nauseous gaze.

"All of his customers would come back. The place will fill to the gills in no time," father said as he began pacing. "This would be a blue chip business move," he said, stopping to tap a finger on the ledge of a curio cabinet to emphasize his point.

Vinny placed his hands on his face, trying to bring the room to a standstill.

"Ask him," father said. "Go see your Uncle Nunzio tomorrow and see what he has to say. What have you got to lose?"

"Probably my last shot at a decent future," Vinny mused.

"Your uncle isn't going to turn you down. Why do you think he's been holding on to that building all these years instead of selling or leasing it? He's been waiting for a family member to finally coming to his senses."

"Do you think he's got enough money to get me started?"

"Are you kidding? He's got so much money it isn't even funny. Do you know how many shares of IBM stock he controls? Lots of them, and that's just one of a slew of investments he's got. Stocks, T-bills, annuities, precious metals, real estate. The guy's loaded."

The room wouldn't stop moving, so Vinny collapsed the recliner and sat upright.

"Now listen," father cautioned, "don't go to your Uncle Nunzio and come right out and ask him to give you money. Just tell him about your intentions. Chances are good he will offer to get you started. Hell, I'll loan you the money if he won't."

Father was turning incandescent. He was getting a little too wound up — and controlling — for Vinny's taste. Already he was suggesting negotiating positions. Then he started spouting off a succession of menu items, pricing schedules and promotional schemes. Even as father's zeal spiraled, Vinny's dwindled, as if their feelings pivoted on a counterbalanced scale. It was father's way. He could be a domineering man, and it was becoming obvious the old man was entertaining more than a passing interest in the bringing Marciano's Mangia House back from the boneyard. He was going to want to play a direct — perhaps central — role in the operation. Forty-five minutes later Vinny's body had gone languid.

"I'm out of gas," Vinny announced. "I need some sleep."

He tiptoed off to the bedroom, only to hear his name being called a mere four hours later. When he opened his eyes he saw father standing at the foot of the bed, showered and fully dressed for the new day.

"Are you going to get up and visit your Uncle Nunzio?"

Vinny's burning eyes strained to read the clock. It was 8:15 a.m. He folded the pillow over his face and kept it there until well past noon, when he finally arose, ate buttered toast and coffee, then showered. A floral cologne was applied before climbing into a fresh pair of slacks and crisp shirt. A tweed blazer capped the ensemble, giving Vinny the closest thing he had to negotiating leverage.

Father was posted expectantly at the front door. His desire to come along couldn't have been any more frank.

"I'll see you later," Vinny said, and he passed by without invitation or eye contact. Father recessed to the kitchen to console himself with a salami sandwich.

Uncle Nunzio opened his front door with a folded newspaper under one armpit and his thick lips wrapped around one of his ever-present Dutch Masters cigars.

Vinny greeted the Great Man. "How goes it, Uncle Nunzio?"

"Terrible. I don't have anything to do. Retirement is boring. You stop working, you start dying."

Vinny mumbled some perfunctory condolences as Uncle Nunzio led him to a table in the breakfast nook.

"Beer? Soda? Coffee?"

Vinny nodded acceptance of the final offering. A pot had already been brewed. Nunzio brought two cups to the table along with a tray holding whipping cream, three different types of sweetener and some chocolates. He kicked things off with a loud slurp of hot coffee. Then he laid his hairy forearms on the table and spoke. "This ain't no holiday so what are you doing at my house?"

"I came to talk business."

"That's none of my business. I told you, I'm retired."

"This would require your assistance."

Uncle Nunzio held up his bloated hands to bring his nephew to a halt. "Before you go on, the only dough I have is the kind used for baking. Almost everything I've earned is all tied up. It's like I don't really own it. It belongs to IBM, stockbrokers, banks, mortgage companies; you know, people who like to play with it. They wouldn't let me have it back if my life depended on it." Nunzio dropped a chocolate in his coffee, stirred and slurped again.

Vinny was having a very bad feeling about the request he was about to make.

"I want you to teach me the family recipes, Uncle Nunzio. I want to reopen Marciano's."

Though his face didn't betray him, Nunzio was too stunned to fire off a witty comeback, and too pleased to take the idea half-heartedly. Despite all that, he wasn't about to hand the family's Holy Grail over to his nephew without getting some assurances and making him sweat a bit.

"So I teach you the recipes, then what are you going to do?" snuffing out his cigar in a crystal ashtray. "Do you have a wad of cash or are you planning to open the joint up with your good looks?"

"Cash is one thing I don't have."

"You don't got recipes, you don't got cash, what do you got?"

"I got a hungry heart. I got a lot of energy. I got an empty wallet that needs filling."

"Where you going to get the money?"

"I'll need some help on that score."

"What about your old man?"

"I'm not sure he's got it. But even so, I don't want him to bank me. He lends me the money and he's as good as my partner. He'll hold sway over me. If anybody's going to be telling me what to do, it needs to be someone who knows the restaurant business. That's you."

"Holy Mary mother of God," Nunzio crowed. "Seven years ago I was ready to give you the restaurant free and clear, and that wasn't good enough. You were too busy growing your hair long and wearing Halloween costumes up on stage. Now that I'm retired you want to charge me so you can open it back up."

Vinny bowed his head and stared into his coffee. Shining back at him was his own grim reflection. "I'll pay you back, with interest. I'll pay you for training time. I'm not looking for a handout. This is a blue chip business we're talking about. Consider it an investment. Charge me however many points you want."

"You know the recipes are Marciano family secrets."

"Of course."

"They can't be shared with any of the people you hire."

"I wouldn't do that."

"You give them away and I'll hate you 'til I die."

"I know their value. I wouldn't cut my own throat."

Uncle Nunzio gave Vinny a long, appraising look, measuring the young man, trying to gauge his sincerity and stick-to-itiveness. "Running a restaurant is hard work."

"I prepared to do that."

"Work, work, work."

"What else do I have to do? My music career is over. The record contract never came through."

Without another word Nunzio left the table and stepped into his home office, which adjoined the kitchen. He pulled out a yellow legal pad and pen and commenced scribbling line after line. Fifteen minutes passed. Vinny grew impatient. He felt like a criminal defendant waiting for a deliberating jury to render a verdict, a decision that would determine whether he had a future to look forward to. Were these the recipes he was committing to paper, or some iron-clad business agreement that piled on more points than a loan shark?

When Nunzio reemerged he was carrying six sheets of tightly rolled notepad paper tucked on his ear, like a teenager's spare cigarette. The men retook their coffee-drinking positions.

"I'm glad you want to re-open Marciano's," the elder of the two said. "I'll come up with some cash and underwrite the start-up phase of the operation; after that you're on your own. I'll teach you the recipes — *after* you've taken the family oath of secrecy — and show you how to run the business end of things."

Vinny let out a big, stale breath he'd been holding for half an hour and began to smile. "Thank you, Uncle Nunzio. This is so cool."

Now he was pointing at Vinny. "There are stipulations. That's what these are." He plucked the rolled papers from the top of his ear and dropped them on the table in front of his nephew. "If I don't think you're working hard enough or I catch you messing with those recipes I'll pull the plug on the deal. People know what Marciano's cooking tastes like. It's up to you to keep that family tradition alive or no dice."

Vinny unfurled the papers to see what Uncle Nunzio had written. Start-up costs were not to exceed $50,000, they said. An 8 percent interest rate would be levied. The menu and pricing had to be mutually agreed upon, and so on and so forth.

"This all looks reasonable," Vinny told his uncle. "But it says here you're going to be the restaurant's ombudsman. What's an ombudsman?"

"An advocate for the public. In this case I'll be an advocate for both the public and the Marciano family. If customers have complaints, I'm the guy who investigates and gets to the bottom of what went wrong. In other words, I'll be rolling through the place willy-nilly and making sure you're not butchering your family's good name. Don't worry, this isn't a salaried position."

Vinny nodded with understanding. "The way I interpret the ombudsman's role is that you'll be there to help me."

"Or to kick your goddamn ass."

Vinny and Uncle Nunzio both put their signatures on the bottom of the final page of the agreement. They shook hands and Nunzio ignited another cigar.

A few months later Marciano's Mangia House reopened its doors with great fanfare. The physical structure was given a thorough cleaning and re-painting. An updated sign was mounted out front. Vinny underwent grueling weeks of training in the art of Italian cuisine, and the official copies of the secret family recipes were transferred to his ownership. Kitchen help, waiters, busboys and dishwashers were hired and trained.

By opening day Vinny was a nervous wreck. "It's sink or swim time," Nunzio told his petrified nephew.

Customers arrived in a trickle, then a deluge. Before Vinny knew what had clubbed him across the back of the head, dozens of dinner orders were lined up and demanding they be prepared to Uncle Nunzio's exacting standards.

The pressure was on.

Vinny ricocheted around the kitchen, routinely messing up customer requests or over-boiling the pasta. Consternation broke out on the floor. Uncle Nunzio got hot and came charging into the kitchen to roar at Vinny, fearful that fifty years of hard work was about to go down the drain in a single night. This only served to compound the boy's stress. He combated his error prone ways by slowing his dinner preparation. Orders started coming out of the kitchen at a crawl and the crowds were forced to wait for up to 90 minutes before being seated. Exceptions were made for medical emergencies, such as the evening a small elderly man rushed into the kitchen sputtering that his wife was hypoglycemic and on the verge of passing out if she didn't get some food, but quick.

A major newspaper article about the restaurant's reopening appeared in the *Sun-Bulletin*, fueling even bigger crowds. The picture accompanying the article showed a smiling Uncle Nunzio with his arm around his shell-shocked nephew. The townspeople swarmed the place, and it wasn't long before people were migrating to Marciano's from around the state, just like the old days.

His nervous system on the cusp of breakdown, Vinny started pulling family members to his side, which afforded him the psychological comfort he urgently needed. First mother and father were drafted into service working alongside him in the kitchen. A few weeks later, Angie and Maria were approached. Excited by the restaurant's resurgent business, they were all too happy to join the effort. I was brought aboard to run the bar. Ginger, feeling left out but not wanting to get her French-manicured fingernails dirty, approached Vinny about becoming the restaurant's official hostess. Several months later Ringo, who was trying to live a life of seclusion and unemployment, was dragged into the enterprise against his will and taught how to make the restaurant's signature pizzas. With the exception of Ringo, we were all taught the recipes and took turns cooking in teams of two during early-morning shifts.

With the full Marciano tribe working at open throttle, the restaurant found its footing and eventually achieved the speed, continuity and consistency of yore. An ebullient Uncle Nunzio never had it so good, basking in the glory without having to do any real work. He became reacquainted with former customers and friends.

Vinny's blood pressure gradually returned to normal and his bout with battle fatigue evaporated. He started spending most of his time in the dining room, where he saw Uncle Nunzio was the center of attention. He witnessed the greatness and legend of the man, watching his mentor work the crowd, slap backs and share guttural laughter. Studying and emulating his elder's techniques, Vinny acquired a smoothness of his own and became a deft conversationalist with a wide repertoire of glib one-liners. Uncle Nunzio taught him how to smoke cigars. As Vinny's star ascended the first pangs of resentment started throbbing among his siblings. Vinny was a celebrity and we were his crew. He absorbed the glory, drank the wine and made sure everybody had a good time. The *Sun-Bulletin* published another article about Marciano's, this one featuring a large color picture of Vinny puffing confidently on illegally imported Cuban cigar. The world had changed. Vinny was raking in the dough; his hard-working and trustworthy family was making everything happen in the foreground and background. Uncle Nunzio gradually pulled back from the restaurant, spending less time playing ombudsman, sensing it was time to fully pass the torch, to give Vinny adequate room to establish his own reputation as a restaurant man of the highest order.

No, he wasn't an international rock star as he had once dreamed, but Vinny was famous and rich by most people's standards. He had become the toast of the Upstate New York restaurant circuit. Moving from table to table, he visited with the regulars and introduced himself to newcomers. He also ensured the dishes being served had achieved the Marciano Seal of Approval. If not, he would take the customer's plate away, goose-walk into the kitchen and scream at his crew to do it over again and do it right.

Vinny was especially charming with the women, suggesting compatible wines, pronouncing menu items with an impeccable Italian accent, kissing the backs of their hands. Women's circles began referring to Vinny as the Italian Impresario. He was establishing quite a reputation as a womanizer (divorcees were his specialty). Vinny further enhanced his personal aura and intrigue by selling copies of the book "The Italians" from a bookrack outside the women's restroom. An excised passage from the book stated:

> "Many women dream of having a souvenir love affair with an Italian man. Sometimes all it takes is a certain look from an aspiring woman to send an Italian man on a new adventure in intimacy."

Generosity and flattery flowed boundlessly from Vinny when he found a woman desirous. Oftentimes it was the women who shamelessly offered themselves up to the so-called Italian Impresario. Most were turned away and had to be satisfied with an aromatic gift bottle of Bordeaux or a romantic poem from Vinny's collection of plagiarized poetry.

# THE RESTAURANT

Angie and I were scheduled to do the morning cooking, but she was running late again. I got started with the daily routine of preparing enough food to feed the hundreds who would show up come nightfall. The tools of my craft surrounded me. There were knives, cutting boards, spatulas and pans for frying, baking and boiling. The gas burners were flaming a mystical blue. The kitchen filled with a multitude of aromas. Small bubbles were exploding off the surface of vats of pasta and pizza sauces.

After two hours, the hired kitchen help came in to complete what I had started and to start manufacturing the non-classified dishes that comprised the balance of the Marciano Mangia House menu. The slow-cooking Bolognese sauce had hours yet to go and careful stirring at the proper intervals was required. The pomodoro and arabiata sauces were also in the maturation process. The brasciol — Italian steak rolls heavily seasoned with basil, oregano and minced garlic — had just been pulled from the oven and were cooling in their aromatic way.

After two hours, the hired kitchen help came in to complete what I had started and to start manufacturing the non-classified dishes that comprised the balance of the Marciano Mangia House menu.

When I returned that evening I was stationed behind our 35-foot Maplewood bar, polishing its high-gloss lacquered finished and restocking bottles.

Angie never showed up. I ate a plate of chicken Marsala and sipped on a cup of imported *Il Perfetto* coffee.

When I returned that evening I was stationed behind our 35-foot Maplewood bar, polishing its high-gloss lacquered finished, restocking bottles and watching Ginger and Maria square off. It was a particularly cold winter day, about one hour before the restaurant's doors were schedule to be unlatched and opened to the public. Ginger was in the midst of organizing her hostess stand and was dressed in her hallmark miniskirt, heels and Wonder Bra. Maria was wrapped in her red apron with white stitching along its edges, pockets bulging with pens, order forms and cash for making change.

The issue of the day was a dead horse Maria insisted on beating over and over to the point of mutilation. In reconstituting the topic, Maria adopted an aggressive stance, sharply thrusting a hip. She might have been a hockey player preparing to brutally check a rival into the rink's turnbuckle. As head waitress, Maria wanted her section filled to capacity forthwith by hostess Ginger. Then, and only then, would she accept Ginger seating customers in sections of the dining room being patrolled by the other waitresses. For umpteenth time Maria enumerated her demands through grinding teeth. Any and all big tippers also had to be seated at her tables, she said, even if that meant forcing them wait for seating while tables were available in other sections. Maria had even penned an updated list of prized customers for Ginger, which she laid on the hostess stand for easy reference.

Maria was particularly obsessed with a customer named Mort Stottlemyre, a major local homebuilder. Leaving big tips was one of the ways Stottlemyre showed off his financial prowess. And he always paid his bill and tipped with cash, for fear than anyone would think he was one of those highly leveraged paper-rich cash-poor real estate developers.

"We're talking double-digit tips," Maria said, adding a little extra accentuation to her hip thruster. "One night he brought in a large party and left triple digits on the table."

Ginger insisted on fairness, reasoning that unless the other servers were treated equally, good help couldn't be retained, causing a decline in the quality of service and ultimately bringing down sales and working against the family's overall interests.

"Family comes first at Marciano's," Maria said. Then she jostled her apron pocket up and down to make her coins chime. "Do you hear that?" she said. "That's how I measure the health of the Marciano's, by the jingle in my apron pocket. Now fill 'er up, sister."

Ginger's method for cooling tense conversation was to apply a calm veneer. She stood straight with arms demurely folded across the midsection, her long black hair draped over her shoulders and down her back. Her voice was even and soothing. "Let's just drop this issue for the time being, shall we?"

Ginger's strategy had a sedative effect on most human beings, but not Maria. She had witnessed her sister's calmer-than-thou routine since girlhood. It was designed to make others look hysterical, and Maria would have none of that. Her nostril flared like a speared bull as she charged. Ginger shrieked while Maria wrenched her into a headlock that left her crying out for the mercy of my assistance.

As I headed around the long bar to bring this feline struggle to an end, I visualized delivering a karate chop to the side of Maria's neck, temporarily paralyzing her and setting Ginger free. Before I could get there Maria had peeled the false eyelashes off Ginger's lids and pulled the foam inserts out of her Wonder Bra, hurling them over the top of the ice machine behind the bar, where they fell onto the dusty backside of the machine's electrical and plumbing apparatus.

"What the hell is wrong with you?" I scolded Maria.

"Just taking Little Miss Perfect's attitude — and knockers — down a peg or two," Maria said, heading back to the dining room.

To move the massive ice-maker and retrieve Ginger's bra stuffers would have been a Herculean production, so Ginger agreed to work the night with a breast reduction. First thing the next morning she could visit Victoria's Secret to purchase some reinforcements.

That brought the encounter to a halt at the precise time that the deadbolt on the side door snapped open and father's over-fed frame trundled in.

"Do you see what time it is," father said, tapping a fingernail against the crystal on his wristwatch. "It's past four-thirty. Our sign and the neon beer logos should have been switched on by now."

"Talk to her," Maria snarled, flashing a gesture towards the hostess stand. Ginger wiggled her miniskirt over to the switches and turned on the electricity.

Then a howling sound came from the kitchen. It was Vinny decrying that a bank bag stuffed with $25,000 had gone missing. He had neglected to lock it in the office safe the night before. As soon as father heard there was some stray currency he aggressively joined the hunt — opening and slamming cupboards, moving boxes and lowering himself with great consternation onto all fours to peek under hot tables and racks of metal shelving. He even stuck his head inside refrigeration units on the off chance someone mistook the cold cash for a perishable. He finally threw his arms in the air and told his son, "I don't know where the hell it is. You find it."

What so irritated father, a man who came of age in the depths of the Great Depression, was that his youngest son could be so cavalier about handling money (even if it did come through the front door in bushels). Father always taught his children the virtues of saving their earnings and buying things on the cheap.

"Don't go squandering your money," he repeatedly advised. "Squeeze every nickel until the buffalo shits in your hand."

The side door flew open again and mother came plodding through. Her head was wrapped in a kerchief and her mouth was complaining about the sub-zero wind that had whipped her on the walk from the parking lot.

"Albie," she called out. "I got here, no thanks to you. You're so damn impatient. Is it possible I have to take a separate car from my husband even when we're going to the same place?"

Father moved to the cash register and started warming up the digits. He made no verbal reply to his wife, opting instead to let the roiling acid stew in his stomach do the talking.

There's only one thing father loved as much as food, and that was money. And that was because money could be used to buy more food. It was a well-known fact that during his drive to work each day, father fantasized about what he was going to consume for dinner that evening. Would it be a veal cutlet or chicken parmigiana? He would talk zealously about his options with Mother Margherita. Perhaps some baked ziti or a two-foot meatball sub. Whatever he chose it would be loaded with plenty of side dishes and eaten with great relish.

"Albie," Mother Margherita would say, "take human bites. You're going to get yourself gassed up like a zeppelin if you don't slow down."

Father's mouth was always too full to reply.

Mother was no slouch on food consumption herself. After taking off her winter gear she marched straight to the kitchen. Or perhaps it's more accurate said that she *tried* to march. Her upper body was marching with head up and arms churning, but her lower body was less cooperative. Her legs seemed leaden and her shoes shuffled along the floor as though lead weights had been attached to them. She forked a couple of sausage links into a bowl and headed to the microwave, shoving the sausages inside, setting the timer and hitting the start button. A crackling sound erupted from the microwave's cooking chamber as sparks went flying in all directions.

"What in blazes," mother said, as she yanked the door open, pulling the bowl of sausages out. When she looked into the microwave's cavity, mother saw something altogether bizarre — a rectangular canvas bag with a metal zipper. The lettering stenciled on it read *M&T Bank & Trust Company*.

"What on God's green earth is this doing here," she said, holding the bag aloft.

"There it is," Vinny said. "Give that to me. It's last night's take."

"It almost became tonight's dinner," mother said.

Vinny took the bag to the restaurant's basement office, dialed the combo on the safe and snapped the door open. He lovingly placed the bag of cash in the safe, where it would stay until he made his next run to the bank. Sitting to the right of the safe was a smaller but no less impenetrable safe bolted into the concrete floor. Vinny clasped the handle and gave it a strong turn to make sure the door was locked solid. In that reinforced steel chamber sat the much ballyhooed and carefully protected secret family recipes that made up the core of Marciano's menu.

When Vinny returned to the kitchen he found Angie standing near the stoves with a club soda in hand and a cigarette idling between her lips.

"Get that thing the hell out of here," Vinny said, pointing at the cigarette with a foot-long boning knife. "If the health inspector walks in with you puffing on that disgusting thing he'll shut me down."

"You've got to be joking." Angie's cigarette bounced up and down with each syllable. Then she pinched it between a pair of fingers to remove it from her lips and held it in front of Vinny's face. "This thing is the least of your worries. Have you looked in the refrigerators lately? You've got new life forms growing in there. Go on, take a good look. I dare you. You've got pizza toppings doing aerobics in there."

Vinny slapped Angie's hand away from his face and sent the cigarette flying into a cauldron of simmering spaghetti sauce.

A bitter, indescribable sound came out of Vinny's throat. He grabbed a ladle and scooped the cigarette off the top of the sauce. Returning the gesture, he held the ladle up to his sister's face, the sodden and dying cigarette was still sitting on the surface, letting loose its final tendrils of smoke.

"This restaurant gets perfect scores from the city health inspector," Vinny snarled, "and all I get from you is falsehoods and negativity about our cleanliness." Then he slung the ladle's contents into a garbage can.

At that moment, Ginger snapped open the deadbolts on the restaurant's front door, and within 45 minutes the place was roaring with patrons. All tables were full and every employee moving fast. There were no reservations at Marciano's Mangia House. It was first come, first served. Ginger simply kept of list of those awaiting tables and platters heaped with our family-style cuisine. They were jammed into the bar area, calling out for drinks and waving large and small denominations through the air. Everyone was bulky in their winter coats. Soon I was madly preparing drinks and making change. When possible, I'd ignite the patrons' tobacco products with an old style flip-top butane lighter. It was one of my signature moves. Some of the regulars wouldn't put their cigarettes, pipes or cigars to their mouths until I had a free hand to offer them my flame.

The horny and confident among the men killed time by flirting with Ginger. Her allure included a repertoire of hair flips and blithe giggles.

Ringo was bent over the pizza bench, scowling at the elongating list of orders. Back and forth his arms churned, massaging the dough, pushing and spreading it into a circle, ready to be ladled with sauce and sprinkled with cheese and toppings, then shoveled on a wooden paddle into the 550-degree oven.

It was no use trying to keep up. Between the call-in orders and requests from the dining room, nobody could work fast enough to stay apace. People were willing to endure the long waits because the payoff was sweet. The wait was made even longer by the fact that Ringo was a slow mover. The job was also particularly ill-suited to his personality. For one thing, Ringo didn't like feeling discomfort, and the pizza bench was all about hard work and lower-back pain. Secondly, he detested crowds, especially crowds of people that were staring at him, and there was plenty of that because making pizzas at

Marciano's was a public task. The pizza bench was right out in the open for the customer's viewing pleasure, all part of the spectacle of dining at Marciano's.

"What the hell are they looking at?" Ringo often complained. "What are they all so curious about? Why don't they just fuck off?"

Thirdly, Ringo was prone to losing his shit halfway through the night and storming out of the restaurant in mid-pizza.

Vinny was unsympathetic to his older brother's countless idiosyncrasies. Indeed, he compounded matters for Ringo because his own shifts on the pizza bench were crowd pleasers — tossing rounds of raw dough into the air and conversing with onlookers about the finer points of the craft. With the audience's expectations heightened, the surly and speechless Ringo became that much more of a bummer. Artless and uncoordinated, Ringo felt certain that if he dared send a round of dough skyward it would most certainly end up landing on his face and getting stuck on the corners of his glasses.

"Repetitive stress disorder," Ringo shouted to his passing father.

"You just keep cranking out those pizzas," father shot back.

Father knew that Ringo used references to such ailments as proof the job was fast becoming physically impossible. With frustration building, Ringo eventually blew his stack and walked out with his white bib-apron still tied around his bulging belly and the baker's cap still jauntily angled atop his head. Vinny threatened to fire Ringo on numerous occasions if he dared to again walk out in the middle of a storming night of business. The threat was a hollow one, though, because Vinny was raised with the understanding that family ties were inviolable. Besides, terminating Ringo would force Vinny to take on more shifts at the pizza bench, since hiring a non-family-member for that position was not an option.

Vinny drifted by to check on Ringo. He brought with him a tall well-iced glass of Coca-Cola, which he set on the edge of the pizza bench to keep his brother cool and his bloodstream leaden with high-fructose corn syrup.

The restaurateur was pleased. The night seemed to be progressing so well, until he turned for the bar and found Maria in front of his face, snorting with exasperation and demanding that Vinny dismiss an employee named Amy Stonebreaker, who served as head waitress on Maria's nights off.

Stonebreaker stood repeatedly accused by Maria of re-seating customers from other waitresses' tables to her own section. Though she was head waitress, Maria wasn't invested with the power to fire her waitresses. The only Marciano allowed to terminate an employee was Vinny, and Maria knew he wasn't about to hand the supple Amy Stonebreaker her walking papers because he was banging the girl with euphoric regularity.

When Maria spat something about sending the "brash little whore packing," Vinny lost all sense of scale and situation. It wasn't that he was particularly defensive of Amy Stonebreaker so much as he was utterly fatigued by his sister's Sally Field impersonations. He grabbed Maria by the arm and sent her spinning against the bank of gas-powered ovens. Vinny pulled open an oven door, hoisted Maria into the air and tried loading her into the blaze. He knew Maria had eaten a serving of mixed vegetables and provolone cheese, so by Vinny's temporarily insane calculation, if he baked her at 550 degrees for about thirty-five minutes she would become the world's first human calzone. Ringo broke up the altercation before Maria could be turned into a new menu item.

# THE RECIPES

    Father appeared bloated with anger by end of the evening, as though his mass was being fed by emotion. He pulled Vinny aside and insisted that an emergency meeting of the Marciano clan be held at the close business. Vinny resisted because he was scheduled to go home and bang Amy Stonebreaker until the wee hours of the morning. Father persisted and my brother eventually assented.

    After the Mangia House had been locked down and scrubbed to its usual hygienic sparkle, we convened in the downstairs board room, each taking our usual positions around the long, rectangular, oaken table, the heads of the grand piece of furniture reserved for father and Vinny — father because of his status as family patriarch, Vinny because ownership comes with privileges. We were all exhausted from the night's long, onerous workload. Vinny was the last to make it downstairs. He was carrying a bank bag stuffed with the evening's cash receipts.

    Father was reddening by the moment. "Hold your horses," Vinny said. "I need to put this away." Heading into the adjoining office, Vinny knelt in front of the safe and whirled the dial right and left through a combination of numbers. A turn of the handle released a series of deadbolts and the door popped open. The money bag, pungent with the unmistakable scent of paper currency, was tossed inside. Having slammed the door securely shut, Vinny reset the dial with a flick of his wrist that sent the dial spinning like a roulette wheel.

FAMILY RECIPES

He was just about to come off his knee when he saw something that kept him fast to the floor. The door on the companion safe to the right appeared to be ajar. It was the slightest of apertures, just enough to be noticeable and arouse curiosity. It was the safe that ensured the secrecy of the secret family recipes. Vinny reached for the safe. As soon as the weight of his hand registered against the handle the door cracked open.

"What the…"

He pulled the door fully open and lowered his head to inspect the contents. The steel box was empty, the contents gone.

*The recipes were missing!*

He lingered for a long chilling moment, his mind dashing through a labyrinth of possible explanations. When every turn of thought led to another dead end, Vinny came to his feet and burst into the meeting room.

"Who the hell took the recipes out of safe?"

Quizzical expressions all around.

"The safe is open and the recipes are gone. Who's got them?"

We followed one another into the office, taking turns staring into the empty reinforced steel chamber, as though one of us had the special vision to see what all others were missing. The only ones who officially knew the safe's combination were Vinny, Father Albie, sisters Angie, Maria, Ginger, and … *me*.

Ringo immediately entered a not guilty plea. "I don't even know the combination," he said by way of providing an alibi.

Ginger piped in, "I certainly hope none of you think I would stoop to that level."

"Well I certainly didn't take them," I said, surprised by the defensiveness of my tone.

"Dammit," mother said, her temperature rising, "I want to know who took those recipes."

Maria said, "Settle down, mother. Why would any of us have taken them? It doesn't make any sense. We all have the recipes memorized. It's not like we need them for reference."

Mother turned to Vinny. "You were the one who misplaced the money last night," she reminded him, "maybe you misplaced the recipes too."

"I checked the safe just hours ago and it was rock solid," Vinny said. "The door was shut and the handle wouldn't budge. Whoever took the recipes did it tonight."

"Well it obviously wasn't one of us," Ginger said. "There's been a robbery."

"Yeah, right," Vinny jeered, "a safecracker just moseyed in here and knew exactly what he was looking for, and the burglar hustles away with the recipes and shows no interest in the bags of cash sitting in the other safe. Whaddayou, crackers?"

Ginger arranged herself in a defiant, cross-armed posture. "Do you have a better explanation?"

Angie launched into a rant that, on its surface, was directed at no one in particular, but whose implications pointed sharply at Vinny and what Angie deemed his resounding incompetence as a manager.

"How many times have I said this needs to be a secured area? That the doors need to stay locked, that nobody outside of the people in this room should have access?" She stamped a foot. "We have budgets and financial reports in here, there are computers loaded with proprietary information. You're all so nonchalant about protecting this place, it's no wonder a thief saw an invitation steal."

Father ordered a search of the premises.

"Somebody misplaced those recipes, now find them," he said. "All of you look high and low. We're not leaving until they're back where they belong."

The ensuing hunt covered every square foot of the building, regardless of how implausible some areas might seem. The office in particular was scoured, including every manila folder in the filing cabinets. We all knew the import and exact nature of what we were looking for — recipes hand-written in Italian by Great-Great-Great-Great-Grandma Marciano two centuries ago in Naples, with a second set of English translations penned by Uncle Nunzio almost 50 years ago on food-stained parchment that he kept in a personal safe deposit box at M&T Bank & Trust Company. The papers had since been laminated to preserve the originals for posterity. They were more than recipes, they were historical documents and family heirlooms bequeathed to Vinny and considered to be under his protection.

During his search, Vinny entered a storage area and came across the metal piping in wood boards that, when assembled, was the scaffolding that artist Enrico Zepeda used to elevate himself to the dining room ceiling to paint his fresco. Then he paused and toyed with the idea of Zepeda being alone on the property every night. He was the only non-family member entrusted with a key and alarm code to the property so he could work by night. He must take breaks, Vinny thought. He had the run of the place. What did he do with his time? What did he really know of the restaurant's set-up and operation?

Vinny knew the documents disappeared sometime roughly between 4 p.m. and midnight, hours during which Zepeda was not on the premises. Still, he could enter and depart at will. Arrival time was about 2 o'clock each morning he stroked the brush for about four hours, departing a 6 o'clock.

Zepeda did not personally remove the documents, of that Vinny was almost certain. But he didn't put it past anybody to be party to a conspiracy. He was certain there was a corrupt covenant of some kind between sisters Angie and Maria. The extent of their chicanery was questionable, but not their duplicity. With nothing more to go on, they were his lead suspects.

After two hours of fruitless searching had elapsed, the conclusion was incontrovertible: the recipes were missing and were not on the premises.

Vinny flushed and felt an extreme urge to pee.

"Call the police," father blurted, cocking a thumb over his shoulder.

Ginger took the lead, marching to the phone and dialing 911. The rest of us shuffled glumly back to the boardroom where we sat around the table sharing our shock and disbelief. Half-hearted attempts were made to unravel this mystery.

Ginger was transferred three times by police officials and left on hold for several minutes before an extraordinary voice came through the handset identifying itself as detective sergeant Clyde Jablonsky. It was a deep, masculine voice, full of rumble, and it quivered Ginger to her core. Ginger's ear seemed to meld with the telecommunications device. She had always liked deep, vibratory sounds and the instruments that produced them, such as cellos, kettle drums and those rarest sets of male vocal chords. She told the man with the baritone voice who she was, the restaurant's name and location, the existence of secret recipes and their stunning theft.

He explained police procedures on a case of this sort, and the dismal chances of recovery. Ginger was getting hot, despite the bleak circumstances. She wanted sergeant detective Jablonsky to just keep talking. She pressed the phone more tightly against her ear to create a seal and increase the absorbency of his bottomless tone. While still holding the phone tightly against her ear, Ginger stood, stepped around the desk swung the office door closed, ostensibly to block out the conversational noise from the boardroom. Ginger sat down behind the desk again and used a free hand to begin tweaking her right nipple, pinching and twisting the hard little knot, rolling it, then twisting some more. She would have been content to continue tweaking as long as the golden-throated detective Jablonsky gave her aural stimulation.

The detective wrapped up his spiel with a promise to be at the restaurant before the clock struck 3 a.m. As Ginger hung up the phone and raised her head she was jolted by the image of Maria standing in the doorway.

"What the hell are you doing?" Maria said. "You're supposed to be calling for help and you're sitting there playing with yourself."

"Oh my god," Ginger said, putting her hands to her cheeks, "the detective who's coming over has got the most *gorgeous* voice. I couldn't help myself."

"You can't go back to the meeting like that, you look ridiculous," Maria said, gesturing with an upturned hand towards Ginger's petite bust line. The over-stimulated nipple was ferociously erect and pointing at Maria in a brash, accusatory way. The other nipple was not at all in evidence. "It looks like your dumplings are winking at me."

Maria always referred to Ginger's breasts as "dumplings" because the term was suggestive of their diminutive size — something Maria wanted to reinforce in her sister's mind. Meanwhile, Maria referred to her own breasts as "jugs," "congas," "dairies," "howitzers," "melons" or "pontoons," any term suggestive of their imperial size and superior womanhood.

"This wouldn't even be visible if you hadn't attacked me this afternoon and stolen my bra inserts." Ginger put her hands over her breasts. "Stop staring at them. I'll put my coat on."

Sergeant detective Clyde Jablonsky arrived a few minutes past 3 a.m.

"Who did I talk with on the telephone?" he asked, the deep resonant sound pouring out of his mouth and taking over the room.

Ginger was momentarily speechless. The voice wasn't the visitor's only physical attribute. Jablonsky was very tall and lean with sharp angles at every joint. The head of dirty blonde hair was long and floppy and he was wearing blue jeans and a well-worn pair of Tony Lama boots that made him taller still. His genuine leather coat and matching gloves creaked with his every move. The brisk smell of animal hide and winter air was all around him.

"That would be me," Ginger eventually croaked, straightening up and shrinking the length of her mini-skirt half an inch.

With practiced ceremony Jablonsky removed his gloves and stuffed them in his pockets, the motion giving us brief view of the semi-automatic pistol holstered under his left armpit. Jablonsky extended a shake in greeting. He squeezed Ginger's feverish hand and smiled.

"I'm here to help," he said, the sonorous voice reverberating through Ginger's body, her Bambi eyes blinking a few times to shake off the trance-like sound. The detective could see from Ginger's flushed cheeks that she liked what she saw. He was accustomed to that. Jablonsky liked Ginger too, especially the long, raven hair. A fleeting thought was already toying with the idea of how sweet it would be to plumb her ever-loving depths.

There was no doubt about it, sergeant detective Clyde Jablonsky was a commanding figure, so much so that it took us several moments to notice the middle-aged woman standing in his shadow.

"This is one of our crime scene investigators," he said, placing a gentle hand on her shoulder. "She'll be dusting for prints."

As the woman snapped open her briefcase of investigative tools, Jablonsky started asking basic questions about the crime's discovery. We started talking over one another trying to explain the inexplicable; all except Vinny, who withdrew into despondence. Jablonsky listened carefully to the overlapping accounts, scribbling a few sentences on his notepad before personally inspecting the safe.

"Yep," he said, pulling his head out of the steel casing, "it's empty all right."

Jablonsky turned his attention to the narrow, transom-like windows just below the office's ceiling. He checked that the locks were clamped shut and ran his fingers along the frames, searching for signs of entry, forcible or otherwise. Then he went outside with his flashlight to examine the areas just outside the window, inspecting for footprints, jimmy marks or any objects that might have been left behind. He came back inside escorted by a fresh plume of chilly air.

"I don't see any evidence of tampering. This was an inside job," he said. "I'm going to want to interview some of your employees."

FAMILY RECIPES

By this time my sisters had slipped into the far corner of the boardroom and were letting out little whoops of excitement over the lawman.

"The guy's carrying a major load," Angie said.

"Armed and dangerous," Ginger added.

"Have him put the cuffs on me right now," Maria said, "and don't come bail me out because that man is radioactive."

Margherita edged over to find out what the excitement was about. "What are you girls doing?"

"Don't you think that detective is a hunk?" Ginger asked her mother.

"A hunk," mother said, "what's a hunk?"

"What I mean is, don't you think he's gorgeous?"

"Oh, for crying out loud, we've just had crime and you girls are carrying on about some man?"

Ginger squeezed her mother's arm and hissed, "Hold your voice down." She peered over her should to make sure the always indiscreet Mother Margherita had not been overheard. "Admit it, the guy could be a movie star. He sounds just like Sam Elliott."

Mother titled her head a bit, as though weighing the evidence. Then she matter-of-factly replied, "He's a handsome man. But what kind of name is Jablonsky? Polish?"

Ginger's shoulders collapsed with exasperation.

"Of course it is," Angie said.

Margherita reacted poorly the confirmation, his lack of Italian pedigree invalidating his many physical attributes.

Ginger said, "For heavens sakes mother, what difference does it make? Did you hear that man's voice?"

When Jablonsky and his assistant finished their work, he handed his card to Ginger, assuming she would continue being his point of contact.

"I'll be in touch," he told Ginger, her cheeks flushing anew. "But, like I said, don't get your hopes up. About the case, I mean."

Vinny was escorting the detective and his crime scene investigator off the property then, once again, convened the family around the boardroom table, his effete body flopped onto the chair. The jarring caused the gold chains around his neck to jangle. They were part of outdated fashion statement, as was his habit of leaving at least the top two buttons of his shirt unfastened so the material cleavage gave view to the chains and pendants, as well as the manly curls of black chest hair.

There were four chains in all. One held a crucifix announcing Vinny's membership in the Roman Catholic Church. Another carried an Italian horn that warded off evil spirits. A third was a thickly braided gold rope that bespoke of his financial prowess. The fourth was a thin gold chain that proved not everything in Vinny's life had to be symbolic or ostentatious.

Angie sneeringly declared Vinny's gold necklace collection a Mr. T Starter Kit, but only when her brother wasn't around.

There was also the matter of the gold pinkie ring with a small, intricately cut diamond bezel-set deep within. The ring ensured that people would recognize Vinny as a tough customer with rough-and-tumble connections. Basically, a fellow one should be loath to fuck with.

It was the pinkie ring that could be heard smacking sharply against the table's oak surface while Vinny pounded the side of his fist to cease all conversation. My brother spoke in a stern yet tremulous voice.

"Listen," he quavered, "no one is to know the recipes have been stolen. Do you understand me? No employees, no customers, no friends, and especially not Uncle Nunzio."

It was only by the grace of some divine power that Uncle Nunzio had decamped just the night before for a three-week getaway in Las Vegas, a lifelong favorite among American vacation spots. He was busy gambling and going to burlesque shows and Wayne Newton concerts. His departure gave Vinny desperately needed time to recoup and repatriate the recipes before the Great Man returned and learned the awful truth.

Ginger promptly ignored Vinny's decree. "I don't think that's right. People will look for them if they know they're gone. Besides, someone might know who took them. Or maybe the person who took them will get nervous and secretly return them."

"Never mind," father said. "Let the police handle it. Whoever it is will spill their guts as soon at that detective starts questioning him."

"Oh no he won't," said Vinny.

Father shot his son a look.

"I told Jablonsky on the way to his car there will be no questioning of anyone. The cops start interrogating employees and pretty soon half the town will know. And I'm not filing a police report, either. I don't need this thing showing up in the *Sun-Bulletin's* Police Beat column."

Ginger deflated with disappointment, haplessly tossing a twisted napkin on the table. "Well so much for the detective getting back to me with investigative updates. There obviously won't be any investigation."

"Yes there will be," said Vinny, "but it's all going to start right here with us, with this room filled with prime suspects."

An hush fell over the room. Vinny could feel the pressure of black, hostile eyes fixed upon him. He surveyed the expressions. Father's visage soured at his son's distasteful allegations. Mother's face fattened with exasperation.

"You louse," she said, "you're accusing your own flesh and blood of stealing?"

"Who else has the combination?" Vinny said.

Angie was pulsing at the temple. "How thick-skulled could you be? What motive could we possibly have for stealing recipes we already know?"

Vinny's eyes darted around the table. "I get the feeling one of you might just be messing with my head. You might even be trying to take me down. If those recipes are lost I'm dead meat. Is there any one of you who doesn't believe Uncle Nunzio would take the restaurant away from me and transfer ownership to one of you?"

Ginger hugged herself. "I feel violated."

"I don't have time for this," Ringo announced, rising from his seat. "I gotta get some sleep." He made a quick exit and we listened to his feet thunder up the stairway and gradually fade into the distance.

"This is ridiculous," Maria said. "We've obviously got a thief on the staff. That's why you need to let the police finish their work on those fingerprints. If there's a fingerprint that doesn't belong to a family member then we have a suspect."

"Be realistic," Vinny said. "Our employees aren't exactly the sharpest knives in the cutting block. They aren't even ambitious enough to try something like this. Anybody smart enough to plan this and crack the safe wouldn't leave fingerprints behind."

"They didn't even close the safe," I said. "That alone would have given them a huge head start. That safe isn't opened more than a couple of times a year. It could have been months before we knew we had been robbed."

Vinny lifted an index finger in my direction. "Exactly," he said. "Somebody wanted me to know they were gone. Somebody's got it out for me and they're not going to get away with it."

The sun was starting its rise as I headed home that evening. My most urgent desire was to tell my wife Sadie all about this latest family drama playing itself out at the Mangia House. That wasn't going to be possible; not because it was the middle of the night. Sadie had a serious problem with insomnia and probably was awake. The issue was that she also had an even more serious personality disorder and could not be trusted with most information. There was really no telling when or where she might disclose information that was supposed to be kept secret. One could be assured, though, that the information was sure to spill at the most inopportune time.

When I got home the bedroom light was on and Sadie was lying crosswise and perfectly still on the bed, as if a tarantula was charting a path across her belly. Her breathing was shallow, eyes staring intently at the ceiling. She didn't bother to greet me, just looked out the corner of her eyes, then returned her gaze to the ceiling.

I offered an insensitive reply: "My god, what's wrong with you now?"

"Go away," she said.

One of the prime features of my wife's personality disorder was the endless cavalcade of psychosomatic physical and emotional ailments. It was the rare day that passed without Sadie fretting that she had contracted a chronic illness or exotic disease. There were at least a couple of doctor appointments per month. Tests were administered and always came back negative, adding credence to what everyone except Sadie believed — that they were phantom illnesses, figments of overactive imagination.

I sat heavily on the edge of the bed. This created too much motion for Sadie's fragile equilibrium. An annoyed glance followed. "Don't be such a cretin."

"All I did was sit."

"Don't you realize how hostile you're being?"

"I'm exhausted, okay? I landed a little harder than I had planned."

"Why are you so late? I almost called you."

"Why didn't you call me?"

"Because I can't hear."

Sadie explained that for the past five hours the sound of an endless freight train was blasting through her left ear.

"It's really loud," she said, "and it won't stop. It keeps blowing its friggin' horn."

I had heard of this condition before. It really did exist, as did all of Sadie's maladies. It was just a matter of time before this one vanished and a new one surfaced. They always came and went without warning or reason.

"Seems like you can hear me now."

"Don't argue with me. Can't you see them in distress?"

"There was a major catastrophe at the restaurant tonight." She let that one pass without comment. I tried prompting her to converse. "I feel sorry for my brother. There was some inventory stolen tonight. We even got the police involved."

That's as much as I was going to tell Sadie. She said nothing anyway.

"I've got to get some sleep," she said. "I can't function like this."

"You don't have a job Sadie."

"That doesn't mean I don't work."

"Yeah, but you can work whenever you feel like working, and you can nap whenever you feel like napping."

"I told you to go away."

"Why don't *you* go away?"

"I can't go anywhere in this condition."

"Maybe you can jump on that freight train and see where it takes you."

Vinny was at home by this time, sprawled across his leopard-skin sectional sofa contemplating the bleakness of his situation. The recipes were missing and the family legacy was in jeopardy, especially Uncle Nunzio's sterling reputation.

He sensed sabotage. Marciano's Mangia House was the source of all good things in Vinny's life — the expansive home, the timeshare on Key West, the fancy cars and fast women, the gold jewelry. They were all underwritten by the volcano of cash the restaurant produced, not to mention the generous livelihoods it provided to his parents and siblings.

Uncle Nunzio would return soon. It would be the shortest three weeks of Vinny's life. The old man had an extremely well developed bullshit detector. Vinny was certain that something in his own manner would alert Nunzio that something was amiss. He might even be compelled to check the vault, and as soon as he found it empty he would likely experience several very severe moments of angina and then keel over dead of a massive heart attack. Vinny could only dream of such fortune. More likely he would confront Vinny, his face a pallid with shock and disbelief, and demand to know where the family heirlooms had gone.

Vinny would lie, of course, claiming he had transferred them to a bank safe deposit box. The needle on Nunzio's bullshit detector would arc to the extreme end of its red zone and he would demand their return to the property. Vinny would succumb to the pressure and admit that his office had been burglarized and the recipes robbed from right under his nose on a busy Saturday evening. A tongue-lashing of epic proportions, and a thunderous slap or two across the mouth would ensue. Less clear was the cost Vinny would have to pay for the most egregious transgression imaginable. He might bust Vinny down to a simple co-owner who would have to share equal stakes in the enterprise with his entire family; in essence, become a mere member of a ruling board that voted on everything from menu changes to employment procedures.

A wave of nausea was unleashed at the thought of having to make peace and build coalitions with Angie and Maria. He would sooner have Uncle Nunzio throw him out of the business completely than to have to kowtow to his sisters. An equal partnership would leave Vinny with a measly

14.3 percent share of the restaurant's proceeds. How could he pay his double mortgage and triple car payments on such chickenfeed?

Nunzio might even insist Vinny surrender his ownership of the restaurant completely. The old man could do whatever he wanted. It said so in the written agreement he had drafted and required Vinny to sign before agreeing to teach his nephew the business and help underwrite its resurrection.

The only remaining question was if Vinny would tell Uncle Nunzio of his suspicions that a member of his own family, a fellow Marciano, had engineered this larceny. The good news of that scenario would be that the recipes were in family hands. Whatever devious motive might have driven a family member to do such a thing, Vinny knew that no Marciano would share the information with an outside party. That would instantly devalue the recipes and work contrary to their own selfish interests.

His suspicion fell squarely on Sister Angie. He hadn't trusted the shrew since they started working together. From day one it had been a struggle, a contest of wills. He knew she had ambitions of her own, separate from the existing Mangia House. What better way to knock him off his pedestal than destroy the very foundation of the business' success? What better way than to set Uncle Nunzio against him? Did Angie somehow know the ironclad terms of his agreement with their grand old uncle?

*Bitch!*

If the real culprit was some thieving outsider, as Maria had suggested, how long would it be before a competing restaurant with the same recipes popped up and started cannibalizing Marciano's business? And what legal recourse would be available? It would be impossible to prove that a competitor was using the very same recipes, let alone that it had pilfered them from the Fort Knox safe in Marciano's business office. You cannot patent recipes. That's a lesson Uncle Nunzio drilled into his head years ago. That's why Uncle Nunzio had always kept the recipes in a fireproof, bulletproof safe, and insisted that Vinny do the same. That's why only Marciano family members were allowed to learn and prepare the recipes. One leak and the loss was irrevocable.

Vinny imagined the recipes appearing one by one in a nationally circulated food magazine such as *Bon Appetite*.

There was probably little chance of ever recovering the recipes, Vinny knew. Still, he wanted the satisfaction of finding out who was behind this heist so he could administer his own excruciating form of retribution. Nobody was going to steal from Vinny Marciano and get away with it. A statement was needed to be made — one so loud and definitive nobody would dare cross him again.

Already he was considering various forms of punishment involving flammable liquids, electricity and a Louisville Slugger baseball bat.

The Tuscan yellow walls of Marciano's Mangia House were painted in a faux finish that gave the illusion that one was sitting along the Italian Riviera basking in golden sunlight and watching transparent clouds drifting past on their way to the Mediterranean Sea. The walls were further embellished with large, colorful reproductions of oil paintings of voluptuous women captured in various states of undress — women in lingerie, in unclothed repose, in bedroom tableaux, in the midst of bathroom ablutions, lazing on the veranda, and standing naked among the begonias. They were rendered in thick splotches of electrifying color, reminiscent of the works of impressionistic icons Claude Monet and Vincent van Gogh. To some they were depictions of blatant eroticism; to me they were artistic studies of the female form.

These were my contributions to the Mangia House. I was a man of few extravagances, but collecting art was one of them. As soon as I ran out of wall space in my home, my collection of framed limited-edition prints spilled over to the bare walls of the restaurant, despite Vinny's indifference for interior decorating and Uncle Nunzio's aversion to change of almost any kind. Many of our patrons liked the effect my burgeoning collection was having on the restaurant's ambiance. It gave the dining room a more European feel appropriate to an Italian *trattoria*.

They had all been produced and purchased from Enrico Zepeda. Oddly enough, Zepeda was a Guatemalan refugee granted political asylum by the U.S. government after he ran afoul of his native country's repressive dictator Alejandro Garcia. Zepeda and his oil paintings were considered national treasures before Garcia's military regime came to power. Zepeda's penchant for rendering portraits of unclad women put him at odds with the new dictator, who was trying to consolidate his power by winning the support of the influential Catholic Church. Though he espoused Victorian values in hopes of earning the church's fealty, Alejandro Garcia lived a lascivious lifestyle, replete with a long-time mistress and the occasional one-night whore.

In defiance of the puritanical dictator's feigned morality, Enrico Zepeda's paintings were rendered with increasing carnality. In particular, he enraged the brutal Garcia by painting the dictator and his tubby wife in an awkward state of copulation. That work earned him a visit from members of the government secret police who beat him with truncheons and warned Zepeda to never again use the nation's maximum leader or his wife as artistic subjects. The offending painting was confiscated and delivered to Garcia, who crushed it under his jackboots and pitched the remnants into a roaring fireplace. He then scurried off to the royal toilet and masturbated.

Zepeda, bandaged and limping, took the incident to Guatemala City's leading newspaper the next day. He proclaimed the primacy of artistic freedom and denounced the brutality of the Garcia regime. But the newspaper's managing editor, firmly constrained by central government censors, sheepishly told Zepeda the incident was not newsworthy and sent him away.

Not to be dissuaded, Zepeda went right to work on another portrait of the dictator. This time Garcia was painted having sex with a prostrating woman whose hind quarters bore the unmistakable dimensions of Guatemala's national borders. The women's visage was equally unmistakable: It was the puckish face of the dictator's long-time mistress, Rosa de la Questa, the nation's most famous actress. What infuriated Garcia most about the painting was that his fully engorged penis was as short and stout as a country mushroom.

These strokes of political heresy came to the public's attention when, during the night, Zepeda secretly hung the portrait in the capitol city's main square, where hundreds of Guatemalans would gather the next morning for coffee and fresh bread. A throng quickly congregated around the portrait. Guffaws and hisses sprang from the crowd. One long-time dissident cried out, "Guatemala's taking it up the ass!"

In the lower right corner were Enrico Zepeda's hallmark initials. Soon a military patrol arrived waving weapons and dispersing the riled crowd. The painting was commandeered and brought to the dictator who again crushed it into several pieces under his jackboots and threw the remains of yet another Zepeda classic into his fireplace, its heavily oiled canvas curling and flaring in the psychedelic flames. Then it was off to his porcelain throne for another bout of self-induced ardor.

Zepeda, well connected to the nation's political underground, used his sources to find transportation across the border into Honduras, where he was stowed on a cargo plane bound for Mexico from where he snuck across the U.S. border. Friends reported the Zepeda residence was ransacked before being burned to the ground. It was replaced by a small stucco government building that today houses the country's Ministry of Arts & Culture.

Zepeda's determination to turn the United States into his adopted country and introduce his work to American art connoisseurs brought him to New York City. He took classes in American Studies at New York University, painted at outdoor cafes, hung in galleries in the Soho district, and received a hero's welcome from the Big Apple's media and intelligentsia. Newspaper and TV reports were frequent and fawning.

Zepeda eventually found big-city living and the pretenses of New York's artistic community stifling, so the Guatemalan started venturing upstate on weekends and became deeply attracted to the rolling glory of the Catskill and Adirondack mountain ranges, ultimately taking up residence in Binghamton. He moved into the city's decaying industrial quarter where a multitude of artists had converted warehouse spaces into live-in art studios.

Though Erinco Zepeda had escaped the tyranny of Alejandro Garcia's regime, his artwork was making some waves at Marciano's. Our clientele was predominantly devout Catholics, and the most devout of all was Father Benito Saragusa, the pastor of Our Lady of the Immaculate Conception, where the Marciano family had logged many years of worship. Father Saragusa pulled Vinny aside one evening and spoke in his most concerned voice yet about the bacchanal that had encroached.

"Look at the place," the priest said, sweeping a robed arm across the dining room. "It's full of children and old women. They don't need to see this kind of stuff, especially when they're eating. What about the men, Vinny? What about their hormones? They don't need to see pornography when they're trying to enjoy their food and live chaste or monogamous lives."

Vinny gazed down at the priest's bony face and evaporating hair. He was a little wisp of man, swamped under layers of black vestments. "Father," he said, "it's not really pornography, it's artwork. Besides, nobody's really looking at them. They're just on the walls to cover some holes up."

"Vinny, we're all Catholics here. If you need to cover some holes, hang some pictures of the Pope and the Virgin Mary." Then the clergyman put a hand over my brother's shoulder, as if to bring comfort to his now troubled soul. "I'll tell you what I'm going to do tonight before going to bed, Vinny. I'm going to pray for you. I'm going to say three Hail Marys and three Our Fathers for you." The priest smiled. "And I'll tell you what I want you to do for me. Before going to bed tonight say five Acts of Contrition. That's my spiritual prescription for you. Then I know you'll do what's right for the congregation."

Before returning to his dinner, Father Saragusa reached up and used his thumb to trace a cross on Vinny's forehead while whispering a holy incantation that included the phrase, "For yours is the Kingdom, the Power and the Glory forever and ever, amen."

A titanic battle had already been brewing among Marciano family members, a civil war pitting sibling against sibling and parent against parent. It was a conflict between family loyalty and professional ambition. Paranoia had infiltrated our relationships, and the recipes disappearance amplified the situation.

Sister Angie and Father Albie wanted to expand Marciano's. Not just to grow the existing business, but to open additional restaurants. Each wanted a Marciano's of their own and had dreams of selling bottled sauces and fresh homemade pastas and pizza dough through the region's supermarkets. There was even talk of publishing a cookbook containing the clan's signature dishes. That the recipes had been guarded for generations and were not allowed to be shared was of little concern to father. His calculation was that, after the initial explosion of condemnations and evil hexes placed on him by his brothers and sisters, and distant relatives in the mountains of Italy, they would quickly forgive after the Marciano Family Trust was established and listed them among the beneficiaries. Father envisioned this trust churning out annual payloads of cash to immediate and extended family members. Father saw money as the balm that healed all wounds and family divides.

He kept mostly quiet about his ambitions, but Angie did not. She talked so openly about splitting off and starting a sister restaurant that Vinny threatened to cut her tits off. New restaurants, bottled sauces and cookbooks all meant the same thing to Vinny: the balkanization of his restaurant's robust customer base. If other Mangia Houses were opened, family members would scatter in all directions. Who would be left at the original Mangia House to cook the family tradecraft other than Vinny? He envisioned endless hours of labor and no days off. His life, like his Uncle Nunzio before him, would become dedicated to nothing other than cookery and full-throttle kitchen and restaurant management. He was living in grandeur just the way things were and didn't want family greed to dilute his splendor. That wouldn't be good for Vinny's job satisfaction. His specialty was the front of the house — mingling with customers and time-honored regulars, and puffing fat cigars at the bar where he regaled the drinkers with sports play-by-play and lurid jokes. Something would definitely be lost if the master of ceremonies was driven into the obscurity of the kitchen.

And Vinny wasn't alone in the anti-expansion camp. Ringo was firmly entrenched there. Anything that augured the breakup or diminishment of the family was a threat to Ringo. He felt great emotional dependence on his siblings and parents and wanted them gathered around him in one concentrated dose, under one roof, all within yelling distance. One business. One location. One unified effort. One family, under God, indivisible, and without fractured endeavors and defections.

Mother Margherita agreed.

"I keep telling your father we're no spring chickens," she told me during morning food preparations. "We're too old to be opening a restaurant and running a business. As it is, the guy works like a bull. He always feels the need to make money and prove himself. I guess he just never got over the fact that his brother got to run a successful business and he didn't. So your brother had a business and you didn't, who the hell cares? You're 70 years old now, support you son."

Later that morning I ran across Angie in the red meat section of the neighborhood grocery store.

"What, we're all supposed to work for *him*?" she said.

I tried to quietly go about my shopping, but Angie steered her cart in my direction and started following.

"What happened to the family tree?" she continued. "Vinny wants to be the trunk of the family business tree, a trunk that keep growing bigger but doesn't sprout any branches. How can that be? We should grow branches that extend in all directions and makes us bigger and richer. We should be reaching for the sky. Let me tell you something, Vinny's not the trunk. Uncle Nunzio's the trunk of this tree, and Grandma and Grandpa are the roots, God rest their souls. Vinny's a branch, and he needs to make room for other branches. That's what families that support one another do."

I looked up and saw Mother Margherita wheeling a cart around the corner. The cart was loaded to the gills with produce, and custom wrapped filets of meat and fish, and it was rolling towards us. Shopping had suddenly become a family affair. Mother pulled her cart head to head with Angie's, as if to prevent a getaway.

"I heard you from the other isle," mother said. "Stop bothering your brother with all your crazy ideas. I told you to compromise. Talk to your brother Vinny about starting a lunch business and you and your father can be in charge of that part of the operation."

"What," Angie protested, "I'm supposed to just have a little piece? He gets to be the big shot and all I get to do is serve a few lousy lunches?"

"It's his business, you jackass."

"That's such a croc. He doesn't even know how to run the place. It's management by absenteeism. He's not paying attention, mother, that's why he keeps all of us around, so every night can be a party for him. The employees are running wild. Do you have any idea how much waste goes on in there? We should be making twice the money we do."

Mother was looking for a can of vegetables to throw at Angie's head. Mother had no qualms about personally leveling stinging attacks against her children, but she bridled at criticism of her children from any other quarter. If one of her kids was attacked, that child was immediately elevated to her favorite offspring, and the attacker was busted down to the runt of the litter.

Having thought better of the severe injury that might be inflicted by a flying can of Delmonte green beans, mother fired back with her voice box instead.

"Stop shooting your mouth off about your brother. He's making a fortune and all you can do is criticize. You think you could do any better?"

"What, you think *he's* the only one who can be successful in this family."

And so it went as I rolled my cart away to finish shopping in peace.

Within 48 hours of Angie's interdiction of my trip through the grocery store, father showed up in my backyard unannounced. It was Saturday afternoon and Sadie and I were grilling. My anxiety started rising as he strolled up to me. Father's mere physical presence made his sons anxious because he was both rotund and bald. He had lost the hair on top of his head. All that remained was a ring of gray hair around the sides and back of his scalp. And his frame was easily lugging an extra 150 pounds.

This left his sons to wonder if they had inherited the same genetic imperatives. Vinny's hair was already thinning at the crown of his head. Though older than both of us, Ringo had a thicket of coiled black hair so formidable it seemed destined to stay grounded for life. My locks were holding their own — for now. Though, judging from the number of hairs in my brush, it seemed shedding season had begun. The critical question was how long my follicles would continue re-growing the strands they were surrendering in such prolific numbers.

On the weight front, Ringo was already losing the battle of the bulge. His stomach was rising like heavily yeasted dough. Vinny had gained a solid ten or twenty pounds since entering his thirties, but he carried it well. All the weight he gained distributed itself evenly over his body, giving him a beefy rather than corpulent physique. The only drawback was that his rings wouldn't come off his fingers without being buttered or lubricated with olive oil. I, like Ringo, took after my father in the weight-gain department. I had not gained but a few pounds since college. Still, every ounce of fat my body retained agglomerated at the belly and in the form of love handles, meaning that even the most trifling weight gain was plainly visible to all around me. Sadie, fearful I'd end up losing hair and accumulating a significant amount of fat, held a vigil over my belly and massaged my scalp occasionally to keep the follicles stimulated and productive.

I nervously smiled and nodded to acknowledge father's arrival.

"You know your sister Angie is right, don't you?" father said. "But she's thinking too small. She's talking about just another restaurant or two. That's just a start. The real money will be made by franchising."

"Franchising?" I repeated, my voice leaden with incredulity.

"Naturally. With franchising we could open hundreds of outlets within a few years if we play our cards right."

"We're a family owned and run restaurant, that's the concept." I grabbed the tongs and worked the grill. "You can't franchise that."

"Listen buster, the thing that makes our place go are those recipes, and those can be cooked in a thousand different places. Not to mention getting our bottled pasta sauces in the supermarket chains. With a national brand name and our products on supermarket shelves, we'll be making money hand over fist."

"Dad, we're already making money hand over fist."

"You're thinking small like your sister."

"We can't franchise. We'd have to give the secret recipes to the franchisees. You do that and Uncle Nunzio will slap you silly."

"Don't worry about Uncle Nunzio, I can handle him," father declared. His chest puffed up. "When millions of dollars in franchise fees come pouring and I set up the Marciano Family Trust, your Uncle Nunzio will forgive and forget. And so won't your other uncles and aunts."

"You think their commitment to a family vow is going to wither that easily?"

"You're damn right," father said, moving closer to the sizzling meats. "It's high time we fully monetized those recipes."

"Monetized? Have you been reading get-rich-quick books again?"

"Never mind what I'm reading."

"Dad, I swear, I going to talk to the city about revoking your library card if you don't stay away from those books. You know they only get you into trouble. How the hell many pyramid and ponzi schemes are you going to blow money on before you learn your lesson?"

My father blushed momentarily. Then he stepped even closer to the grill, right into the clouds of smoke coming off the fire so that his clothes and what was left of his hair would take on the smell of flaming food. It was clear that he had come under the sway of something even more primal than money. The irrepressible appetite that was the most powerful force of his existence came growling back life. His nostrils flared.

"What do you have on that barbecue?" he said.

Father was ghostly figure now, made slightly opaque by the billows of smoke engulfing him. He joined Sadie and me for t-bones and chicken breasts. When our repast was completed, after father had gnawed every steak and chicken bone smooth and clean, he turned to me and said, "Don't tell your brothers what I told you. I don't want them getting upset."

Then father and his head full of dreams wandered away.

A few evenings later, while I was counting my tips at the bar, Ginger sashayed over wearing a new miniskirt and larger than usual bra inserts. She was normally long gone by time the place had emptied out. Tonight she had stayed behind to talk with me about the issue that had set Marciano against Marciano.

"Christ almighty, Ginger, I don't have time for this shit. I want to get home. I've got a wife with a vibrator waiting for me there."

"Just stay out of it," she advised of the family conflict. "I'm not getting involved and neither should you."

"Hey, you're talking to Switzerland," I said. "My constitution forbids me from taking sides. I keep telling everybody I'm officially neutral and all anybody can do is talk to me about this and try to convince me of the brilliance of their stance."

Ginger, who often suffered from conversational deafness, prattled on.

"There's no winning on this one. You'll be resented by half the family, whichever side you take. I've got my own opinions about this, but I'm keeping them to myself. I'll share them with you because I know you'll be discreet. This family needs to stay the course right now. A breakup would not be a good thing. Everybody's underestimating the role of chemistry in our success. We have the perfect chemistry going right now."

"It resembles nitroglycerin," I said.

"If we decide to reformulate that chemistry there's no telling what might happen. Remember how *The Beatles* broke up thinking they were all going to have fabulous solo careers? And what happened?"

I shrugged and sipped my tonic water.

"Even the most successful of them was only a shadow of the Fab Four. And you know why? It was their lack of chemistry with other players. *The Beatles* had just the right blend that produced special music, even when they were fighting like terriers and tabbies. That's what we've got, and I'd hate to see us piss it away on a bunch of solo careers. Maybe someday, but it would be foolish to work at cross-purposes right now. That's a recipe for disaster. Together, we're worth millions; apart, this family will probably end up in a tailspin. We're practically there now."

My sister looked over her shoulder to make sure we were still alone. "That's between us. I don't want Angie and Maria to start having conniptions."

I reached up to my pursed lips and placed an imaginary lock on them.

"Maria and Angie have a secret agreement."

"How could it be secret if you know about it?"

"I overheard them in the ladies room one day. They didn't know I was sitting in one of the stalls?"

"I don't see how that's possible with all the perfume you wear. They must have smelled your signature scent."

"As I said, I was sitting in one of the stalls."

I gave Ginger a flummoxed look.

"There was a BM in progress," she said.

"Did you say a BM?"

Ginger became irritated. "A bowel movement, okay, there was a bowel movement in progress. So I guess my signature scent, as you call it, must have been masked."

"This is remarkable," I said. "You've spent your whole life pretending you've never so much as had a gas leak let alone taken a smelly shit. To what do I owe this newfound entry into the human race?"

"Oh, stop it."

"If you were in there creating a hazardous waste site they must have smelled the consequences."

"For chrissakes, I don't know what to tell you about that. They must have thought it was a hit-and-run visit and the air still hadn't cleared. Do you want to hear my story or not?"

"Enlighten me?"

"Maria has promised to go to work for Angie if she starts her own restaurant and builds up a clientele as large as Vinny's got. Maria apparently wants some assurances that her tips won't take a hit by jumping ship. Maria also insisted that the deal's off if I become the hostess at Angie's place. She wants some boot-licker she can control running the hostess stand."

Ginger used a lot of unnecessary motion walking over to the jukebox, where she deposited a couple of coins and made some selections. Soon, *Strawberry Fields Forever* was streaming out of the machine.

The truth was that, for all the notions of building a regional food empire, nothing was likely to happen because we were not a very entrepreneurial bunch. Entrepreneurism meant taking risks, and that was foreign to our nature. Mother and father were products of the Great Depression and instilled in their children a life-and-death terror of playing even the most rational games of chance. Basically, we grew up paralyzed by fear. Vinny's decision to take over Uncle Nunzio's restaurant, though ann act of valor by Marciano standards, was about as sure a business bet as one could gamble on, given the restaurant's history and Uncle Nunzio's personal training and assistance. All one really had to do was hang the Marciano flag and start cooking the same food that had been served under the name for the past forty years and the enterprise's long-time customers would re-appear in legion. Besides, Vinny was young and broke at the time and didn't have anything to lose.

Father Albie, his ample belly leading the way, approached Vinny later that day with that look on his face. It was that look that said *I've got a notion*. Not just a run-of-the-mill notion, a bright idea. Vinny looked as though he wanted to make a fast exit from the scene. He hung tight and listened anyway.

Father volunteered to go on eating campaign at competing Italian restaurants — targeting rival establishments that had the greatest incentive to rob the Marciano treasure chest. The idea was to ensure that none of the pilfered recipes were suddenly being turned out by those kitchens.

Vinny's face turned blank.

"Listen buster, I know you think this might've been an inside job. It makes a lot more sense that a competitor stole those recipes. What good are they if they don't start using them? This could be happening right under our noses we wouldn't even know about it unless I get out there and start poking around."

Vinny shrugged. "You really believe they would be that obvious?"

"They see all the business we're doing. They know they don't have a chance against us without those recipes."

Vinny nodded in acknowledgement rather than agreement.

"I'll need an expense budget," father said, "something on the order of several hundred dollars a month."

Vinny's frame buckled ever so slightly. "Do you really think this is the time to start spending more money? Who knows how much money I'm going to need for investigators? This just adds overhead. Aren't you the one who's always telling us not to squander money, to squeeze every nickel until the Buffalo shits in our hand?"

"This is different. It would be tax-deductible money well spent; certainly better spent than some of the funds being spent around here." Father pointed to the ceiling. I was listening to the exchange from the bar. Father cut a momentary glance my way, then back to Vinny. "What I'm talking about is a pittance by comparison."

It wasn't that father needed the money to go on an eating campaign; the expense account simply added an aura of legitimacy to his "volunteer" assignment. Now he was on a mission to eat his way to some grand revelation.

"So you're okay with this plan?"

Vinny shrugged his shoulders again, even more languidly. It was a gesture that said "no" while his mouth said, "What exactly is your strategy? How will you go about doing this?"

"Simple. I'll do some drive-bys. I'll check to see if they're suddenly attracting more customers. I'll check out the menus." Father lifted a finger in the air. "I can smell those recipes a mile away. My nose will be the first detector to go off. If I see something suspicious, I'll order and give them the taste test. Most of these places over-cook the pasta. It's a bunch of mush. The salads are soaked with dressing and the meats are almost never seasoned properly. I don't know how these people stay in business. And the service … *bah*. Some of those servers visit the table so often you can't even eat in peace. Once my order arrives I want to be left alone to focus on my food."

A deep sigh came from Vinny. "Okay, let's give it a try. Keep the cost down."

I couldn't stand it anymore. I had to tear the duct tape off my mouth and pipe in: "Sounds like a wild goose chase to me."

Slowly, father turned my direction and made a clatter by kicking the leg of a barstool.

"I wasn't talking to you buster. I'm having a conversation with your brother. Mind your own business."

"It is my business when my seriously overweight father is talking about restaurant hopping. I know you, dad. You binge. You can't help yourself; you will clean your plate off. You can't be racking up calories."

"Oh my aching back, you sound like your mother."

"You already have acid reflux so bad you have to sleep sitting up. You keep eating that pomodoro sauce and it's full of acid. Didn't your gastroenterologist tell you that stuff gets your throat as electrically charged as a car battery? Mom says he scoped you. Your esophagus is already scorched with first-degree burns. Don't you ever learn your lesson?"

"These doctors don't know their ass from a hole in the ground. I wouldn't go to them at all except that your mother insists."

My eyes dropped to father's belly. Although it was very big it was not squishy. Just the opposite, it was hard to the touch. I was not sure if that was indicative of positive health or a sign of liver problems. I called his domed belly "the movable feast." His appetite was the "irresistible force" and it had created the "immovable object." We all wanted father to drop a couple hundred pounds, even though we had a hard time imagining him a thin man. Round was the only shape we associated with him. Most of us didn't think we would like a slimmed-down version of father. What would that look like? Would he still be our father or just half the man he used to be? We were accustomed to father playing a big role in our lives. Two hundred fewer pounds, that's the kind of change that could be disturbing. It wasn't anything we spent time thinking about, really, because nobody believed father would ever drop the weight.

"Let father be father," Maria liked to say. "The man knows how to digest a meal. Love father for who he is. God bless that appetite."

When father returned later that day his shirt had sauce stains.

"Nothing so far," he said.

Under my breath I mumbled, "What a waste of time and money that is."

Father stared at me as if he wished he had skipped sex the night I was conceived. He kicked the leg of the barstool again. This time he almost lost his balance, wobbling along with the barstool.

Mario Fabrezio, the mayor of Endicott, was a regular at Marciano's and he was in the restaurant again on this evening. He always came with an entourage and tonight was no exception. As usual he filled the largest table in the dining room, a circular one with eight seats. As he and his party settled in, Fabrezio started carrying on as if he was one of King Arthur's Knights of the Round Table. The mayor was in a suit and tie, too. He never went anywhere without a suit and tie, nor did he ever turn down a speaking engagement or ribbon-cutting ceremony.

Endicott, New York was a small town, but to listen to Mario Fabrezio talk about the place you would have thought he was Fiorello La Guardia running Manhattan. He loved running his little town in his trench coat. He had a real passion for politics, regardless of how small the stakes might be, and he had been re-elected several times and had already been mayor for eleven years. When among confidants he called himself Mayor for Life. Why not? Mayor Fabrezio had a City Council that rubberstamped every decision he made, so he basically ran the city by fiat.

Being mayor wasn't even a full-time job. It paid a small salary. Mayor Fabrezio earned his real daily bread as an insurance broker with State Farm, and maintained an office in Endicott and another one across the river in Vestal. He had been hustling insurance for a long time and had built up a substantial clientele, thanks to his ebullient personality and mayorship.

Vinny walked over to the mayor and started rubbing his shoulders as a greeting. My brother was putting on a good show of being carefree. Then he directed the table server to pull two bottles of the best Chianti from our stock. The mayor dropped a lot of money at the restaurant and Vinny found ways to reciprocate in decent measure. Besides, most of the Marcianos had auto, home, health, dismemberment and life insurance policies with Fabrezio's brokerage, so a brisk stream of dollars was flowing in both directions.

As he often did, the mayor ordered two pizzas as appetizers for his cohorts. Ringo had the night off, so I was scheduled for the pizza bench this evening and got right to work on the mayor's order, hand tossing the dough, ladling the rich tomato-herb sauce, scattering the cheese, and sprinkling the finely cut oregano and basil leaves. When it was done baking to perfection we lightly splashed it with an extra virgin olive oil squeezed and bottled in our ancestral Abruzzo province of Italy.

Most pizzerias make two foolish mistakes. They use too much cheese and they use mozzarella, thinking that is the brand of cheese that melts, bubbles and browns the best. Don't get me wrong, a good mozzarella is a beautiful thing and we used it on our margherita pizza, in accordance with tradition. The problem is that mozzarella doesn't have a sharp enough flavor, not compared with many other options, which is why all other pizzas we produced were baked with a very strategic and carefully balanced blend of four cheeses — asiago, fontina, provolone and romano. But that's a secret, as are the percentages because we didn't use all four in equal proportions.

Uncle Nunzio had been baking pizzas this way for more than fifty years. They were thin-crust with an airy texture. Hell, we didn't even call them pizzas on the menu. They were "hot pies," just as our family called them in the Old World. It was one of the things that set us apart. And we didn't put to-go orders in boxes either. That was another thing that set us apart. The hot pie was placed on a circular disk of cardboard and a sheet of white butcher paper was wrapped around it and twisted at the top. A lot of people considered this a gimmick, but it wasn't a gimmick at all. It allowed the steam to escape and kept the hot pie from getting soggy, which is why our hot pies tasted so good cold, and why they reheated so well. It also gave us a nice visual signature. People always knew a Marciano's hot pie because people carried it by choking a hand around twisted top of the white butcher paper.

The mayor and his guests demolished the hot pies within minutes. Then they ordered a second appetizer, one that was actually listed on the appetizer section of the menu. It was an eggplant dish, thin-sliced, layered with gorgonzola cheese and highly acidic tomatoes, then seasoned with wild marjoram. A pesto sauce reduction was drizzled over the top. Vinny called it vegetable art.

That was followed by veal parmagiana and pasta entrees. For dessert they shared an entire sponge cake topped with ricotta and sprinkled with candied fruit and dark chocolate shavings, then smothered in a white chocolate sauce.

The wine kept flowing and as the mayor imbibed more Chianti he started roaring like the lion he believed himself to be. Everybody thought he was just a little bit crooked, but nobody had ever proven anything. Vinny liked the guy, mainly because the mayor liked Vinny, and Vinny liked people who liked him. It reinforced his high opinion of himself. Vinny and the mayor had that in common.

The Marciano family knew that, corrupt or not, Mayor Fabrezio could always be called on for a favor. That lightbulb was already glowing above Vinny's head. After dessert and before the check arrived, Vinny pulled the mayor aside to have a private talk. He explained the situation and made an earnest request that Fabrezio allow sergeant detective Clyde Jablonski — and any other resources of the Endicott Police Department — to work on the case without it being part of the public record, ensuring it wouldn't show up in the newspapers. Though my brother didn't know how truly discrete the mayor was, the situation called for this measure.

"No problem," the mayor blustered with his usual dose of joviality. "I'll talk to the police chief. He works for me."

Technically the chief of police worked for the city manager, but Vinny knew the mayor had adequate influence to carry through with his word. Vinny shook Mario Fabrezio's hand and beseeched the mayor to treat the matter with the highest level of discretion.

When they returned to the table the mayor turned to Vinny and said: "I'll take care of business tomorrow."

The two men clinked glasses and sipped wine. Vinny picked up the evening's tab.

I found Vinny staring at the dining room ceiling, obscured as it was by the burlap coverings strung across nearly its full expanse to keep the fresco a mystery to all but a few of us until the Grand Unveiling would take place. Vinny could not shake the circumstantial suspicions he was feeling toward Enrico Zepeda and his nightly occupation of the place.

"I want to go see Zepeda," he told me. "Both of us. For a progress report."

Vinny's suspicion was palpable, even though he had never voiced it. "Zepeda?"

"The artist," he said.

"The accented one."

"How long does it take to put the scaffolding together and climb to the top?"

"He fell off it one night," I said. "In the morning I found him lying semiconscious on the floor."

"He fell?

"Nothing got broken. No bones, no furniture."

"How does a man fall from up there?"

"He was looking at the ceiling to long. Got disoriented. There was some disequilibrium."

"I thought he was lying on his back like da Vinci."

"That's a myth," I said. "Da Vinci didn't lie on his back when he painted the Sistine Chapel. He stood there. Just like Zepeda."

The front door to Enrico Zepeda's residential loft and working studio was a huge slab of wood set on rollers, top and bottom. It might have been the entrance to a small airplane hangar. It was ajar in anticipation of our visit, as I had texted our intent to a stop by. I pounded on the huge door with the side of my fist to announce our arrival. Zepeda's heavily accented voice beckoned from within.

It was the first time Vinny had been to Zepeda's space, a converted warehouse, and he was taking a cool survey of the place. The air stung with the smell of oil paint and turpentine. Zepeda was a man consumed by passion for his artwork. There wasn't room for anything else in his life, with the exception of Guatemalan politics and his hatred for that country's dictator. Actually, there was one other thing — Zepeda's strong, prurient interest in naked women. That was made obvious, too, by the artist's subject matter.

What interest would he have in recipes? The man would stand at an easel for hours, went into a trance and often forgot to eat, yet he still had a blubbery midsection because of his sedentary profession and lifestyle. Painting did not involve a lot of movement, and like most non-Americans, Zepeda had no affection for exercise.

"Did you say a 'progress report' in that text you sent me?" Zepeda's expression was filled with incredulity.

"Vinny wants to see the rest of the value sketches you've made."

"Of course," Zepeda said. "I'll start a pot of coffee."

Vinny moved along the edges of the vast room, one side of which was almost entirely giant, louvered windows that gave a wide view of the rustbelt ruins that was Binghamton, New York. It had seen better days. The Industrial Revolution had been good to Binghamton, while the Information Age had left it behind. Now the population was shrinking and the turn-of-the-century buildings were decaying; a dingy city frozen in time. It was a beautiful city in its own way, not unlike the historic cities of Europe. At least it could be romanticized as such. It was, after all, founded and built by European settlers.

I was talking to Zepeda, who seemed distracted. The artist glanced over his shoulder every now and again to pick up on Vinny's movements. Vinny lingered by a stack of file boxes, the only place in the room where documents of any kind might be kept.

When the coffee was done brewing Zepeda poured, then gestured to Vinny with a steaming cup. "Please, have some."

We all sat and sipped our coffees. It was a lethally strong brew.

Next, Zepeda was on the move. He went to the corner of the room with the filing boxes and grabbed a very long roll of paper, like a blueprint paper you might find in an architect's office. He unfurled it on a large open area of the floor, then slipped off his boots and walked on it in his wool socks, pointing out the various features of the penciled sketches. His damp, wool socks left moisture prints behind.

"I'm painting from the inside out, as you know. This entire center area is already done, now I'm working on the perimeter."

"This is quite detailed," Vinny said, "almost like paint by the numbers."

Zepeda smiled. "With something this extensive, absolutely. Planning is essential. My imagination takes shape in pencil first. Then come the oils. As you see, in the center we have creation, surrounding that is triumph and celebration, and beyond that we have lust, strife, conflict and the human condition. I've never tried to convey so much in a single piece of work. It's extraordinary."

Zepeda looked at Vinny. "Thank you for the opportunity."

Vinny forced a smile and nodded.

"Do you feel properly briefed?" Zepeda asked.

"I think so," Vinny said. Then he asked: "Are you enjoying yourself?"

"This is the most excited I've ever been about a piece of work. Except for the time I besmirch that asshole president in Guatemala, and he sent his goons after me. But this is different. This isn't revenge. This is love. This is passion."

When we got to the Mangia House we found detective sergeant Clyde Jablonsky leaning against the bar, along with his leather jacket, blue jeans and boots. Standing close to the lawman's commanding presence was Ginger, prattling away about her ill-fated days as a modeling student in the Windy City. She wanted to make sure Jablonsky knew just how glamorous and worldly she was.

Ginger's complexion had turned primrose and she was giving the detective adoring expressions. He was looking down into her face with a devious smile. *It said, I'm not hearing a word you're saying but I'm keen to all the possibilities.*

"The hell you doing here Jablonsky?"

"Ginger tells me you had a conversation with the mayor."

"Oh she did," Vinny replied, giving our sister a sharp glance.

Just as Vinny was preparing to tell sergeant detective to get out, another set of words were escaping Jablonsky's resonant voice box: "I haven't gotten any word about this yet from the chief, though I do have some information for you."

Vinny took a cigar from the humidor he kept behind the bar. I flipped open my butane lighter and ignited the end of it. Jablonsky gazed at us strangely, as if we were auditioning for some type of synchronized act on a variety show.

"I'm listening," Vinny puffed.

"A restaurant's opening on the outskirts of town," Jablonsky said. "Construction's been underway for a while. I've been wondering for months what the building was going to house. They finally put a sign up that has the place's name and bragging about having authentic Italian recipes."

Ginger started waving a hand to clear the air. "Do you have to smoke that disgusting thing?"

"Where is this place?" I asked.

"Twist Run Road, just past the Cider Mill. I thought it was a bit out of the way, but the owner claims the town is growing in that direction. I don't know. I don't see it, but it's his dime."

Vinny puffed hard on his cigar and let a ribbon of blue smoke escape his lips and spiral past his face. "You spoke with the owner?"

"That's what I'm trying to tell you. I popped in to talk to the guy, more out of curiosity than anything else. Asked him where the recipes were from, and then the shit started coming out of him. He stuttered his way through a few dishes — some veal, chicken and pasta entrees that sound similar to yours. And, of course, there's pizza. Thin crust."

"Cigar?" Vinny asked Jablonsky.

The detective shook his head.

"They're Cubans. I've got Montecristos and Cohibas."

"Last time I checked those violate our embargo against communist Cuba and are illegal in the United States."

Ginger threaded her arm through the detective's in a girlish *he's-my-hero* fashion. Then she leaned up against his body, creaking the black leather jacket. I'd never seen my sister get this cozy with a guy so quickly. Ginger had always played the aloof hard-to-get type, but it was apparent she was falling hard for this guy. Jablonsky had somehow buried all her resistance beneath his lush baritone. The detective had all the qualifiers on Ginger's list. His tall, lean body had more angles that a geometry book. He was also macho and unflappable, and his voice sang out like a deep, rich musical instrument with every word he spoke.

"I'll admit to fracturing a few federal laws in my time," Vinny said.

Jablonsky gave Vinny a stiff look. The detective didn't like Vinny's type, a cocky young man who thought the rules only marginally applied to him, that he was somehow given special dispensation to cross the line when it served his notions of expediency or pleasure. Jablonsky was a man who believed in rules, and that they should be enforced. That's why he became a cop.

Vinny said, "I don't think federal trade laws are your jurisdiction, so why don't you tell me some more about this guy you intimidated."

"I shouldn't even be giving your case a second thought. Officially speaking, the crime doesn't even exist. That is, unless you want to change your mind about this filing a police report and pressing charges against any perpetrators I find."

"As you know," Vinny said, giving Ginger a momentary, penetrating glance, "I discussed this with the mayor. This should now be an official off-the-books investigation."

"I haven't gotten a single word about that from anyone at the department."

Vinny stiffened. Then he relaxed. "Oh well, sounds like you're doing fine without the marching orders."

"It was strictly happenstance. I saw this new place and I stopped."

"So what's the guy's name? You must have picked that up."

"Sure I did," Jablonsky said, reaching into a pocket to retrieve a small notebook. "It's right in here," he said, flapping its pages in the air before returning it to his pocket.

"So what it is?"

"Confidential."

"Unusual name."

Jablonsky shifted his long frame and the petite Ginger went along for the ride on his hip.

"Find the culprit and get my recipes back. I got a finder's fee of five grand ready to be deposited in your bank account."

Jablonsky gave Vinny a bemused smile and shook his head. "No can do." The detective's eyes kept dropping to Vinny's assortment of gold chains, which were becoming entangled with the curly hairs on his chest.

Vinny took the cigar from his mouth and blew a toxic conflagration of smoke over the aspiring couple's heads. "Did I say $5,000? I meant $10,000."

"What do you think, you're talking to some cop from Mexico? We've got rules and regulations at the department, and we actually follow them."

"I read somewhere that incentivized cops almost always solve crimes. That's why police shootings never go unsolved."

Jablonsky hardened his expression.

"C'mon," Vinny said, "this is just little off-the-record commission for you. The mayor's going to see to it that you're on the case anyway. Might as well get some extra scratch for your efforts."

"Save your money. You'll need it to buy more illegal and over-priced Cuban cigars."

Vinny blew another plume of cigar smoke towards the ceiling, where a slowly circulating overhead fan pushed it back down on our heads. "If you really want to help me, give me the name of a good private eye."

The two men tensely held one another's eye contact for several moments, each man believing they had leverage over the other. Vinny, the taxpayer, brought a *you-work-for-me* attitude to the situation. Jablonsky, the lawman and romancer, took an *I-have-your-sister-in-emotional-and-physical-custody* stance to the matter. It was Jablonsky who finally broke the standoff when he finally pulled the notebook back out of his pocket and tore a page from it, set it on top of the bar and started scribbling. He startled Vinny by stuffing the note in the breast pocket of his shirt. "Give this guy a call, but don't tell him I sent you. I'm not recommending the guy."

"You're sending me to a guy you can't recommend?"

"Let me put it this way, this investigator gets things done, he just doesn't exactly do it by the book. He's a former cop who got in a lot of trouble for using rough and tumble tactics. Hurt a few people pretty bad."

Vinny smiled.

"Shall we?" Jablonsky's voice rumbled down to the still primrose-faced Ginger. She dislodged herself from the detective's hip and told Vinny, "My set-up work is complete. I'll be back in time for opening."

When the newly-minted couple disappeared behind the closing door, Vinny retrieved the piece of paper Jablonsky had stuffed in his breast pocket and read it. Then he nudged me and said, "C'mon, let's pay this private dick a visit."

A couple of days after she and her family had been accused of stealing the recipes, Angie took hold of a meat hammer and set about the regular chore of pounding several dozen veal cutlets to tenderization. The stainless-steel hammer looked like a one-handed sledgehammer but was much lighter. Its doubled-headed hammer was also studded rather than smooth, so much the better for breaking down fibrous meat and making it suitable for cooking and eating.

Angie was especially good with the meat hammer because she had a huge reservoir of pent up rage dating back to her incidence with the umbilical cord during the birthing process. Her rage was compounded on this day by her brother's recent allegations, so she was lowering the boom on the veal with more ferocity than ever.

*Whack! Whack! Whack!*

Most cutlets require just 20 to 30 good strikes per side before being moved along in the process and the next cutlet placed on the wood hammering block. But Angie had lost all sense of time and count. She was well past 100 strikes and just kept hammering away on the same piece of veal, her hammer strokes booming through the kitchen.

Veal parmagiana was one of our most popular dishes. They arrive at the tables sizzling on a platter accompanied by a half-portion of homemade pasta and the freshest green vegetable our suppliers had available. But if Angie's bludgeoning wasn't put to a stop the night's special was destined to be veal pate on bruschetta croutons.

*Whack! Whack! Whack!*

The racket got Mother Margherita's attention. She shuffled over to Angie's corner of the kitchen and noticed that she had been pounding the same slab of meat for the last fifteen minutes and was so thoroughly bludgeoned that it was turning to mush.

"Hey, take it easy with that hammer," she said. "We're making veal cutlets, not Spam."

"What?" Angie said, giving her mother a twisted facial expression. "What did you say?"

"Look at the damn thing. You've turned it into a piece of road kill."

Unfazed, Angie turned back to the cutlet and started swinging the hammer again. She might have been blacksmith beating a horseshoe into shape.

*Whack! Whack! Whack!*

Mother saw a daughter out of control, playing out another of her endless internal dramas. She knew that Angie had a way of taking a bad experience, internalizing it and stewing on it until she had mentally inflated the episode to intergalactic proportions. Angie saw a slab of veal that, from the moment she slapped it on the chopping block, had a spitting resemblance to Vinny's smug visage. He was staring up at her, his face full of conceit and allegation. As Angie hammered away she silently repeated the incantation, "I wanna to smash his big fat face!"

By this time flecks of creamed veal were starting to fly with every strike. Several had glued themselves to the lenses of Mother Margherita's glasses, while others clung to strands of hair that had just been dyed at the beauty salon that morning.

"Stop beating that poor thing," mother cried.

Angie was in deep in a psychotic spell and was still busy pulverizing Vinny's image. She pounded the meat even harder, her own face and blouse speckled by flying bits of creamed veal.

*Whack! Whack! Whack!*

The audacity of my little brother, Angie thought. The insolence! To accuse me of stooping to the level of a common criminal. To accuse me of stealing from my own family. The bastard had gone too far this time.

*Whack! Whack! Whack!*

Mother Margherita was beside herself. "That's a delicate piece of meat you fool!" She pinched her daughter's earlobe between a pair of fingers and twisted.

Angie stopped only long enough to knock her mother's arm away and offer a look of such furor it seemed she might turn the kitchen tool on Mother Margherita's sagging old body.

*Whack! Whack! Whack!*

"Stop hitting that meat, you jackass!" Mother edged closer and got hit in the face with a fresh spray of creamed meat.

Angie ignored her still, lifting the hammer even higher above her head in preparation for delivering the most devastating blow of the afternoon. It never landed. Mother grabbed Angie's arm in mid-air and the two women started wrestling for control of the utensil. Though Mother Margherita was the elder of the two women, her grip was still strong and she also had leverage over her shorter daughter. Mother twisted the stainless-steel hammer until it broke free of Angie's grasp and she was able to take possession.

Angie made a move to get the hammer back. "Let me do my job," she cried.

Mother Margherita pushed her away and raised the hammer above her head and said: "Back off! Back off you maniac, before I use this thing to soften that stubborn skull of yours."

Angie decided to take the wiser of two paths, retreating slightly.

"Now get the hell out of here," mother ordered. "Go take a tranquilizer. I'll take care of the veal."

Angie, her face red and sweaty from the exertions, stormed out of the kitchen and went missing for several minutes. Mother threw the mutilated slab of veal in the garbage, wiped down the surface with a clean rag and put a fresh cutlet on the chopping block. She started pounding.

Minutes later a murderous scream came from the dining room. Mother, father and the rest of us went running to see what the commotion was. A second scream split the air and led us to the back corner of the dining room, where we found Angie curled in the fetal position underneath a table.

Angie had turned, as she always did, to her primal scream therapy in an effort to blow off the steam that had accumulated.

Mother, infuriated that her daughter would behave like this in front of a restaurant full of employees prepping for work, unhinged a fire extinguisher from the wall and blasted her daughter with its contents for a three-second count. When she finally released the trigger, Angie was frosted white with a layer of sodium bicarbonate. She coughed and spluttered for air.

"How many times do I have to tell you to do your screaming at home?" Mother Margherita said. "And only after you've covered your face with a pillow."

"Why you sack of shit," Angie finally shot back after catching her breath.

"You still haven't learned your lesson," mother said, pulling the fire extinguisher's trigger again and blasting Angie with a second coat of white frosting.

"There," Mother Margherita said, "now cool your jets."

"That's enough," Father Albie said, yanking the extinguisher from his wife's hands before she could cut it loose with another hale of the fire-suppressing agent. He remounted it on the wall and ordered Ginger to get the Hoover and vacuum up the mess.

He turned to his youngest daughter and said, "Go home and clean yourself up. Take the night off. Hurry up before the customers start showing up."

Maria helped her sister off the floor, escorted her to the car. Angie, coated with creamed veal and white frosting, made the unsteady drive home, letting loose two more primal screams along the way.

Vinny was a conflicted Catholic. Many things troubled him about the church, such as its insistence regarding the Pope's infallibility in matters of faith. Its stand on contraception. The prohibition on marriage in the priesthood. Disclosures of rampant pedophilia among the clergy.

My brother also complained that he got none of the benefits and all of the side effects of being Catholic. Chief among the side effects was guilt, and Vinny was feeling plenty of that after accusing family members of stealing the restaurant's recipes. That act had aroused so much guilt that Vinny did something he hadn't done in a long time.

He went to confession.

From the time my brother walked through the grandiose front doors of Our Lady of the Immaculate Conception Church, the sweet and sorrowful memories of Christian worship came swirling back to him. The smell of the smoldering incense. The racks of burning candles. The arresting solemnity of the structure's silence. Houses of religious devotion seemed to have a different quality about their silence; there was a significance and profundity about it.

Vinny dipped his index finger in a small dish of holy water hanging on the wall and was almost surprised it didn't burn. The sign of the cross was made, leaving a moist spot on the center of his forehead.

He moved gingerly through the church's cavernous open spaces and looked around at all that was holy around him — the biblical images portrayed in stained glass, the statues of the Madonna, the huge gilded cross, the vestments draped over the altar. It was a huge and historically important church. The structure's beauty and good fragrance were tinged by the inevitable echoes of sin and punishment.

There were people lined up against a distant wall, awaiting their turns in the confessional. They seemed burdened by the indiscretions they were about to unload. Vinny seriously considered walking out. He didn't even like being seen in this light, as a person who did sinful things that needed righting. He took pride in his insouciance toward his actions, regardless how wanton. But he decided it was worth sticking around just to continue inhaling the glorious fragrance of frankincense and myrrh.

It took 19 minutes for his turn in the confessional. Then there was more waiting while Father Benito Saragusa was attending to the sinner in the confessional on the other side of the priest's chamber. It all felt incredibly foreign. Vinny didn't go to church very often anymore. It didn't jibe with his lifestyle. Father Saragusa's sermons had a wicked habit of sounding custom made to pass judgment on some unsavory act Vinny had engaged in the night before. They had a way of reminding him just how prodigal he had become.

The small window through which priest and parishioner communicated slid open. Vinny could see the shadowy chin of Father Saragusa through the dark screen that was supposed to protect the confessor's identity.

"Forgive me father for I have sinned," Vinny whispered in a raspy voice he considered a disguise. "My last confession was at a year and a half ago."

"What!" the priest snapped. "Do you want to go to hell?"

"I'm here to confess that I may have falsely accused my family of committing a crime."

"Is that you, Vinny?"

"Dammit, father, I hate when you do that," Vinny said, his voice returning to normal. "You did that the last time I came to confession, which is why I haven't been back for so long."

"There's no need for that, Vinny. You've come to me with a tortured soul; let's not make your situation any worse."

"This is supposed to be an anonymous confession between a priest and a parishioner. Now you've broken the spell."

"You're guaranteed privacy," the priest said. "not anonymity."

"Why do you think the church builds dark, soundproof booths? Why do you think we're talking through a screen?"

"How could I not recognize your voice? I know my flock. I cannot blindly attend to my parishioners' needs. It would be irresponsible. As pastor of this church I'm in spiritual charge of the congregation, of which you're a member. At least you used to be. Where the hell have you been?"

"Can't you at least for appearance sake create the illusion of anonymity by pretending you don't know who's in here?"

"You're in the sanctity of the confessional, Vinny. Don't let my knowledge of your identity bother you. I'm a man of God and a Catholic, which means I'm sworn to secrecy. I ask again, where the hell have you been?"

Silence…

"Okay, let's get on with it. At least you're here and I should be grateful for that. You got as far as telling me you accused your family of a crime. Tell me what happened, Vinny."

"I told you, I accused my family of committing a crime, and I don't really know that any of them did."

"What was the crime?"

"It was theft, okay. I accused them of stealing something. I accused them of stealing, even though I have no evidence of that."

"Accused them of stealing what?"

"What difference does it make? Stealing is stealing. It's a sin."

"Why split hairs, Vinny? You came here to fully disclose your confessions to God. To get the full advantages of confession you need to let it all out. It doesn't just cleanse the soul, it's good for your mental health. It eases the conscience."

"I'm not here to confess a sin, Father, not have an encounter session."

"You're beleaguered, Vinny. I know that because it's very rare that something weighs on your mind so heavily that you're driven to confession. Full confession offers tremendous relief to the beleaguered."

Vinny wouldn't budge, partly because he had suspected that Father Saragusa was a gossip, that church members' confessions had a way of leaking out. Saragusa had always been heavy-handed about people attending confession. Vinny suspected that was because the priest had a voyeuristic streak, and the information he received at during confession gave him fresh grist for the rumor mill.

"Was money stolen, Vinny?"

"Knock it off, Father. I'm not going through a process of elimination with you. I've said all I'm going to say. If you do this again I'm going to go straight to God with my confessions from now on."

"I shouldn't press," the priest said. "There's always next week. Come back after you've clarified your feelings and you're ready to confess the rest."

"Have any of my family members been to confession during the last couple of weeks, father? Have they admitted to anything that sounds like the incident I'm referring to?"

"How could you even ask such a question?" the priest said. "You know the confessional is sacred. Everything said here is between me, my parishioner and the Holy Ghost."

"If I knew my accusations were correct it would go a long way towards putting my mind at ease. I'm assuming if one of my siblings or parents stole anything they would come to see you on-the-double to confess and get a fresh start."

"Focus on your actions, Vinny, not theirs."

"You must hear some pretty wild stuff in here, Father."

"I've long said if one wants to contemplate infinity all he need do is consider the stupidity of man."

"You must find it hard to keep all these secrets you collect."

"By time confession's over, I've handed them over to God the Father and I don't even remember what I've been told anymore. There are no secrets to keep. Now … can I count on you coming by next week?"

"It's hot in here."

"You used to be one of my altar boys, helping me orchestrate mass every Sunday morning. What happened, Vinny? I never see you in church anymore. I feel that you have strayed so far from the flock."

"I'm busy, father, you know that. I've got a business to run and it takes all my time."

"Perhaps it's me. Perhaps I've been a poor shepherd for your soul."

"Oh please, Father, not more Catholic guilt. I'm not participating in that. I might not show up often but I put more than my fair share in the collection basket. From what I can see you're putting that money to use. I see new pews, stained glass and marble facings on your Roman columns." He didn't mention that the priest's new black limo hadn't gone unnoticed either.

"We've added some new pews, yes, but the stained glass and marble just look like new because we finally had them steam cleaned."

"I do what I can."

"You could do more, Vinny. It's important that you attend my masses. Other people will see you there. That will attract others and the parish will grow. You're a man of influence in this community, and I'm asking you to put it to good and godly use."

"I'll do the best I can, Father, that's all I can promise. Is my soul clean now? Has it been washed?"

"I want you to know that if you're having a crisis of faith I'm here for you. It's important you know that. Not just for mass or confession, either. The door to the rectory is open to you any time you need to sit down and talk. About anything, I mean. We can talk about the Yankees or the Knicks."

"I'll keep that in mind, Father."

"What else do you have to confess?

"Nothing."

"Aren't you forgetting something?"

"Don't play games with me, Father. What are you talking about?"

"How about the pornography on your restaurant's walls? It still hasn't been removed, and there are many parishioners exposed to those scenes of debauchery when they come to your place of business."

"Father, I told you, that's not pornography it's art. And my customers and your parishioners don't seem the least bit bothered by those paintings."

"Well, what do you expect them to do? They have to eat, so they ignore them."

"I'm not going to go round and round about this with you Father. Now I'm going to ask you again, has my soul been cleansed by this confession?"

Father Saragusa let out an exasperated sigh. "Say three Hail Marys and three Acts of Contrition this evening and you will be reborn of soul."

"That's what I wanted to hear," Vinny said.

"I haven't seen your brother Mickey at mass either. I see Ringo at mass every Sunday. Same with your sisters and parents, but no Vinny or Mickey. What's Mickey's excuse?"

"All I can tell you is he says he needs something more."

"What is that supposed to mean?"

"Something more than the Catholic Church can give him."

"Mickey seems to be having what we call a 'wilderness experience.' People sometimes get restless or adventuresome and wander away from the flock, thinking they're going to find something more befitting or exciting. After fumbling around in a wilderness awhile they find their way back to the church. They come back to what's comfortable and dependable. Bottom line, the Truth always wins out, and the only place a person finds Ultimate Truth is in the church through Jesus Christ our Lord and Savior."

"He's involved with a meditation group," Vinny said. "One of those groups where they sit around and say 'Om' together."

"I know. He told me. What's that all about? He's not going Hindu on me, is he?"

"No claims of religious affiliation that I know of. He believes in the good in all faiths. I guess he's taken a portfolio approach to religion."

"God is not something you spread you bets on," the priest said. "Come to mass Vinny, and bring Mickey with you. Good acts are recognized by the Lord."

"Tell me again that my soul is clean."

"I must go now. I have people waiting. They expect absolution."

The address given to Vinny by sergeant detective Clyde Jablonsky led us to a historic section of the city's downtown. The area was full of badly aged buildings from the turn of the century. They were constructed of red bricks whose color had been faded and stained by decades of punishment from inclement weather and air pollution. The windows were so opaque you could not begin to see what was taking place inside. Some windows were cracked and taped over. The ridges of many buildings were lined with pigeons that defecated freely, scorching the upper portions of the once majestic structures with stark white streaks of bird shit. In some areas, moss and ivy had sprung to life and were migrating up the walls. Tiny shards of broken glass glinted in an almost ornamental way along the sidewalks. Why the city had not taken more care in preserving its historic roots defied explanation.

Vinny pulled his Jeep Cherokee to the side of the road, wondering why this hot-shot investigator was hole up in such a dilapidated district. He shut the motor down and we stepped out of the vehicle, taking extra care to make sure the vehicle was locked its alarm system activated. The building's lobby was a threadbare and moldering affair. I pushed the button to summon an elevator. There was a distant mechanical clatter of cables, pulleys and sliding doors. After waiting for some time it was decided the elevator was not going to show. We took the stairs to the fourth floor. On our way up we passed an agitated man headed the other direction wearing a blue jumpsuit and a tool belt.

Our rubber-soled shoes moved quietly along the corridor until we reached suite 412. The door was open and the investigator was standing twenty feet away with his back towards us, peering out the office window at the parking below, keeping an eye on his 1967 Buick LeSabre. It was fully restored in royal blue paint and white-walled tires. We would later learn that on a couple of occasions he found would-be vandals messing with his car and chased them off by pulling his snub-nosed .357 revolver from his armpit holster and firing a couple of rounds into the dumpster just a few strides from the LeSabre.

The detective was a big man and had a hitch in his stance. The tweed blazer and its elbow patches had seen nattier days. His office was sparse to the extreme. A desk, a phone, an answering machine, and one battered four-drawer filing cabinet. We smelled a whiff of hard liquor. It was 2 p.m. Based on this unimpressive montage, I gave Vinny a screwed up look and motioned for him to follow me out of the place, leaving the statuesque detective standing in suspended animation. When I shifted my weight for locomotion the floor creaked. We froze as the investigator turned and saw us.

"Yes?" he said.

The man's face resembled the lunar surface, cratered from a catastrophic case of teenage acne. I swore he could see a miniature of Neil Armstrong's legendary footprint in the hollow of the investigator's cheek. I could not help but think, "That's one small step for man …"

We stepped into the office. "Wes Fitzgerald?" Vinny said.

"Who wants to know?" Fitzgerald took a few lumbering steps towards the strangers. I could feel the aging floorboards flexing under the man's weight. Fitzgerald had plenty of reason to be paranoid. His years of law enforcement and private investigation made a tremendous number of enemies, several of whom had sought retribution over the years.

Vinny did more than stand his ground, stepping up to the detective and extending a hand. Fitzgerald warily engulfed it in his own hand.

"Vinny Marciano," he announced. "This is my brother Mickey."

I extended my hand and the investigator put a squeeze on it that announced he had the strength to crush my knuckles into dozens of bone fragments if provoked.

"As you can see, my identity is no secret," Fitzgerald said, lazily motioning towards the door, which had a frosted panel of glass with stenciled lettering that spelled out:

**Wes Fitzgerald**

**Private Investigator**

We took our places on respective sides of the desk and exchanged some preliminaries.

"I think my girlfriend's having an affair." Vinny's statement caught me by surprise, both because he did not have a girlfriend at the moment, and because that was not the purpose of our visit.

"How do you know this?" Fitzgerald said.

"All the signs are there."

"Such as?"

"She's losing interest in sex — at least with me. When I ask her what she's thinking about or where she's been, I get elliptical answers."

It was obvious from the sudden daze in Fitzgerald's eyes that he didn't know the definition of the word elliptical and was doing his best not to let on.

"I'm also worried about her safety. There's no telling what kind of man she may come across. It's important she has some protection."

"You sound unusually charitable for a guy whose girlfriend is supposedly polishing another man's knob."

"I care about her ... indiscretions and all. I figure we can work it out."

"You might consider seeing a florist instead of an investigator. A dozen red roses can do wonders for a woman's disposition and sex drive."

"Don't worry about the florist," Vinny said, "he's getting his share of my business."

"How'd you find me?" Fitzgerald was looking askance.

"You're in the book."

"Very scientific of you."

"We're just talking about tailing somebody. I didn't think an executive search firm would be required."

I looked back and forth at the men, following their game of verbal ping-pong. Judging from their hardboiled repartee the both of them had seen too many second-rate noir crime films.

Fitzgerald rubbed a hand across his badly scarred face. He was not sure how to regard this latest client. Nothing extraordinary about a distrusting man wanting his girlfriend tailed.

"Are you sure there isn't something more you want to tell me?"

Vinny shook his head. Fitzgerald needed another paying gig, so he laid his suspicions aside. Besides, he liked following women.

"I'll need a photograph," he said.

Vinny dug into his wallet for a two-by-three-inch color mug shot of Sister Angie. He slid it across the desk like he was dealing a playing card. Fitzgerald picked it up, took one look and let out a pretty-girl whistle.

"Detective," Vinny said, "do you mind?"

"Relax," Fitzgerald grumbled. "It can't be any secret to you that men find your girl attractive. That's why you're here, isn't it?"

He handed Vinny a yellow legal pad and a Bic pen.

"I'll need her home and work addresses, and her daily schedule. I'll also need a deposit. My fee is $100 per hour, plus expenses."

"How are you going to go about keeping tabs on her?" I asked

"My techniques are proprietary," Fitzgerald said. After a pause he shrugged and added, "Some of this stuff is pretty obvious. I'll make sure she actually goes to work in the morning, see how she spends her lunch hour and make sure she heads right home after work. Those are the three keys points of opportunity during a working person's day. If you go out of town without your girlfriend, let me know. You give her a bigger playground and that means I have to put in some extra hours."

Vinny handed over a $500 deposit check.

"My work will start after this thing clears," Fitzgerald said, tucking it in his breast pocket.

We left Fitzgerald's office and found the elevator sitting there with its doors open. It seemed to beckon. We got on board and pushed the first floor button. After the doors closed the elevator car gave us a few seconds of undulation but didn't go anywhere. The doors slid back open. I hit the first-floor button again. The doors closed and the elevator did another palsied rendition of the rumba and threw its doors back open. Then we heard the workman in the elevator shaft below pounding hard on something metallic. We made a fast exit to the stairs.

"What the hell?" I said to Vinny as we pulled away from Wes Fitzgerald's office. "Angie's photo? And what's with the bullshit story?"

"I don't trust the big ugly son-of-a-bitch," he said.

"Then why'd you just pay him to stick his nose up Angie's ass?"

"Fitzgerald will never go to work on that case. I gave him a check from a dead bank account."

"I saw you take that right out of your wallet."

"I carry a couple of dead ones around because you never know when you'll need to write a hot check."

"Wouldn't it have been simpler to just not hire the guy? We could have just said 'No thanks' and walked out."

"I think he would have pegged us as a couple of perps from past arrests and thought we were casing him for revenge. So I talked a little bullshit, wrote down some fake info and gave him a bad check. It was cleaner this way."

I shook my head. "He didn't even notice the family resemblance."

"Yeah, real observant guy." Vinny chuckled. "We won't be hearing from Mr. Wes Fitzgerald again."

"We went there on a referral."

"Yeah, and what did Jablonsky really say about the guy? He was a crooked cop and now he's doing dirty work as a private dick. Jablonsky didn't even want us to use to drop his name. What does that tell you?"

I rubbed my face. All seemed tense.

When we got back to the restaurant we went right to the kitchen for the evening's final food preparations. While slicing eggplant and Portobello mushrooms, a wan-faced waitress came in to say there was someone at the front door who wanted to see us.

"We're not open," I said. "The place is locked."

"I know," the waitress said. "He's on the outside of the door. He's banging on it. I told him we're not open. He won't leave."

Vinny dropped his knife and headed for the door. I tailed him. Through a small, reinforced window at the top of the door we could see the scarred mug of private investigator Wes Fitzgerald scowling through the glass. Vinny snapped open the deadbolts and let him in. The investigator was waving the check Vinny had given him.

"I called the bank to make sure you had the funds to cover this," he said. "Turns out the account has long been closed."

"How the hell do you know where to find me?" Vinny said.

"Your license plate. I'm funny that way. I'm an investigator. One of those sneaky things I do. Come to find out the vehicle is registered to Marciano's Manga House. Nice place," Fitzgerald said, looking around. "Heard of it often. Too bad I've never had the pleasure of eating here."

"We open at five."

"That's a shame because I've worked up quite an appetite tracking you down. The address on this check was also null-and-void. Some apartment building they've since turned into a hotel."

"I'm impressed," Vinny said.

"What's the big idea wasting my time and dropping a rubber check on me?" The big man's voice rose on a plume of stale alcohol.

Vinny motioned Fitzgerald over to a two-person table. I sat and watched from nearby, conscious of the revolver holstered beneath the Irishman's blazer. He seemed ready to explode. I didn't think he was crazed enough to shoot anybody, though a good pistol-whipping seemed well within his package of options.

"Look, I'll be candid with you, Fitzgerald. Your low-budget office on the bad side of town didn't exactly instill confidence in me. What are you doing in that dump?"

"Appearances," Fitzgerald sniffed. "Is that all this is about? The building's owner is a friend. He gives me the space for free because I double as onsite security for him. It's an informal arrangement. If some asshole causes trouble at the building, I put an end to it — quick."

"There's not so much as a computer in your office."

"Do I look like the kind of guy who's going to do my own typing? The information I needed to run you down come out of a computer. I have other people do the girly work."

That brought a rare few moments of silence to Vinny's lips. "I wasn't bullshitting when I said I was impressed a few minutes ago about how fast you found me."

"If that means you still want me to tail your girlfriend it's going to be cash up front from now on."

"There is no girlfriend," Vinny said.

"Jesus Christ," Fitzgerald said, "you're in more serious need of brain surgery than I thought. I'm outta here."

The private eye stood to leave.

"Wait," Vinny said, standing and moving toward him.

Fitzgerald gave my brother a *don't get too close if you know what's good for you* look.

"Please," Vinny said, extending a hand of invitation back toward the table.

Fitzgerald eyeballed.

"There's the potential for some very good money," Vinny said. "I promise you that."

The private investigator slowly returned to the sitting position. "I'm listening."

"My restaurant was robbed. It wasn't money that was stolen, it was some very important documents taken right out of the safe in my office in the middle of a busy night of business. I have no idea who took them, but there's reason to believe it was an inside job."

"You can never trust fucking employees."

"It's worse than that. I suspect the thief might have been a family member — or a team of family members."

I tried to interrupt Vinny but he waved me off.

"Doesn't surprise me," Fitzgerald said, glimpsing at me. "Can't tell you the number of cases I've handled where family has stolen from one another.

Didn't anybody ever tell you never to do business with family? Family is trouble. They don't even consider it stealing. It's more like inheritance."

"There are some significant tensions and ambitions between me and some of my siblings. Even between me and my father. Let's just say they need to be considered among the field of suspects."

"Tell me about these documents," Fitzgerald said.

"I can't be specific. They're highly sensitive."

Fitzgerald rolled his eyes. "How the hell am I going to find them when I don't even know what I'm looking for?"

"You'll know them when you see them."

"Oh yeah, how's that?"

"They're five-by-seven-inch pages. There's twenty-four of them and they're laminated."

"There are a lot of laminated documents in this world. Hell, your restaurant menus are probably laminated. I don't work blind."

"These pages are handwritten in Italian."

Fitzgerald shrugged. "Alright, you scored a point there. But like I said, I don't work blind — especially for a guy who's already pulled a fast one on me."

"Let's just refer to them as the 'missing documents.'"

"You got a fucking screw loose, you know that? I'm ready to walk."

"I'll pay you a $10,000 bonus for their safe return and identification of the person who robbed them from me. That's on top of your hourly fee and expenses."

Fitzgerald gave an appreciative whistle at the lavish bonus. "Now you're starting to talk my language, jive bo."

"I also expect that you'll do your level best to hunt down any copies that have been made and hand them over to me to be destroyed."

"That all sounds great except for one thing. I don't work blind. Stop fucking around and tell me what I'm looking for."

"I just told you."

"I'm walking," Fitzgerald said, standing and heading towards the door.

"Alright, already! They're recipes!" Vinny looked around and lowered his voice. "They're secret family recipes! They're mine and I want them back."

Fitzgerald stopped and turned.

"Are you happy?" Vinny said. "That's what I need you to find. And nobody can know what I just told you, got it?"

Fitzgerald came back to the table and lowered himself onto the chair with a creak, "I think you just hired yourself a private eye. Never had a case like this. Sounds interesting."

"Wait here," Vinny said.

I followed my brother down to the office scolding him the whole way for turning an armed and dangerous-looking alcoholic loose on the rest of us. Vinny ignored, opening the cash safe and counting out $1,000 in fifties and twenties. We returned to the dining room and he set the stack of cash in front of Fitzgerald.

"This is twice the deposit you asked me for earlier today."

Fitzgerald thumbed through the bills. He pulled out a fifty and held it up to the light. "You don't have printing press back there do you?" he said, cracking his first smile of the day.

Vinny let that one go past.

"Come by my office tomorrow at the same time and we'll go over the details of the case," Fitzgerald said. "I'll need the names of anyone and everyone who might be a suspect. Family members, employees, customers, vendors x anyone who might have access. I'll draw up my standard contract for your signature, including the part about the $10,000 bounty fee," Fitzgerald said.

"I might even have some extra copies of the agreement laminated and written in Swahili for preservation purposes."

It was another brittle Sunday dinner with the family. The conversations were tentative, appetites muted. When we concluded, Angie asked Maria to take a drive. Endicott and the whole of Upstate New York was a frozen sheet of ice. If one's car broke down in the wrong place a person could freeze to death in this weather. Angie pointed her Infinity and full-throttle heating system westbound along the Southern Tier Expressway until the two women rolled into the rural town of Apalachin, population 1,131. Eventually, Angie turned onto McFall Road and came to a halt in the driveway of a stone house with a shingled roof. The place looked slumped to one side with what appeared to be structural damage.

"Check it out," Angie said.

"What?"

"Do you know what this place is?"

"No clue."

"This is a history piece of Italian-American history."

"You've been drinking."

"No, seriously. Something really big happened here more than 50 years ago and it made headlines all over the country — maybe all over the world."

Time passed. Angie had shut the motor down and freezing temperatures were already penetrating the vehicle. The fingers and the tip of Maria's nose were starting to tingle from the sub-zero air.

"Think about it," Angie said. "Take your time."

After another interval of silence, Maria finally felt something dawning. "*Cosa Nostra?*"

"That is correct," Angie said. "This is where they got busted. The notorious Apalachin Meeting was held right *here*. Can you believe it?"

Maria's eyes were wide. "Are you sure?"

"Of course I'm sure. It's in the history books. It's in old newspaper clippings. Can you believe we've lived here our whole lives and never visited?"

"It's just that it looks so plain, so … *middle class*. I would have expected mafia bosses to go for a little more luxury; maybe a ballroom at the Waldorf."

"The house is bigger than it looks, and the property is more than 40 acres and has five auxiliary buildings. I've been reading up on it," Angie said, and then she spoke in a steady non-stop rhythm for the next seven minutes, explaining the storied background of the visually unremarkable house.

The incident dated all the way back to Nov. 14, 1957, Angie began explaining. Vito Genovese and Frank Costello were battling at the time to take control of the Luciano crime family. Costello had it, Genovese wanted it. After much bloodshed Genovese emerged victorious and he called for a nationwide meeting of mob leaders in hopes that the other families would acknowledge his status as the new Godfather of the Italian crime syndicates. But the meeting of about 100 mobsters and their consiglieri had not gone very far before it fell apart. New York state troopers noticed a suspicious number of expensive cars with out-of-state license plates converging on the small town, and when they found the cars parked in the driveway of a home owned by Joseph Barbara they started taking down license plate numbers. Steaks were still sizzling on the backyard grill when the mafia dons noticed the presence of law enforcement. Panic instantly ensued — many of them fleeing into the woods in their pinstriped suits, white fedoras, pointy shoes and gold watches. The troopers caught about 60 of them, including a guy whose coat got hooked on a barbed-wire fence. During questioning, many insisted they had gathered to cheer up their friend Joseph Barbara, who recovering from a heart attack. When all was said and done, the troopers had apprehended mafia leaders from New York, New Jersey, Tampa, Los Angeles, and several other locales. The bust made national news and forced J. Edgar Hoover and the FBI to finally acknowledge that organized crime families existed and their influence was more widespread than the feds had imagined.

"In a sense, this is where the mafia was born," Angie said, speaking with a verve Maria had not heard since before the Grand Theft had decimated her zeal for living.

"It's not like you to be interested in history."

Angie couldn't wait any longer for Maria's curiosity to find greater depth. "Don't you want to know why I'm interested?"

"Well, we are Italians after all," Maria said.

"Okay, what I'm about to tell you is 100 percent classified," Angie said. "Agreed?"

Maria nodded her assent.

"Hans and I made an offer to buy this place."

Surprise was all over Maria face.

"Like I said, 100 percent classified, so what I'm about to say does not go any farther than *you*."

Maria was speechless.

"You are looking at the future Maciano's Macaroni & Mafia House." Angie gave Maria a *whaddaya-think-of-those-meatballs* expression.

Already tingling from the icy air, now Maria was also tingling from Angie's pronouncement. "Are you *serious*?" Her voice was rising with excitement.

"I've never been more serious about anything in my life." You know I've had my sights set on opening my own place, why not a place that brings Italian food and history together? I have to admit, Mickey got me thinking with that ceiling fresco that a businessperson can really put a stamp on a restaurant by making it to an attraction of some kind. Something special, like a piece of art, or maybe a historic location" she continued, tilting her head toward the mafia house.

"I love it," Maria said. "Just think of the nostalgia."

Angie's smile got broader. "I knew you would. Think about the marketing possibilities with this joint."

Maria's hands went to my temples. "Oh my god, my head is spinning. The ideas are already flying." She sat straight and looked squarely at her sister. "An all-male staff of waiters dressed like mafia dons. Violin cases on the walls."

"Entrees named after the crime figures," Angie added. "'Chicken Cacciatore Castellano' and 'Gnocchi Genovese.'"

"Lamb Chops Luciano," Maria countered.

"Trafficante Truffles," said Angie.

"Spaghetti Gigante."

"Al Capone Marscapone."

"Gotti Giambotta."

Maria gazed back at the house. "No way is this going to happen. Uncle Nunzio will never let this happen."

"Don't be so sure. Even Uncle Nunzio might be able to wrap his head around this one. The sensation being caused by the fresco has opened his eyes."

"The mafia is a scarlet letter in American-Italian history," Maria said. "You know how the Old Guy is about Italian pride."

Angie's eyes darted three different directions before saying: "The way I look at it, if I have to wait until Uncle Nunzio drops dead, that is what I'll do. In the meantime I can buy the place and rent it out until Hans and I can convert it."

"Is that even possible? Planning and zoning isn't going to let you turn a residential home — and a piece of city history — into a commercial enterprise? Think about the neighbors and the traffic."

"I know members of the county Board of Supervisors, and I have influence with them. It's called campaign contributions. That's one of the few things I've learned from our *shit-fer-brains* brother and the way he throws money around. I've already had meetings with some of the supervisors. Besides, think of what this will mean to Apalachin, New York, to have this place in operation, to have this place turned into a piece of *living* history. The room where Cosa Nostra met will be a private dining room for private parties. Think about that. Who isn't going to what to be renting the place out?"

"John 'Flippin' Gotti," Maria said.

"Al 'Fucking' Capone," Angie countered.

"Joe Bananas"

"Carlo 'The Big Bat' Gambino."

"A 1957 Cadillac Coupe DeVille parked out front, just like the mobsters liked to drive back in the day."

"We need to watch more mafia movies."

The sisters stepped out of the van and a freezing wind immediately assaulted them. They pulled their winter gear tighter and toured the property, stork-stepping through a foot of snow. At the house, they cupped their gloved hands around the sides of their faces, peering into the windows to get an interior view of the house, which was just as unremarkable as the exterior.

They hustled back to the Infinity. Angie reactivated the motor and heating system. They thawed.

"I see blood and destruction," were the next words out of Maria mouth. "I see Vinny plotting your murder. I see a *48 Hours* mystery episode on CBS. You will never get away with this. He will burn this house down. He will place a *malocchio* curse on you," Maria said, referring to the Italian superstition of the Evil Eye.

Angie's hallmark agitation returned. "You said you loved the idea. Now you're predicting Armageddon?"

"It will tear the family apart for eternity."

"Don't be so sure. Father will follow the money. Mickey is a marketing guy and will love this concept. Vinny will dash off to the Adirondacks and never be heard from again, for all I care. The guy thinks I'm mentally unstable, but he's the one whose mental health is dangling from a thread. How many times have I told you that? Besides, I'm not doing anything different than he is doing; I'm just doing it more smartly. He has it coming."

Maria said, "Nobody two-times Vinny Marciano, you know that."

"I'm not afraid of him and all his bluster."

"This must be what the Civil War was like," Maria said. Family member versus family member. Mother will put a Mastiff-size shock collar around your neck to keep her from doing this — and your primal scream thing."

Angie jutted her chin at the suggestion.

Vinny and I were doing the morning cooking when the call arrived.

The hot oil was bubbling around the meatballs. Chopped and seasoned vegetables were sautéing. Gallon-sized cans of tomato puree were being poured into aluminum vats.

Proving that we were our father's sons, it was impossible for us to cook without also eating. We had already consumed a couple thousand calories each — dipping bread in pasta sauce, popping meatballs in our mouths whole, chopping sweet sausage and bell peppers and folding them into three-egg omelets. The only thing keeping us from bloating to the size of Father Albie was the high metabolism of youth.

My brother refused to work with dull tools, so he made a practice of manually sharpening the knives at least a couple of times per week. He ran the blades at 20 degree angles along a nine-inch sharpening steel until they had the glint of surgical steel.

My brother became a cutlery fanatic after watching Daniel Day Lewis's performance as a butcher in *The Gangs of New York*. Acquiring an expertise with blades struck both macho and professional chords in Vinny. After taking a cutlery course in New York City and leaner the finer points of the tools, Vinny gave the restaurant's entire knife collection to Goodwill and spent thousands of dollars replacing them with high-carbon stainless steel knives, the most expensive and longest lasting made. He insisted they slice through meat and produce with a surgical ease and accuracy.

Like Daniel Day Lewis in his role as the butcher, Vinny took ritualistic pleasure in the repetitive scraping of knife blades against the sharpening post. Forth and back, he slid the knife blades, in two-toned syncopation. It was the most meditative thing my brother did.

"A knife's your best friend during food preparation," Vinny said. "That's a fact. If it's not sharp it's a danger to you. It'll slip right off the food and onto your finger. And I'll tell you something else; a sloppy cut from a dull blade will do you a lot more harm than a fine incision from a sharp one."

I started flavoring and stirring the tomato puree.

"Are you listening to me?"

"Yeah, I hear what you're saying. It's a stabbing pain right in my ear."

"You don't know how many times people have asked me if I own a gun to protect this place from some after-hours intruder. I tell them, I don't need no gun. I've got my cutlery. Somebody wants to try to roll me and I'd be happy to carve out his windpipe with my paring knife or cut his dick off his groin with my boning knife. And when I'm done doing that I'll slice his ear off the side of his head, put it in my pocket and keep it as a souvenir. That's what the wiseguys used to do — back in the day — when they needed to send a message."

The phone rang. It was like an explosion going off. The ringer was kept at maximum volume so it could be heard over the dinner hours' clamor.

Vinny set down his tools and walked to the phone. "Hello." There was a pause. "This is Vinny," he said, his manner tinged with the annoyance of a morning ritual interrupted.

Then he started wildly snapping the fingers of his free hand to gather my attention and motioned me to pick up the other phone. I dashed to the pizza room and held the receiver to my ear. There was a woman's voice on the other end.

"You heard me," it said. "I've got your recipes."

Vinny was growling now. "Who the fuck is this?"

"Don't be stupid Vinny."

Vinny and I looked at one another. *A woman!* I mouthed at him.

"How do you know me?"

"Everybody knows you, Vinny. You're a big man about town." Her voice sounded young, and it was breathy and full of humidity. "But you're a nobody without these recipes."

"I don't know anything about any recipes."

"You know exactly what I'm talking about. You've been freaking over them for days."

"Yeah? And exactly how would you know that."

"I'm the one who took them, pal, took them from right under your nose. Cracked open that two-bit safe of yours and made off with them."

"You're bullshit. A lot of people know what you just said."

"Sorry that I didn't close the safe door, but I wanted to make sure you knew they were missing."

Vinny and I were making eye contact again. That comment all but assured we had been contacted by the genuine perpetrator. Vinny complexion blanched to a ghostly shade.

I closed my eyes and listened carefully, hoping to ID this voice. It didn't sound like anybody we knew.

"I want my recipes back." Desperation had crept into my brother's tone.

"You can have them back. I want to give them to you. They're yours in exchange for $500,000."

"Half-a-million clams!" Vinny croaked. "You're off your rocker."

"Don't plead poverty with me. That's not a lot of money for a man of your means. Sell one of your homes or automobiles. That'll be a good start." A condescending snigger slipped past her lips.

"I'm telling you, I'm not that liquid. I don't have that kind of cash."

"Don't start haggling with me," she said, putting an extra cushion of humidity under her words, "or the price goes up."

"Those recipes belong to me," Vinny snarled, recapturing his bad-boy rage. "I don't pay no ransom for my own property. You just turn them back over to me, sweetheart, and save yourself some pain and suffering."

Unperturbed the caller said: "Here's the deal. I'll be back in touch with you soon with instructions for the exchange."

"I don't pay no bitch no nothing!" Vinny roared.

"Suit yourself. Just understand the consequences. If you don't deliver the $500,000, I will send copies of your recipes to every Italian restaurant on the Eastern Seaboard and will destroy the originals."

My brother's voice dropped to a taut whisper. "You *cunt*."

"I'll run them right through a paper shredder."

"Nobody does this to me!"

"I'll be in touch," the voice said. Then there was a dial tone.

Vinny was spitting with fury. It sounded like he was going into anaphylactic shock, causing his throat to constrict and his words, barely squeezing past the esophageal grip, came out sounding like a walrus. It was a roar of satanic proportions.

"What bitch does that voice belong to!" he said. "What bitch does that voice belong to!"

"Beats the shit out of me," I said.

Vinny was on the phone again, pounding out Wes Fitzgerald's number on the keypad. I picked up the other receiver to listen in. The call must have roused the private eye out of a deep slumber because he sounded like a bear emerging from hibernation. Vinny started screaming at him to call the phone company and have the ransom call traced. Judging from the crash I heard, Fitzgerald must have fallen off the side of the bed. He started to roar back but nothing he said could be understood. Vinny got his bearings long enough to give a brief explanation of the call.

"I'll see what I can do," Fitzgerald said and hung up.

Next my brother hammered out Clyde Jablonsky's number. The sergeant detective answered on the second ring and Vinny started screaming at him too.

"Put a trace on the call," he demanded. "I want the name and address of the asshole who stole my recipes. And I don't want this showing up in the newspapers."

"I make no promises," Jablonsky said. "I don't control the press. I'll be there within the hour."

# THE INVESTIGATION

Vinny was a wild animal while waiting for Fitzgerald and Jablonsky to show up. A world-class chauvinist had just been swindled and taunted by a woman. He never would have guessed the villain had tits, unless it was one of his own sisters, and this chick didn't sound anything like Angie, Maria or Ginger. This chick, whoever she was, had been in his place of business, slipped past everyone and entered his inner sanctum. A safecracker no less, dialing her way into Fort Marciano and making the heist, then slipping out of the building without suspicion or incident. Who was this mystery woman? The question was well on its way to becoming an obsession.

Jablonsky arrived carrying an armload of electronic equipment.

"The phone company couldn't trace on the call," the sergeant detective said. "It was too short."

"What's with the wires?"

"I'm going to hook this up to your phone. It's tracing and recording equipment. Next time she calls you switch this gadget on and it will track where the call's coming from."

"She's hitting me up for half-a-mil, as if I've got that kind of money sitting in my checking account."

"Let's see how she wants the money delivered. If it's a drop, we'll make up a bag with fake money and try to catch her in the act. If it's an electronic transfer she's after, we'll set up a dummy transaction with the financial institution involved. That's assuming it's within U.S. law enforcement jurisdiction, or a country with a friendly government. Let's just hope she doesn't want the money to go overseas to some uncooperative state like Cuba or Sudan."

Vinny was looking dyspeptic.

"Whatever her plan is, we'll trick and bag her. We certainly won't use real money. No point in that."

"I want my recipes back," Vinny said, his voice cracking.

"We have to keep things in perspective."

"They're family heirlooms."

"It's not like we're dealing with a human life."

"Yes we are. My Uncle Nunzio's going to exterminate me if I lose the family jewels."

I stepped closer to Jablonsky and piped in. "If you don't catch her and she finds out it was a trick, it's bye-bye recipes."

"Are you ready to risk half-a-million dollars? Even if you play by her rules there's nothing that says she doesn't keep your property, or destroy it."

"Have you ever handled a ransom case before?" I asked.

"No. But I'm reading up on it."

"Oh, Christ," Vinny mumbled.

"Listen," he told my brother. "I'm going to hook this equipment to your office phone; that way it will be out of sight and nobody will be asking questions."

Vinny was dazed.

"Don't worry, I'll show you how this works. It's easy."

We headed down a flight of stairs to the office.

Jablonsky was still figuring out how to hook up the tracing equipment when we heard somebody banging on an upstairs door. Vinny found Wes Fitzgerald standing there. The man didn't look so hot. His face was badly in need of a chemical peel, and his disposition would have benefited greatly from about eighteen undisturbed hours of sleep. There was also a ball of cotton stuffed in one ear.

Don't ever screech at me like that again or I'll box your goddamn ears so hard they'll ring until fucking New Year's."

"I was a little panicked at the time," Vinny said.

"What's the unmarked police car doing in your parking lot?"

"I've got a detective on the case too."

"I'm putting extra effort into this one because of that $10,000 finder's fee. I want that money. I don't need any keystone cops getting in my way."

"Don't sweat it. You help the cops solve this case and I'll pay you the full ten grand. So don't turn this into a competition. I want cooperation and teamwork."

"Who'd you get from the cop shop?"

"His name's Clyde Jablonsky."

"Not that fucking guy," Fitzgerald said.

"What's the problem?"

"He's one of those stocking-stuffer cops. A real pretty boy. All hair and leather. I mean, you've seen the guy; is there any evidence on that face that he's ever taken a punch? No real cop's got a nose that straight."

"I'm sure he knows what he's doing."

"You better not be thinking about cheating me out of my finder's fee and claiming Pretty Boy solved the case."

"We just got done discussing this, Fitzgerald. You need to listen. You ought to learn to stop talking in threats. It doesn't make for a very congenial conversation."

"Irish blood boils at low temperatures."

Vinny brought Fitzgerald downstairs.

Jablonsky, who had just figured out how the tracing equipment worked, looked up and saw the private dick. He played dumb. "Fitzgerald, what are you doing here?"

"Consulting with my client."

Jablonsky looked at Vinny. "You got the department on the case now. No need to spend extra money on a hired hand."

"My client wanted somebody with a little more experience," Fitzgerald said.

"We've got a whole team of people at the station. Hundreds of years of experience in total."

"Right, like you guys are going to devote a lotta time and manpower to a simple theft like this one."

"You shouldn't disparage us, Fitz. You used to be a member of the brotherhood yourself."

"Yeah, until I got sideways with the pinheads in the city bureaucracy."

"What actually happened?" Jablonsky asked, feigning ignorance again. "All I've heard is the rumors."

"Let's just say solving crimes was not my superiors' top priority."

By this time Jablonsky and Fitzgerald were standing face-to-face a few feet from one another. Both were tall. Jablonsky was the angular masterpiece of geometry; Fitzgerald the thicker, stronger, less well-conditioned of the two. The private eye's sagging alcohol-reddened complexion contrasted nastily with the young sergeant detective's boyish, blow-dried presentation. Then again, next to the hard-living private eye just about anybody would look like a male model. For Jablonsky, the leather jacket and boots was a strategic ensemble, rugged accoutrements to help the young man look more Tommy Lee Jones than Brad Pitt.

A stare-down ensued. It was pure eye-to-eye combat. Cops were trained in this intimidation tactic. Neither was flinching. The younger man's eyes were clear and steady. The older man's were bloodshot and only half-conscious.

"Vinny, step over here with me," Jablonsky said, finally breaking eye contact. "I'll show you how to use this equipment."

We gathered around the phone. Fitzgerald leaned his big, disheveled frame in the doorway.

"You don't answer incoming phone calls," Jablonsky told Vinny. "Let somebody else do that. If the call's for you, pick it up down here. The second you hear it's that lady's voice, hit this switch. Two things will happen. It will record the call for later analysis, and it will send a tracer out to find the call's origin."

"Look at you, messing with that police department toy," Fitzgerald sniffed.

Jablonsky shot a searing glance over his shoulder. "Law enforcement has advanced a bit since you were on the streets wailing away on skulls with your baton."

"Whoever this caller is, she's probably disguising her voice," the private eye said. "I wouldn't even assume she's the real thief. Might be fronting for somebody else. Criminals have been known to work in cahoots."

Jablonsky turned back to Vinny. "Keep her on the phone as long as you can. It usually takes several minutes for a successful trace. You talk fast. Don't do that. Take your time responding. Don't argue. Ask questions to keep her talking. When she gives you the instructions, tell her you want to go over them again to make sure you've got it right. With any luck we'll find out where she's placing the call from."

Fitzgerald was grumbling again. "I hate to tell you, but this lady isn't calling from her living room for your convenience. If you're able to trace the call at all it's going to lead you to a telephone booth or some other public place where you'll find 300 sets of fingerprints, none of which will prove anything."

"It gives us something to go on, Fitz." Jablonsky was getting hot. "A location. Somebody might have seen something. We'll have a recording of the call. We can pay attention to speech patterns, phrasing, word choice. That might match someone Vinny knows. There might be background noises that give us clues."

"Perry Mason couldn't get background noise or mumbo jumbo about word choice admitted in court. So you might as well touch the wrong wires together and short-circuit that worthless contraption right now."

Jablonsky swiveled in the chair to directly face Fitzgerald. "Why don't you hit the streets and start indiscriminately torturing passersby and see if you can force a confession out of someone?"

"I don't care how you guys do it, I just want this person caught," Vinny said. "I want the death penalty."

"We don't have the death penalty in the State of New York," Jablonsky said.

"Thanks to a succession of pussy governors," Vinny said.

Fitzgerald waved the comments off. "Don't give it a second thought. When I get my hands on her, she's going to wish she had a cyanide capsule in one of her molars.

Vinny climbed into the passenger seat of my Range Rover and we headed out. It was time to see in Enrico Zepeda again and discuss plans for the Great Unveiling of his ceiling fresco. As we rolled down State Route 17 towards Binghamton I called Zepeda but got no answer. Then I sent a text message and got no reply. We decided to forge ahead through the cold and snow because, regardless of anything else, Vinny wanted to eat at a steakhouse not far from Zepeda's residence and studio, a place named The Cattleman that served thoroughly aged beef and sautéed mushrooms in a red-wine sauce that was second-to-none in terms of the richness of its flavor. It also traded in a very good selection of craft beers and boutique wines from small vineyards.

The giant door to Zepeda's place was fully shut when we arrived. I pounded with a side of my fist. Zepeda's heavily accented voice beckoned from within. I shouldered the edge of the door and pushed hard. The immense assemblage of lumber rolled open slowly and loudly. Vinny and I stepped inside and froze. There was a naked young woman reclining languorously and motionless on a chaise lounge in the middle of the studio. Zepeda motioned towards us to proceed.

"Come, come," he said. Zepeda was standing behind an easel, his hands occupied by a palette and paint brush. "It's okay, my friends, she's a professional model."

I muscled the door back into the closed position and approached.

"Please," Zepeda said, "make yourself at home. I need just a few more minutes and this will be complete."

Vinny and I happily whittled away the time, transfixed by the shimmering image of feminine grace before us. We moved closer to the artist's subject. She had one leg lying flat, the other bent forty-five degrees at the knee. Hands were folded in a delicate stack on her perfectly flat tummy, just above the navel, which was filled with a round semi-precious yellow stone. Her head was turned away from us and her eyes stared dreamily out a snow-dappled window. A space heater was humming nearby to keep the unclad woman comfortable.

"Tell me what you think," Zepeda said, waving us to his side of the easel.

We stepped behind the canvas to observe. Though amply breasted, Zepeda had pumped up the model's breasts to roughly 50 percent larger than their actual size. And the folds of her vulva were equally enhanced.

"Very nice," Vinny said. "But these are out of proportion." He pointed to the breasts and vulva.

"That is my interpretation," Zepeda replied, mildly irritated. "I paint what I see with both my heart and my eyes."

There was a stirring on the chaise lounge. The naked beauty was getting restless.

"Jasmine, you're done," Zepeda crowed. "Come take a look at my portrait."

The model stepped into a raspberry jumpsuit that zipped up the front and tousled her hair on her way to the easel.

"Hey, nice boob job," she said. Zepeda smiled and nodded approvingly. "And it looks like it's mating season too," she said pointing to the portrait's swollen genitalia.

Zepeda chuckled. "Very funny. Now, seriously, what do you think?"

"I think you did an awesome job," Jasmine said. "You owe me a complimentary copy of your limited edition prints."

She gave Zepeda a long, warm embrace. Zepeda's hairy, spectacled face winked at us over the model's shoulder.

"Jasmine, allow me to introduce you to my friends, Mickey and Vinny Marciano."

"Oh, you two are brothers," she said.

"What was your first clue," Zepeda said, "the matching noses or last names?"

Jasmine shook my hand with both of hers, sending a tingle up to my elbow.

"Mickey and Vinny are famous in town. They run Marciano's Mangia House."

I reached into my wallet and handed the model a business card. It gave only my name, affiliation and contact information. It didn't include a title, mainly because I didn't know what to put there. "Bartender" sounded too blue collar. Calling myself a "chef" just because I cooked and made pizzas a couple of days a week would have been overstating things. I wasn't an owner or partner, just a well paid employee. A title like "vice president" sounded pretentious and "associate" sounded meek.

"What do you do at the restaurant," she inquired.

"Tend bar, make pizzas and do some cooking. Not exactly what I expected to be doing after earning a bachelor's degree in sociology," I said with a thick air of defensiveness. Vinny smirked.

"A college degree?" she said.

"Yes, in sociology."

Jasmine tilted her head daftly and phonetically echoed, "So-she-ol-oh-gee?"

"That's right," I said. "It's the study of people and societies. It's all about how we interact as individuals and civilizations."

"Sounds like a trip," she giggled.

Not to be left on the sidelines, Vinny handed her a business card as well. Vinny's card clearly identified him as the restaurant's "proprietor," dwarfing my status.

"And you're the boss," she said, "smiling at Vinny." My brother and his pinky ring filled her field of vision while I diminished to sidecar status.

"Let me give you one of mine," she said, retrieving cards from her athletic bag, handing one to each of us. It read:

### JASMINE STARLING
### Model, Actress, Consultant

A mobile phone number and e-mail address were also listed.

Vinny and Jasmine started prattling away. Zepeda put an arm around me, led me towards his kitchen area and offered me these words of consolation: "Vinny's single, you're not."

The artist started preparing a pot of coffee. When the naked model and the restaurant proprietor had finished sniffing each other's moist territories, Zepeda escorted the former to the exit and offered his assistance with the front door.

"I apologize for just popping in like this," I told Enrico. "I called and texted but didn't get any replies."

"Nonsense," Zepeda said. "What could I possibly be doing that is more important than a visit from friends?"

"I don't know. You might have a naked woman lying in the middle of your living room."

"Don't worry about her. She's paid to be naked," Zepeda said in his refried Spanish accent. "I remember during my days in Guatemala I once paid a model to pose naked for a party I hosted. She stood like a statue all night and was the absolute center of attention. There must have been a hundred people there. And you know what's funny? The women were more fascinated with her than the men. They all gathered around looking her up and down, circling her like a pack of hyenas. One of the ladies had too much to drink and tweaked the model's nipple. She never flinched. I was so proud of her I paid her double. You mark my words, I'm going to do that again some time. I'll be sure to invite you."

We sipped our coffees. Again, it was a lethally strong brew in the Latin American tradition. The conversation turned to the Great Unveiling and Zepeda surprised us by insisting that a system of wall-mounted Xenon track lighting had to be installed in the dining room to properly illuminate the fresco. He went into a lengthy explanation that Xenon were the best because they produced light that was the closest to the rays of the sun, revealing the truest colors.

"Without lighting the fresco will go mostly unnoticed." Zepeda voice took on a new authority. "People don't look at ceilings unless they are directed. It's no different than pieces of art in a gallery, they require illumination to be brought into full relief."

Vinny looked to me. "Why did I come here?"

"Ernesto," I said, "this wasn't part of the contract."

"I know. It was an oversight, and for that I sincerely apologize. I will pay half the cost of the lighting. It's that important to me."

"There are monthly power bills," Vinny said. "This is a continuing cost."

"The fresco will more than pay for itself," Zepeda said.

Vinny's fingers reached for his temples.

The artist wasn't budging. "Without these lights the ceiling will be so dimly lit the fresco will look like a Rembrandt."

"Rembrandt sounds good to me," Vinny said.

"I'm not a fan," Zepeda replied.


Angie and Maria arranged a classified meeting with residential homebuilder Mort Stottlemyre. It was held in his mobile office, which had been plopped on the site of his new 266-home 513-acre subdivision his development firm had under construction. Mort needed to be on site to keep a watchful eye on progress and to make sure his men were strategically violating certain portions of the state's Uniform Building Code to keep construction costs on budget.

The girls figured at this restricted and remote site there was no chance of anyone finding out about the meeting. Angie's husband Hans Sprink insisted on coming along because he considered his wife too emotional about business dealings to make sound decisions. Angie was worried that Hans would blow his nose in front of Mort.

Mort Stottlemyre was so excited about having the Marciano girls over that he had lunch catered. A white tablecloth was spread and real silverware set out. Gourmet sandwiches and salad were quickly passed around.

The builder invited everybody to start eating by forking mouthfuls of salad with Italian dressing into his face.

"You are not going to believe what this place is going to look like when I'm done. Every buyer will feel like Ben Cartwright living on their own private Ponderosa," he said, quoting the company's marketing brochure. "I love ranch-style living like I love your pasta, girls, so believe me when I tell you that this place is going to be Home on the Range. Every home is going to be strategically situated among these rolling hills and the border of every property will have wood-cut rail fences as demarcation lines. The smallest lots will be two-acres big, and some of the larger lots are zoned for horses. That's why I'm calling it *Rancho en los Cerros*. For those of you who don't *habla Espanol*, that means Ranch in the Hills. Hell, I've cut out a six-and-a-half-acre homestead for myself. It will become my new residence. Pool, hot tub, home theater, solarium. It won't be more than a five-minute walk to the clubhouse and activity center. This housing development is going to be my Picasso."

As they continued eating their lunch, men in hardhats shuffled in and out, poring over site plans, architectural blueprints and suppliers' catalogs, looking for places to cut corners and enhance the profitability rating and borrowing power of Stottlemyre Residential Development Corporation. Of course, Mort Stottlemyre didn't call it cutting corners. He emphasized "economies of scale" and "efficiencies," such as the use of cheaper materials and finishes, single-paned glass and less insulation.

Little crusts of dried mud kept falling off their work boots as the construction crew foremen came and went. Maria kept glancing their way. Mort was thinking she was getting distracted by all the activity.

"Guys," he yelled to the men in the hardhats. "Take it somewhere else. I need some alone-time with my guests."

After the crew vacated, the builder starter talking again. "Seriously, you girls should think about buying a place here. I'm practically giving the first few models away just for promotional purposes. No hard sell. You just let me know. Anywhoo, what can I do you for?"

Maria shifted in her seat and said, "Actually, Mort, we are here to talk business, though we thought you might be the one writing a check rather than us."

Stottlemyre face dimmed, though he maintained his frozen salesman's smile. "I'm listening." He forced the words through a locked jaw.

"Mort, we know you love Marciano's food. You've always been very complimentary. So … I'll get right to the point. Angie and I are talking about opening a second Marciano's. We're looking for a lead investor. We'll be putting some of our own money in, of course, but we don't have enough between us to do the job in the first-class style it deserves. We thought, as successful as you are, you might like to diversify your line of business by getting into restaurants, and your construction company could help with construction."

Mort Stottlemyre's smile was starting to regain its normal voltage. "I like what I'm hearing, girls. Can't say yet whether I can swing it just yet, well, with *Rancho en los Cerros* running full throttle and all. But it's sure worthy of consideration, and I'm flattered that you came to me. I love the idea of having a stake in the restaurant world, especially in tandem with the Marciano brand name and product. I mean, your family is the Gold Standard when it comes to *I-talian* dining."

Angie cleared her throat to take the floor. "Let's not get ahead of ourselves," she said. "Before we even started discussing our plans we should have said that this meeting is absolutely top secret. That's why we came to your place, Mort. What we are talking about can never be repeated, not even to other members of our family."

"Especially not to other members of our family," Maria added.

"Whether you do the deal or not," Hans Sprink piped in.

"It would cause huge problems," Angie said.

"Girls, deal with non-disclosure documents for a living. I insist on them. So do my investors and lenders. So you can be assured what's said here stays right here," he said, tapping an index finger against his temple."

Maria leaned forward. "How much time do you need to think about this, Mort?"

"Put together an offer sheet for me. You know, how much money you'd like me to invest, what my ownership stake will be, who will be the officers of the company, how profits are divvied up and when they get dispersed. So on and so forth."

The Mangione sisters were looking a little dazed.

"I'll handle that part of the deal," Hans Sprink said.

"Is that why you're here, Hans? Chief negotiator?"

"He's here because he's married to me," Angie said.

Stottlemyre guffawed. "We all have our place in life, Hans."

"My wife doesn't have a business head," Hans said. "I'm here to protect her interests and mine. We want a win-win-win situation. That's the only way a business deal really works.

"As long as one of those wins falls into my column." Stottlemyre gave his visitors a big smile, revealing that a few dozen dark-green flecks of basil and oregano had become lodged in the crevices between his teeth.

"Mort, we were even thinking you could have your own table for entertaining clients," Maria said. "It would be available to you any time you needed to do some wining and dining. We were even thinking of a corner booth with drapes that draw closed for privacy."

Mort Stottlemyre' eyes turned luminescent. "That would be awesome," he said.

"We want a big place," Angie said, her sibling rivalry rising. "And classier in every way."

"I like what I'm hearing. I like the idea of Stottlemyre Construction involvement in the site's preparation. We'll make damn sure the work is top shelf and the price is fair. I especially like having a table for my business dealings. Let's think in terms of that corner booth and drapes you mention, Maria. Or even a small private room. I've already got designs flying through my head. This could be really cool."

"But you're a residential construction company," Hans interjected. "Have you ever done a commercial or retail project before?"

"Ah heck, there's nothing to that. Construction is construction. Just give us the blueprints and we can erect a structure faster than a Frenchman makes love. You know … lickidy split." He smiled again, giving the Marciano sisters a sickening view of his green-speckled teeth.

Hans reached into his pocket and pulled out a white, monogrammed handkerchief. Angie stiffened. She had many pet peeves, but none greater than people blowing their noses in public — especially her husband. Angie was prim in her belief that anytime one carries out a biological function that involves waste matter exiting the body, it should be done in the privacy of a bathroom. She had asked Hans repeatedly to never blow his nose around other people, especially when she was present. But Hans had blown his nose in public his entire life and had never gotten the message. It wasn't that Hans Sprink was shunning his wife. He was simply a guy full of involuntary actions.

What mortified Angie most was that, after blowing, Hans felt compelled to take a gander at what had come flying out of his nose.

Hans held the hanky to his nostrils and blew hard. A duckish honk cut through the mobile. Hans held the hanky open a few inches away from his face to examine the catch of the day. Then he neatly folded up the contents and stuffed them back in his pocket, as though for safe keeping and later use.

Angie laid a hand on her fork and contemplated the pleasure of burying it in the side of her husband's neck. Her normally olive complexion had deepened to red. Excusing herself, she headed to bathroom where she did a few minutes of deep-breathing exercises to calm herself.

The meeting quickly broke up after her return. Angie Mangione and Hans Sprink were in their car now and heading home. Angie sat still, silent and red-faced on the ride. With the automobile's air temperature dropping rapidly, Hans Sprink deduced that he had unwittingly done something to upset his wife, but the offending act escaped him. Perhaps it was his contention that she didn't have a head for business.

"Penny for your thoughts," Hans said.

She glared and replied, "No amount of money of is going to get you into my head right now."

The silence resumed until they got home. Angie paced the living room several times, picking up speed on every lap, before finally blowing her top.

"Why, if you insist on blowing your nose in front of other people, do you have to look at what comes out of your nose? Do you have any idea how gross that is? What in the *hell* are you expecting to find in there!"

This was the day we discovered relations between Ginger Marciano and Clyde Jablonsky had turned carnal.

Earlier that day Ringo reported spotting them having a romantic lunch on the patio at a pretentious French bistro that served dishes such as quiche Florentine and a smelly fish stew called bouillabaisse.

Ginger was looking and behaving in a way she hadn't looked and behaved since she lost her virginity shortly after her seventeenth birthday. To the unfamiliar eye she was under the sway of a very powerful narcotic — stuck in a euphoric dimension that was all her own and from which she wanted no retreat. Glassy-eyed, impervious to the clatter and distractions around, over-sensitized and fully exposed. Skin was flushed to primrose, as though it had just been scrubbed bare with loofah sponges at the local spa.

I heard saxophone music playing.

There was no question that Jablonsky had eaten this little biscuit whole.

Even Enrico Zepeda, who was painting overtime that day and still plying his fresco to the dining room ceiling, sensed an unusual presence. He brought his brush to rest and peeked down from his perch.

The lunch had been leisurely and besotted with wine. Kind and flattering words were exchanged. Both testified to their mutual attraction and respect. Jablonsky maintained his tough, bad-boy exterior and was mostly quiet. Ginger was talkative and anticipatory. She invited the new beau to her plush condominium with the controlled electronic access and surveillance cameras at every turn.

Herbal tea was served. Jablonsky went along with the gag to keep the mood intact. After the tea ceremony was finished, a tour of the condominium was staged, terminating at the bedroom, which Ginger had spent the morning preparing. There were fresh silk sheets on the bed and Ginger had carefully tousled the lavender comforter and pillows to invite use. There was fragrant potpourri on the nightstand; she went to the matching nightstand on the opposite side of the bed and lit a trio of votive candles. Then she moved in on Jablonsky, tugging at the thick leather belt wrapped around his jeans. He ran his hand into her hair, then stuck his nose in and smelled Prell shampoo. He lowered his lips to meet hers. Soon they were under cover, his long body playing African rhythms against Ginger's petite frame. It was all whimper and whiplash after that.

An hour had elapsed since the conclusion of that interlude, but mother could see that her daughter was still supercharged with hormones. It worried mother that, even for an Italian girl, Ginger's thermostat was constantly set at an unusually searing temperature.

Mother finally approached. "You were with him, weren't you?"

"Who's him, ma?"

"That detective."

"His name's Clyde, ma."

"Yeah, I know his name, especially his last name. What have you been doing?"

"Ma, I had the most wonderful afternoon. We had lunch at Chez Vous."

"I suppose you had a good time?"

"Oh my god, ma," Ginger said, bringing hands to cheeks, "I think I've finally found Mr. Right."

Mother's face and heart sank and she let out an oft-heard lament: "For the love of Jesus, here we go again. Can't we have a decent wedding in this family?"

"Chill out, ma, I didn't say anything about marriage."

"No, not yet you didn't, but what do you think Mr. Right means? I've already seen this too many times. Angie runs off and marries a German, Mickey marries an Irish girl, Ringo won't give women the time of day let alone marry one, and Vinny's always running around with that Stonebreaker girl — and who knows what the hell kind of name that is."

"You had your Italian wedding when Maria married Shekko."

"He's Sicilian. That's not the same thing. Those people are *chadrools*."

Ginger threw her arms in the air, frustrated that mother had chased away the euphoric spell. "I thought you'd be happy for me, ma."

"He's not one of us," mother said. "He's Polish. He's barely European."

"Look, if it makes you feel any better, he's only half Polish."

"What's the other half?"

"Bulgarian."

"Oh brother, from one loser country to another."

"Stop it. I don't want you criticizing him. He's everything I've been looking for in a man."

"Yeah, what's that?"

"He's tall and lean and handsome. He's strong and masculine and smart. He knows how to take control of situations. And he appreciates who I am."

"You need to find someone you're compatible with. Italians are compatible. They eat the same food, they worship the same god, they behave the same way. They have common values."

"Ma, it's the 21st century. We're so past all that stuff."

"There's nothing old fashioned about people keeping with their own."

"When I marry it's going to be for love, not for someone's gene pool."

"I'm just telling you a fact. You're going to hear the Dumb Polack jokes. So are your children. Then what are you going to do?"

"I just met the guy. Can we leave children out of this discussion?"

"Well, you said Mr. Right. What am I supposed to think?"

"I'm sorry I said anything."

"Where did you two go after lunch?"

"I had him over for some tea."

"That must have been one hell of a cup of tea. You walked in here looking like you had just seen Christ on the road to Damascus."

Ginger got her smile back, gratified that the ardor she felt for this man was shining through her. "No," she said, "no visions of Christ, I'm sorry to say. But this was the closest thing I've ever had to a religious experience."

"You jerk," mother said, appalled by the implications of her daughter's comment. "Did you sin?"

Menopause hit Mother Margherita with devastating force about a dozen years ago. The quantum mood swings and manic tirades it induced were still fodder for many a family horror story or joke. Though most of her symptoms passed as soon as her physician found the proper elixir of hormones, one particularly annoying symptom persisted.

When mother got hungry she got cranky, and that was putting it mildly. But matters were compounded by the fact that she would get cranky before realizing that she was getting hungry. So by time she realized her body wanted food, mother was often convulsing with anger and committing emotional atrocities against those around her.

Maria and Angie were well acquainted with this biological time bomb. At approximately 5:30 each day, mother would begin making abusive statements (precisely when the dinner rush was starting to mount and they could least afford to get sidetracked in the kitchen).

"Hey, there's orders piling up," mother said one night. "Can't you jackasses move any faster?"

Maria, attacking the birth of Godzilla in its infancy, remarked, "Ma, are you hungry? Tell us what you want, we'll fix you something to eat."

"Well ... what do you got?"

Angie, "What do you want, a menu? You work here. What the hell kind of question is, 'What do you got?'"

Mother's face filled with more contempt than her mouth knew how to express.

"Ma," Maria interrupted, "here's a menu, ma. Pick anything you want I'll make it for you."

"Just forget it." Mother slapped the menu down and directed her gaze toward Angie. "I wouldn't want to inconvenience you, you louse."

Within minutes, though, the hunger pangs were again licking at mother's belly and driving her mood into further depths of irritation. When Maria returned to the kitchen with another customer order to post, mother inconspicuously sidled up to her favored daughter of the moment and whispered, "Maria, you got time to make me a few raviolis?"

"Angie," Maria shouted over the clatter, "boil up an order of raviolis for ma."

Mother elbowed Maria in the ribs. "Jackass," she continued whispering. "Do you have to let the whole kitchen know? I didn't *her* to hear that."

Minutes later mother's mood had taken a striking turn for the better as she ploughed into a bowl of cheese raviolis with creamy pesto sauce.

Father came walking into the kitchen with a newspaper spread between his arms. "There's an article in today's paper that says boxes of the Tarantino brand of ravioli are being recalled by the company because there have been reports that some are contaminated with botulism," he said.

"Oh my god," Angie said, "that's the brand I bought."

Mother made a clatter dropping her fork into the bowl. She searched her daughter's face for an explanation.

"We ran out of the homemade raviolis," Angie cried, "so I had to run to the store to buy a commercial brand."

By this time mother had already made substantial incursions into her bowl of raviolis. She spit her current mouthful back into the bowl and wailed. "Christ almighty. What are you trying to do, kill me?

"Let me see that article," Vinny said as he, Maria and Angie all gathered behind father and craned their necks to read along.

Offended by the lack of attention she was receiving, mother clutched her stomach in hand and started groaning loudly and staggering around the kitchen. Ringo shrieked and dashed over to stabilize his quaking mother. Father kept reading his newspaper.

"Thank you, my son," mother weakly remarked while Ringo escorted her to a chair onto which she languidly collapsed. "You're the only one I can count on at a time like this."

"We've got to get her to the hospital," Maria said. She went to the basement and returned with a blanket. After spreading it evenly on the floor, they guided mother onto the center of it. She lay on her back, groaning and rolling her head from side to side. She invoked the aid of Christ and requested her rosary beads.

The blanket was turned into a makeshift hammock when they each family member grabbed opposing corners and hoisted mother into the air. They shuffled her toward the back door of the kitchen, but were forced to set her back down when Angie started buckling under her weight at the same time that father was experiencing stabbing chest pains.

"Call an ambulance," father ordered.

Ringo, who typically suffered paralyzing anxiety attacks when confronted by crises, moved stiffly to the phone and summoned the paramedics.

Ginger and the waitresses were told of the situation by Maria and directed to quickly collect all plates of ravioli. The restaurant's patrons started fretting when they saw food being retrieved without explanation. Their angst worsened when flashing red and blue lights appeared in the window and three paramedics and a gurney came in the front entrance and strolled across the dining room. The lead paramedic hesitated halfway through and asked the first waitress he saw, "Where's the food poisoning victim?" The inquiry got the paramedics where they wanted to go, but it also caused an outbreak of panicked catcalls from the suddenly queasy customers.

"Food poisoning," one echoed.

"What is going on back there?" another man demanded.

"Waitress," a woman who had just overeaten cried out, "am I going to get sick?"

A lawyerly type wearing suspenders boomed, "If a single member of my family comes down with so much as a loose bowel I'm going to own an Italian restaurant."

Ginger bristled. "All right, that's enough. Everybody just sit down. There's nothing to freak out about. We've had a little incident in the kitchen that has nothing to do with the food you're eating."

Her statement was immediately undermined by four fully-uniformed members of the fire department who came strolling through to offer the paramedics whatever support might be needed.

"Go back to enjoying your food," Ginger said. "The situation is under control and there is absolutely nothing for any of you to worry about."

Nonetheless, the whirling red lights atop the waiting ambulance continued flashing against the dining room windows at synchronized intervals. It was a color and tempo familiar to all, and begged to differ with Ginger's assurances.

Ginger hustled to the kitchen and found Angie standing over mother's body with her voice and hand raised high over her head. "You mean to tell me you clowns know how to handle medical emergencies but you don't know the difference between the front and back door?"

The paramedics gathered around mother and started asking her questions, most of which Angie supplied the answers to.

"Mam, how old are you?" a paramedic asked.

"She's sixty-eight," Angie said.

"What are your symptoms?"

"She's got terrible stomach pain."

"Don't listen to her," mother said, "she's the one who orders the inventory. There must be fifty different brands of ravioli on the market and, wouldn't you know it, my daughter picks and feeds me the one made with poison."

They applied pressure to different areas of mother's abdomen and asked about tenderness. Regardless of where they touched or how little pressure they applied, mother crowed with agony.

"Heartbeat and blood pressure are about normal," one of the crew members said. "Other vital signs also show no indication of failing health. There isn't even any discoloration of the eyes."

FAMILY RECIPES

"Yeah, but abdominal pains appear to be some of the most severe I've ever seen," his colleague said. "We have to take her in. Radio ahead."

They grabbed hold of mother's limbs, hoisted her upon the gurney and swathed her up to her neck in a blanket. Angie and Vinny stood abreast to cordon off the paramedics path back into the dining room.

"Out the rear door with you," Angie said, shooing them off with the backs of her hands.

At that moment Uncle Nunzio was making what he reckoned would be a triumphant return from three exhilarating weeks in Las Vegas. As his Cadillac DeVille pulled into the parking lot, he was greeted by the flashing lights of two emergency vehicles. Uncle Nunzio came barreling through the front door, not sure if his one of the gas ovens had blown up and set the restaurant ablaze, or his brother had been felled by a heart attack and was doing the floppy chicken on the kitchen floor.

Some of the regulars called out to him as he staggered his way toward the kitchen.

"Thank god, Nunzio," one acquaintance hollered.

"What's going on back there?" called out another.

Nunzio burst into the kitchen just in time to see mother's gurney being wheeled out the back door.

"Albie," he said, grabbing his brother's arm, "what is it?"

Father pulled the newspaper out of his back pocket and pointed at the article. "Food poisoning, we think."

Father climbed into the back of the ambulance to make the ride to the hospital emergency room at his wife's side. I climbed into Maria's car along with Angie and Ringo and chased the speeding ambulance to the hospital.

Uncle Nunzio marched up to Vinny and whacked him over the head with the newspaper section. "How the hell many times do I have to tell you to keep up on the raviolis? We can't be running out of any goddamn food.

You don't think these people know the difference between our homemade raviolis and these machine-stamped pieces of crap?"

"My half-wit sister's in charge of inventory," Vinny haplessly argued. "She can't seem to count."

"Don't give me any of that nonsense. You're in charge. You take responsibility. It all falls on the boss." Uncle Nunzio swatted his nephew over the head again with the newspaper, messing up the top of his hair. "I outta crown you."

Uncle Nunzio headed to the dining rooms and started settling down the patrons. Those who had eaten raviolis were gathered. There were almost two dozen people.

"This wasn't our food," Nunzio told them. "My numbskull nephew got some store-bought stuff that we're not sure about. It's getting checked out right now at the hospital. I'll be getting a call soon and will be able to tell you if anything's wrong."

One woman sank into a chair. "I'm an old woman. I don't have much of an immune system left. I'm don't think I can survive a bout of food poisoning."

The lawyerly-looking man handed the frightened senior citizen his card, and gave one to her next of kin as well.

The clutch of cardiac distress was now rising in Nunzio's chest. Heart disease wasn't unknown to the Marciano clan. Grandfather's ticker had run out of beats by time he reached 60. And grandmother went the same route after outliving her husband by 11 years. The family diet was rich in animal fats, oils and cheeses. If the U.S. Food and Drug Administration was privy to the grams of saturated fat per serving, it probably would have required a Surgeon General's warning be affixed to the menu. Fortunately, you could still get away with some things in America, and slowly debilitating and killing people with delicious foods was one.

The emergency room was almost dead still. A rubber-shoed nurse led the Marciano children behind a draw white curtain. There, father was sitting in a chair, smiling smugly at his disabled wife. She lying on her left side with a lubricated plastic tube shoved down her gullet and into her stomach. A pump gently humming nearby, suctioning the contents of mother's digestive tract through the plastic tube and depositing them in a container sitting on a small stainless steel table. It was obvious that mother had swallowed several of the raviolis almost whole.

"They're pumping her stomach," father jovially explained. It was the first time all day that his wife wasn't beating her gums.

An oxygen line was strung under her nose and around her ears, electronic sensors were taped to the upper chest to monitor heartbeat, and saline was being intravenously fed into the bloodstream through one arm while a nurse was taking a blood pressure reading off the other.

A physician appeared from behind the curtain. He was dressed in green surgical scrubs, having just sewn back together an unfortunate hiker who had ended up on the sharp end of a buck's antlers. He was wearing a cap and had a mask tied over his mouth and nose. Hands were protected by a fresh pair of latex gloves as they reached for a small platter of sterilized instruments.

Mother's eyes flared with apprehension, as she imagined the doctor taking hold of a scalpel and cutting deeply into her ravaged torso. But the doctor picked up only a small gauge needle and a small glass vile. He snapped the two together and jabbed the needle in mother's arm to extract a blood sample. He ordered one of the nurses to take the vile of blood and the contents from mother's stomach to the hospital's testing lab.

The remaining nurse connected the tube to a different machine that repeatedly pumped lukewarm salt water into her stomach and vacuumed it back out.

"*Ow wong do oo hav tuh kee dis toob in we?*" mother mumbled around the tube.

"We to have keep flushing your stomach until the fluids are coming out are clear," the nurse said. "We want to make sure any poisons are out of your system."

The doctor removed his mask and pulled the group of us aside. Speaking directly to Father Albie he said, "What's strange is that your wife ate less than an hour ago and is reporting severe abdominal pains. But the symptoms of botulism take hours to appear. And she showed no evidence of any other botulism symptoms, such as double or blurred vision, drooping eyelids, difficulty swallowing."

Father said, "What are you getting at, doctor?"

"Has your wife been feeling okay emotionally?"

Angie immediately piped in. "I know exactly what you're getting at, doctor, and I think you're onto the real problem. My mother needed attention. We're a very dysfunctional family. We're all messed up."

"That's enough of that nonsense," father said.

"You saw what happened, dad. Ma, was fine until she heard about botulism, then her imagination ran wild." Angie looked back to the doctor and said, "She's very psychosomatic."

"Look," the doctor jumped in, "it's not my intent to in the middle of family disputes. My advice is to give your mother extra care and attention. Sometimes that's all it takes. You don't know the number of people we see in this emergency room repeatedly even though nothing's physically wrong with them. So do what you have to do to keep your mother feeling content."

We returned to mother's bedside. A few minutes later the doctor was back and reported that no nerve toxins were found in the raviolis or blood sample.

"Mrs. Marciano, you don't have botulism," he said.

A nurse yanked the tube out of mother's throat. She choked momentarily and sat up.

"Are you sure I'm okay?" mother asked the doctor.

"Absolutely. Our testing was thorough."

"Oh, thank god," mother remarked, holding a hand over her heart. "I pray and pray all the time for all of you," she said, gesturing toward us, "and forget about my own spiritual needs. It's a wonder I'm alive at all."

"If it isn't botulism," Maria said, "then what does she have?"

"It may have been nothing more than gastro-intestinal distress. Judging from what we pumped out of your stomach, Mrs. Marciano, it looks like you were eating much too fast. That could have traumatized your upper GI tract."

"How many times have I told you to stop inhaling your food?" Angie scolded.

"Take small bites," the doctor ordered, "and chew them thoroughly before swallowing. Remember, digestion begins in the mouth."

Mother promised to slow it down as the doctor shined a flashlight in her eyes, then poked at her stomach in find any sore spots.

"We normally keep a patient around a few hours for observation," the doctor said, "just to make sure."

"Never mind that," mother said, sitting up. "The pain is gone and I'm alright. I'm going home."

"As you wish. But I want you to come back immediately if the abdominal pains return or you start experiencing dry mouth, muscle weakness, difficulty swallowing — or pretty much anything out of the unusual."

We all gathered around and congratulated mother on her swift and complete recovery. The color was returning to Ringo's face. Father shuffled to the nearest phone and called his brother with the news. Still, Nunzio personally collected up all the boxes of frozen raviolis and dumped them in the trash.

As father and the nurses cleaned the lubricants and adhesives off mother's body, we quickly excused ourselves to dash back to the shorthanded restaurant. Within thirty minutes we caught up on orders and had the place running like normal.

About that time father had paid the hospital bill and gotten mother to the car. Mother's stomach was, of course, empty again. It had been pumped clean. That brought mother into the kitchen snorting like a bull. Father was looking tormented from the ride.

"Ma," Angie said, "what are you doing here? You should be home lying down."

"Oh shut up. You can't chase me off that easily."

Angie and Maria cleared a path as mother charged for the kettle of spaghetti sauce. She scooped two meatballs out and crash-landed them on a plate. A fork was used to crush and stuff them betwixt a slice of Italian bread. Mother bit deeply into the sandwich. Through her bulging cheeks she said, "What the hell's wrong with him," pointing with an elbow at Ringo, who was slumping on a couple of produce crates.

"You nearly gave me a goddamn heart attack," Ringo said.

"Aye, watch your tone," mother said, "or I'll have Angie make you some raviolis."

General Alejandro Garcia was dead. It said so on the front page of my morning newspaper. The Guatemalan dictator's government had been toppled by revolutionary forces that had won the allegiance of several divisions of the country's military. Garcia had been taken into custody, tied to a chair, interrogated and savagely beaten. Then he was shot dead with a bullet through the back of the head.

The Latin American strongman's thick features were stretched across the mug shot accompanying the story. Below that was a picture of the bearded and deliriously smiling Enrico Zepeda, who was quoted in the story condemning his longtime nemesis and calling the change of power in his native land a victory of good over evil.

"Sadie," I shouted up the stairs to my wife, "come quickly."

Startled, Sadie came bounding down the stair in a short chiffon robe to find out what the commotion was about. There were still creases along the side of her face from the wrinkles in her pillow. She read the story over my shoulder while her throat made sounds of shock and fascination.

Before we could finish reading the article the phone rang and Enrico Zepeda's voice was on the other end. He had been on the telephone all night talking with the instigators of the *coup de etat*, several of whom were his personal friends and members of the secret underground that helped him flee Guatemala for the United States when the dictator sent the death squad after him.

We invited Zepeda for coffee. He arrived wired from lack of sleep and started pacing the kitchen like a deranged animal. A cup of coffee in one hand and the other left free to punctuate his political commentary. Loudly he spoke about the historical turning point represented by Alejandro Garcia's overthrow and execution-style murder.

"After seventeen years my country is finally freed from the torturous rule of that madman. It's going to be the rebirth of a nation."

What the newspaper didn't report, Zepeda said, was that the artist's dearest friend was among the two dozen people in the room with Garcia while he was being spat upon and brutalized. He participated in the festivities by yanking a painting depicting a biblical scene off the wall, marching up to Garcia and saying, "This is for what you did to Enrico Zepeda." He smashed the painting over the prisoner's skull. Garcia's bloodied head came busting through the center of the canvas but the frame stayed rapped around his neck like some sort of bizarre Elizabethan collar.

After everyone had taken turns teeing off on the fallen dictator, the opposition leader held a silver hollow-point bullet in front of Garcia's face and said, "Here's your ticket to hell, you sick bastard." Then he loaded the single shot into his pistol's chamber, stepped behind Garcia, cocked the hammer and consummated the overthrow by pulling the trigger and putting a bullet through his brain. The exit wound left a circle the size of the Holy Eucharist on the victim's forehead. Garcia's lifeless body slumped in the chair.

The coup leader was not without a sense of humor. Seeing Garcia bound and battered with the destroyed painting around his neck, Guatemala's new president barked, "I want this sonofabitch embalmed just the way his is and taken to the National Museum of Art and put on display for all the people of Guatemala to see how art imitates life."

Zepeda's mind was returned to the events of the day. He quickly whipped himself back into a political frenzy.

"There will be a celebration," he said with a demonic chortle, "and you two will be invited."

Then he set his coffee down and headed for the door. On his way out he shouted "*Viva Guatemala!*"

Clyde Jablonsky showed up late that evening after the crowd had fizzled. The sergeant detective was in his in full regalia: denim jeans, cowboy boots and his black leather jacket with extra zippers. There was also the ever-present bulge of a firearm near his left armpit. He gave Ginger a full-body hug, engulfing her within his limbs and giving her a nose full of musk oil and leather. He refrained from kissing her, though, figuring restraint was a wise path at this stage of the relationship. I offered him a Perino draft. This time he accepted. Halfway through the beer Vinny strolled by.

"Jablonsky, let's debrief," he said, waving the detective to a quiet table on the far side of the dining room. Vinny stared at Jablonsky, shifted in his chair and said, "I'll be blunt. I've got a problem with you spiking my sister when you're supposed to be investigating her as a potential suspect."

The cop was annoyed. "I would expect a little more delicacy when talking about your own sister."

"I've got an excuse. My vocabulary's limited. I'm not a college boy like you."

"Has some kind of announcement been made that I should know about?"

"Nobody had to say anything. My sister walked in here this afternoon looking like she was tripping on acid. You've got her mesmerized. Ginger's not usually the type to fall big for a guy. She's more the I'll-stay-mildly-interested-as-long-as-you-show-me-a-good-time type. You're different for some reason. You've got her full of passion. Don't ask me why. I guess she's always been a sucker for tough guys."

"I'm just pleased I make her happy," Jablonsky said, taking another swig from his beer mug.

"Help me get my head around this one. Ginger is still a potential suspect, and now you're bedding her. Wouldn't any police agency label that conflict of interest?"

The detective shrugged. "You've got a valid point. If you really think Ginger's a suspect I can turn the case over to one of my colleagues."

"I have a suspicion that your fellow cops just might have an interest in protecting you and anybody you're interested in protecting – like, say, a significant other."

Jablonsky leaned back and crossed his arms, leather coat groaning. "There seems to be a trust issue here. We can call the whole department off if you like."

Vinny looked off and gave the notion consideration. "Never mind that," he finally said. "I've got that big, ugly private eye on the case as well. I'll make sure he gives a little extra focus to Ginger — and you."

The two men turned to look my way as I rushed to the table.

"Phone call," I said to Vinny. "Sounds like our girl."

My brother swallowed dryly, then headed downstairs to the office with Jablonsky on his tail. The tracking and recording equipment was hidden under a towel to keep it out of Uncle Nunzio's view. Vinny whipped it off and threw it on the floor and buzzed me via the intercom to let me know he was ready for the call to be transferred. As soon as it rang the trace/record switch was activated. The office was equipped with two phones, so Jablonsky picked up a receiver to listen in at the same instant Vinny answered.

"Vinny Marciano speaking."

"I forgot to tell you not to get the police involved."

Her voice was instantly recognizable from the first call. "You're a real pro, you know that?"

"Did you call the police?"

"For what? You think they're going to loan me half a mil?"

There was a pause from the caller, so Vinny spoke again. "What's your name? I mean, what should I call you?"

Jablonsky slowly nodded his approval.

"There won't be any need for civilities. We're going to get of this deal done and our communication will be permanently severed."

"Will it?" Vinny said, trying to sound bemused. He still believed he might know the person on the other end of the phone, maybe closely. Maria and Angie had already left the evening. He imagined one of them speaking into the phone with a handkerchief held over the mouth to alter her voice.

"Did you get the half-million together?" Her voice still had that sultry corona around it, though it lacked the conviction and confidence of her first call.

"It's not neatly stacked on my desk, if that's what you mean. Tell me where you want it dropped and I'll bag it."

"Cooperative, aren't we? You seem to have had a change of heart."

"Those recipes are everything to me."

"You were lying about the police, weren't you? That's why you're so willing to make this drop, isn't it. The cops are ready to make a sting."

Jablonsky mouthed the words talk slower to Vinny.

I ... don't ... even ... like ... the ... cops?

"What's wrong with you?"

"Nothing's ... wrong."

"Then why are you suddenly talking like you've been dipped in molasses?"

Vinny shrugged. "I ... don't ... know ..."

Jablonsky made a spinning motion with his finger, urging Vinny to speed back up.

"... what you mean," Vinny finished.

"You're a bastard, you know that? You're making a big mistake trying to fuck around with me. You're dealing with an alpha bitch. You hear me boy? You don't play me, I play you."

Then came the dial tone.

Wes Fitzgerald was hiding in the landscaped bushes taking a piss when he spotted Ginger Marciano bursting out the front gate of the Atherton Mill condominium complex and moving quickly towards her car.

"Shit," Fitzgerald growled.

He shook the last drops of urine from his penis, tucked it back in his shorts and ran towards his car, forgetting to zip his trousers. The detective's honking blue Buick LaSabre rocked under his weight as he slid behind the wheel. The vehicle's aging eight-cylinder engine coughed back to life with a smoky carbon monoxide plume from its tailpipe and gave chase. Ginger was already flying down the street in her high-revving matchbox-size Mini Cooper convertible. The sports car's small, agile chassis weaved easily through lanes of traffic.

"Fuck me," the detective snarled. The interior of the car smelled of vomit after a particularly bitter night of drinking at his neighborhood tavern. Fitzgerald got so shit-faced he managed only to stumble into his car, where he immediately passed out. He woke 43 minutes later just long enough to throw up all over the passenger-side floorboard, then conked out for a couple more hours before regaining consciousness and weaving the car back home.

This morning he did a half-assed job of cleaning up his spill. The car still smelled so putrid it made Fitzgerald want to vomit all over again. That wouldn't do much good, though, because there was nothing in his stomach to regurgitate. There was no way he could choke down any breakfast in his condition, so the dry heaves would be the best he could muster — which would be far worse than spewing his favorite brand of bourbon and Coke.

He was trying to keep two cars between the LaSabre and Ginger's Mini Cooper, as was his policy when following a suspect. He was doing pretty well until one of those goddamn oversized sport utility vehicles pulled into his lane and blocked the view of everything on the road. How pleasing it would have been to pull out the .357 and blow the back tires off that Winnebago of a vehicle. The way Fitzgerald was feeling he was just as likely to tuck the gun barrel under his chin and blast gray curds and whey all over the roof of the car.

The LaSabre swung into the other lane. Fitzgerald gunned the engine and flipped off the driver as he passed. Ginger had opened up about a five car-length lead. Fitzgerald struggled to keep pace without running innocent motorists off the road — or, worse, making it obvious to this Italian hussy that she was being bird-dogged by a man in a vehicle that stuck out like a bad toupee.

Fitzgerald was falling farther behind and become annoyed. His head felt a fresh surge of pain with every beat of his heart. As the Mini Cooper pulled away he became more aggravated, causing his heart to beat harder and squeezing waves of blood more forcefully into the arterial passages of his brain, multiplying his pain.

"Dumb degenerate cunt."

More daring attempts were now being made by Fitzgerald to make up lost ground. People were getting cut off, horns started honking. Just as he was getting within a respectable distance, the Ginger cut a sharp left turn down a side street.

"Motherfucker."

Fitzgerald nearly tore off the steering wheel in frustration when a torrent of oncoming vehicles forced him to come to a full stop until traffic cleared and he could make his left turn.

The quiet side street was deserted, the Mini Cooper nowhere in sight. The private dick slowly cruised up and down several blocks looking into driveways, parking lots and still more side streets.

Where the hell had Mrs. Houdini gone?

The detective was embarrassed by his entanglement with the morning traffic. As a law enforcement officer he had been trained in the fine art of tailing a suspect. This wasn't exactly a textbook performance.

"Bitch."

Fitzgerald reluctantly called off the hunt and navigated the car towards his favorite neighborhood tavern. Returning to the scene of last night's crime, the detective was prepared to sooth his aching melon and rotting gut with some hair of the dog.

Enrico Zepeda was thrown into a manic state by the overthrow and slaying of arch-enemy Alejandro Garcia. He was now operating without sleep and spoke on the telephone constantly. Countless interviews with the revolutionary artist were being conducted by newspapers and radio stations across the Western Hemisphere. Leaders of the new Guatemalan government invited Zepeda to join their meetings via teleconference to assist in drafting a new democratic constitution and planning elections. A trip to his native country was being scheduled to participate in the installation and inauguration of the new regime.

What little time those activities left Zepeda he devoted to planning a post-revolutionary celebration. His final act of defiance against the fallen dictator would be a party that challenged Garcia's false piety and puritanical utterances. Zepeda named it the Libido Ball. It would be a costume party filled with attendees wearing attire that was, at the least, suggestive, but preferably charged with sexual invitation and innuendo.

Vinny immediately volunteered to host the event at his palatial home. The day of the party Vinny needed help moving some furniture to accommodate the crowd. I obliged while complaining of lethargy.

"I got something for that," Vinny said. He disappeared and then returned with a handful of pills and gelatin capsules of various color. "Take these. It's a vitamin package I've been taking. It's specially designed to boost your mitochondria."

"My *mito* what?"

"Remember your biology? The mitochondria is the little energy factory found in each cell of the body. Take these and it will boost your energy production."

I smirked. "This sounds like a marketing gimmick."

"All I can tell you is it works for me. Just give it a try. They can't hurt you, they're vitamins."

I slipped them into my pocket.

When I returned home I found Sadie in her favorite posture, lying on the bed with a sock over her eyes to block out the light. I'd never known a woman to spend so much time in repose — and almost none of it sleeping or copulating. Sadie was an insomniac and was almost always suffering from some type of physical distress that doctors found impossible to diagnose, mainly because her symptoms were moving targets. One day she's immobilized by ovarian pain. The next an irritable bowel kept her chained to a toilet. Today she was moaning about a painful headache that was throbbing behind one eye.

Sadie always felt better when I lay down beside her, so I did. Soon we had dozed off. When I awoke the room was dark, except for illumination from the digital clock that told me were had already missed the start of the Libido Ball. I roused Sadie. She insisted I attend without her. I demanded she get her ass out of bed.

We had not spent any time planning our costumes and there was no time to improvise, so we simply dressed in street clothes and tooled across town.

Immediately upon walking into the Libido Ball my penis became a problem, as it went into an almost instantaneously aroused state. The instigator was the young woman sitting naked high atop the impressive rock and flagstone waterfall that was the centerpiece of my brother's living room. The motionless woman had struck a sensuous and contemplative pose, reminiscent of a less intellectual version of Rodin's sculpture *The Thinker*. Long chestnut hair fell down past her shoulders while water gushed up from below and ran in smooth currents around and between her shanks.

There was something terribly unusual going on. This was the biggest, stiffest, most urgent erection I had produced since a teenager. My blood-engorged cock felt stretched so thin it was ready to burst into a glorious red fountain.

Luckily, a chair was nearby, which I quickly perched himself upon to conceal my physiology. I had foolishly worn boxer shorts to the party. The feel of my genitals swinging freely brought a stimulus of its own, but to be under the influence of a party full of people dressed to appeal to prurient interests posed an immeasurably larger problem.

What had I been thinking? A very tight pair of jockey shorts was called for under these circumstances. Between my free-range testicles and the scantily dressed crowd it was going to be a long night with many ups and downs.

Sadie, unaware of my plight, drifted into the crowd, which was moving to the sound of a live Latin jazz quartet. Cocktail waitresses from a catering company were dressed in Playboy bunny attire and carrying trays of hors d'oeuvres. Two bartenders in vests and bow ties were mixing and serving drinks from behind a fully-stocked bar. Three Dobermans belonging to the man of the house were cruising warily among the guests, making sure none of this bizarre menagerie disturbed their master or got near their food supply.

Enrico Zepeda, the master of ceremonies, was concealed by nothing more than a loin cloth and a pair of fuzzy slippers. He spotted me sitting like a wall flower in the house's foyer and came over.

"Enrico," I said, "you look like you escaped from a Margaret Mead encampment."

"Try again," Zepeda said.

"I give up."

"Would you believe the Son of God?" Zepeda replied, pointing to the stigmatic streaks of red lipstick along his ribcage. "I was also going to be wearing a crown of thorns but the people at the floral shop couldn't get it woven in time."

"You certainly don't sell yourself short."

"Well, you know what they say: power is the ultimate aphrodisiac. I want every woman in this place to know that I can wash away their sins if they simply feast on my Holy Eucharist."

"Why you sacrilegious prick," I ribbed.

"That's no way to talk to your Personal Savior and Lord. Now get your balls in the air and join the party."

"In a few minutes," I said, still trying to reduce the inflammation of my penis. "I'm just going to observe for a little while."

"A perfect vantage from which to enjoy the glories of nature," Zepeda said pointing to the naked rock climber I was trying to ignore.

"Nice touch."

"I thought so. She's one of my models. You and Vinny met her at my studio."

Now I had to give the woman with the perfectly scooped breasts another look. Then it dawned. "Oh, yes, that's ..."

"Jasmine," Zepeda said. "Jasmine Starling."

"Yes, I remember," I said, exciting myself all over again.

Zepeda looked me up and down. "I see you really went all out for the party. Bugle Boy pants with a pair of loafers and a pullover sweater. Who are you supposed to be, the new poster boy for The Gap?"

"Sorry to be a party pooper. Sadie and I ... we're not much for costumes."

"That's a shame. It could spice up your sex life." Zepeda sipped champagne from a large silver chalice that was supposed to be the Holy Grail. "Well, I best get back to my apostles," he said. Zepeda's fuzzy slippers made flapping sounds as he walked away.

A few minutes later Shekko Lombardi walked through the front door with my sister Maria on a leash. It was clasped to a spiked leather collar around her neck. Maria had never looked happier in her black hot pants, red bustier and leather choker. Shekko was in lion tamer's garb and carried a short whip. There was also a military-issued pistol holstered on his hip.

Zepeda was back, greeting them with applause. "Nice show," he cheered. "Just make sure she doesn't urinate on any of the furniture or hump my guests' legs."

With my penis finally in partial remission, I got out of the chair and joined the crowd. The place was packed. More than three dozen of Zepeda's friends had made the four-hour drive from the New York City to celebrate the demise of Alejandro Garcia. There were locals as well, including some Mangia House employees. An effigy of Alejandro Garcia, sculpted by Zepeda, was hanging from the ceiling with a rope around its neck and a wretched little hand arthritically wrapped around a pathetically small penis.

Soon I was standing near Vinny, who was in a chef's apron and hat. He had a spatula in one hand and a small frying pan in the other and was insisting to those around him that the hearts of women, like men, were inextricably connected to pleasures of the stomach.

I positioned myself in a way that sealed him off from the rest of the crowd and said, "Hey, what was in those vitamins you gave me?"

Vinny lost his battle to fight back a devious grin. "Why do you ask?"

"Because I've got a hard-on for the ages." I glanced down to my crotch. "It's all I can do to keep this thing from reaching out and shaking everybody's hand."

Vinny took a gander of his own. "You look normal to me."

"That's because the hand in my pocket is wrapped around the damn thing. I've got it pulled over to the side. I'm going to have to spend the rest of the night looking like I'm making change."

Vinny was laughing now and carrying on like a man who had scored big on April Fool's Day.

"What is it, you bastard? What did you do?"

"The vitamin cocktail I gave you included a little something extra."

"*Tell me.*"

"A doctor I know gave me a free sample of the latest erectile dysfunction drug. It's called Emectus. Supposed to be the most high-octane one yet."

"Thanks a lot, asshole. As if I needed it. What are you doing with it anyway? Are you having problems making it straight?"

"No way. Never. I just gave it a try to see what the buzz was all about. It's awesome."

"When the hell is this stuff going to wear off?"

"Who knows? You're young and virile so you might be bouncing on your pogo stick the rest of the weekend." The harmless swipe I took at Vinny's face was easily evaded.

He was laughing again in that mocking way that he had perfected. "The side effects listed on the package say medical treatment should be sought for erections lasting more than four hours. Can you believe that? It's got to be the first time in history a drug's label has sent men stampeding to the pharmacy in hopes of experiencing its side effects."

"You just ruined this party for me."

"Relax. Just let it go and let it show. Tell people it's part of your costume, that you've come to the party as John Holmes. They'll think you packed your pants. If you're lucky a few women will want to grab hold to find out what kind of construction material you used."

The conversation ended when I turned to investigate the source of a British accent. It was Ginger wearing a regal gown and a Princess Diana mask. Her long, black hair was twisted flamboyantly at the crown of her head.

Zepeda noticed her at the same time. "Well!" he boomed. "Good evening your Royal Highness!"

Ginger offered the Guatemalan a gloved hand, which Zepeda took between his paint-stained fingers and kissed with aplomb.

"I understand there's a new cavalier in your life," Zepeda said. "Will I be making his acquaintance this evening?"

"Unfortunately not," Ginger lilted. "He's out with the rest of the bobbies keeping our Piccadilly Circus safe from the rogues."

I walked my penis to the bar to get a drink. On the other side of the living room I saw Sadie having an intense discussion with Amy Stonebreaker, who had donned animal skins of a pre-Columbian design.

Hans Sprink, stuffed uncomfortably in a tuxedo, sidled my way. "Get a load of Shekko," he said. "That gun he's toting around looks real. I hope to god it isn't loaded."

I shook my head. "How is it possible that even in the middle of a costume party Shekko Lombardi is the most surreal character in the room?"

We observed as Shekko spotted Zepeda and immediately walked over with his wife in tow and started recounting his days as an Army Ranger in the Vietnamese jungles when he and his men supposedly exterminated an uncooperative rural warlord.

"It was just like *Apocalypse Now*," he said.

Every few minutes Shekko wound up the whip and lashed his jubilant wife across the buttocks and thighs.

"Do that again," Zepeda beseeched.

A heavyset woman in fishnet stockings and a suede jacket was producing big laughter in the corner. She was part of a small group listening to an effeminate man in a feather boa claiming to have had a homosexual affair with Zepeda. His name was Benjamin Francois and as he spoke he waved around a cigarette in a long holder.

"I didn't know Enrico swung both ways," said the fat woman in the fishnets.

"That's what I said the first time we shared the saddle," the man lisped. "My actual words were, 'I didn't know men were on your palette.' And I'll never as long as I live forget Enrico's response. He said, 'Anytime I discover that I have an inhibition I seek to eliminate it immediately.' So, I guess it might be a stretch to call him a switch-hitter. He was just dabbling, though I'm quite delighted he had the good judgment to choose me for his dalliance."

Sadie, disgusted by the Frenchman's indiscretion, walked away and tracked down Angie, who came dressed in her wedding gown.

"I've been dying to wear this dress again for years," Angie explained. "I paid a fortune for it and think it's just beautiful. It was either wear it here tonight or force Hans to remarry me."

"Where's Ringo?"

"Are you kidding? You know he's anti-social. He wouldn't show up for party — or anything that involved a crowd."

"I saw him yesterday and he told me he'd be here."

"Ringo speaks with forked tongue. He's always telling people he'll show up, then he bails out at the last minute. And I do mean the last minute. He pulled up out front about an hour ago, looked at the house and drove off. He does that; makes him feel included in some way."

"He should have come in."

"Naw, he'd be miserable. It's not just the crowd, Ringo's afraid of dogs. Vinny always promised to lock the Dobermans in the basement, but Ringo's convinced they're going to break loose and pick him out of a crowd of one hundred people to attack."

"The boy is a bundle of strange phobias."

"Who you telling? I grew up with the guy. The older he gets the more things he's afraid of. The oddest thing is that he doesn't fear death but he's afraid of everything else. I keep telling him the worst case scenario with all his phobias is death, which is what he longs for, so what's to be afraid of? The guy can't wait to get to heaven; thinks he's got all kinds of special rewards coming, like he's the big winner on a game show. I think he half expect Bob Barker to greet him at the Pearly Gates."

Sadie tapped Enrico Zepeda's bare shoulder as he coasted by.

"Enrico, I think it's offensive that you have a naked woman in the middle of the living room," my wife said.

"You must mean the living sculpture."

"Okay, the living sculpture. I find it offensive."

"And why is that?"

"It's exploitative."

"This is the Libido Ball, my dear, it's all about exploitation. We exploit ourselves for the enjoyment of others."

"Why not exploit a naked man?"

"That's not my preference."

"What does that have to do with it? I thought this was supposed to be a piece of living art, not a statement of sexual orientation."

"It is indeed."

"So it could just as easily be a naked man, couldn't it?"

"I suppose so. Would you enjoy that?"

"Yes," Sadie said, looking towards Angie and getting a supportive nod from her. "I think I would."

"Good," Zepeda said, "hold my drink while I remove my loin cloth."

"Enrico, you are impossible."

Zepeda smiled and gave Sadie a peck on the cheek, then he picked up the Latin rhythm of the band and danced away.

After a couple of hours elapsed the jazz band's tempo accelerated and the crowd grew tipsy and rowdy. I saw a woman with a bandanna and man in a Hawaiian shirt pawing at each other as they disappeared into a bathroom.

A band of women congregated around the mermaid in the rock fountain to get a closer look. Their inhibitions diminished by a surplus of alcohol and their bravery increased by their number, the cutting remarks started flying.

"Those tits are fake," said a flat-chested woman. "I know a pair of saline bags when I see them."

"Looks like she's heavily invested in the Collagen Corporation too," another chimed in. "Look at those lips. Shot full of the damn stuff."

"No shit. She's going to look real cute in a few years when it's running down to the cleft in her chin."

The fat woman in the fishnet stockings decided to weigh in: "These young girls kill me, parading around in their birthday suits and fake parts, thinking they've got the world by the tail. Well I've got news for them, I've been to plenty of Vegas burlesque shows and, believe me, girls who look like her are a dime a dozen."

A sarcastic voice added: "My, what a neatly trimmed little triangle," staring at her crotch. "She must have just gotten a fresh shave on the *Howard Stern Show*."

Zepeda grabbed me by an elbow and brought me closer to the crowing women. "What did I tell you?" Zepeda said. "Nobody likes looking at naked women like other women. That's why women's magazines are full of nudity. The comparisons are constant. And listen to them. Have you ever heard anything so venomous? This scene you're looking at is going to be the inspiration for another Zepeda painting. I'm going to title it Beauty and the Beasts."

The voice of the fat woman in fishnets was cutting through the air again. "Look at her sitting up on her rock pile all high and mighty. Who does this chick think she is, Rapunzel?"

Jasmine Starling had some choice thoughts of her own, but they went unspoken. She remained motionless and outwardly unfazed, which antagonized her assailants all the more.

"She's so young, but look at that poise," Zepeda marveled to me.

Shekko Lombardi suddenly pulled the pistol out of his holster and started waving it in the air and shouting revolutionary slogans. He had dropped the whip and the leash, setting Maria loose.

"Down with the dictator!" Shekko declared. "Revolution runs on empty bellies! No justice, no peace! Power to the people!"

He was getting louder and more crazed with every slogan. Maria was begging him to stop. "*It's a Vietnam flashback*," she cried.

"Give me liberty or give me death!" Shekko shouted. "It takes a revolution to make a solution! No fears, no tears! *Viva Guatemala* and let them eat cake!"

Then Shekko Lombardi fired four rounds of ammo at the hanging effigy of Alejandro Garcia. The saxophonist screeched to a halt along with the other band members. Most of the crowd dove for cover. Even the unflappable Jasmine Starling shuddered momentarily.

Vinny marched over and screamed at his gun-toting guest: "Moron! Get out out here, and take your weapon with you!"

"It's blanks," Shekko said, pointing innocently at the smoking weapon.

"The only thing full of blanks around here is your head."

"Look," Shekko said, aiming the gun at Vinny's chest and firing off another round. Screams were offered from across the room. The sheer horror of having a loaded weapon discharged against you at point-blank range rocked Vinny back on his heels. Now the Dobermans had surrounded Shekko and were crouched in attack position, growling in concert and crinkling the tops of their snouts and baring fangs.

"Get out now," Vinny said, "or I'll call the police and have you brought up on charges."

Shekko huffed and returned the weapon to its holster. Carefully tip-toeing between the Dobermans, he regained control of his wife's leash and gingerly walked her out the door, escorted by the gurgling canines.

Apologizing to the jazz band, Vinny ordered its members to again kick-up the sound. He urged all the guests to banish the ugly incident of gunplay from their minds and resume having a jolly time. But most were too shaken to recapture their frivolity. Some were looking to the door, half expecting Shekko Lombardi to come busting through with his weapon reloaded with live ammo and laying waste to the place. Women were clutched to their men and insisting they go home. The skittish Hans Sprink was nearing hyperventilation.

Ginger, still obscured by her Princess Diana mask and mock British accent, said to Vinny. "I had no idea he was so bloody unstable. Two or three drinks were all he had."

"Too bad your boyfriend wasn't here to cuff him," Vinny said. "I just might bring that bastard up on charges. I certainly have plenty of eyewitnesses."

Sadie and I were preparing to leave when he heard a woman call my name. I turned to discover it was Jasmine Starling, who had just climbed down from her mount, toweled dry and was now concealed in a robe. Stunned that she had remembered me, I was now face to face with the young vixen and alarmed that my resurgent penis was going to turn this into a three-way conversation. Though my pocketed left hand was still firmly wrapped around the organ, I could feel that it was reaching new degrees of inflation.

"Don't you recognize me with some clothing on?"

"Of course I do, I'm just surprised you remembered me. We only met for five minutes and it was a long time ago."

"Let's just say you're a memorable guy, Mick." Jasmine used a sly smile to put an exclamation mark behind the comment. "Haven't had a chance yet to come by and have you fix me a drink yet, but I'm planning to."

My cock throbbed at the notion. "I'm impressed. You even remembered my profession."

"Yeah. And what is that subject you got a degree in — the one with the weird name."

"Sociology."

"That's it. I still remember the definition you gave me: the study of people and society."

"Very good."

"I remembered because it sounded interesting. Maybe I'll even take a class some day."

"I think you'd enjoy that," I finally responded.

Jasmine stretched her arms high above her head. The movement caused her robe to part lasciviously. My cock torqued again. My hand pressed even harder to keep the body part in check. "You must have gotten stiff sitting up there like a statue for hours."

"It's really no big deal. My mantra and I went transcendental. I must have repeated it three thousand times tonight. It's still going through my head."

"Now there's something we have something in common. I meditate too. What's your mantra?"

"I can't tell you. It's a secret. It was given to me by Mahareshi Mahesh Yogi. I paid $350 for it."

I smiled with amusement. Jasmine looked around.

"This is one hell of a house," she said. "A waterfall in the living room — that's way cool."

"Yeah, my brother's got a flair for spending his money."

"He's really kinky too. Before the guests got here your brother kept trying to talk me into doing weird things with those Dobermans. He wanted to video me with his camcorder."

My eyes rolled. "That's Vinny for you. The man dreams of a world without boundaries."

"Tell me about it. It's not just him. When a girl takes off her clothes, men start thinking she's willing to do anything."

As the small talk rolled on I became aware of a tremendous energy field emanating from over the right shoulder. My head swiveled to see Sadie standing very straight and prim, waiting by the door prepared to leave. Her body was angled in a geometric effort to set herself apart from her husband. Her head was subtly titled back and nose held high as if defiantly maintaining her dignity in the midst of my outrageous flirtation with the naked woman from the waterfall. I suspected that Sadie knew I was battling an inopportune erection.

The tension was not lost on Jasmine. "I guess you better go," she said.

I nodded and returned to my wife. Together we embarked on a sub-zero ride home.

Then came talk about lie detector tests.

Vinny first brought up the subject during our weekly family dinner. It was Sunday, the one day of the week the restaurant was closed in observance of the Sabbath; the day we met at mother and father's home at the designated time to break bread and spend time like a traditional family.

This week's repast consisted of broiled steaks seasoned with oregano and served with a side of penne pasta in a light cream sauce. The vegetable of the day was steamed broccoli. Salad would be served after the main course, as was a family tradition. Mother always told us that salad was an excellent "eliminator."

None of the in-laws were in attendance. Shekko Lombardi rarely attended because he never got along with the Marcianos. Hans Sprink was traveling on a quality control assignment for his company. My wife was still stranded in bed trying to ward off her latest symptom, having something to do with a headache that had blinded her on one eye.

We ate mostly in silence. Like all good Italians our concentration was on our food and we ate aggressively. The one exception to that rule was Ginger, who whittled away at her servings in a deliberate, microscopic manner. Her utensils were lightly and carefully gripped in the prim manner taught her during finishing classes at the Chicago modeling school she helped bankrupt. Each bite was thoroughly chewed a minimum of twenty times before swallowing. It was all part of her health and longevity regiment, a means of keeping her digestion and elimination in regular working order and helped prevent the production of gas, something Ginger found unattractive and un-ladylike. She always finished eating 22 minutes later than the rest of us, significantly delaying salad and dessert, the latter of which she skipped ninety percent of the time anyway.

Halfway through the meal Ringo paused eating to conduct the ritualistic cleansing of his glasses. He pulled the plastic-framed spectacles off his face and held them up to the light. One of his many idiosyncrasies was an obsession with keeping the lenses dust free. He hit the left lens with a blast of air from his mouth to clear it of some particles. Satisfied that his vision was no longer impaired, he used both hands to return the glasses to the bridge of his nose. The act was carried out with extreme care and precision, as though gluing together pieces of a model airplane kit. Ringo took longer to reattach glasses to his face than any person I had ever seen.

"How are those recipes coming along?" father asked Vinny.

My brother shrugged.

"Are you getting any closer to finding them?"

"Clyde's working on them," Ginger interjected.

Vinny gave her a lingering, incredulous stare.

"You know your Uncle Nunzio is back from Las Vegas. All sorts of hell is going to break loose if hears they've been stolen."

FAMILY RECIPES

"Albie, leave the boy alone," mother said. "You don't think he knows that?" Then she continued wailing away at her food.

"Any chance you're going to find them before your uncle starts getting suspicious?"

"Maybe ... with a little cooperation."

Father gazed at Vinny until he felt compelled to elaborate. "The private investigator I hired has a lie detector machine, and even knows how to operate it. He wants us all to take the test."

The clatter of dinner came to a standstill. A queasy pall descended over the room. Some blood ran cold. Some ran hot.

Maria angled an eating utensil at Vinny's face from across the table. "Don't insult me."

"I'm not going to let that big ugly cuss touch me," Ginger followed, "or subject me to humiliating questions."

"I don't steal," mother declared, "and I don't lie." The authority of her statement was sharply undermined by the partial floret of broccoli that tumbled from her mouth as she spoke.

"Tell that investigator to go jump in a lake," father said.

"Why is this such a big deal?" Vinny said. "Nobody at this table's got anything to hide — do they?" He gave everyone a look.

"Those machines aren't accurate," Maria said, "that's why they're not admissible in court."

"We'll do this as a family," Vinny said. "I'll go first."

Now Angie piped in. "You and that *chadrool* are dreaming up more inane methods to discredit us."

"If you don't go along with this you're obstructing the investigation," Vinny said, dropping a fist on the table. His pinkie ring let out a loud crack against the wood.

"I don't want to get involved," Ringo said.

"It's a way to eliminate yourself as a suspect," Vinny told him. "You pass the test, you come out smelling like a rose."

The magnetic pull of the dinner plate had already distracted mother and father.

"Why would you suspect us and not one of the employees?" I said.

"They're suspects too. Let's just establish that none of us took the recipes so we narrow down the investigation's focus."

"Start with the employees," Ringo said.

"No. I don't want this thing spilling out into the open before it has to. We have to think about what this could mean to the restaurant's reputation. Secrecy is paramount."

"I'll take the test," Maria said, "I don't give a shit."

"You'll do nothing of the kind," Angie shouted, coming halfway across the table and dipping a breast in the pasta sauce.

Maria looked to Vinny and said: "I'll ace the damn thing, roll up the machine's printout and stick it so far up your nose it will tickle your widow's peak."

Angie was nearing Primal Scream agitation. "Why don't you tie your girlfriend up to that machine and see what she's got to say? See if Stonebreaker can produce a steady line on that machine. She's the one who wants to become a gourmet chef; that sounds like motive to me."

"She's not the only one with motive around here," Vinny clucked.

"What are you insinuating?" Angie said, dipping her napkin in a water glass and started cleaning the pasta stain from her blouse.

"You don't think I know some of you want to discredit me with Uncle Nunzio?" Vinny was looking back and forth at Angie and Maria, making plain the targets of his allegation. "You don't think I know some people in this room have designs on opening another Marciano's?"

"The recipes are all right here," Angie said, tapping an index finger against her temple. "I'd hardly need to steal recipes if I wanted to open another restaurant."

Vinny turned up the intensity of his insistence. But he got back every bit of that intensity and more, partly because he was badly outnumbered. But numbers always added up to zero for Vinny.

Father combated the anxiety of the moment by picking up his steak bone and gnawing it perfectly clean.

Vinny grabbed the Chianti bottle and refilled the wine glasses, as if to medicate the situation. Everyone was drinking but Ringo, who claimed alcohol exacerbated his mental handicap.

"I think that big ugly cuss was following me the other day," Ginger said between sips from her wine goblet. "Can you imagine, he was tailing me in that blue ocean liner of a car he drives, as I'm not going to notice. How stupid."

"Look, the police department did the fingerprinting and that was inconclusive," said Vinny, determined to stay on subject. "Nobody's fingerprints were on that safe but ours. That means we need to take the next step. Go deeper with this investigation."

I said, "There were no fingerprints because whoever stole those recipes had enough brains to wear gloves or use a pot holder to turn the dial."

"You don't know that," Vinny said. "None of us know anything. We need to sort things out. We need to eliminate suspects. That's what the lie detector is for."

"I'm not going to do it," Ringo said with his characteristic finality. "I get nervous around other people. That will make me fail the test even though I always tell the truth."

"There's nothing to get nervous about. The investigator just wants to ask some questions."

"He's going to ask me trick questions." Ringo's momentous voice was rising fast and ready to crack some plaster.

"Ringo's right," Ginger chimed. "It's an interrogation."

Vinny shot an acidic glance at his big sister. "Like you know so much about this stuff."

"I know a thing or two about interrogation. He'll start out asking you what our favorite color is and finish by spluttering in our faces and trying to get us to say things he wants to hear."

"Is that what your boyfriend did on your special date the other day?"

Ginger whipped a crumpled napkin at Vinny.

Ringo got up and walked out of the room. Mother called after him. "What about your salad?"

He sat down in the living room, took hold of the stems of his glasses and adjusted them ever so slightly. It was the most trifling of adjustments, but it put Ringo's face back in its comfort zone. Then he turned on a New York Giants football game just in time for kickoff.

Mother went to the kitchen and returned with a huge wooden bowl. The conversation quelled while she tossed the salad in front of us and we watched the playful tumble of iceberg lettuce leaves, tomatoes, black olives, cucumbers and radishes. All of the vegetables glistened in a fine coating of vinaigrette dressing.

Winter was biting down even harder on Endicott, New York. The cold was bitter enough for Uncle Nunzio to break out his huge plum-colored overcoat. He looked like a giant eggplant walking through the side door. His head was kept warm by a matching fedora hat. The fedora's black band matched his wingtip shoes with the skid-proof soles, nicely tying together the ensemble.

After racking his coat and hat, he silently observed his nephew from a distance. Vinny was perched on a barstool puffing on a smoking-hot cigar and watching retired linebackers arguing on ESPN.

The air of exasperation came in a blast through elder man's nostrils. The scene was typical. As soon as Nunzio had discontinued day-to-day involvement in the business, Vinny embraced all the celebrity and financial rewards of his occupation and offloaded every task and responsibility to siblings and parents. It was all wine, women and song with this boy. He continued examining his nephew, searching for the slightest reverberations of genetic kinship. If they existed at all they were undetectable.

"*Vinny!*" Nunzio waved him into the dining area.

The old man was looking uncharacteristically somber, putting Vinny on guard during approach. Before Vinny understood what was happening his uncle had him cornered and had stuck his big face just inches from his own. It was still ruddy from the sub-zero wind chill factor.

"I'm hearing things," he said.

Vinny met his uncle's inquiry with a gulp and a croak. "What?"

"I said I'm hearing things."

Vinny did his best to regain his nonchalance, even though his brain was spinning like a centrifuge in search of deceptions and excuses. "I've been hearing things too. Like the price of olive oil is going up. We all hear things. What things are you hearing?"

"I'm not talking about that. I'm hearing things about the restaurant. I'm hearing things about what's been going on here."

"I dunno how to respond to what you're saying, Uncle Nunzio. Could you be more specific?"

The exchange had become a disturbance. A server setting up a nearby table had cast a glance and cocked an ear.

"You come with me." Nunzio headed down the restaurant's creaking flight of stairs, past the storage area and board room and into the business office.

"I've been hearing from customers about a stranger among us. A man with a badge and gun and a lot of hair. They asked me what's going on and I don't know what to tell them. So now I'm asking you, what the hell is going on?"

"Oh, is that all you're talking about? That's Ginger's new boyfriend. You haven't met him yet. He's a detective with Endicott Police Department."

Uncle Nunzio squared his body and took Vinny by the shoulders, looking unflinchingly into the younger man's face. Vinny shriveled under his laser gaze.

"Don't you two-face me Vinny. You hear me? Don't you two-face me boy. I've got instincts like shit's got stink. I know when I'm being bamboozled. Now you give it to me straight up."

"What?" Vinny opened his hands to the heavens, trying to regain his innocence, but the word had again come out of his throat as a croak.

"You're up to no good, and don't tell me otherwise. I know people, and I damn sure know my nephew. You come clean. You try to carry off some scam and I'll tan your goddamn hide."

Vinny made another stab at ignorance and innocence. It still wasn't working. He had gone sheepish and couldn't carry it off anymore. His body collapsed into his office chair in an involuntary act of surrender. "The recipes are missing," he said, swiveling shamefully away from his uncle. "They've been stolen."

As soon as the words escaped his mouth, Vinny felt a surge of relief. Only then did he realized just how enormous the burden of secrecy he had been carrying for the past three weeks. The pressure of keeping the theft from his uncle had lifted in the most merciful way.

Uncle Nunzio was seeing spots. He went down on one knee before the safe — a highly athletic maneuver for a man of his age and girth — and started dialing to release the safe's stainless steel bolts. He cranked the handle, swung the door open and stuck his hand inside, feeling around its metallic emptiness. His head snapped around. With his bulging eyes and lashing tongue he was looking positively reptilian.

"Where are they!" He pushed hard against the top of the safe to heave himself back onto his feet.

"I don't know. I've got a private investigator and a police detective working on it. Somebody called me and claims to have them. She's asking for ransom.

"*She?*"

"I don't recognize the douche bag's voice."

Uncle Nunzio stood there, a hand on hip and another on his forehead, adrift in disbelief for the situation. For him this was the Marciano clan's 9/11. Monuments had fallen. Eternal vows broken. The world had forever changed. The fifty-year history of the restaurant went hurtling through his mind. He had retired with a pristine record. He had thought about turning down his nephew's request to reopen the restaurant because he worried about his legacy, worried about becoming the restaurant industry's equivalent of the athlete who tries making a comeback, only to tarnish his past greatness, like the heavyweight champion who comes out of retirement because he misses the limelight, then gets pummeled and knocked unconscious by an unranked ham-and-egger. He wasn't sure about Vinny, either. He considered his nephew too bound to pleasure, too unacquainted with long hours of self-sacrifice and grueling workloads. The kid played in a rock and roll band, for crying out loud. That's why he made Vinny sign a binding prenuptial agreement that said ultimate control over the restaurant still rested in the hands of its founder, Nunzio Marciano. It invested him with the right to strip Vinny of any degree of power he deemed fit.

"You goddamn knucklehead. First you nearly poison our customers, and now this. Why didn't you just burn the goddamn place down?" He pulled an ampoule from his pocket, shook free two nitro pills and quickly inhaled them to counteract the gathering encampment of pain at the center of his chest.

Alarmed that he might also be held responsible for precipitating his uncle's death, Vinny sought to ease his distress. He explained the efforts being made to recover the recipes, pointing in the direction of the kitchen towel that hid the phone tracing equipment from view.

Nunzio whipped the towel off the desk top and saw the electronic box with its dials and switches and digital numbers and wires connecting to the phone. In a fit of rage he wrapped the towel around the top of Vinny's head until it looked like an amateur turban. Still holding the two ends of the towel, he jerked Vinny's head around before unraveling the towel in a one smooth motion.

Vinny was too embarrassed to resist his uncle's verbal and physical assaults.

"I spent months teaching you the business, showing you the ropes. I invested money in you, Vinny, and this is the thanks I get? You've destroyed your family's heritage."

"I'm going to fix this. I'm going to make it right."

Uncle Nunzio wrapped the towel around Vinny's head again, this time covering his entire face and yanking the boy's head to the nine corners of the earth. From the outside Vinny looked like a prisoner of war. On the inside he was running short of oxygen and reached for the towel. Sensing his nephew's deprivation, Uncle Nunzio quickly but roughly un-bandaged him.

"Stop messing up my hair," Vinny said. "You're always going after my head and messing up my hair."

"You find those recipes." A thick, index finger pointed at the tip of Vinny's nose. "You return them to that safe, and I mean soon. I want all of them, intact."

In his fiercest tone Uncle Nunzio explained that the price of failure for Vinny would be a loss of control over the restaurant. Ownership would instead be transferred, in equal shares, to the members of Vinny's nuclear family. They, after all, were the ones doing the work, Uncle Nunzio insisted.

It was the worst of all possible outcomes for Vinny, the most complete humiliation his mentor could inflict. The several thousand pounds of barometric pressure that had lifted upon his confession of the recipes theft were quickly reassembling themselves atop Vinny's drooping shoulders.

The rosy color drained from his frostbitten face, a pasty-white Uncle Nunzio careened from the room and scaled the stairs with labored footfalls.

A bleak cloud of darkness was still swirling around Vinny the next morning. Uncle Nunzio was making his presence felt. He spent the entire day stalking the restaurant. From afternoon until evening he moved in and out of Vinny's field of vision. Seeking to re-establish order, Uncle Nunzio slapped a firm and guiding hand on the place, howling orders and course corrections to everyone doing their jobs with less-than-Nunzio exactitude.

"Mickey, one ounce of booze per cocktail. Every beer gets half-an-inch of suds on the top. Consistency," he said, giving his hands a double clap."

"Maria, make sure your bus boys clean those tables off pronto. I don't want to see dirty dishes lying around. We need to turn these tables over. Customers are going to be waiting. Empty chairs mean empty wallets."

"Angie, did you double check to make sure there's enough homemade raviolis for tonight?"

"It's been done," she said.

"Well go back and check again."

"Look at the way the top of that sauce is bubbling, Albie. I don't want anything sticking to the bottom of that pot."

Father turned down the flame and picked up a long-handled wood spoon and stirred.

"Margharita, make sure those pasta orders boil for exactly ten minutes before straining, and not five seconds longer. Five minutes and thirty seconds for the home-mades. We serve *al dente* around here."

We all knew why Uncle Nunzio was in such a state. We all knew what had transpired because Uncle Nunzio had talked with father about his encounter with Vinny. Father told mother. Mother told everybody.

Angie had long decried Vinny's aloof management style and the leniency given to non-family employees. Then again, Angie only liked the strong hand of management when it wasn't second guessing her work. Between father and Angie they both thought restaurant would collapse if not for their intervention at the captain's wheel of day-to-day decision making that Vinny had long since abandoned.

Father was aglow for another reason. He figured the recipes would never be returned, meaning his dream of nationally franchising Marciano's would make perfect sense. Once it was established that the recipes were gone for good, father would approach his brother Nunzio about quickly taking full advantage of their worth by getting them in the mouths of people far and wide, before the person who stole the recipes had a chance to capitalize on the theft.

"Are you kidding me," mother told father. "Nunzio wouldn't share those recipes with a bunch of franchise partners in a million years. He has sworn to keep them in the family. Hell or high water isn't going to change that."

"The horses have already left the barn," father countered. "Anyway, I can do whatever I want. I'm a Marciano too."

"Your brother is the keeper of those recipes, Albie. He knows that if you start some kind of franchise against his wishes you'll both end up cursed by the Evil Eye."

Legend said a hex was placed on the recipes a few generations ago, meaning anyone who violated the oath of secrecy would come under a spell that brought with it all manner of bad luck.

"You don't actually believe in that nonsense, do you?" father said. "That's an old wives tale. It's something they used to tell us kids on Halloween to scare us."

"All I know is that your great uncle got sideways with the family and ended up spending the rest of his life in a Rome insane asylum. So don't be taking leave of your senses unless you want to end up in the nut house."

It was totally uncharacteristic of our uncle to be less than cheery, especially right after his annual pilgrimage to Las Vegas.

I retreated to the back dining area and sat alone in a booth, closing my eyes and trying to meditate on serene imagery. Floating ducks, billowing clouds and hang gliders drifted past. Silently I repeated to myself, "I am an open channel for the Divine Light and Creative Energy of God." It was a mantra I'd picked up in a Shakti Gawain book. I wanted to see Light or hear Celestial Music. I would have settled for a sense of inner peace. It was no use. I was too distracted to concentrate. My visualization quickly blurred and dissipated and was replaced by the surly visage of Uncle Nunzio.

Soon the premises were filled with the chatter of arriving employees and their evening preparations.

Wes Fitzgerald muscled his way through the front door and took a seat at the bar. Despite the extreme cold he wore just a turtle neck pullover and blazer — the same tweed blazer with elbow patches he was wearing the day Vinny and I dropped into his sparse office. It was as though the man was impervious to the elements. A pack of non-filter Camels were dropped on the bar. One was pulled free and set precariously between his lips. I ignited my Zippo and applied it to Camel's tip. Fitzgerald cupped the flame between his hands to warm them and drew, pulling the cigarette tight between his lips and sucking the flame right into the tobacco. The ground leaves flared and curdled. A second later the private investigator was chugging smoke like a Civil War locomotive. There was a boredom and harshness about the man.

"You here to talk to Vinny?"

"I'm here for a bourbon and a menu," he said.

Though we weren't officially open yet, I poured the liquor.

"Make it a double."

I set the drink down and slid a menu next to it. "Take your time deciding. The kitchen doesn't open for twenty more minutes."

As Fitzgerald slugged away at his drink, I kept surreptitiously peering his direction. So formidable, this hulking, ragged man, yet so shiftless. Fitzgerald's attitude fell under the headline, *Doesn't Care* — not even for his own wellbeing. His was a mind that didn't believe life amounted to enough to quiver over losing it; and a life of cowardice would certainly be a destiny worse than death. There was only one way for Fitzgerald to live, with a fist in the face of any and all enemies, real and perceived.

This fascinated me because I was scared just standing across the bar from him.

He reviewed the menu's contents. "Homemade spaghetti with extra meatballs."

I gave him a lingering glance. I wrote it on an order form and walked it to the kitchen, posting it above the gas range.

"We've got an early bird," I said to father.

He looked at the order, tilting his head back to view my writing through the reading portion of his bi-focal lenses.

"Start boiling water," he said to the kitchen help.

When I got back to the bar Fitzgerald also had his head tilted back, but it was to finish the last of his bourbon. An avalanche of ice cubes broke free and hit him in the face. He quickly turned the glass upright and set it down, going back to his cigarette as though nothing awkward had happened, as if it was natural to have a half dozen ice cubes scattered around him. I used a towel to whisk them off the bar. Without seeking his permission I replenished the ice and poured him another double.

Movement in the window at the far end of the bar took my attention away from my customer. The pane of glass looked out on the western end of the parking lot, where Ringo was bringing his Chevy Lumina to a standstill. He was late, as usual. Fitzgerald joined me in observing Ringo as he sat wide eyed in his car, looking in all directions before removing himself from the vehicle. He walked quickly and vigilantly toward the front door.

"Somebody chasing him?" Fitzgerald asked.

"He's afraid of dogs. Never been bitten in his life, but he's convinced he will be if a dog ever gets near him. He literally doesn't spend any time outdoors. When he goes for a walk it's at the mall, where dogs aren't allowed."

Fitzgerald gave me a strange look and flicked the ash off his cigarette.

As soon as Ringo closed the front door he relaxed. Out of danger, he started moving like a bovine, oblivious to timetables.

Having spent a lifetime around Ringo I'd concluded that he was struggling through his first incarnation as a human being. How else was it possible that his hierarchy of needs was so basic? How could anyone of his means think only in terms of food, shelter and personal safety. How else could he be so utterly devoid of any desire to achieve some modicum of status, significance or self-actualization?

Fitzgerald and I watched Ringo mosey an involuntary path into the kitchen, where he took up residence at his mother's side. Anytime mother was around, Ringo was joined at her hip — never having overcome the dependency that comes from once having suckled at her breast for sustenance.

He said, "I'm here, ma," announcing his arrival, as if there was something surprising or unusual about his presence on this particular day and time.

"Thanks for the press release," father interjected, "now get the pizza bar set up. We're almost open. The phone's going to be ringing like a dinner bell soon."

When mother didn't respond Ringo slightly reworded his announcement. "Ma, I'm here."

"I can see that, Ringo," she said. "What do you think, I don't have eyes?"

"Aye," father said, "what did I just tell you. Get to work on that pizza bar."

Ringo gave father a sour look.

"What's your problem?" father had to ask. "You look so miserable it isn't even funny."

"You know what's wrong. I'm handicapped."

Father waved him off.

"I'm handicapped," Ringo repeated with added emphasis. "My brain doesn't work like a normal person's. You know that. I'm severely depressed. I'd like to throw myself off the top of a building if God would have me."

"Oh, don't start with that nonsense again."

Mother said, "Now leave him alone, Albie. You know how he is. Don't provoke him."

"I'm handicapped," Ringo hollered.

Father ignored the comment, stirring away at his sauce.

"Why don't you ever *believe* me?" Ringo sniveled.

Already he was warming up to another meltdown and walkout. It was a scenario that had played out umpteen times before. It started with Ringo getting disagreeable with everybody who speaks to him. With each exchange his volatility increases until he finally blows like the rear tire on an eighteen-wheeler, sending his tractor-trailer-sized body veering out of control. Then came the mad dash for home, where he would console himself with the soothing sports commentaries of ESPN announcers.

But for now he was persevering. Taking the tubs of pepperoni, sausage, mushrooms, black olives and roasted red peppers out of the refrigerator and setting them in their respective pizza table compartments. Ringo was already dreading the crowd of gawkers who would soon gather.

Uncle Nunzio wandered by and said to Ringo, "Pay attention to how you stretch that dough. Make sure those pizzas come out round. I don't want any footballs. Tip 'em on their end and you should be able to roll them down the street."

Ringo thought this would have been another good opportunity to scream at somebody and decry his lot in life, if the words were coming from anybody other than Uncle Nunzio. Even Ringo respected his uncle's exalted place in family lore. It was only under the most extreme of circumstances that he would give grief to the Great Man.

By now the kitchen's air was coming alive with the scent of extra virgin olive oil and sizzling minced garlic.

"Oh, how I love that smell," Uncle Nunzio bellowed, regaining his usual cheer. It was all reminding him of his days as a full-fledged restaurant operator and the thousands of hours he logged making pizzas in front of the crowds.

Through a service window connecting the kitchen to the bar, Fitzgerald's steaming bowl of home-made spaghetti with extra meatballs arrived. There was an approving nod as I set the food between his arms. A basket of fresh bread was also delivered. The investigator put his head down didn't come up for air until after he had inhaled his order, including the entire basket of bread. He dropped his fork into the empty bowl with a clatter.

"That was one hellacious bowl of grub," he said. The next five minutes were spent licking at and sucking the crevices of his teeth for leftovers.

I tipped the bottle to refill his glass once again.

The doors were open. The light chattered that had begun the evening was quickly rising to a tidal roar. The bar was filling with waiting customers.

As he came under the sway of the bourbon, Fitzgerald voice became louder and sloppier. The lower lip was starting to protrude and glistened with a surplus of saliva.

Vinny came through the bar on his rounds and was startled to find Fitzgerald toying with a pack of Camels. My brother looked at his watch and said to Fitzgerald, "We don't have an appointment, do we?"

"I came by to eat," he said. Then, holding up his fourth glass of double bourbon, added, "And drink."

Vinny stepped up, but not too close. It was Fitzgerald's natural state to look beastly, but after enough alcohol to send him three sheets to the wind he was a virtual horror show.

"This place is huge," the drunken investigator slobbered. You must have a fucking army in that kitchen keeping up with it all."

"It's a hell of a payroll," Vinny acknowledged, "and you're the latest and most expensive addition." He consulted his watch again and said, "What the hell, while the night's still young why don't we take ten minutes to discuss if you're giving me my money's worth."

Fitzgerald slid off the stool and came to his unsteady feet. He and his bourbon glass followed Vinny down to the restaurant's underground where they took seats at the boardroom table. The investigator looked around the windowless room while Vinny gathered his thoughts.

"We could suffocate down here," Fitzgerald said.

Vinny rested his elbows on the arms of the chair and made a thoughtful steeple of his hands. "I'm getting tired of waiting for this cunt to call again and give me instructions on how to get the money to her."

"Tell me about it. I'm getting tired of waiting to collect my finder's fee." He sipped from the bourbon glass. A rivulet escaped his lips and ran down a crevice of his chin. He was content to let it linger. "My friend at the phone company got me the records I needed. No one in your family placed the ransom calls. Neither did that Amy girl you're boinking. The times don't map. Of course, those are just their home phone records. Most people aren't stupid enough to make ransom demands from their residence."

Vinny's steeple crumpled with disappointment.

"I've been doing some tailing, too. Nobody's made stops at phone booths or any other suspicious places so far."

The Irishman sucked at his bourbon glass. He already smelled like a distillery.

"Your sister Ginger likes to zip around in that little red sports car of hers. Damn ... she near got me into a head-on collision the other day. Not much to report on her, other than she and that pretty-boy detective are spending plenty of time together — mostly behind closed doors." He let his drunken head roll loosely around his neck. "Can't say that I blame him, your sister's a foxy little thing."

"What about Angie?"

"She goes home and grills meat every night for her husband and bakes cookies for the children."

"Are we talking about the same sister?"

"The one with the big breasts."

"Angie and Maria both have big breasts."

"Yeah, but I'm talking about the one who's always showing off the nice aerial view of the goods."

"You're talking about Maria."

"Fine, Maria. She's a regular Susie Homemaker. That guy she's married to strikes me as being mighty dangerous. You can see it in his face."

The comment reminded Vinny that he had become so accustomed to Shekko that he had forgotten how daunting his brother-in-law's appearance could be to the uninitiated.

"Did some time in 'Nam," Vinny explained.

"I'd say so. Looks like he drank some Agent Orange and left a few of his crackled marbles back in the jungle. Some weird shit goes on in that house after hours. He carries his wife into a dark area of the house. It isn't dark for long, though. A blue strobe light starts flashing real fast."

"It reminds him of the firefights he got involved in near the demilitarized zone."

"The strobe chops everything up, but I can still make out some shadows. I see these movements, like he's swinging something around."

"Whips, probably. He likes to flog my sister with them. Nothing too severe. Soft leather straps. No skin is broken. It's just enough to flush her and get the two of them horns up."

Fitzgerald shrugged. "I guess I'll have to give the guys some points for style."

"What else?"

"Far as I can tell your sister Angie spends most of her time away from here eating popcorn and drinking red wine."

Vinny smiled and nodded. "You're good."

"You aware she sees a shrink?"

"For at least 15 years."

"Not making a lot of progress, is she?"

"I can't figure her out. She's into this 'scream therapy.' The psychologist teaches her how to scream to purge her psyche of all the trauma she's suffered from being a member of the Marciano family. But she just keeps screaming. Claims she's accumulating traumas more quickly than she can scream them out of her system, and she blames all of us for that. The method has already been discredited by the American Psychological Association, but she'll have none of that. 'We come out of the womb screaming,' she tells me. 'What more proof do you need that we've been traumatized?' Angie wants our whole family to start screaming. I told her, 'Have you listened to us lately? All we do is scream.'"

"Your sisters aren't the only ones into the weird stuff. Your brother Mickey's involved with some fringe religious group."

"It's not a religion really, just a meditation group. He's a yin-yang kind of guy."

"All I know is I heard them chanting yesterday and it sounded pretty outlandish. Some robes and haircuts and they would have been Hare Krishnas."

"Don't waste your time with either one of my brothers."

"Yeah ... and why is that?"

"Neither one of them could possibly be involved. This is way too ambitious an undertaking for Ringo to even think about doing. And Mickey's too worried about his karma to do anything unethical."

Fitzgerald sniffed at the notion. He couldn't imagine someone worrying about anything as lily-livered as karma, even though he wasn't really sure what it was.

"I'll lay off, but take my advice, don't rule anybody out. It's often the person you least expect who did the deed."

Vinny gave him a reluctant shrug. "Point taken." He reached into his pocket for a piece of paper and handed it to Fitzgerald. "That's the list of all my employees. Let's go back to your friend at the phone company and see if any of these people placed calls that sync with the ransom demands. At the bottom you'll see the name Mort Stottlemyre. He's a housing developer who comes in the restaurant quite a bit. I caught him having a little tryst the other day with Angie and Maria. They all acted like they were just having a friendly visit, but that was horseshit. I could tell they were up to something. I wrote down his home and business numbers for you."

Fitzgerald scanned the list and shook his head. "It's going to cost you. A hand full of phone records is one thing, but a list like this is going to require some scratch."

"Man you are tapping me out."

"It won't be anything extravagant. This guy's not supposed to be handing out private phone records, you know. He's taking a risk, so he expects at least some reward."

Fitz stood up and wobbled. Then he headed up the stairs using the railing to pull his booze-soaked body up the stairwell and returned to the bar. He waved to me for one last double-bourbon. All the barstools were taken, so Fitzgerald stood and clutched his drink. His head floated above the rest of the buzzing crowd, many of whom still had mufflers wrapped around their necks.

As Vinny passed through the bar he heard one customer say to another, "It's true, I diagnosed my wife's ailment on BrainTumor.com."

When the weather is cold, people feel compelled to overeat. They fill their bellies to warm their bodies. The warmth and sensuality of the delicious food comforts the mind in ways that counteract the depressive effects of cruel winter temperatures.

It was a simple equation — the lower the mercury slid down the thermometer, the more numerous and ravenous our patrons. We had been overrun the last two nights by human waves of growling stomachs. We were girding for an even bigger mob tonight, given that it was the Friday evening kickoff to the weekend.

Shortly before the dinner bell was schedule to ring, real estate magnate Mort Stottlemyre came through the door in a cloud of arctic vapor. Though his visit was unscheduled, Maria noticed him instantly and helped in removing his winter coat. Underneath he was expensively dressed in a 100 percent wool business suit with 100 percent cotton boxer shorts and Hathaway shirt and a 100 percent silk tie. Mort fancied himself a man who always gave 100 percent to whatever he did.

Maria sat him in a distant corner booth that offered prying eyes few lines of sight. Then she retrieved Angie from the kitchen for the confab. Mort set on the table the investment proposal given to him nine days earlier by Angie and Maria. It proposed a 25 percent ownership stake for Mort in return for several million dollars in the purchase and renovation of Marciano's Macaroni & Mafia House.

Angie eyed the document nervously. Why did he bring it into the restaurant? What if Vinny walks over and casts his prying eyes upon it? Or what if it gets mishandled, ends up on the ground in the parking lot, and is scooped up by illegitimate hands? She suggested taking the discussion to a remote location, the Queen of Beans Coffeehouse down the street.

"We can all have cappuccinos," Angie said. "My treat."

Mort quashed the idea, complaining that he was hurting for time due to an after-hours meeting with his bankers.

"Even the little bit of extra time it takes to get to Queen of Beans will set me back," he said. "Besides, it takes a good fifteen minutes just to bundle up in the winter gear and take of all off again."

Angie looked around to make sure they were still alone.

"I'll be quick, Angie, and discreet."

Maria gently elbowed Angie to bring her attention back to the table and said, "What did you think of our offer, Mort?"

"I cannot tell you how flattered and appreciative I am that you came to me with this deal, ladies. You have the best dining experience in the world, as far as I'm concerned, and the opportunity to diversify my investment portfolio by expanding into the restaurant business on your coattails made this one of the best deals that's ever crossed my desk."

The Marciano sisters broke into broad smiles. Maria, in particular, was wearing her excitement like a sable cape.

"I love this business. You know there are few things I'd rather be doing than eating. And the fact that you offered to give me my own reserved and personalized table just goes to show how sensitive you are to how business gets done these days. You really hit me right here with that one," the developer said, patting an open hand against the center of his chest.

Maria held her hands forth in a magnanimous gesture. "That's because you're a trusted friend, Mort, and we know you're a great businessman. It makes so much sense to get you involved."

Angie leaned out of the booth to ensure their conversation was still being carried out in privacy. Maria grabbed her arm and pulled her back into an upright position. "You're being rude. Listen to what Mort has to say."

Mort lowered his voice in saying, "Don't even sweat it, Angie. If anyone approaches this table my conversation immediately turns to Rancho en los Cerros. As far as anyone's concerned I'm familiarizing you with the project and making a sales pitch. I'll go right into my spiel. Hell, I'll sell a home or two to your family members if the occasion presents itself."

Maria said, "Pay no attention to her, Mort. She's a worry wart. Go ahead with what you were saying."

"Well, you can see I'm smiling. I'm a happy guy. I read your plan three times, it excited me so much. This is such a high-profile business and the notion of being involved puts me on Cloud Nine. I could be a big shot, hanging out with the crowds like you two. It's not that way in real estate development. Once you put something up nobody remembers who the builder was, nobody remembers your name or has reason to contact you, unless they want to sue, of course."

"So you obviously see this as a really fine deal," Maria said, trying to move the conversation towards finale.

"I really do. That's why it pains me so much to let a juicy plum like this slide past me."

Angie and Maria's faces fell.

"Oh, no. Now I can see I've disappointed you. I've erased your smiles. I'm sorry ladies, but I just don't have a choice right now. Financially, I'm leveraged to the hilt. All my eggs are in the Rancho en los Cerros basket. That's the kind of confidence I have in this project. I'm letting it all ride. Any other time and I'd be all over this deal. Ownership in a new Marciano's, are you kidding me? My own table? This couldn't be any sweeter. It's all about the timing."

Angie's peripheral vision picked up a fast-moving object. It was Vinny, and he was heading for the table. There was a horrified expression on Angie's face as she looked at Mort Stottlemyre and held a hand to the side of her mouth so Vinny couldn't read her lips.

"My brother's coming," she hissed.

Mort turned the investment proposal face-down as Vinny arrived at the table.

"Vinny," Maria said in a tenor that sought to restore a casual atmosphere to the table, "do you know Mort Stottlemyre?"

"I've seen you in the restaurant a million times, but we've never been formally introduced," Vinny said, clasping and pumping the man's hand five times. "You're the homebuilder."

"You got that right." Mort was visibly pleased that his reputation had preceded him.

"What's the occasion of this meeting?" Vinny asked, gazing around the table. Angie was still looking like she was tied to the railroad tracks.

"I'll admit that I'm trying to sell your sisters some homes in my new housing development. Maybe you've heard about Rancho en los Cerros."

Vinny went blank.

"It's been in the papers," Mort said. "The biggest most luxurious thing I've ever done. Right on the edge of town near the big IBM plant in Glendale."

"Okay," Vinny nodded, "I've driven past it a couple times. Saw the bulldozers pushing dirt around. I didn't realize that was your development. Is that one of your sales brochures," he said, pointing at the secret proposal.

"This?" he said, placing the tip of a finger on the back of the document. "Naw, this is just a financing plan I'm presenting to my bankers." He hastily tri-folded the document and tucked it inside the interior pocket of his suit coat and out of view.

"You don't have your financing in place yet and you're doing all that construction?"

"Financing comes in phases these days, Vinny, especially for a project as big as Rancho en los Cerros. They want to see some milestones achieved before they disburse the next lump of funding. It offers them some extra protection and ensures that my guys are working their asses off on the project, building as furiously as nails can be driven through lumber. Not that we're making that much progress in this freezing weather. Things always come to a crawl this time of year."

"What do those Spanish words mean?"

"Ranch in the hills." Stottlemyre smiled. "Say, Vinny, you're a swinging young fella. We've got a few units that are smaller scale bungalows that make swell bachelor pads. They have all the amenities but are geared more towards singles." As Mort leaned forward in his enthusiasm the suit coat crept up his arms, revealing the cuffs of his white Hathaway shirt. Vinny could see they were monogrammed with the initials M.S. "Comes with hot tub and sauna and bedroom skylights and wall mirrors. Nobody will stay single for very long living in that place, I guarantee it."

"Interesting, but I'm not in the market — for a new home or wife.

Mort chortled in an unnatural but good-natured way. "Where are you living now, Vinny?"

"I've got a fifty-five-hundred square foot home up in Crestview Heights."

"Whoa, living in the fancy neighborhood in a big home. In that case, forget the bachelor bungalow, we've got ranch style spreads with major square footage and acreage."

"I don't know, it sounds like you're still trying to get your financing in place. Better take this one step at a time."

A discomforting moment of silence ensued.

"Speaking of that," Mort said, consulting his watch, "I've got to get over to that meeting pronto. You never want to leave a group of bankers sitting around talking among themselves. They might come up with reasons to hang onto their money."

The group exchanged civilities as Mort Stottlemyre reloaded his body with winter gear and bid his farewell. As soon as the home builder was out the door, Vinny turned to his sisters.

"What were you three really discussing?"

"I don't know what you're talking about," Maria said.

"Yeah, right. Look at Angie. She looks like she's come down with the flu."

"Stop talking about me like I'm not standing right in front of you. I feel perfectly fine. My body temperature is 98.6 degrees, except when talking to you."

"So what was really on those pieces of paper he was hiding from me?"

"What difference does it make what we discussed with Mort?" Maria said. "It's none of your business."

"Anything happening on company time is my business."

"You heard him. He's got a financing plan to present."

Vinny paused and gave them a appraising glance. "You two are up to something. You're always up to something. It usually involves messing with my restaurant."

"You're rude, you know that?" Maria said. "Busting in on a conversation you weren't invited to."

Angie said, "It's worse than that, Maria. He's a paranoiac."

"Now I'm a paranoiac? That's a laugh."

"It's a clinical condition," Angie said. "Look it up."

"More pop psychology from my neurotic sister."

"I can't deal with people like you."

"Of course you can't. You're too anxious and irrational to get along with anybody."

"You need medication. I prescribe a trip back to the bar, where you can continue drowning yourself in alcohol."

By eight o'clock the kitchen was running short on the evening's hottest entree, veal parmigiana. Angie had to pull more cutlets from the walk-in cooler and start tenderizing them for cooking. She took hold of the stainless-steel meat hammer and started lowering the boom. As usual the force of the pounding was fueled by Angie's surplus of bottled rage, though she wasn't creaming the meat this time. It wasn't long before she caught sight of mother coming towards her. She checked to make sure there wasn't a fire extinguisher in her hands. Angie still hadn't forgiven mother for frosting her with sodium bicarbonate a couple of weeks ago. Angie's mental wounds from that episode were still fresh and oozing.

"Is everything okay with Maria," mother asked. "Something seems to be bothering her."

"Ma, what do I know? You think I'm my sister's keeper?"

"Well, I know you two talk."

Angie slapped a new cutlet on the table and started whacking it. She wanted to say to her mom, *Why are you always worried about everyone in this family except me?*

"She never tells me what's going on in her life," Angie said. She would have liked to tell mother the truth, that Maria was still getting over the sting of having their restaurant proposal turned down by Mort Stottlemyre. So was Angie, for that matter, but Mother Margherita had not bothered to notice.

Angie knew that telling mother about the new business proposal would cause a battle royale. She was always on Vinny's side anyway, and couldn't keep a secret if victory in World War III depended on it. Word would spread and she and Vinny's already bellicose relationship would mushroom into full conflagration.

Mother looked down at the cutlet Angie was striking, then walked away.

When Maria entered the kitchen to pick up the next round of orders, mother intercepted her.

"Everything okay between you and Shekko?" she mumbled.

"Oh Jesus, ma, how come you're always asking about my marriage? Shekko's very happily married. My god, the man's a roaring fork."

"Where did you come up with a queer term like that?"

"Ma, just never mind."

"You said Shekko's fork is roaring, what about yours?"

"What brought this up? Why are you asking?"

"You've been looking so blue these last couple of days."

"Well, whatever you're seeing is misleading. I couldn't be happier. Now step aside before this food gets cold."

As Maria came rushing out of the kitchen she nearly collided with Vinny, who was cruising through the dining rooms doing what he called "walk-around management." He found Uncle Nunzio working the crowd at full throttle, just like the old days. The response from adoring patrons — some whom dated back decades — restored the man's customary joviality. Vinny hung back, not wanting to putrefy the moment by allowing his mere presence to remind Uncle Nunzio what a bummer his nephew had turned out to be. And he certainly wasn't going to join in the merriment. Having a good and carefree time while disaster swung like a pendulum over his skull would have been unbecoming to the extreme. This was a time for glumness. So Vinny disappeared into the recesses of the restaurant and let the old man do his thing until he ran out of gas shortly after nine o'clock. Then Uncle Nunzio donned his overcoat and fedora and bid his family and fans adieu.

Vinny relaxed as soon as he witnessed the door close behind Uncle Nunzio. He came to the bar, where I lit his first cigar of the evening and set a martini in front of him. He knocked a couple more back as the crowd dispersed and the crew went into cleanup mode. We were just beginning to wonder why Ginger was still hanging around at such a late hour, when detect sergeant Clyde Jablonsky showed up and used his height differential to hyper-extend Ginger's neck vertebrae with a forceful kiss. The kiss came from on high and leveraged downward upon Ginger's waiting mouth, flexing her neck backwards. It was more than a kiss, it was a lip-lock that smothered Ginger's face and froze the moment. The act was a testament to how fully their relationship had already burgeoned. They had gone from peck to pucker to swapping saliva in a remarkably short time for a woman of Ginger's forbearance.

Vinny found the detective's boldness an affront, especially in the midst of a serious case that involved the entire family. It was becoming clear that he also was being swept up by the splendor of the relationship. His judgment was impaired.

Shocking, though it was, it shouldn't have come as too much of a surprise. This guy met all the criteria on Ginger's list. And when all else failed there was The Voice, the rich baritone. Ginger wanted to join its rough and tumble world.

One could just imagine Ginger staring dreamy-eyed into the mirror and reciting "Mrs. Ginger Jablonsky" to herself, and being tickled by the alliteration between first and last names. The agreement of sounds! The strength and repetition of it all!

"Ready to go?" the sergeant detective said, after breaking off the kiss.

He assisted in hoisting Ginger's winter coat upon her shoulders. Then the couple faded into the dark frigid night.

Vinny went back to confession. Again, he found himself standing in the foreboding church of his youth, the hulking stone and stained glass edifice that is Our Lady of the Immaculate Conception. Incense and candlelight and solemnity surrounded him. All the hallmarks of faith and guilt were in evidence. The smallest sounds amplified themselves in distant echoes.

The air chilled to a supernatural temperature.

When his turn came, Vinny closed himself in the soundproof booth, just a screened window away from the adjoining chamber from which the judgments and strictures of Father Benito Saragusa would flow.

"Forgive me father for I have sinned, my last confession was two weeks ago."

There was a prolonged moment of silence.

"Father?"

"Yes, I'm here," Saragusa said. "What are you here to confess?"

"I'm not sure. Can't we just talk?"

"I'm listening."

There was another prolonged silence. "This is Vinny, Father."

"I know it is."

"You didn't say you knew it was me."

"The last time we talked you said you wanted me to pretend I didn't know it was you."

"Never mind what I said."

"I was trying to abide by your wishes."

"It just feels silly for me to pretend you don't know it's me. Why play that game?"

"Agreed. I'm ready to hear your confession."

Vinny hesitated. He could still feel the cool moistness of the holy water he had dabbed on his forehead upon entering the grand front doors of the church.

"All I know is that my life has gone to shit. Excuse my language, Father. I haven't been a good Catholic."

"Could you be more precise?"

"For one thing, I fornicate something terrible. I fornicated last night. I fornicated again just an hour ago."

"Aren't you dating that Stonebreaker girl?"

"I wouldn't call it dating. I'm" — Vinny rummaged his vocabulary for an acceptable verb — "having carnal relations with her. She's just the most frequent of many."

"This does not surprise me. You've always had a thing for the girls. They are a great temptation to men, especially a young fella like you."

"There are so many women. They all look so beautiful to me. The blouses. The skirts with slits up the back. The bangles and the chokers." The words practically gurgled from Vinny's throat.

"You're handsome man. Popular in your community. Financially successful, too. Those are blessings from God. Those characteristics make you especially appealing to women. Don't turn these special gifts into excuses for sin."

"I could never be a priest."

"Remember that these women come bearing forbidden fruits."

"Sweet apples and fresh cut figs." The words came dreamily off Vinny's tongue.

"The mind has to stay focused on higher thoughts."

"Taking a vow of chastity would be impossible for me. I don't know how you do it, Father."

"Ask God to relieve you of your desires."

"They're too powerful."

"God is more powerful."

"Where do you think these hormones came from?"

"Let's not be putting the Creator in a difficult position. God challenges us with many in-bred urges. The desire to eat, for instance. Is the drive to eat food any less powerful than the drive to have sex? I don't think so. Many of our brothers and sisters have lost control of their food cravings. This is no license to blame God the Father."

"I've taken advantage of the young women under my control. I've become sexually cunning."

"What goes through your mind when you see an attractive woman?" Saragusa asked, listening keenly.

"Sinful and exciting things. The kind of things I wouldn't describe to my priest."

When Vinny looked hard he could see the priest's shadowy mouth and chin through the dark mesh of the screen. They drew closer when the conversation took a prurient turn.

"You've got to miss women, Father. It's just isn't natural for a man not to be attracted to the opposite sex."

"All men are surrounded by the temptations of Eve. We mustn't allow ourselves to be turned into the fallen Adam."

"Women look up to you too, Father. You're an authority figure. You wear a uniform. There's got to be many who throw themselves at you."

"I don't want to discuss my job."

"How can you resist, Father?"

"You're being inappropriate."

"You must have broken your vows at least once or twice."

"That's enough."

"Would you have something to confess if we switched places."

"You seem to be forgetting who's wearing the black robe and white collar. In matters of faith and sin, I'm the arbiter of what is just and unholy."

"But has it happened?"

"Stop it right now!" the clergyman hissed. "You're out of control."

Vinny went silent.

"I think we've exhausted the subject," Saragusa said, his voice cooling. "Let's move on to other issues. The last time you confessed you told me about a theft. Did you find out who took your money?"

"It wasn't money. It was something more valuable."

"Something sentimental?"

"I wouldn't discuss it then and I'm not going to discuss it now."

Vinny wanted to tell Father Saragusa. He wanted someone who understood the importance of those recipes to sympathize and commiserate with him. What was a priest good for if not to comfort a parishioner in tumultuous times? Still, suspicions about the clergyman's penchant for gossip kept Vinny mum.

"My uncle hates me."

"Nunzio?"

"Yes."

"I don't see how that's possible. Your uncle is a great man — a loving man."

"I've allowed something unforgivable to happen."

"What are you talking about?"

"I can't go into it."

"Whatever it is, you must be misinterpreting. The Nunzio I know is not even capable of hate."

"You've never seen him like I just saw him."

"There must be some mistake."

"I'm telling you, something epic has happened."

"You're making it difficult for me to help you, Vinny. Why all this secrecy, all these mysterious references? Tell me and the Lord what you're talking about."

"I can't."

"Don't you trust me?"

"Trust isn't the issue," Vinny lied. "There's too much shame. I'm not ready to expose myself. I need time. Maybe you can usher me through this process."

"I'm doing the best I can, considering the little cooperation I'm getting."

"I can only deal with this one small step at a time."

Father Saragusa sighed. He had more cooperative parishioners waiting to fully disclose their peccadilloes.

"How's Ringo? He was at mass Sunday but was looking like his stomach was bothering him."

"Nothing has changed. Still drowning in melancholy. Keeps telling us that God has given him too much to handle in this life. He longs for death and his ascension into the Kingdom of Heaven."

"Your brother's a man of great faith."

"My brother shouldn't have been allowed to own a Bible. He's taken all the heavenly glories the book talks about too seriously. All he's focused on is the end game."

"God bless him."

"We haven't dealt with my female problems, Father. You're the expert in this area. What should I do?"

"Find a special one and marry her. Give her all your passion and devotion."

"I couldn't be faithful."

"You must. You can't spend the rest of your life fornicating and tainting women."

"Don't you have a prescription other than marriage?"

The priest exhaled. "I'm going to give you a Biblical quote. Use it like an incantation. Repeat it at least a dozen times a day. The words are from St.

Paul, who said, 'Now the works of the flesh are manifest — adultery, fornication, uncleanness, lasciviousness, and the like. They which do such things shall not inherit the Kingdom of God.' That's not the saint's exact quote. I've cleaned it up a tad to make it easier to remember and repeat."

"What's that supposed to do?"

"You need to keep reminding yourself what's at stake, Vinny. The pleasures of the flesh are fleeting. The gratifications of the spirit are eternal."

"So I'm supposed to just keep repeating it."

"Say it every time unclean yearnings visit."

"I've already forgotten what you said."

"I'll e-mail it to you."


Sergeant detective Clyde Jablonsky used the best of his rational thinking to finally convinced Vinny that even Amy Stonebreaker should be interviewed about the crime. It didn't matter that Vinny thought there was zero chance of Amy's involvement. The more people interviewed the more eyewitness accounts that could be gathered, the more leads on people who are out of place or seen in suspicious places on that fateful evening.

Jablonsky suggested Amy Stonebreaker meet him at the police station, a venue that would give him maximum leverage and access to resources. Amy Stonebreaker surprised him by agreeing without hesitation. There was nothing about her behavior that suggested nerves; she was a poised young lady. She could be spellbinding, too, and Jablonsky wanted to make sure he didn't become mesmerized and blow the interview. The detective's interrogation technique was to gently get to know the suspect through the use of personal questions. The idea was to build trust and warmth and a comfort level that convinced the person they were safe in disclosing whatever was on his or her mind. Stonebreaker surprised him again by opening up almost immediately and sharing highly personal information. Jablonsky got the full story of her arrival and coupling with Vinny.

She had just moved to the area from Troy, New York, and was a fanatic for the food business. Her ambition was to learn to run a professional kitchen and save enough money over the next few years to attend the Culinary Institute of America in Hyde Park, New York, where she would become a master chef and eventually author cookbooks and, one day, host her own nationally televised food program.

Nothing would have pleased her more than being named assistant chef. Vinny had to explain that only family members could prepare Marciano's main courses because preparing the secret family recipes was a clandestine activity. That left the assistant chef with the trivial duties of sautéing vegetables, garnishing plates and tossing salads. Not exactly the education she had in mind. Still, Amy Stonebreaker's passion for food was genuine, and that impressed Vinny. She saw food as something perfectly romantic, the centerpiece of family life and yet hedonistic all at the same time.

"What else can you say *that* about?" she said.

Though the assistant chef's position, per se, didn't exist, Vinny was not about to let Amy Stonebreaker slip past. She had a lusty wholesomeness like he had never seen before, and a bright and passionate voice. She shined without making any effort to do so.

Vinny hired Amy to fill a waitress's position that did not exist. That placed her under the grueling auspices of sister Maria. Sparks started flying almost immediately as Amy Stonebreaker and the head waitress took an instantaneous dislike to one another. Amy didn't care for Maria's *you ain't shit if you ain't family* attitude. Maria resented any woman she was forced to hire by Vinny's fiat. She saw the new girl as a consummate manipulator. She also knew that, in time, Amy Stonebreaker would become the latest in a long line of women who proved that Vinny's sexual impulses were utterly out of control. The two were already speaking in flirtation.

Ginger wasn't a fan either, because Amy Stonebreaker challenged her status as resident sex kitten.

Amy looked Jablonsky in the eyes and said: "Maria hates me. So does Ginger."

"Because you're younger and more beautiful?" he inquired, then twitched as soon as the words left his mouth, realizing the statement's implications.

Stonebreaker looked past Jablonsky's shoulder and into a nonexistent distance. "Is not just youth and looks. Ginger is very possessive of her brothers — Mickey and Ringo included. There's a sense of ownership there. It's a strange relationship."

Jablonsky shrugged his shoulders.

"Sorry about that. She's your girlfriend. I really shouldn't be talking smack about her."

Jablonsky shrugged again.

"I trust we're speaking in confidence."

Jablonsky's body began to tingle. "Of course," he said. It was the first time Jablonsky felt desirous of another woman since meeting Ginger Marciano.

"Mickey likes my legs. He says they're lean and muscular. He calls me Secretariat, though never when other people are around. The other guys call me Amy Ballbreaker. I guess because I'm disinterested in every man in the place — with the exception of Vinny, of course.

Too bad, was Vinny's attitude. He issued a hands-off policy when it came to Amy Stonebreaker. That infuriated Maria, who complained her authority was constantly being undermined by her kid brother, and now by this *vamp*.

Amy Stonebreaker started reporting to work early and dropping by to talk food with Vinny in the restaurant's basement office. During her first visit she was wearing a wispy cotton skirt and carrying an armful of books about food preparation and design. Vinny was gratified and aroused. His understudy made several more unannounced stops over the next few weeks. It wasn't long before she visited afterhours to profusely thank Vinny for the employment opportunity and the contributions he was making to her education. In communicating her earnestness, Amy Stonebreaker took Vinny's hand and held it warmly between hers. Then she kissed the back of it and pressed it lovingly against her cheek. Encouraged by Vinny's failed defenses, she took his index finger into her mouth and gently sucked. Vinny reciprocated with an act he had contemplated since the day Amy Stonebreaker's miniskirt and boots walked through the door. Spreading her legs right where she sat, he planted kisses up and down the tender flesh of her inner thighs while Amy Stonebreaker purred and restyled the boss's hair with her hot slender hands. Pulsating with desire, Vinny snapped shut the deadbolt of his office door and went to work on his ravishing pupil.

Jablonsky could have listened to Amy Stonebreaker's stories all day in that velvety voice of hers. She kept tousling her hair while testifying; not in a nervous way but in a lascivious one. There was a microphone on the table recording audio, and a camera mounted in the corner of the room shooting video, capturing every word and action. She wasn't the least bit disconcerted that the instruments were capturing every word, movement and expression. Jablonsky wondered if Vinny would be embarrassed or prideful about all these disclosures.

At this stage in her story, everything pointed to a spectacular conquest for Vinny until Amy Stonebreaker pulled down the front of Vinny's underwear and his engorged 10-inch cock came springing out.

"Good god," she shrieked, scurrying across the room, "where did you get that penis?"

Pride of ownership steamrolled across Vinny's face. "Some people are just born with it," the Boy Wonder crowed.

"I'm not going to stick anything that big inside my vagina — or any other hole."

"Why not?" Vinny said, his expression going hapless. "I thought you'd be happy about it. Women love this thing."

"Well not me. That thing looks like it came from a deli case. It must be a foot long."

Vinny wasn't about to tell her it actually terminated two inches shy of a foot. Let the illusion play, he figured. "You don't have to use the whole thing," he said. "Most women can't. We can go halfway or two-thirds of the way with it."

"I don't know," she said, staring mistrustfully at the beast, still reaching across the room toward her. "It's not just the length it's the … *circumference*."

"Look, just take it in your hands and get a feel for it," Vinny pleaded. "Take some time to get used to it. It can be quite friendly. It really can."

Amy Stonebreaker, young and petite, was still treating it as a foreign object poised to impale her.

Vinny said, "Let's go for a ride. I'll take you to the exact spot where I lost my virginity."

"Yeah right."

"I mean it."

"You're being silly," she said.

"Honestly," Vinny said, wrenching it back into briefs and cinching his trousers closed.

He drove her to the flood wall and held Amy's hand as they walked her to the precise cluster of shrubs where Rachel Spring had robbed him of innocence years earlier and sent him cartwheeling through puberty.

Vinny spread a waterproof tarp on the ground, slipped out of his pants and briefs and reclined on its cold surface. Amy Stonebreaker took Vinny penis in her hands and started playing with it. The excitable organ expanded quickly.

"It's so big," she said. "It's so hard. It isn't just a penis, it's a … a *shaft*."

Vinny lay there, hands laced behind his head, smiling at the night sky. The stars were shining down upon him. As poetic fate would have it, the Big Dipper was in evidence, devouring half the night sky.

"What can I say, I got lucky. The guys in my junior high phys-ed class started calling me Tripod."

The young woman's comfort level was rapidly rising, her interactions becoming more carefree. She grabbed his scrotum and began to massage its contents.

"So you started casting magic spells on the girls with your big wand."

"I can't tell you the difference it made. I just swelled with confidence. Almost overnight I was bigger, stronger, more athletic and masculine, smarter, better looking. I just knew I was destined for great things."

"Mamma Nature super-sized you," she cooed, "didn't she, Tripod?"

Jablonsky was so captivated by the things that Amy Stonebreaker had to say that it took a full hour before he even began quizzing her about the night in question.

The Boeing 777 rolled ponderously across the tarmac at New York's LaGuardia Airport and made a looping right turn towards the runways. The decals on the sides of the jet advertised that it was operated by the Italy-based carrier Alitalia. The 777 made a hard right onto the embarkation point at the head of Runway 2 where it came to a standstill and awaited radio communication from the control tower, its giant engines exhaling a blurry wake.

Once cleared for takeoff the pilot gunned the engines and sent the wide-body jet rumbling down the 7000-foot-long thoroughfare, picking up speed by the second. All 279 passengers were jiggling in their seats, among them Nunzio and Vinny Marciano. The Marciano men had extra jiggle room, in fact, because big bucks had been shelled out for the more spacious seats in the first-class cabin.

Just when it seemed the 777 was going to run out of asphalt, the aircraft finally lifted off the ground with a mighty torque and pulled its nose skyward. The jet groaned and shimmied as it strained against the laws of physics. Rapidly it ascended towards the low-lying clouds. It veered leftward and set its coordinates on a flight path scheduled to terminate in Rome, Italy in precisely eight hours and forty-seven minutes.

Vinny looked out his window and watched Manhattan shrink with distance and eventually become obscured by clouds. He turned to his uncle, who was still shaking like gelatin from the turbulence. Other than that, Nunzio was his normal cherubic self.

The flight attendants had already served drinks to the pampered first-class passengers. The Marciano men had consumed two rounds of red table wine before the plane had even left the gate. As soon as the aircraft started leveling off and smoothing out, the flight attendants were back on their feet again in their crisp, blue-shirted uniforms, pouring more wine and setting bowls of salted nuts on the shared consoles between the premium seats.

Vinny nibbled and sipped with normality, though he was in disarray. His mood was dismal but he did his best to feign anticipation each time the Great Man looked his way. He was confused about the exact reason he and his uncle were making this long, extraordinary trip across the Atlantic. Uncle Nunzio sprung it on him just one week ago. The announcement came in the form of airline and train tickets dropped on his desk. It was time to visit the Old Country, was all Nunzio had said. Vinny's resistance was immediate. There was the restaurant to think about. Just days before Nunzio had ordered him to redouble his efforts, get more directly involved in the details of day-to-day operations, and get the enterprise back on track. Now he was whisking him away. Where was the logic? What kind of corrupt covenant might Angie and Maria hatch in his absence? That's to say nothing of the blackmailer, who might call at any time. If that douche-bag though she wasn't being taken seriously there was no telling what the reaction might be. She might do something incredibly ugly, like destroy the recipes or, worse yet, post them on the internet for the whole wide world to see.

It wasn't as though Vinny hadn't been to Italy before. He'd blown through Rome, Florence and the canals of Venice on a whirlwind tour a few years ago. Then he remembered how Uncle Nunzio's face turned lugubrious after learning that Vinny had stayed in Rome's Beverly Hills Grande Hotel and spent more time in dance clubs and going to American movies than at visiting trattorias and lionized ruins. He had reproduced the American experience in a foreign country.

It didn't help that he had brought some young women he liked at the time, a gal of Chinese descent named Penelope Chang who wasn't interested in any kind of history, let alone the accomplishments of a bunch of dead Romans. She wanted to run for the glitz, and Vinny wasn't one to deny a woman anything she found stimulating.

So now Uncle Nunzio was insisting that Vinny go back, this time under his tutelage. And the point wasn't to visit the country's classic cities and tourist destinations. This time Vinny would be spirited to the mountainous Abruzzo province east of Rome to the tiny town of Castiglione, the community from which Grandpa and Granda Marciano hailed, and the place where the succulent family recipes and cooking methods has been perfected over generations. It was still home to more than two dozen clan members, and Vinny was about to meet every one of them. With any luck the boy would acquire a true appreciation of what had been bequeathed to him, and understand the importance of honoring thy family.

One glance at Vinny's fancy, gelled hairdo reminded Nunzio just how swollen with arrogance and showmanship the boy's head had become. Who did he think he was, Rod Stewart? The boy had gotten soft. Success had come too easily. He had lost sight of the dedication, grueling work hours and attention to detail that his uncle had devoted to turn Marciano's into a gastronomical institution of the highest order.

Nunzio concluded long ago that Vinny wasn't in the business for the artistry of food. Just look at his track record. Everything he knew about cooking Nunzio had taught him years ago. Since then he'd done nothing to embolden his culinary skill. There were no cooking classes and few attempts to develop new recipes; not that Nunzio would allow him to pepper the menu with experimental dishes. But a passion for the craft, however misguided, and an eye towards invention would have helped convince Nunzio that his nephew had become a member of the profession for reasons other than getting rich and lubricating women.

But it was even worse than that. Nunzio had borne witness to the unraveling of ethnic pride. Vinny's ability to speak the language had gotten so feeble he could barely be called bilingual. Did he even consider himself an Italian anymore? He had become so … *Americanized*.

He didn't even know that Italy was the greatest country in the world. The Americans knew how to build wealth and exercise military might, but the people of Italy knew how to *live*. Their society was still centered on people and families and the good food they gathered around. Italians still believed that having a conversation with a friend was more important than closing a business deal or achieving some personal self-help goal. Family values had disintegrated in America. No wonder the whole country was taking pharmaceuticals just to cope with being alive.

He glanced at Vinny again. The kid was gazing out the window and looking terribly unhappy under that landscape of sculpted hair.

Too damn bad. Nothing but good could come out of Vinny meeting other members of his gene pool. How can you understand who you are if you didn't know where you came from? Besides, the whole trip, including travel time, was only going to take a week, Nunzio thought, and he was paying for the whole shebang, so what was there to snivel about?

When the aircraft reached its cruising altitude of 44,000 feet the alcohol's effect was amplified. That wasn't any big deal for Vinny, who pounded down the drinks nightly. Uncle Nunzio, though, was a modest imbiber. The excitement of the trip put him in a celebratory mood; it was occasion for extra drink. Before he knew what knocked him, Nunzio was pitching and rolling in his seat as though he had come under the sway of a malfunctioning gyroscope. The histamines in the wine turned the skin tone of his face from its normally rosy hue to something resembling a Roma tomato.

Sensing the onslaught of inebriation, Nunzio traded the red wine for club soda with lime. His billboard-size smile and communicable laughter lit up the first-class cabin. He was working an easy crowd because most of the passengers were en route to vacations and already predisposed to mirth.

He had the flight attendants going too. They found the jolly old coot charming and prized his facility with their language. Besides, his eyes literally twinkled.

On schedule, the aircraft ground to a halt at Roma-Fiumicino Airport. Nunzio and Vinny retrieved their bags, loaded a luggage cart and were accosted by an over-anxious taxi driver. They checked into the Boscolo Exedra Hotel where they dropped their bags and hopped back in the same taxi for the ride to Taverna Angelica, one of Rome's finest restaurants.

"Now we eat real food," Nunzio told Vinny as they settled themselves in the candlelit dining room. "Best food in the city."

Nunzio did all the ordering in perfect Italian. Vinny was surprised by how tiny the place was. It had just twenty-six seats, allowing the chef to concentrate on each individual dish, according to the menu. The results were impressive. Vinny went for the pasta primavera with tender spring vegetables grown by local farmers. Nunzio ordered a plate of veal medallions. The cattle had been grass-fed and freshly slaughtered.

"My god," Nunzio said, "there is nothing like the taste of freshly slaughtered meat. It's almost impossible to get this stuff back home. We've gotten so far away from honest farming and cattle ranching."

Vinny used a fork to point at his uncle's plate. "That's not good for your ailing heart. High fat content."

"Ahh, that's a bunch of nonsense. Besides, if you're worried about fat take a look at your own plate and all that creamy primavera sauce."

"It's full of vegetables to counteract that. Here's another cholesterol buster," Vinny said, raising his wine glass.

"I couldn't even look at that stuff after getting boozed up on the flight. I was flying higher than the plane. Thought for a few minutes I was going to have to head to the lavatory and upchuck." Nunzio used a sharp knife to slice apart more veal. "Stop staring at my veal like it's a cemetery headstone. All that talk about fat's a bunch of malarkey."

Vinny chucked. "Those silly medical researchers."

"I have my own theory about food and health." The veal was steaming in Nunzio's cheek.

"Okay," Vinny said, "let's hear it. I'm in the mood for a little science fiction."

"No fiction about it. The mind and body work together, that's a scientific fact. Notice how happy people are always the healthiest? Eat what makes you happy, that's what I say. When you're happy you're healthy."

"You better get happier because your heart's been giving you fits."

"Ahh, my heart's fine."

"What are you, kidding me? How many heart attacks have you had? Three? Four?"

"That's what the doctors say but I think they got it wrong. It was a few bad cases of indigestion."

"Since when do they prescribe quadruple bypass surgery to treat indigestion?"

"Those goddamn doctors are always trying to run up the bill. Unnecessary surgeries are done every day. Besides, if I did have a problem it's been taken care of. They put a clean set of tubes in my chest. The pressure's off and the blood is flowing free. Now pipe down and let me concentrate on my food."

When they finished and walked out of the restaurant Nunzio announced, "I gotta go pray."

He walked half a block to a Catholic church and trudged down the central aisle and kneeled in the first pew. Vinny did some praying of his own but it was ten rows back. He looked at the back of his uncle's head and wondered if his supplications would include some divine grace regarding the errant recipes.

Seventeen minutes later Nunzio was done worshiping and making demands of God, and they were back in a taxi and heading towards the Boscolo Exedra Hotel. Vinny was pleased by what he saw there. It was a genuine five-star Italian hotel and there was no doubt why it earned such an esteemed ranking. The lobby had white Roman columns and a vaulted ceiling. It was filled with regal cream-and-butter-colored furniture. There was a champagne bar lit with red and blue lights and the sparkle of cascading crystal chandeliers. Hotel staff members were numerous and attentive.

The rooms were equally luxe with their kind-sized beds and brocade bedspreads and curtains. The bathrooms had gold marble walls, floors and counters. Vinny especially like the oversized shower.

The two men said goodnight to one another and plowed their bodies under the high-thread-count sheets, blankets and comforters. They woke to a complimentary breakfast and steaming cappuccinos. The Stazione Termini train station was just half-a-mile from the hotel. They climbed aboard the 10 a.m. train for the three hour ride to the Castiglione Cosentino station.

They had a private booth where they could sit comfortably and face one another. Even without the wine, Nunzio was pitching and rolling in his seat again as the train clattered and rocked its way across the Italian countryside. It didn't bother Nunzio in the least, as he snored the entire way. Vinny marveled at his uncle's ability to doze off within 60 seconds, even in the most inhospitable of venues. The station stops and constant clatter and motion of the train did nothing to disrupt his sleep, which was so deep it seemed induced by an anesthesiologist. The Great Man sat upright in the seat with his head and stomach lolling from side to side and his fluttering windpipe putting out a consistent 30-decibel rhythm.

Vinny was fretting, too nervous to sleep, uncertain what to expect when he met blood relatives with whom he had nothing in common except food and some imperceptibly twisted strands of DNA. How was he going to survive an entire week with people he didn't know and could scarcely communicate with? The hours would pass like days as they sat around and reminisced about people Vinny he had never met and events that didn't interest him.

Worse than that, the visit was humiliating to him on its face. Here he was about to show up at the cradle of Marciano civilization holding his uncle's metaphorical hand; the retarded child being escorted to Special Education classes where he would be taught Italian 101. Lesson one, don't betray your family's trust. Lesson two, appreciate the things you've got and never had to work for. Lesson three, learn the language you dumb shit! Lesson four, you've flunked out, give the restaurant back to your uncle.

What agonies we suffer in the name of family, Vinny lamented.

As the train slowed to its final stop, Vinny kicked his uncle's shoe and brought him snorting out of slumber. As they stepped off the train and onto the platform, Vinny saw passengers were being greeted all around them. He turned to say something to his uncle about catching a taxi into town when a pretty middle-aged woman appeared in front of him and said, "Vinny Marciano?" She beautifully enunciated every syllable. Vinny nodded.

"Tessa Marciano," she said, placing a kiss on each of his cheeks, then hugging her breast bone against his.

Vinny looked to his uncle, who had been surrounded by three men. They were also hugging and going cheek to cheek. A minor celebration has broken out. Tessa took Vinny's hand and walked him over to the others. Uncle

Nunzio made introductions. They all seemed silently fascinated by Vinny's highly-enriched hair.

The group climbed into two vehicles and drove to the tiny town of Castiglione. When they arrived at Tessa's small home for lunch the place was jammed with more than two dozen Marcianos representing three generations. They all clapped and cheered as their American guests arrived. Vinny's eyes misted. The scene was overwhelming. He and his uncle were being greeted as conquerors from mighty America.

Everybody was seated at two long dining room tables for an early Sunday dinner. A spread was set before them, and all the food was familiar — grilled peppers and eggplant in olive oil, spaghetti with pomodoro sauce, macaroni with tuna and olive oil, sliced pork, spicy sausages, baked fish. Bowls filled with five different kinds of cheese were passed around. All the family's major food groups were washed down with an ambrosial Marciano-made red wine.

Vinny examined the crude label on the wine bottle and turned to his uncle. "Why didn't we ever do a private label wine like this?"

Nunzio shrugged and gave him a mischievous grin. Between the drink and convivial company he was back on the road to intoxication. "What a terrific idea," Nunzio said, followed by a burst of his epidemic laughter.

"I'm serious," Vinny said. "We could have them produce extra qualities of this stuff and ship it to us in New York."

"Don't get ahead of yourself. We haven't been here an hour yet. There's still plenty to observe and learn."

As was the custom in Italy, all the men were sitting and all the women were on their feet, engaged in the selfless exertions of food preparation and service. The din never fell below a roar. Italians had an incredible stamina for conversation, Vinny decided, far higher than what he had witnessed from Americanized versions of the breed. The talking and motioning was ceaseless. They were all speaking Italian at a torrential pace, making it impossible for Vinny to interpret quickly enough to track the conversations.

Uncle Nunzio had no such deficit. The revelry revolved around. The Great Man who had made the Marciano name famous in an important region of the mighty United States, and he was participating zealously in the repartee.

"All this for us," Vinny said in his uncle's ear.

"This isn't a special event. This happens every Sunday in Castiglione. The only difference today is that two more seats were wedged around the tables."

He skipped a few beats to appreciate the stunned look on Vinny face and said, "Welcome to the *real* Italy, my boy."

The leader of the local Marcianos was a large, loud middle-aged man named Enzo. He did the most talking and stood every time he spoke, as though addressing an auditorium filled with strangers. So wild and unpredictable were Enzo's gesticulations that he inadvertently backhanded a few women and children. There were elders he would respectfully defer to. The eldest of those was a 97-year-old woman named Masina, who walked with the aid of a cane. Though still robust, her voice was too weedy to break into the conversation, so when Mesina had something to say she pounded her cane into the floor until everybody shut up.

Vinny studied the faces. Family resemblances emerged. The Roman noses. The unbroken eyebrows that grew a path right over the bridges of the men's noses. The fulsome breasts. The olive-black eyes and the full lips.

After the women cleared the plates, they brought in baskets of fresh fruit and plates of baked desserts.

They spoke of Grandpa and Grandma — Salvatore and Pia Marciano — in hallowed terms. They were heroes in their ancestral home, youngsters who had bravely ventured forth to the Land of Milk and Honey and established a Marciano appellation in the United States. They made themselves a new home and one of their clever sons had hit the jackpot with food, using the family's very own recipes.

When the meal ended the music was turned on; it was Italian language remakes of Billy Joel songs such as *Piano Man* and *Scenes from an Italian Restaurant*.

The dinner was followed by a slow-motion walking tour of Castiglione. The village was remote and primitive. People somehow managed to survive without cable TV, internet access and satellite dishes. There was no business district, per se. All the homes and other structures were made of stone. There was a general store, a saloon and two churches. Grandpa and Grandma Marciano's house was still in the family. We were taken inside and shown a kitchen outfitted with very old appliances.

One of the centerpieces of town was the Marciano's restaurant, which had been in operation less than twenty years. Though very small, all of the Marcianos rendezvoused there the next evening for a dinner. The signature family recipes were served. It delighted and frustrated Vinny that they were even more delicious than he and Nunzio were able to turn out at the New York restaurant.

"All of the meats were freshly slaughtered and the fruits and vegetables picked from the countryside farms just hours before cooking," Enzo announced while standing and flailing his arms. Nunzio interpreted for Vinny. "Country living has its advantages."

Nunzio dropped a heavy hand on the table and said to Vinny, "Can you believe that with all this good food they didn't open a restaurant until long after Marciano's became a big hit in the United States?"

"We didn't know what was possible," Enzo said. "But what are you going to do in a little town like this? We only have a few thousand people. You probably feed that many people in a few days."

There was an area behind the restaurant used as a makeshift winery for production of the Marciano vintage. A barrel tasting was hosted for a Chiati that had been aging since before the new millennium. Hints of plumb and strawberry surged across Vinny's tongue when he sipped and swirled.

"Why hasn't this been bottled yet?" Vinny said in broken Italian.

Enzo shrugged. Then his arms started to windmill as he said, "Every year we taste and it gets better and better. We figure when we do a tasting that isn't an improvement over the year before it has reached its peak. Then we bottle."

"You know, we never really fought until we opened that restaurant and started working together," Enzo said in Italian spoken slowly enough for even Vinny to translate.

It was Angie and Maria's turn to do the morning prep work. They went through the scrupulously choreographed motions, and Angie was pleased by the efficiency of their morning collaboration. The pasta sauce was slow-cooking, the lasagna baking, the pizza dough rising and the rotisserie was turning and roasting whole chickens to a crispy skin tone. Most of the birds would end up shredded and turned into chicken cacciatore.

For their mid-morning break the girls camped at their favorite dining room booth. Additional companionship provided by their ever-present cigarettes and coffee. Maria's hair was tightly bound in a red and white bandana. Angie's face glistened with her daily quota of jojoba moisturizing cream.

Conversation was unusually slow in coming, partly the result of the residual sting inflicted by Mort Stottlemyre's unexpected rejection notice. He had slammed the door on their investment offer, at least until his *Rancho en los Whatever* was constructed and its Spanish-style homes sold off. That would take at least a couple of years, and whatever youthful exuberance Angie and Maria had for restaurateurship could dissipate by then.

Besides, Angie was desperate to get out. She was tired of indentured servitude and the mounting family tensions. The issues were insoluble and that made defection all the more urgent. She was all the more convinced of this with Vinny an ocean away in Italy. The restaurant's entire electro-magnetic field had changed in his absence. Angie could breathe again. For the first time she was getting a sense of what emancipation would be like, and it was sweet.

While Angie's spirits soared in her silent reverie, Maria seemed especially disconcerted, fidgeting in her seat, shifting the weight ratio between one cheek of her buttocks and the other.

"Why are you so jumpy?" Angie said.

"It's not that. I can hardly sit. Shekko was corn-holing me all night."

Angie touched a hand to her forehead, wishing she could somehow retract the question. "My god, how can you let him up there?" she said. "Is nothing off limits in your bedroom?"

"Bedroom, my ass, he did me in the woods on Roundtop. We haven't done it up there since we were teenagers. Shekko told me it makes him feel like a youngster again."

"The two of you were at it all night?"

"We got interrupted. Some high school kids came along and heard me whooping. They thought a crime was in progress and called the police. We got out of there fast."

"So your big, macho husband is afraid of the cops."

"He doesn't give a shit about cops. I made a run for it because I was afraid that Jablonsky hunk was going to show up and find my skivvies hanging in the tree branches."

"Can you believe Ginger is balling that guy? Talk about hitting the jackpot."

"She won't tell me anything, not even how long his thingy is," Maria complained. Then she waved a gathering cloud of cigarette smoke from her face. "Listen, we've got to talk business," Maria said. "We need to change the plan. Forget an investor, and never mind the mafia house in Apalachin. I want a place that fits our requirements. We've been thinking too big. Let's just lease a place, then we can move in fast and get going. I'm sick of sitting around and waiting."

The side of Angie's fist hit the tabletop and the coffee cups and ashtray jumped. "I'm not going to get into another situation where I'm under somebody's control — like a landlord."

"Then it's never going to happen. It's too expensive to buy that mafia house and do all the renovations. We're not going to find a person willing to put up that kind of money."

"We have a plan," Angie said. "We even typed up a business proposal. It's a good one. All we need to do is find the right investor."

Maria turned sideways. The angle gave restraint a slight edge in its struggle against eruption. Edgy moments passed. Jaw muscles twitched at the effort required to keep her mandible from swinging back into action. Maria suddenly felt exhausted by the prospect of decamping with her sister to open a second incarnation of Marciano's.

Angie was a complicated and volatile creature, and she was blind to the fact that, under any circumstances, starting a second Marciano's would be a delicate enterprise with many moving pieces. There was Uncle Nunzio to consider. His reaction couldn't be predicted. Father Albie was an advocate of expansion, though the sudden partitioning of family members could strike a dishonorable chord.

"We're not going that direction anymore. Aren't you listening to me?" Maria said, still bobbing and weaving to keep pressure off her inflamed hemorrhoidal tissue. "Even if we could find an investor it's going to be a bad deal for us. Pay attention to what Hans has been telling you. An investor means giving up a big chunk of ownership. I'd rather move into an old place and keep all the money. We can work our way up from there."

"I'm not going to start at the bottom. Did Vinny start at the bottom? Are we Marciano's or not? How stupid it would look for the new Marciano's to be in a second-rate location," Angie said, though in the privacy of her skull she understood that sister Maria's reasoning was sound. Leasing was the most expeditious way to launch the new Marciano's. But that was beside the point. Angie wanted more than just her own restaurant, or even autonomy from

Vinny. The ultimate goal was total supremacy. That couldn't be achieved by cooking alone, because the recipes would be identical. Overshadowing Vinny would require an act of architectural splendor and fanfare so historically and culturally significant that it rendered the original Marciano's bourgeois by comparison. That would be the mafia house in Apalachin.

Oh yes, she dreamily noted, there's more at stake for her than freedom, ownership rights, a Good Housekeeping Seal of Approval and the Malcolm Baldrige National Quality Award. This was an opportunity to take down her shit-finger brother, to prove that all the theorems she had proposed (and he had rebuffed) over the years would add up to a superior operation — a place with better food, happier employees, less spoilage, stronger contracts with vendors, higher profits and a perfect sanitation score from the New York State Department of Health. Angie had not subscribed to the *Harvard Business Review* for nothing. She was up on all the data, all the latest thinking, all the most pertinent organizational management tactics and the latest wisdom from workplace psychologists. She saw the chinks in Vinny's operation. The lighting in the kitchen was too bright. The walls weren't painted a motivational color. Improper music was being played at an agitating volume. The amount of square footage per employee had them feeling sequestered. That was to say nothing of how undisciplined and poorly trained the staff members had become.

It was a euphoric state of consciousness that was short-lived. It vanished when Maria said, "Look, I wasn't going to bring this up today, I was going to do this in stages. But it's probably best if I lay all my cards on the table and get your hysterics over with now."

Angie started doing the chin-jutting thing again.

"I've changed my mind about the kind of Marciano's we should open. I say we open a place that just does lunches — and my mind is made up about that. We either do a lunch place or you can count me out."

Just that fast Angie realized that Maria was turning her master plan into a smoking pile of dog shit. A stream of profanity came spluttering out of her twisted little mouth. Maria's spine flexed backward in retreat, until her head came up against the back of the booth. She could smell the gloriously roasted *Il Perfetto* coffee grounds on Angie's over-heated breath.

Maria scampered from the booth and beat a wheezy retreat to the kitchen.

Vinny and Nunzio spent their nights at Enzo Mangione's home. He had an extra room with two beds. The stone house's insulation was non-existent and the winter weather was bitterly cold at this mountain elevation. Chilly air flowed into the guest bedroom like a cooling system had been switched on. The host armed his guests with stacks of heavy wool blankets to pile on. Soon, Vinny could hear his uncle snoring under the crush of bedding.

The ensuing days were replicas of one another. Food, drink and conversation were had in excess at a different Marciano household, followed by sluggish walk through town. Day one had been exhilarating. By day two the excitement was gone. Day three felt mundane. By day four a state of alienation had beset Vinny. He felt like a mute listening to conversations running at too fevered a pitch to comprehend and participate. At fifteen minute intervals Nunzio clued him into the topics under discussion, but Vinny's attempts at the language were so broken and sporadic as to be meaningless.

How could there possibly be so much to talk about in this little middle-of-nowhere town?

He combated the boredom with large quantities of the family's delicious wine. Mostly, though, he kept watching Tessa. He felt an affinity for this woman. She was so full of warmth. Her face was kindness personified, and she moved with a modesty and grace American women lacked. There was also a mystery about her. She was very attractive and he wanted to keep staring at her, and yet she didn't arouse his normally irrepressible sex drive. It was as if she was too pure a soul to elicit such primeval instincts.

He was already looking forward to Tessa hugging him goodbye, again feeling her nurturing breasts compressed against his chest.

After days of discreet observation, Vinny finally accumulated the gumption to approach Tessa and attempt communication. He had silently rehearsed his opening statement. He said in Italian, "Is there any chance of your coming to America one day and visiting the restaurant?" She shrugged her shoulders, picked up a cookie tray and held it forth.

"Biscotti?" she asked.

Vinny wasn't sure his statement had translated properly, so he took one of the hard, dry cookies off the plate and walked it back to his chair.

When departure day finally arrived, Vinny packed furiously. He wanted desperately to get back to Rome, the land of internet connections and full-scale lodging accommodations. Most of all he wanted to get back to New York and the restaurant so he could do a damage assessment; find out exactly what kind of havoc Angie and Maria had inflicted.

The goodbyes with all the clan members were effusive. Everybody was hugging and kissing and thanking one another, as if they had just won Academy Awards. Vinny waited to say goodbye just to one, the sweet and kind face of Tessa Marciano. When that moment finally came, he squared up to her. As always her hair was tied back to keep it off her face and out of the food. He took and kissed the back of her hand and said in practiced Italian, "I'll never forget your kindness and hospitality."

"*Lei è benvenuto*," she said, which even Vinny knew to mean, "You're welcome."

And with that, Vinny kissed each of her cheeks and they hugged each other tight. Vinny concentrated on the sensation of her breasts flattening and spreading across his chest. They brought back the infantile sensation of swimming in a warm, fragrant bath of amniotic fluid.

Enzo drove them the short distance to the train station. Before bidding him ado, Nunzio handed Enzo an envelope fat with American dollars to be distributed among the clan. It had become a tradition with Nunzio. The family looked forward to his visits both because they loved him and because he reciprocated for their kindness by showering them with the kind of money that wasn't easy to come by in a tiny Abruzzo village.

A wistful expression came over Nunzio's face as the train pulled out of station and started clattering towards the Italian capital. Already he was missing his tribe members.

After a half-hour of reverent silence he turned to Vinny and said, "That's quite a family you've got. Not the kind of people you would want to disappoint."

Vinny understood the verbal dagger's point but kept his reply in a positive vein. "They're beautiful people. I felt like royalty the whole week."

"It's a lovely countryside town."

"Thank you for not mentioning the stolen recipes."

"I would never do anything to break their hearts."

Thirty-three minutes later Vinny started asking about Tessa. "Who's her husband," he said. "I never figured that out."

"Tessa's parents are Umberto and Manuela, but she lives in a small place of her own."

"A single woman living alone; isn't that unusual in Italy?"

"It is. Nobody talks about it. She's the funny one in the family."

"What's so funny about Tessa?"

"I'll tell you and then you forget you ever knew. I never want it coming out of your mouth."

Vinny's posture recoiled slightly at the dark implications.

Nunzio gave a conspiratorial glance to the left and right and hushed his tone. "She doesn't like men. She was caught years ago messing with women from another town. A goddamn threesome if you can believe that."

"Tessa's a lesbian?"

Nunzio grabbed his nephew's forearm and squeezed. "Keep your voice down," he hissed. The old man peered into the adjoining private compartments to make sure the comment hadn't stimulated any prurient interests. "What do you think you're in New York City or something? Everybody in this part of the world knows each other."

Nunzio looked out the window a moment at some passing farmlands. He whispered, "The answer is yes, it's the L-word. When it was discovered the priests were called in and something resembling an exorcism was held. It didn't do any good. As far as we know she doesn't mess around with the girls anymore, but she still doesn't like the boys."

Vinny shook his head and wondered how much he really knew about women. It was then he realized it wasn't so much kindness he had seen in Tessa's face as sadness. The sadness of a woman scandalized by her own desires; trapped in a body and a Catholic society that knew no variances. She belonged in Rome where she could freely partake of the fruit of her own gender, away from the judgments and disappointments of family. But this was Italy, a nation with traditions that said an unmarried woman did not live a life separate from blood relatives.

"I'm shocked," Vinny said. "I had no idea."

"Why would you? It's not like she's wearing a scarlet letter on her apron."

"There never are any signs with women. They're a mystery."

"It don't matter," Nunzio said. "She's one of us and we love her just the same."

"A lesbian," Vinny marveled to an invisible passenger.

"Stop saying that word."

Father Albie's eating campaign was finally exacting its toll. Even by his gargantuan standards, this binge was unprecedented. It all stemmed from his determination to hunt down knockoffs of Marciano's special dishes, retrieve the recipes and bring the perpetrator to justice. This required visitations to every Italian restaurant in the region to taste-test any entrees that resembled those served at Marciano's.

We all knew that, however noble father's intentions, his search was also a remarkably handy excuse to eat like a rhinoceros. Now he wasn't feeling well, which is to say he was feeling even less well than usual, which is to say burdened by the usual symptoms of obesity. They had achieved a new level of acuteness. Energy was depleted. Joints aching. Feet and ankles swollen. Breathing labored. Varicose veins bulging.

Mother Margherita, worried about her husband's health and wearied by his complaints, made an appointment for a blood test at the offices of Dr. Mohan Ganjoo, father's longtime physician. A medical technician took father into a small room nauseatingly stocked with glass vials, gauze and syringes. Two of those vials were filled with his blood and sent to a local laboratory for testing. Within seventy-two hours father's phone was urgently ringing. Dr. Ganjoo was on the other end demanding that Albie come to his office on the double for an emergency medical appointment. Father could hear Ganjoo aggressively rifling through the paper results of his blood test.

As Father Albie entered the examination room later that day with his badgering wife glued to his side, he was reminded how much he detested the antiseptic smell of medical facilities. It reminded him of isopropyl alcohol, which reminded him of cotton-balls and sterilization, which reminded him of hypodermic needles, the kind used for tetanus, diphtheria and flu shots — as well as to draw blood for testing. He abhorred needles.

The nurse directed him to step onto the scale. The metal stand grunted under the load. The nurse slid the weights along their measurement tracks until the scale balanced out at a whopping 373 pounds, a personal record.

The nurse's final order was to strip down to his undershorts and await the doctor's arrival.

The unveiling of Father Albie's body was a deliberate and precarious affair, especially with the assistance of his ham-fisted wife. Everything hurt and the basic agility required for disrobing had been smothered by the mass of stored fats. The man had become a prisoner of his own reserves.

The next thing Albie remembered was sitting on the examination table in his super-sized boxers. The thin sheet of protective white paper crinkled with each breath taken. The table's foam padding was fully compressed.

Even Father, who long ago resigned himself to being a life-long shopper at Rochester Big & Tall stores, was distressed by his record-setting roundness. He felt like a continent sitting there and spreading out across the table's surface. He had never felt so ... *gelatinous*. Albie frowned. The world wasn't built for the fat. It was hard to fit into cars and clothes and the much ballyhooed "stadium seating" at movie theaters.

Fretful Mother Magherita was sitting nearby, coaching her husband on what to tell the doctor — all of which father tuned out until she got to the part about his bowel movements.

"I know what I'm doing," Albie snarled.

Just then the doorknob turned and Dr. Mohan Ganjoo stepped into the room in his white coat. The mandatory stethoscope was clasped around his neck. The doctor was a dark and disheveled man from Bengal, India. His mussed hair and rumbled clothes suggested a person too preoccupied with science to practice self-conscious grooming. One imagined his living space piled high with stacks of moldering medical journals. Father appreciated this aura of commitment to the profession. He also liked the way the doctor showed his caring by scolding him during each visit and prescribing impossible lifestyle changes to restore maximum health. Of course, those were gentle, almost loving scoldings. Based on the tone of the call he had received from the doctor, today's visit would probably be more akin to a brow beating.

As always, there was a smile on Ganjoo's face, though this time it was unusually tentative. He nodded his acknowledgement to the couple and then turned his attention to the chart he was carrying. A slow ticking sound came from his mouth that, when translated into English, meant, *Shame on you*. Then he re-read the numerals from the blood test and shook his head.

He stuck the stethoscope's antlers into his ears and walked toward father. The receiving end of the instrument was placed against the patient's domed belly. The doctor listened thoughtfully to the chemical reactions taking place within. There were the usual squishing sounds of digestion in progress, as well as the severe growling sounds of a pack of jackals. Then there were the extraordinary sounds, such as the staccato of great gas globules machine-gunning their way through and around the volatile mixtures of decomposing food items. Sucking, slurping and slopping sounds were being made, as well as several other adjectives beginning with the letter *s*.

Ganjoo backed away, as though to avoid being consumed by the quagmire. "Octopuses are mud wrestling in there," he said.

He removed the stethoscope from his ears and began speaking in his high-pitched, squealing Indian accent. "Let me be clear that this is a doomsday prognosis," he said, holding the medical chart and blood-test results aloft. "All your vital signs and key indicators are telling me you are already dead."

Mother Margherita inhaled one cubic foot of air. The doctor turned toward her. "He's entered the Red Zone, Margherita."

"The Red Zone!" Mother ominously repeated, coming to her feet.

Father wasn't a man who caved easily to illogical fears, yet there was something altogether logical and horrifying about being read your death sentence by a credentialed physician.

"We are talking extreme obesity." Ganjoo turned back to father and said to him in piercing tones, "How dare you come in here in this condition after all the warnings I have given you. As the physician responsible for your health, this is a slap in my face. I must insist that you start showing me proper respect. The doctor-patient relationship is a two-way street. I cannot have a successful practice if my patients ignore my orders. What does that say about me as a physician? It tells other patients I am not persuasive enough to lead my patients to fitness. Soon even my healthy patients will begin to mistrust, then my practice will be in very serious state indeed."

"Doctor," mother said, "what about the pain he's feeling?"

"His body is under extreme pressure. The human skeletal system is not made to support such tonnage. It's like setting a Winnebago on a suspension system built for a Honda Civic. The joints are being compressed and will not tolerate this much longer. Ligaments, tendons and cartilage will begin to fail. The groin may rupture. The human girdle can only sustain so much weight for so long, then it lets loose. Next thing you know a few miles of intestines have fallen into your pants. Getting all that stuff recoiled and back into the torso is not as simple as rolling up a garden hose, you know."

The little Hindu backed away from father, as though he needed a wide-angle perspective to bring his patient's girth into full view. "Well, don't just sit there gaining weight," he squealed. "What do you have to say for yourself?"

Father held up his arms up to express how hapless he felt. "What can I say? As far back as I can remember I've always had an unstoppable desire to eat."

"Yes, but why is this desire growing so precipitously? You have packed on forty-three pounds since we last visited."

Mother said, "I try to stop him doctor. What can I do? He's a raging bull when he gets around food."

"Shall I describe in graphic detail the wreckage taking place in your body?" He reached down and squeezed Albie's swollen calf to accentuate the bundle of varicose veins bulging at the skin's surface. Green and puffy and billowing, they resembled a ghoulish facsimile of the Hanging Gardens of Babylon.

Mother neared tears. "There must be something you can do, Dr. Ganjoo."

"The burden is truly your husband's. He must begin following my orders. If not I will have no other option than to prescribe gastric bypass surgery."

This time mother inhaled two cubic feet of air.

"Let me be clear. Your husband is now member to a small group of patients who I must categorize as Code Red. Do you understand such medical terminology? It means death is imminent unless severe measures are taken."

Mother brought her hand into prayer position and gazed towards the heavens. Even though as she saw were acoustic tiles she howled, "Holy Mary mother of God!" She had read that the chances of dying from that brand of surgery were frighteningly high, and she told the doctor so.

The doctor's piercing, high RPM voice started spinning again. "This is true. About one-in-ten do not make it. But we have to play the odds at this point. Albie's risk of sudden death is much higher than one-in-ten. That means the operation is a very sensible alternative."

Margherita potted herself back on the chair, as though the statistics being bandied about were too much to bear.

"Using that surgery I can reduce Albie's stomach to the size of a golf ball." The doctor's voice had risen to an even higher pitch. His already sharp verbal inflections were being delivered at even more acute angles. "The problem is stomach tissue is very elastic. Stuff it with food and it will stretch. Stuff it with more food and it stretches larger still. Unless your meal times can be accompanied by discipline the golf ball will soon return to the size of a beach ball. Then, we're right back where we started."

Mother's mind wandered in its state of shock. Father wallowed in the shoals of self-pity. Dr. Ganjoo resumed his examination by wrapping a Velcro strap around father's upper arm and pumping it full of air. Just as it reached the crushing point, Ganjoo released the air valve and applied the stethoscope to the front side of his elbow joint to detect the heart beats.

"Your blood pressure is higher than the Space Needle. Have you ever been to Seattle?" He didn't wait for Father's answer. "A lovely city. I doubt you'll ever make it there."

Albie was looking spooked but offered no defense.

"Have you ever heard of the Seven Deadly Sins?"

Father assumed the question was rhetoric and didn't reply.

"They're called *deadly* for a reason. One of them is gluttony, which is defined as an inordinate desire to consume more than that which one requires."

Father looked to the floor and shook his head in defeat.

"Your body's a time bomb. My guess is that the detonator will be a colossal myocardial infarction."

"A what?" Mother said.

"A massive heart attack, most probably caused by a clogged aorta."

Mother was at the Wailing Wall again, letting out all the associated sounds of misery.

"I'm going to write prescriptions for several pharmaceuticals you need," Ganjoo told Albie. "They are strictly emergency measures. The only long-term solution is for you to stop eating so much. You will receive a call tomorrow from a nutritionist. Meet with her. She will give you a customized diet that will drop your intake to eight-thousand calories per day. Then we'll work out way down to five thousand."

Such small numbers gave father visions of starlings at a bird feeder. How, he wondered, can I possibly subsist on such skimpy rations?

"If you do not take me seriously this time, Albie, if you cannot bring your appetites under control I highly recommend you get your affairs in order. Then, give serious consideration to gastric bypass surgery."

Mother stood and gave her mostly naked husband a pathetic look.

"Get dressed. I will meet you two at the front desk."

As father leaned his mass forward to dismount the table a peal of flatulence, the likes of a throttled Harley-Davidson 1200, escaped his shanks.

"Albie!" Mother shrieked.

Father's humiliation was total.

Dr. Ganjoo grabbed an aerosol can and sprayed the vicinity with some Glade. It was the brand's Country Garden scent.

The doctor exited the room. Albie began the arduous process of getting dressed. He sat on a chair to pull his slacks up his legs and over his buttocks, because doing this from a standing position carried the risk of keeling over and smashing a hip, or compacting his wife to the verge of death.

Mother Margherita tugged the socks back onto her husband's swollen feet. She was stuffing too much sausage into too little casing. She pulled a shoehorn out of her purse for leverage in cramming his feet into a distressed pair of shoes, which she double-knotted for safety.

When they got to the front desk the attendant docked father's credit card for the visit and handed him a receipt. Dr. Ganjoo appeared again carrying four slips of paper, each prescribing a different drug. There was Lipitor to lower the runaway cholesterol level, Inversine to ease his stratospheric blood pressure, an anticoagulant named Coumadin to thin the blood and keep it from clotting and causing a stroke or heart attack, and Prilosec to reduce the heart burn caused by acid reflux.

Albie Marciano, dead man walking, exited Dr. Ganjoo's office with his fistful of prescriptions.

When Vinny and Uncle Nunzio stepped off the train in Rome it was back to Taverna Angelica, where the elder man ordered another plate of veal medallions. Vinny prayed that Nunzio wouldn't need to worship again after this meal. He just wanted to get back to his hotel room, an enclosure with insulation, a heating system, a soft mattress and a half-dozen feather pillows. Vinny envisioned soaking in the marble tub, steam fogging the bathroom's 100 cubic feet of wall-mounted mirrors. He also needed to place an international call to inquire about the status of criminal actions being taken against him by that cunt making ransom demands.

Vinny paid the tab this time. Then Nunzio started strolling down the street.

"Where you going?" Vinny called out.

"C'mon. Vatican City is just three blocks from here. Let's take a refresher tour of St. Pete's Basilica."

Vinny trudged along, the gastrointestinal acid digesting both his dinner and the lining of his stomach.

"I always feel so holy when I walk through this place," Nunzio said, looking up at the globally revered grandeur all around him. After circling the interior of the huge basilica, he hunkered down in a pew for prayers. They lasted twenty-three minutes this time.

Finally, it was back to the Boscolo Exedra Hotel. Again they had rooms across the corridor from one another. Vinny placed a call to father. With Nunzio hovering nearby, Vinny threw in some superlatives about their time in Castiglione for his uncle's sake. An approving smile came across the old man's face.

Nothing had changed in New York. The restaurant was still packed every night, the blackmailer had not called and, as far as Vinny could discern, Angie and Maria had not launched an insurrection.

Give me the phone, Nunzio said, reaching out a hand.

"Albie," he shouted into the mouthpiece, "we had an unbelievable time. You should have seen your son's face. He looked like Adam after biting the apple. Yeah, that's right. It was pure enlightenment. Is Ringo keeping his shit together? No walkouts? Is Angie keeping the shelves stocked? How about Margherita, she's not putting too much dressing on those salads is she? Okay, I'll tell you all about it when I get back."

Vinny took the phone back. "Dad, you would have loved it. We ate like pigs. I gotta go. God love 'ya."

Sodden with food, drink and travel fatigue, Nunzio bade his travel companion a good night.

"I'm going to go for a little walk," Vinny informed him. "It's been a long time since I've been to Rome."

As soon as Vinny reached the lobby he approached the concierge's desk. "Where do young people go to dance in Rome," he asked.

The concierge spoke good English. He told Vinny, "There's a nightclub about seven blocks from here that's famous for its dance music. Very rhythmic. It attracts young people from all over the world."

He unfolded a street map and highlighted in yellow the route from hotel to club. Minutes later Vinny was at the front door of a place named Tabu forking out twelve euros just to walk through the front doors.

There was a disc jockey playing music so loud it forced most of the oxygen from the room. He ordered a bourbon and ginger ale and watched the kaleidoscope of bodies on the swarming dance floor. It was good to be immersed again in the pulse of modern life. There were exotic women everywhere and all of their inhibitions had been checked at the door. Some of what passed for dance was more fittingly described as seizures. That was of little consequence to Vinny, as he felt a familiar stirring behind the zipper of his jeans, which reminded him that he had not been laid in a week. That was the longest stretch of sexless living Vinny had done since his penis dripped with a yeast infection that sidelined him for a ten-day course of antibiotics seven years prior.

Vinny moved towards the dance floor. After a week parked in a chair and eating and drinking to excess, he felt as though he was oozing out of his clothes. He stepped into the writhing crowd and got his big ass moving. Suddenly the strobe light kicked on and cut the scene into 240 rapid-fire scenes per minute, making even the lamest dancers look like they belonged on *American Bandstand*. Vinny hip-hopped up to three Italian girls who were dancing and smiling at one another. Their expressions slackened when the flashing face of a strange male invaded their space with a chest full of curly hairs and gold chains and pendants. Everything Vinny tried to say was immediately smothered by the enormously amplified sound. So he put his lips close to their ears and shouted that it was his last night in Rome before flying back to America. They didn't speak English, so he resorted to his second language, broken though it was.

The disc jockey finished his latest number and the music stopped, giving Vinny nine seconds to make his case. If Vinny was lucky, the women would see this as the perfect opportunity to jump some Yankee's bones for the night and never have to face him again. Before much could be accomplished the music roared back louder than ever. He started screaming in their ears again, trying to impress them with the luxurious five-star hotel room at his disposal. He was saying something about room service and the extra-large marble tub. The young women tired of splicing together the snippets of Vinny's tortured Italian without much success. They consciously drifted away and vanished in the swarm.

There was another woman within eyeshot dancing alone and wearing a skirt buoyant with undulations. Eye contact was being made and her smile was an obvious invitation to approach. My god she was hot, glistening with a thin sheen of perspiration. Vinny's arms and legs did the locomotion as he moved closer. Christ almighty, he thought to himself, he had spent so much time on trains during the past week he was beginning to move like one.

She imitated his movements and they looked on track for a head-on collision. She was deft with the feet, though, and moved sensuous figure 8's around her new dance partner, mugging him licentiously each time her face passed by his. When the song ended the band announced it was taking a break. Vinny spoke tormented Italian. She didn't understand. English didn't work either. As they sent incomprehensible words past one another, Vinny figured out she was French and visiting from Paris.

The mademoiselle got the drift, too, straightening Vinny's collar and announcing, "*L'Américain*."

He motioned to the bar, expecting to ply her with some libations. She motioned towards the door before taking his hand and leading him out of the club, through a few side streets and into her hotel. As soon as the door to her room closed she started kissing Vinny as though he had just returned from a foreign war. Then their clothes started falling to the floor. Vinny had never been with a woman who couldn't talk to him. He liked it. It removed a complication, a bigger one than Vinny had ever realized. This is what it must have been like for cave dwellers. Besides their grunts and crude gestures they must have communicated with touch — and Frenchy was doing a lot of communicating with her taste buds. She was all over Vinny and quickly unsheathed his mighty penis. The young French woman held hands against her cheeks in astonishment. "*Ooo la la*," she said.

As she sunk the entire appendage between her splayed legs the air came out of her like the sound of a falling soufflé. She froze for a few moments while the elasticity returned. A few tentative movements followed. Soon, though, she gained momentum and was bouncing and rotating on Vinny's lap, her long black hair waving and shimmering like the stormy surface of the Mediterranean Sea. The combined scents of Tanqueray and aroused womanhood perfumed the room. Then she let loose with an urgent stream of

French phrases that Vinny didn't comprehend but he was sure had salacious intent. In the distance the oscillating sound of a foreign police siren could be heard. Its teeter-tottering sound grew louder by the second, ricocheting off the city's edifices. Vinny turned his head and glared at the windows and saw the pale blue silhouettes of revolving lights. They were growing in intensity. The vehicle was coming closer and closer. Vinny was sure the French beauty's dirty cries of depravity were picked up by someone in the adjoining hotel room, who called the police to rescue the woman from the horrors going on next door. Louder and louder the siren sounded. Vinny was having trouble concentrating on the intercourse and keeping his cock inflated. Next came the screeching of rubber tires as the police made a hard turn down their street. The authorities were right on top of them now. Vinny felt like tossing Frenchy off his lap in mid-rotation and making a naked break into the night.

The police car produced a deafening and blinding sound and light show as it flew screaming past the hotel room windows. Vinny's woman for the evening reached completion at precisely that moment and crumpled onto his torso. The siren mercifully faded into the urban distance. Vinny's muscles relaxed. The tourist on his chest panted a few moments, only to push herself upright again and go back into motion. Now she was crying out again in her native tongue with even greater urgency. It was about the sexiest thing Vinny had ever heard, primarily because he convinced himself the proper translation was, *"Fuck me you American stud!"*

She went off a second time, almost as quickly as the first. Then made a gymnastic dismount and stripped latex off Vinny's thing. She grabbed the stupendous organ with both hands and started stroking it furiously, rushing to get the butter churned and smeared on her baguette for an early morning breakfast. Vinny's body went rigid and his toes curled as he gave forth everything he had with great gushes. When the waterworks finally ended the Frenchwoman was half covered in goo. She held her open hands at her shoulders and declared, *"Viola!"*

Vinny walked back to the hotel, footfalls echoing off the ancient apartment buildings. Flaming smudge pots surrounded a couple of road-construction sites. They flickered rapidly as a chilly breeze blew past.

The nameless French woman was still all over his mind. Her alluring scent lingered in Vinny's nostrils. His gooey crouch buzzed like a hornet's nest with residual stimulation. It was about the most exciting encounter he had ever had. The woman was absolutely beside herself. The volume and madness of her carnality. It was all very primitive.

If only he had brought his pocket recorder, the one he often used to secretly archive the maelstroms of love. Without a record, who would believe his recounting of this tale? Who wouldn't think there were several generous helpings of exaggeration? It would come out sounding like the proverbial fish story. I caught one *thisss* big…

There was a friend back in Endicott who spoke French. He could have interpreted the woman's yowling pronouncements. What had she said? Did Vinny really want to know? It couldn't have been bad, not with the response he was getting out of her. How much of it was real, Vinny wondered. Her motor skills certainly didn't indicate drunkenness, but the billows of Tanqueray suggested otherwise. Perhaps she was just putting on a spectacle for *L'Américain*, showing Uncle Sam a thing or two about love Froggy Style.

The wrenching two-fisted hand job. The volcanic conclusion. The soggy aftermath. Whatever the underlying motivations, this bout of four-alarm sex had reactivated Vinny's nearly indomitable sense of self.

He thought about going back for a second round, then quickly dismissed the notion. The time was very late and concern was growing that Uncle Nunzio was knocking on his hotel room door for a bed check. It had been a hell of a long walk. At least an hour had elapsed and counting. Vinny realized he was lost. He yanked the walking map from his pocket and stood by a street lamp, only to realize he was utterly disoriented by the city's network of curving streets and piazzas. He marched on, engulfed by the dark shadows along the residential streets. They were abandoned except for the occasional whine of a motor scooter zipping past. Manhole covers released steam from the Roman underground, giving a mystical quality to his isolation.

Finally an elderly man came hobbling along with the aid of a cane.

"*Calle de Cassi*," Vinny said into a startled face.

The man spoke wheezing Italian and offered hand signals to indicate the lefts and rights. Vinny counted them off and walked quickly to execute the moves before memory failed.

The glow of the big thoroughfare increased in intensity as he approached. When he turned left onto *Calle de Cassi* and Vinny lifted his head and saw the grand hotel. He also noticed its façade was getting painted with flashes of blue light. Then the ambulance came into view, maybe the very one that went screaming past the French woman's windows and nearly turned him flaccid. A gurney was being rolled towards the vehicle. Laying on the gurney was a man with a great dome of a belly. A thunderbolt of alarm cut across Vinny's torso as he recognized the shape and the brilliant head of white hair. He broke into a sprint, running to the edge of the gurney where he was braced by a couple of medics.

"That's my uncle," he protested, shunting them aside. He climbed into the ambulance to accompany his uncle on what might become a fateful ride to the nearest medical center. Nunzio's face was a toxic blue and he was rubbing the center of his chest with one hand.

The Great Man winced in pain. For the fifth or sixth time in the past twenty years he was on the verge of exiting the mortal stage.

"*Momma Mia*," Vinny said, "I told you not to eat that veal."

Past his swollen tongue Nunzio managed to force out just one word, one syllable at a time: "In-di-*ges*-tion."

Ringo was back on the pizza bench and the inner calculations were back at play. With Vinny and Uncle Nunzio off the continent for an unexpectedly prolonged time, Ringo had again resorted to phantom ailments and bogus affronts as pretexts for angrily walking off the job in mid-pizza.

Already he was pulsing at the temples, feeling trapped again between the fire-breathing gas ovens to his rear and the clutch of gawking customers to the front. What, he wondered, was so fascinating about watching a pizza being made, even one with a statewide reputation?

Though it was an unusually slow night, Ringo was working much harder than he cared to. So he began carefully scanning every statement and action in search of something to get upset about. He was disappointed that it was such a tranquil evening and there wasn't the slightest provocation within sight or earshot. If all else failed, of course, there was the time-tested stratagem of intentionally fucking up a pizza order so when it got sent back he could use that as an excuse for erupting and making yet another ill-timed exit. But he had just pulled that tactic from his repertoire a couple of nights ago and he didn't want his methods to become any more contrived than they already were, so he decided to fall back on his self-induced affliction.

Ringo's hands were suddenly aching. It was deep, painful throbbing. The more he spread the dough and distributed the toppings, the more acute the pain. It wasn't the first time Ringo had imagined that his hands were wrought with agony. He had insisted on a few other occasions that he had come down with a case of arthritis — this despite his youth and no family history of the ailment.

Contorted and lacquered in sweat, his face started to resemble a royal flush. Ringo had somehow figured out how to raise his body temperature, turning his skin an emergency-room crimson at will. The grouping of customers could see Ringo's head glowing hotter with each passing moment. For some the suffering became too ugly to watch and they drifted back to their dining room tables. He had become known among regular customers as the crazy pizza maker.

Ringo used the wood paddle to shove one last pizza pie into the oven, and then quickly removed his apron and slam-dunked it into the dirty bin. "I gotta go," he told his parents, who were doing their own sweating on the cooking line. "My hands are hurting." Ringo quickly scurried out the back door to avoid a scolding, but Father Albie made a surprisingly agile rush out the back door in pursuit. He searched his mind for some parting words to hurl at the boy, something that would make him feel guilty or condemned. Before he could find anything, Ringo was behind the wheel of his car and spinning gravel.

Father stood for a few moments, cooling in the frozen night air. To his left the tumultuous Susquehanna River was flowing past, chunks of ice colliding with one another and moving rapidly towards Binghamton, and eventually through the Pennsylvania cities of Scranton and Harrisburg, before dumping its contents into the Chesapeake Bay.

He consulted his watch. It was 9 p.m., the schedule tip-off time for tonight's Knicks vs. Celtics game. Ringo's time of departure was no coincidence. The soothing play-by-play of Marv Albert awaited him. Sports were the boy's singular interest in life, his only refuge. He liked the numbers, the finality of it all, the blackness and whiteness of its outcomes. There were winners and there were losers. There where champions and also-rans. There were very few gray areas to confuse one. And when things did get confusing, there were the instant replays and coach's challenge to resolve the disputes.

Ringo prized all major sports, though NFL football easily rose above the others. It was the king of sports, supplanting baseball as the new national pastime. It was strategic, competitive and had a rich history with storied franchises. Most of all, it was a contact sport. A *hitting* sport. The harder one hit the better. The crack of helmets, shoulder pads and bones gave vicarious play to Ringo's own unfulfilled desire to lay a devastating crack-back block on all those who vexed him, especially those who forced him to work for a living.

How, Father Albie wondered, could it be that he — a bona fide workaholic, of all people — had produced a lazy boy? What scuffed chromosome or over-twisted strand of DNA had produced of son without industry? What type of cosmic folly was this?

Father directed his youngest daughter Angie to take over the pizza bench, which she did with great agitation. She had her own work to do. Besides that, Angie didn't like being told what to do under *any* circumstances, and she especially resented having to sub for her brother, who she thought belonged on the fourteenth floor of the county psych ward.

She thumbed through the growing stack of orders and grabbed the airy slabs of dough. Each was given a deep-tissue massage.

This would be a setback for her workload and force her to work overtime hours. She was paid a flat salary, not hourly like Ringo, so the extra hours would go uncompensated. The money Ringo forfeited during his walkouts should be paid to his replacement, Angie reasoned, but she had already fought and lost that battle numerous times.

Angie's resentment billowed. That fucking brother of hers had done it again, created havoc and displacement. This family is so dysfunctional. She would try again to convince father to commit the entire clan to group therapy.

Father didn't believe in the therapeutic value of talking about your problems with strangers. Besides, the Marciano family was locally famous and had an image to uphold. There was zero confidence that a therapist of any credentials would keep his or her mouth shut about the crazy and very public family he or she was trying to disentangle.

Pure horseshit, Angie told herself. She was in therapy with a male psychologist who was prudent beyond his professional commitments. For years she had been processing and applying salve to her emotional wounds. She would have long been finished with her recovery if her family wasn't continually inflicting new wounds upon her psyche. She would never be able to make herself whole until family relationships were detoxified.

Slab by slab of gooey dough, Angie persevered, making pizzas until deep into the night, when Marciano's Mangia House finally stopped taking orders. After cleaning up she swung by the bar to add some Bailey's Irish Cream to her cup of decaf coffee for the ride home. By then it was 10:45 p.m. and there were just a few people left on the stools. I was on the phone trying to talk Sadie into staying up until I got home. She tried coaxing reasons out of me.

"What do I get if I stay up?" she purred.

A server showed up and called out his order. "Something pleasing," I said before hanging up.

I started fixing drinks and answering half-hearted questions from Wes Fitzgerald, who was fast becoming a fixture at the bar. It was as though he believed by just hanging out at the crime scene the perpetrator would eventually walk up and confess.

"Did you see anyone at all suspicious that night?" he said between slurps of his drink.

"Isn't it a little bit late for a question like that? The crime was committed weeks ago and you're just now asking me if I saw anything?"

"Memory's a funny thing. Things we think we've forgotten can suddenly be jarred loose."

"I don't remember a thing from that night."

"Maybe you're not trying." He scrutinized me with his hostile gray eyes.

My anxiety was rising. The asshole had just shot to hell a month's worth of meditation.

"Can't we just have a good time?" I said.

"I'll tell you who's having a good time, that chick who smuggled the goods. You can hear the criminal pleasure in her voice every time she calls to make her prissy little demands."

Fitzgerald was already slurring and using too much saliva to get the words out. I kept my distance from the spray, though I couldn't put enough space between us to escape his whiskey breath. It reached across the bar and reminded me that the only thing that stood between me and this goon was highly flammable vapor.

"Be a good little bartender and fix me another bourbon and water." Fitzgerald was heavy-handed in slapping down another small stack of bills.

Sitting at the other end of the bar just out of earshot were Ginger and sergeant detective Clyde Jablonsky. Ginger's hands were wrapped around the lawman's bicep; he flexed it a bit more tightly and gave her a smile of appreciation.

Fitzgerald looked the scene over. "I'd like to puke."

I set a fresh drink in front of him. "You're losing your appreciation for young love, Fitzgerald."

"Love, my ass. Pretty Boy is a player. He's real good with the phony affections."

"You think he's toying with my sister?"

"I'm saying the guy gets a lot of ass. No man sidelines himself while he's in his prime."

"Kind of flattering thing to say about a guy you have no use for."

"He's a cop. The badge, the gun, the uniform, the billy club. Women go crazy for that command and control shit." He slurped more bourbon. "Look at me. I'm no Burt Reynolds but you wouldn't believe the pussy I got back in the day. My handcuffs got a lot more use in the bedroom than on the streets."

Dreading that Fitzgerald was about to launch into graphic tales of conquest, I turned my attention to the television mounted in the near corner. The Knicks game was were well into the fourth quarter and the tempo was picking up.

"Christ almighty," Fitzgerald said, "who thought of such a dumb sport? Grown men running around in shorts like a bunch of fairies."

"Dr. James Naismith," I answered.

He raised his eyebrows, impressed by this morsel of trivia. "I guess that makes you a basketball fan."

"They're the most finely conditioned athletes in the world."

"Sure they are. Conditioned to do what? Run across a plank of lumber and jump up and down. Hell, the cheerleaders do that."

He pinged his glass with a fingernail. It was already empty. When I placed the refilled glass in front of Fitzgerald he pointed at the TV and said, "That's not a man's sport. Football's a man sport. Boxing and hockey are men's sports. If there isn't any bone-crushing involved it isn't a manly game."

"Somehow I'm not surprised by your assessment."

Fitzgerald gave me a look that said my very use of a word like "assessment" proved that I had been feminized by my taste in sports. Or that I was already feminized and therefore attracted to sissy sports like basketball. It was a chicken-and-egg mystery.

I looked the other way and saw Jablonsky nosing his face through my sister's long hair in search of her neck, where he got a snout full of her new hormone-based perfume. Jablonsky woozily retreated after overdosing on the fragrance.

As I walked their direction Ginger pulled closer to Jablonsky, taking fuller possession of her trophy boyfriend. Though she clung to the male, it was Ginger's loins that were humid with sexual power. She had always believed herself capable of seducing and taking custody of any man. Jablonsky was proof of her theorem. Off the market he had come. And, as a woman, she could give him an inexhaustible supply of what he desired most — keeping him tame and domesticated around other women. She was the Queen Bee.

"Hate to disrupt your chemistry experiment," I said, "but I talked to my brother this morning about our problem."

The detective gave me the subtle smirk that had become one of his signatures — seventh behind his leather jacket, square-toed boots, police-issued firearm, hipper-than-thou stride, floppy dishwater blonde hair, and fourth degree black belt in the ancient martial art of kung fu.

"He's asking about progress on the case."

"Right now we are lying in wait. Like a cheetah in a field of antelope."

I tilted my head, trying to figure if there was any other way to interpret the words that had just entered my ears.

"You know the cheetah," Jablonsky said, "the fastest of all land animals."

"I guess that's the Marlin Perkins *Wild Kingdom* analogy."

Ginger's eyes moistened with a surge of adoration.

Now I wanted to puke.

"The perpetrator made her demands known. Now she's got to tell us where to make the drop. That's when I become the cheetah in the tall grass and she becomes the antelope."

Ginger liked the analogy so much she crawled up her boyfriend's arm.

"You're quite the cat," I told Jablonsky. "The problem is we haven't gotten a call in more than a week. What if this antelope has drifted off never to be heard from again?"

"Think positive," the cop said. "Greed always prevails."

Fitzgerald started braying for another bourbon and water. His mood was blackening with each additional ounce of whiskey. Normally, I'd cut off a drinker before he became even more inebriated and dangerous. Fitzgerald was a different case. The man's penchant for confrontation was swirling around him like an emotional disturbance. His hand would have wrapped too easily around my neck and given me the chiropractic adjustment of a lifetime. Jablonsky would have felt professionally obligated to intervene, and escalation would become inevitable. Having the leather-clad Jablonsky at the other end of the bar with a pretty girl wrapped around his bicep and a loaded weapon in his armpit didn't help. Jablonsky's angular youth reminded Fitzgerald of things he would rather forget, that he was far into the aging process and was rapidly becoming a paler copy of his previous self. He couldn't command a room or a woman's attention like ten or twenty years ago. It was a sobering realization that he aggressively smothered with great depths of intoxication.

I wished Vinny was around because he had the balls to tell Fitzgerald to pack it in.

"Why don't you take a break," I said. "Too much alcohol isn't good for you. It dehydrates the body. How about a club soda?"

Fitzgerald slid his glass toward me. "I'll suck on the ice cubes."

Twenty-two days after leaving for Italy, and fifteen days later than expected, Vinny and Uncle Nunzio returned to American soil. We all gathered at the restaurant for the Great Man's triumphant return. Opera streamed from the sound system while we moved silently, concerned about the man we were about to be reunited with. Yes, our Lazarus-like uncle had done yet another elusive dance step around The Grim Reaper, but we were yet to find out what toll had been exacted.

A frosty plume of air billowed through the front door when they arrived. We stared fixedly as the while cloud dissipated and a large shape stepped through. An oversized eggplant-colored overcoat and matching fedora materialized before us. The man under the hat, the man who had just suffered a massive heart attack looked as though ... *he had been vacationing at an alpine health spa!* There was nothing of the calamity. His shoulders were pulled back and his chest elevated as if to show off his reclaimed cardiac muscle.

The old man greeted us with aplomb, taking his fedora in hand and holding it forth in salutation. He might have been Mikhail Gorbachev setting free the communist masses, if not for the hair and absence of a port stain on his forehead. The fat ladies singing recorded opera were seemingly aware of the moment and rose to their highest, most grandiose octave. Maria's nostrils flared.

"Long live Uncle Nunzio," we all chanted in Italian. *"Zio Nunzio lungo vivo!"*

Limelight beamed from all around him.

Vinny stepped out from behind his uncle to give us a victory smile, one that took some pride in bringing our uncle home alive. There has to be something good in this for me too, Vinny figured. All those hours of bedside vigil had to count for something. Surely his uncle was seeing that his nephew had been dutiful and patient in his ministrations. Surely, short of the recipes becoming part of the public domain, his uncle would allow him to retain full and unalloyed ownership of the restaurant. He had earned it. He had taken up where his uncle left off. The place was setting revenue records. So what if he flunked family history and the ancestral language. Those were shortfalls that could easily be ameliorated, if not outright ignored.

Nunzio held up a hand to silence the chants. "Never count me out," he said. The voice was strong and zealous. "I always make a comeback."

We applauded and took turns approaching Uncle Nunzio to kiss his cheeks and express our concern. His Old Spice aftershave ornately seasoned the air. Ginger helped shed his overcoat and exhorted him to adopt her low-fat vegetarian diet. Angie and Maria offered to team-up to fix their uncle something to eat. Maria suggested a seafood risotto. "The shrimp and scallops were just pulled out of the Atlantic," she said. He smiled and then assented with a minuscule nod.

Angie headed to the kitchen, where she used a strong arm to stir and stir the rice mixture with all it component parts and sea creatures.

Father asked his brother, "What did the doctors say about your ticker?"

"They said I got a heart like a buffalo. Any other man would have been dead."

"Oh, listen to you," Mother Magherita said. "We heard you turned blue."

Vinny said, "A couple of angioplasties and the man's golden."

"It wasn't just the doctors who pulled me through," Nunzio said, augmented the words with a wagging finger. "You can chalk this up to the restorative powers of Italian culture. The food, the drink, the language, the love."

"Hey buster," Ginger said, "all those prayers we said didn't hurt either."

"I mean, look at me. I feel stupendous. Two weeks in that hospital and I didn't lose a pound. The Marcianos came down from the mountains with pans of food and flasks of wine. When they weren't around I sent Vinny out to my favorite Roman restaurants to pick up to-go orders."

As the family feted, the lissome form of Amy Stonebreaker could be seen discreetly working the perimeter, setting up tables for the evening dinner crowd, waiting for an appropriate moment to offer her boss a proper greeting. First, though, the family had to have their due. As the gathering dissipated, Vinny made his move, hustling her into the coat room for a fast round of cloak and dagger. He kissed Amy hard on the mouth and petted her nerve centers with heavy hands. He insisted on knowing how many men she slept with in his absence. Just two, she told him. Vinny felt a pang of jealousy at being outscored two-to-one, though he consoled himself with the certainty that his encounter was far more memorable than her two put together.

Nunzio looked up at the dining room ceiling. Much progress had been made by Enrico Zepeda. The fresco was almost complete. Nearly the entire ceiling was filled with images. There were soft yellows, burnt oranges and verdigris. Celestial bodies floated overhead and from behind them a heavenly light glowed. Cherubs with small wings and tiny penises were in flight, angels sang, saints wept and demigods mustered fury. It was all there — the agonies of those pursuing an elusive Creator, and the riotous ecstasies of those surrendering to fleshly temptations. Zepeda had struck a precarious balance between the sacramental and the bacchanal, God and Lucifer brought into perfect equilibrium. What was life if not a bundle of contradictions and ambiguities and opposing forces?

It was not the Sistine Chapel, but for the first time Nunzio felt connection. Though he never liked the idea of spending thousands to turn the ceiling into an immovable piece of art, he was coming around because what he saw brimmed with biblical influence.

Nunzio's neck was going stiff. He made the sign of the cross across his forehead and chest, then sat and consumed two dishes of seafood risotto. Fatigue began to creep, so he excused himself and headed home to rest.

As the honored guest exited the building the phone rang. I answered from behind the bar and immediately recognized the balmy young voice on the other end. Pressing the mouthpiece against my stomach, I wildly snapped my fingers to get Vinny's attention.

"The call's for you," I said. "It's the one you've been expecting."

Vinny lips turned bloodless. "Put her on hold."

I complied and said, "She's waiting on line one."

Vinny made an unsteady move for the area between the kitchen and the bar, where a flight of stairs led to his basement office. His descent was shared by a cavalcade of his siblings who crowded into the office.

"Privacy," he said, jostling us back out of the room and bolting the door shut.

I went upstairs and placed an emergency call to sergeant detective Clyde Jablonsky, urging him to get to the Marciano's Mangia House forthwith.

Vinny sat. A deep and controlled breath was taken. Then there was deep and controlled breath number two. He activated the recording and tracing device and picked up the phone. "Vinny Marciano speaking."

"Welcome home Vinny."

It was her, there was no question. The same damp enunciation. "Who's speaking please?"

"Aren't you clever? It's the one you can't get out of your mind, the one with her hand wrapped around your testicles."

"Welcome back from where?" Vinny said, quizzing the caller.

"Italy, of course."

Vinny's brain went on tilt. The room unhitched itself and started to spin and wobble. She's right on top of him, he told himself. Knows my every move. When I shit, she smells it.

"How did you know that?"

"I keep a very close eye on you."

"This is crazy. You have something that belongs to me, now give it back."

"Yes," she cooed, "that's exactly what I want to do. We have some unfinished business. You owe me a large sum of money."

"I have no proof you really have the recipes."

The caller recited a few pasta sauce additives, including mashed capers and pureed sun-dried tomatoes.

The bile migrated from Vinny's stomach to throat, its alkaline taste registering on the tongue. "So you read Italian," he said.

"I read your mind," she said, "and I know what you're trying to do. Don't antagonize me or the price will go up."

"Why this taunting? I've already agreed to give you the money, now tell me where to deliver the ransom and let's get this over with."

"Very soon. Just a few more preparations and you'll receive my instructions. They will be explicit and foolproof. They will be followed exactly. I hope you're good at following instructions because if you screw them up I'll assume a double-cross. Don't think about getting the cops involved because they won't be able to help you. Besides, they'll never catch me."

"When will we meet?" Vinny asked. She produced a condescending giggle. "Have we met before? Did I do something to offend you? Is that what this is about? It all seems very personal."

"You're not recording this phone call, are you?"

"Of course not."

"You're such a liar," she said with a girlish lilt. "Lying's a sin."

"I'm not."

"Oh, shut up. You most certainly are. You would be an idiot not to. Maybe you're not as smart as I thought."

"When should I expect your call?"

"Tell your uncle I hope he's feeling better."

A dial tone signaled the end of the conversation.

Vinny hung up the phone, walked into the restroom, bent over a white porcelain toilet and vomited until the lining of his esophagus sustained second degree burns.

After cleaning up he went back to the recording device, replayed the conversation, went back to the restroom and vomited again. This time he experienced none of the nausea and discomfort associated with regurgitation because he had already dissociated and was observing the scene from above, having left his body and drifted up to the whirring ventilation fan. A fresh geyser of terror sprang. If he was floating, he was lighter than air, something approximating vapor, which meant the fan could suck him out of the room, haul him through the ductwork and blow him outside the building, separating him from his body for all eternity. Looking down Vinny saw his physical body in its wretched state. He had heard of this happening to people in cases of extreme anxiety or temporary death. If he was up here, who was running things down there, where one idiotic move could ruin his future? Don't do anything stupid, he wanted to shout to himself, if only he knew how. All he was capable of doing was floating, which didn't take any effort, and praying that he didn't come under the pull of the spinning blades just above what seemed to be his right ear.

Behind that panic ran a second, cooler train of thought that contemplated the irony of how people spent their whole lives searching for incontrovertible proof that they existed independent of their body, only to find themselves horrified at the prospect of not having a body. How does one act without a body? Everything needs a container. What could spirit do when it's not suffused with flesh and blood?

Before Vinny knew what happened he was back in his body, doubting he had ever really left it. His head was balanced over the toilet bowl's rim and he was gasping for air and staring into the fetid water. Hallucination, he thought, brought on by temporary psychosis. When his breathing returned to its usual pace and the burning sensation in his esophagus subsided, Vinny took a head count, making sure every Marciano was accounted for and acting normally. If anyone was in cahoots with the blackmailer, they must have known the call was coming, maybe even tipped her off that Vinny was back in the Mangia House. That person would surely be trying to look as inconspicuous as possible, and that wasn't normal behavior for a Marciano.

The inquiry turned up nothing. The next sound Vinny heard was the arrogant tempo of boots against a hardwood floor, and he knew Clyde Jablonsky's footwear was announcing his arrival. Vinny turned and there he was, a tall order of denim, leather and strategically tousled hair. Everything about him said he was ready to take charge. But take charge of what? He was too late. The conversation was over. All that remained was a rude and interminable dial tone. It spoke of no one and led to nowhere.

"What are you doing here?" Vinny said.

"Mickey called, said it was an emergency."

Vinny fired a serrated look at me. "My whole life has become an emergency," he told Jablonsky.

"Did you get a recording?" the detective asked.

Vinny nodded. "Listen for yourself."

I followed Jablonsky to the office. Vinny stayed upstairs, fearful of more regurgitation at the sound of his saboteur's voice.

Jablonsky came back to the main floor, his cocksure stride intact.

"Do you get it now?" Vinny said. "It's someone very close to me. She knows where I come and go."

"Listen to me," Jablonsky said, setting a reassuring hand on Vinny's shoulder. It's good news that she's close. That means we're within striking distance. She's vulnerable and doesn't even know it. The instructions for the drop are coming soon. That's when we'll corner her."

"Oh yeah, the cheetah," I said.

"What cheetah?" Vinny said.

Jablonsky shook his head. "Never mind that."

The third grand opening in Marciano's Mangia House history was staged on Saturday, December 3. The first had taken place back in 1946, the day Uncle Nunzio opened Marciano's. The second was seven years ago when Vinny reopened the Mangia House. On this evening, after months of painstaking planning and work, the grand opening of Enrico Zepeda's ceiling fresco was finally happening.

It event was a lollapalooza. Art and culinary critics from New York City newspapers and magazines were in attendance, including scribes from the *New York Times*, the *Wall Street Journal* and even *Vanity Fair* magazine. City and county dignitaries were milling about, as were local business leaders. Mort Stottlemyre was swirling a drink in his hand.

The dining room was swarming though not roaring. This is a different kind of group. They conversed in hushed tones out of reverence for artistic sensibilities and the heavenly scene floating high above them. The expensive new system of wall-mounted track lighting gave the sprawling depiction of celestial glow.

Everyone was looking up. Most of them were conversing eloquently about nothing.

"It's so expansive," one said.

"Total sensory overload," added another.

"I see terror. I see nostalgia."

"It's was all there, predator and prey locked in eternal battle."

At the center of all was the artist himself, Enrico Zepeda, and a man named Jimmy Greenspoon, the artist's manager and the proprietor of Exposure, one of Manhattan's most famous galleries and home to more original Zepeda canvases than any gallery. A charmed theatrical aura surrounded the two men, as well as a large throng of admirers and acquaintances. Zepeda was pointing skyward, explaining the nuances and intricacies of this milestone piece of work, by far the largest "canvas" he had ever produced. I was certain this was going to be the advent of a new era for Marciano's Mangia House. For the first time I wasn't feeling like just another family-member-turned-employee. Now I had made an indelible and enduring contribution to the family business. The Mangia House wasn't just a place to eat anymore, it had become a landmark with repute far beyond the local area, a place where art aficionados and gourmands would find special meaning.

For Enrico Zepeda it was the work of a lifetime. Thousands of people would be exposed to this brilliant and touching rendering of creation, Catholicism and human temptation and frailty. It was an electrifying scene rendered in the dazzling colors and bold brushstrokes that were in Zepeda's signature style.

There was a second, smaller throng and these were the people surrounding Uncle Nunzio. My uncle had arrived dubious and expressionless. He didn't see the need for such an addition to the restaurant. To his way of thinking it was extravagant. Uncle Nunzio's mood changed as soon as friends and dignitaries approached and turned him back into the bellowing social animal that was his true nature.

The dining room had been mostly cleared of its usual furniture and replaced with cocktail tables. Around the exterior were food stations. Piles of the restaurant's signature entrees and appetizers were everywhere, as were manned stations where made-to-order pastas and sautéed meat and vegetable dishes were tossed together. Father was busy seizing the moment, his ravenous, dripping tongue eating its way around the room while mother hectored and tried to pull him away.

"Can we get some pictures," called out one of the photographers. The swarm surrounding Zepeda and Greenspoon parted and the photographers opened fire. Greenspoon — a small, twitchy man with closely cropped black hair and a tight fitting skinny-suit like The Beatles wore on the Ed Sullivan Show — jerked spasmodically in the direction of every camera flash. It was as though he was electronically connected to the pulses of light. Then the photographers turned their cameras towards the fresco and started clicking again.

Vinny and I were both dressed in tuxedos. My brother walked up and put an arm across my shoulders. Both of us were holding a glass of Prosecco, the sparkling Italian wine that was our people's answer to French champagne.

"You know," he said, "this would not have happened without you."

My head bowed with modesty and embarrassment, though I wanted to hear more.

"This is all you. I never would've thought of this. You had to sell me on the idea. Then we had to sell Uncle Nunzio. I think what you've done here is amazing. I cannot thank you enough."

Then my brother hugged me. I had never heard Vinny be so articulate and charitable. This soirée was touching him in an unexpected way.

The glow of the moment lasted only until Father Albie sidled up, looking pretty sharp in his tuxedo, black bow tie.

"What a colossal waste of money this is," he said. "It's bad enough you spend all this cash on a painting, look at all this food and drink you're giving away. None of this was necessary."

"Dad you just don't get it," Vinny said. "I'm sorry to say that but you just don't get it."

"I know when my son is squandering his money. We could have just told people that the restaurant has some new artwork and to come out and see it. At least then they would have paid for their own dinners. Doesn't that make a lot more sense? Look at all these people carrying on like this place has just been turned into a goddam Sistine Chapel."

My chest was tightening. I turned and walked away. I didn't get very far when I ran across Sadie, who had given me minor assistance me in planning the festivities.

"I'm responsible for this event," Sadie cried.

"All the more reason not to be acting like a spastic colon," I snapped. "Be happy. It's a big hit."

Sadie stormed away. As I watched her trail off, she brushed past Father Benito Saragusa in his white collar and black vestments. Saragusa was staring up at the ceiling fresco with his mouth hanging open, his eyes shifting in his face. There was full catastrophe hedonism floating just 15 feet above Saragusa's bald head. When he came upright again he rubbed his neck and shook his head. After making the sign of the cross, the priest started moving through the crowd with great purpose, looking for somebody, looking and looking. When he found Vinny the little clergyman used a hand to clasp my brother's shoulder and turn him.

"Vinny, what in hades is this?" He gestured towards the heavens. Vinny reflexively looked up and then right back down and into the priest's eyes.

"What? It's a fresco. Mr. Zepeda's latest work of art."

"I know about Mr. Zepeda's so-called works of art. I've been trying to get them off these godforsaken walls for years. You don't listen to me."

The air came out of Vinny at the thought of yet another lecture from Father Saragusa about female nudity and men's prurient interests. Only a Catholic priest could look at that fresco consider it a source of sexual stimulus.

"Father, take a closer look," Vinny said, pointing out elements of the tableau. "There's a depiction of the creation day, the resurrection of Christ, the Virgin Mary, and look at the angels and the trumpets being blown."

"Yes," Saragusa said, "and look at how they're being desecrated by those milky breasts and scenes of violence. I count at least five little penises on those cherubs. Can't this man ever keep people's clothes on while he's painting them?"

"Father, this is not the night for one of your sermons. I'm having too good a time, and so is everybody else here. You're taking his artwork too seriously."

Saragusa glanced at the fresco once again. "The temptation. The hormones. I'm starting to think that you've got a dirty mind, Vinny, that your dirty person. It's an insult that you invited me to witness this."

"I didn't invite you, Father. You came to the restaurant to have dinner, not realizing that we're not open to the public tonight. I didn't want to turn you away so I told you to stay."

Saragusa's face turned acidic. Vinny motioned towards one of the makeshift bars. "Please, Father, grab yourself a glass of red wine and enjoy yourself. There are plenty of sacraments up there, let's drink to those."

Instead, Saragusa made some hand gestures that normally would have been a blessing, though it looked more like an exorcism in this case. Then the little clergymen turned and walked vigorously out of the building.

In time, the attendees were brought to full attention and Jimmy Greenspoon and Enrico Zepeda were handed microphones. Greenspoon spoke first.

"This is artistic brilliance writ large," he said, motioning toward the fresco. "This man is not just a successful painter, he is a painter of consequence. The first time I cast eyes on his artwork I was astonished. His creativity is without reserve. I knew I had to represent him. Enrico Zepeda's ascent in the New York art world has been unlike anything I've ever seen. He has amassed an amazing body of work, and this installation may well be his crowning achievement."

Zepeda cleared his throat. "Some thought this was a Sisyphean task. And, indeed, it took months for me to complete this. There were times I had my doubts, but there you have it. What you see are the poetics of sin, spirituality and temptation. They blend beautifully and their co-existence is mandatory because one cannot exist without the other."

The artist's Spanish accent bathed the room as he described the tableau broadly and then minutely. When he heard the first mumblings of a restive audience, Zepeda wrapped up his comments.

Then Mayor Gayland Fabrezio stepped up dressed in a three-piece suit, while his small retinue of assistants stretched out the ribbon. Uncle Nunzio, Vinny and I lined up to one side of the mayor. On the other side were in Zepeda and Greenspoon. The mayor, his head topped by a shock of thick white hair, read a declaration that said "whereas" this and "whereas" that. The important language noted that Marciano's Mangia House had been designated a historic monument by the Endicott City Council. As such it would be preserved in its current form in perpetuity, and that included the new fresco. The mayor handed of the declaration to Uncle Nunzio, owner of the property. Then he handed the giant scissors to Vinny, who thanked the mayor and, with little hesitation or ceremony, cut the ribbon in half to a burst of cheers and applause. Photographic pulses of light were again chopping up the scene. Honored guests and dignitaries gave one another hearty handshakes and congratulations.

As the grouping dissolved, Angie walked up and said, "You didn't invite that big, ugly detective did you?"

"You mean Jablonski?"

Angie snorted. "I'm talking about that drunken Irishman."

"Naw. I don't think you fit in here."

Angie started talking about missing documents, and the overall worthlessness of her brother's management style. I tried to throw her off course, but the bile kept bubbling from her throat. The conversation curdled. We finished our interlude in silence.

I was reactivated when Amy Stonebreaker came floating past in a bustier that accentuated her diminutive bustline. She looked lovely with her hair mostly pinned up and loose tresses falling to her bare neck and shoulders. Vinny walked up to his girlfriend and twisted her head to plant a kiss on her lips. Amy could tell by his manner and exhilaration that Vinny was tuned-up for another night of violent athleticism in the bedroom.

Then Vinny came up behind Uncle Nunzio and gave his shoulders a rub before leaning forward and saying, "What do you think, boss?"

"Primo," Nuncio crowed.

That favored term would be used by Nunzio several more times during the next few weeks as exuberant publicity of the event and fresco brought tidal surges of new business. Nightly and weekly sales records were broken. I was flying high.

Zepeda visited the Mangia House a few times during that period to observe and re-experience the excitement of its unveiling. He complained of the emotional letdown that is the aftermath of any climactic event.

It was also during this period that Vinny pressed Zepeda hard to agree to an "interview" with Wes Fitzgerald. Zepeda had never said *no* or *yes* to that idea. He just offered the excuse that he was too consumed by the fresco to divide his attention between that and anything else. With that behind him, the artist felt an obligation to Vinny.

Zepeda had seen Fitzgerald and took an immediate dislike to the man. Fitzgerald was a junkyard dog as far as Zepeda was concerned — sneering and crude. He told me the detective's face was full of hatred and mistrust. Fitzgerald reminded Zepeda of the thugs that slain president Alejandra Garcia used to send after him. He could taste blood in his mouth. The whole idea of answering some investigator's questions felt accusatory to Zepeda. Vinny insisted that wasn't the case, that Zepeda might have seen something that would help the Fitzgerald solve the case.

When the artist assented it was with certain stipulations. He would pick the date, time and location. That would be Saturday at noon in a Binghamton coffeehouse named Laveggio Roasteria. Zepeda wanted an environment that would cool the big, angry detective's penchant for antagonism and violence. If anything did go down, there would be plenty of witnesses. Zepeda figured he had already faced down gangs of Garcia's thugs in Guatemala, so one American detective wasn't going to intimidate him. Of course, he was younger back then, brash and in better shape. So, just in case, Zepeda attended the meeting with a small canister pepper spray in his front right pocket.

"You've been avoiding me," Fitzgerald grumbled. "Why?"

"What is your next question?"

"You didn't answer the first one," Fitzgerald said, revealing dishwater-colored teeth.

"This is absurd," Zepeda said. "October 9 was a long time ago and I don't remember anything of that day.

"You'd be surprised what people remember when they put their mind to it — and what they learn about themselves when they're being interviewed. That is, when they cooperate with the process."

"In this case I'm learning more about you than me."

"I'm learning some things too. People who get combative usually have something to hide. That's something experience has taught me. Now where were on October 9?"

Zepeda didn't answer.

"You were on the roof."

"I'm a painter. You have me mixed up with the roofer."

"You know what the hell I mean. Where were on October 9?"

"Is that a special day for you?"

"Something valuable to me went missing that day," Fitzgerald said.

"Valuable to you?"

Fitzgerald's cold reply came back: "Yeah, to me."

"Are you talking about documents? Pieces of paper? What do those pieces of paper say that has you so riled up?"

Zepeda discreetly reached into his right pocket. The move registered on Fitzgerald's face, and Zepeda noticed that Fitzgerald noticed. That didn't keep Zepeda from wrapping his hand around the canister of pepper spray. It was good that Fitzgerald noticed. That meant he knew Zepeda was armed with something. He didn't know what, but he figured the cop's imagination was outlandish and was conjuring notions of something more dangerous than pepper spray, maybe even something lethal. Cops saw that shit every day; it wouldn't be a surprise.

Fitzgerald's immense hand was now wrapped around the paper cup of steaming black coffee. Zepeda considered that one jut of this idiot's hand and sixteen ounces of steaming hot coffee would be splashed across his mug, eyes and face scalded, and the goon would be on top of him, wailing away. Just a few pile-driving fists would almost certain require a trip to a maxillofacial surgeon to reassemble bone fragments and suture lacerated skin. Fitzgerald could blow out of the coffeehouse before most of the customers knew what was happening. And who was going to step in front of the onrushing man of his size and intimidation to detain or question him. That would come later when the cops visited him, and that would be little more than a police fraternity party. Fitzgerald would be released without charges, just a cop excused by his fraternity brothers for good naturedly crossing the line. This is exactly why Zepeda opposed the idea of dealing with a sick fuck like Fitzgerald. This guy would have made a good member of Garcia's death squad. He told Fitz that.

"You think so? Thanks for the compliment, pal. That's a good reason not to play your sissy games with me."

"You're sick, you know that? You're sick and you don't even know it. Not only are you sick, you're intoxicated. What was that additive you put in your coffee? Some brandy for lunch?"

Fitzgerald surveyed the crowd, as though calculating the odds. "You want to make this simple or difficult? I can do this either way," he said, broadening his arms just enough that the ratty lapels of his blazer parted and flashed on his holstered revolved. A pistol-whipping could come in no time flat. "I like doing it the hard way. That's my favorite. But you won't like it, that's a fucking guarantee Picasso."

We had just finished watching *Raging Bull* for the eleventh time on Vinny's giant high-definition TV screen and were again marveling about the acting partnership between Robert De Niro and Joe Pesci that had persevered for decades through movies such as *Goodfellas* and *Casino*. We sprawled on his living-room sectional and sipped away at the last of our second bottle of Chianti. Then my brother's mood turned dark with a recounting of the chain of events that had befallen him this winter. Time was running out, and he considered it increasingly inevitable that Uncle Nunzio would take action, dethroning and humiliating him by placing the restaurant back under his own control — or, far worse, putting the two-headed monster of Angie and Maria in charge.

Vinny mused that he would probably move out of state and open an Italian supper club. If that failed to enrich him at a level he was accustomed to, perhaps he would enter the porn business while he was still young enough to make a name for himself. Then he started complaining about how the sex trade was all free on the internet and there was probably no money to be made banging and abusing women.

"I should have gone for it years ago, back when people were still going to the Triple X cinemas and buying videos. At least no one could have stolen my dick."

Vinny's cell phone started chirping like a sparrow. He gazed at the screen and smirked. "It's Frankenstein." He answered on speaker with a, "Yeah, what?"

The detective's gruff tobacco-cured voice said: "Yo, I've got the recipes and the scumbag who stole them in custody. You're not gonna believe this."

Vinny bolted upright and my brother's face flushed red. *"Who is she?"* Vinny was shouting. Finally, the call he had been waiting for. "What does she look like? Don't let her get away!"

"Believe me, this one isn't going anywhere."

"Who is it?"

"You have to see it to believe it."

"Don't fuck around. Tell me who it is?"

"Let's just say the perpetrator's indisposed at the moment."

"I want to know who the fuck it is!" A blood vessel in Vinny's temple was pulsing.

"Don't get your jockey shorts in a bunch. I've got the person in an abandoned warehouse that a friend gives me access to for these purposes. I'm in Binghamton. Get your ass to 932 Upper Front Street, pronto."

The line went dead. Vinny was having conniptions grabbing his winter coat and wrestling his body into it, sweeping the keys off the counter as he hustled for the door. I dashed after him.

Vinny broke every speed limit along the way by multiples of two and sometimes three, and he spent most of the drive gurgling in satanic verses about what he was going to do to the cunt. Beneath the gurgling I could also detect an odd undercurrent of relief in his voice.

Halfway to our destination, Vinny called Fitzgerald.

"I wanna know what this bitch looks like before I butt-fuck her for punishment."

"Better reconsider that one," Fitzgerald said.

"What do they say?" Vinny barked. "The recipes. Read some to me."

"I can't read the fucking things, they're in *I-talian*. You have to do your own translation. And make sure you bring a goddam check. And it better be good this time or I'll wring your guinea neck."

The line went dead.

Vinny glanced over to me and nodded, realizing that Fitzgerald had the genuine articles in hand. I rummaged inside a large, blue duffel bag Vinny had slung between the seats when we climbed into the van.

"Leave that stuff alone," he told me.

I ignored him and started taking an inventory. A miniature Adirondack aluminum baseball bat. Brass knuckles. Rope. Switchblade. BernzOmatic trigger-start handheld torch.

"What the hell is *this*," I said, extending the butane torch next to his face.

"Put it back. It might come in handy."

The abandoned warehouse was a dingy four-story brick shell. It was situated in one of those parts of Binghamton that nobody went at night. A faint light was glowing within. The back entryway was slightly ajar. It seemed as though the door might fall off as Vinny wrenched it open. Fitzgerald's voice blasted the air. "Second floor," he shouted.

We scaled the metal staircase and followed the brightening glow into a large open space. A light was hanging from the ceiling. A chair had been positioned below it. Standing next to the chair was Fitzgerald, and sitting in the chair was a shadowy figure with wrists and ankles duct-taped to the arms and legs of the chair. We moved closer and our eyes bulged with the recognition of who we were looking at. There, sitting in the chair, with a head that looked as though it had been used for a soccer match, was Father Benito Saragusa. He looked to be only half-conscious and was having trouble holding his head up straight. There were several contusions and at least one abrasion on his face. Below that he was attired in his ceremonial black robe and white collar, though the collar was askew and looked ready to pop out of his neckline. What little hair he had was seriously mussed. Fitzgerald had obviously had his way with him.

"*You!*" Vinny said.

"There must be some kind of mistake," I said. "Where's the girl who's been calling?"

"There is no girl," Fitzgerald said.

Vinny shot a blazing look at Fitzgerald.

"Disappointing, I know. I found this." A small electronic box was being held aloft in his hand. "It's a voice synthesizer. Adjust the setting just right and this thing could make me sound like Shirley Temple. I hooked it up, spoke through it myself and my voice came through all breathy and girly, just like your caller," he said, tilting his head toward the sad, little man bonded to the chair. "That's when I started tearing this guy's residence apart. He doesn't know much about hiding contraband."

Vinny grabbed the synthesizer from Fitzgerald and stuffed it in the duffel bag.

Saragusa was madly trying to communicate through the rectangle of duct tape glued over his mouth. "*Mother of God*," I said, rushing to Saragusa and stripping away the tape.

"*Ugh*," Saragusa gasped. "Mickey, Vinny, oh thank God. Help me. This man is crazy."

Fitzgerald told me to keep my hands off his prisoner.

"Water," the priest said, "I need water."

"You're in an abandoned warehouse," Fitzgerald said, "there's no running water. This place barely has electricity."

"I'm so sorry," the clergyman groaned. "It's not what you think. I'm not really a criminal."

Fitzgerald let out the closest thing he had to a laugh. "That's one of the things you learn in my business. Nobody thinks they're a criminal, even if they've knocked over Fort Knox."

"I'm a sinner," Siragusa admitted, "I know that. I have sinned. I'm a man. I wanted to be a demigod. In the end, I'm just a man. I aspired to so much more. You have no idea."

"These were in his living quarters too," Fitzgerald said, dangling a stethoscope. "He must have used this to listen to the tumblers fall when cracking your safe. I'm telling people all the time that a safe is no barrier for real criminal. But this fucking guy," Fitzgerald said gesturing with the stethoscope, "ain't no real criminal. It all makes sense, though. Nobody suspects a priest of a larceny like this. He took advantage of his station in life and snatched you blind."

"Whoa," Vinny said, his hands in the air. "Back up, man. You went to the church? To the rectory? You were in his residence? What the fuck?"

"I took my feeble old mother to the novena on Tuesday night. They had a parish gathering in the church basement after the service and were serving some food and drink. I smelled something in the air, not quite the pasta sauce, but there was something familiar, and the collared one started acting suspicious as soon as he saw me milling about. I mean the shit was coming out of his ears. I got suspicious. So I showed up later at his residence, unannounced. We talked while he was holding the door between us. I suggested we get more comfortable. He didn't want to let me in, so I lowered my shoulder and bulldozed past him and tied up the little guy. Then I started asking all the relevant questions and roughing him up. He didn't confess, but I knew." Fitzgerald looked over at the priest and said, "You need to go to confession

Father. Take some of your own medicine. You definitely have something to set straight with God."

Fitzgerald also explained that — despite the sport he made of sergeant detective Clyde Jablonsky's telephone recording machine — Jablonsky has given him copies of the recordings of the breathy girl demanding ransom, and Fitzgerald spent a lot of time listening and analyzing them. There were words and phrases that sounded suspiciously like the same ones used during Saragusa's sermon at the novena. Then came the odd behavior at the basement gathering, and that was all he needed to decide a surprise inspection of the premises was warranted. The voice synthesizer and stethoscope turned up quickly.

"That's when I got really aggressive and physical with the questioning and started tearing the place apart. Let me tell you, he didn't put a lot of thought into hiding your recipes. Just slipped them behind a row of books. Of course, why would a priest think anybody would show up and search his place? After all," he said looking over a Saragusa, "we trust priests don't we? That's when I gagged and strong-armed him into my car and headed over here. The mouth gag came loose during the drive and this guy started squealing, 'Where are you taking me?' I told him, 'Somewhere where I can take your confession.'"

Vinny's hands covered his face. I could hear a muffled *oh my god* slip through.

My nose felt as though it was bleeding. Adrenalin flowed. The place was saturated with violent impulse. I would have taken over the room if I had been a physically dominant man. But I was slight by comparison with my muscular brother and his home weight room, and half the size of the pickled sociopath with the revolver holstered in his armpit. If I possessed a firearm at that moment I might have actually used it.

"What about copies?" Vinny asked.

"There are none. I searched for those too. Nothing. As *laisse faire* as he was about hiding the originals, I doubt he put any thought into making copies and hiding them any better, on-site or off-site. But who the fuck knows for sure? Maybe here's got them stashed in the rectory with the nuns. Feel free to interrogate him for answers to that mystery. Or I could go shake the nuns up." He flashed a Halloween smile. "Maybe rap their knuckles with a metal ruler."

The decimated body glued to the chair started moaning and pleading. "Vinny, please, this man is a monster. You've got to help me. It's not what you think."

Vinny rushed Saragusa went into a spastic rant. "How could you do this to me? How could you do this to Uncle Nunzio? He's the most loyal parishioner you have? He must have stuffed half-a-million dollars in your goddam collection baskets through the years. He's going to be devastated when he hears what you've done. You're a priest! Thou shalt not steal! The sins of the father! The penalty for sin is death!"

Fitzgerald said, "Even I know *thou shalt not steal*, Father. That's the eighth commandment. There's only ten, you little twerp."

Vinny grabbed the priest by his vestments started shaking him, causing his head to fly all around. "You knew what was happening. I was confessing to you and to God in the holy chamber. This is the biggest breach of trust I have ever known." Vinny reared a fist back, as though ready to slug the priest, instead throwing a mock punch that *whooshed* past the front of the Saragusa's face, scaring the wits out of him.

"You *conned* me, you little bastard. And you toyed with me inside the confessional. You *knew* what you had done was tearing the family apart, and you still kept on. You must have been laughing like a jackal when I wasn't around."

"No," Saragusa moaned, "that is not true. And look what you have done. How could you send this gorilla after me?"

I pulled Vinny's arm to separate him from the priest. "We have to let him go. This isn't right. He's a good man. It was a momentary lapse in judgment."

"Are you nuts?" Vinny said.

Saragusa was stirring again. "Vinny, please, I can explain."

I walked up to Saragusa and put my hands on his wrists and leaned my head close to his battered face. He averted my eyes at every turn. The man who had spent his life commanding the attention and fealty of audiences had been plundered and dishonored. I could smell his fear. "Father, just come out with the truth. Do you admit that you did this, Father?"

"I confess," he said. "I did it, but I can explain."

Fitzgerald chuckled. "Every criminal has their extenuating circumstances."

The priest cried, "For the love of god, Vinny. Can't you see what he's trying to do to us? He's trying to turn brother against brother."

Fitzgerald whacked Saragusa in the back of the head, titling the holy man's white collar further ajar.

"Stop that!" I said. "The man's heart is going to stop. My god, Vinny, put an end to this right now. Whatever he did, he's a priest. The man has spent his life doing good things. You have to forgive him for this."

The detective gave me one of his routine, ugly expressions and said, "Don't you know anything about human nature? Men, like horses, need to be broken." Then he turned back to Saragusa with a fresh threat: "You could be dead real easy, and I know how to get rid of dead bodies. They'll never find your corpse, I can guarantee you that."

There seemed nothing in this world that the vulgar private-eye did not feel entitled to violate. I reconsidered my non-belief in the existence of evil.

Vinny extended a hand toward Fitzgerald and said, "The recipes."

The detective rubbed the fingertips of one hand together to indicate it was time to remit payment for his solving the case. My brother dug into a coat pocket and handed him a slip of slip of paper. In an act of superstition, Vinny had filled out the $10,000 check weeks ago, thinking it would want to be cashed and somehow supernaturally make events transpire to that end.

Fitzgerald took the check and inspected it, holding it up the weak lighting before pocketing it. The recipes were tucked inside the back of Fitzgerald's pants. He pulled them out and even from a distance Vinny could recognize them. "I'll hold onto these until the check clears," Fitzgerald said, flapping laminated documents in the air.

"Fuck that noise," Vinny said. "They cannot be out of my possession any longer." Fitzgerald put the hand holding the recipes behind his back and gave Vinny his best *who-says-so?* look. Vinny was raging as he moved in. Fitzgerald extended an arm to keep him at bay. The two men scuffled. I moved closer but knew better than to get involved, unless that crazy motherfucker detective reached for his firearm. Then I saw the recipes still flapping in his hand. He was too pre-occupied trying to show Vinny who's boss to even notice that I had snatched them and moved across the room. I waved them at Vinny and he broke free of big Irishman and dashed over to take possession, girlishly clutching them to his chest.

"Ah, what the fuck," Fitzgerald said. "I know where to find you."

Vinny carefully examined the laminated sheaves of paper and confirmed authenticity. Then he stepped up to the bound man in the chair and said, "Forgive me father for I have sinned," and slapped Saragusa across the mouth.

"Now you're talking," Fitzgerald said. "Hit him again, harder this time. You'll feel better if you slap him a few more times. Release some of that anger. It works real nice for me."

"You are one sick bastard," I told Fitzgerald. In a seethe he strode toward me. Vinny headed him off.

"And you're just a weasel," he shouted past Vinny's shoulder.

I kept pressing Vinny to let Father Saragusa go, appealing to his sense of the legal jeopardy that we could be facing if accused of participating in a kidnapping.

"Oh, please," Fitzgerald interjected.

My brother looked me in the face, his eyes slightly tearing. "Do you have any idea what I've been going through?"

"It's over now," I said. "You have the recipes. Be grateful you've been made whole again. Find it in your heart to forgive."

"Listen to Mickey," Saragusa pleaded.

Vinny turned to the prisoner and then back to me: "I don't know if I can. Forgiveness is one of my greatest weaknesses."

"Forgive me Vinny," Saragusa croaked pathetically. "Think about your soul."

"I can't watch this anymore," I said turning away. "It's too sad. It's too sick."

I was already toiling with the moral dilemma of whether I would turn state's evidence on my brother if he killed or maimed. I didn't really think Vinny would kill somebody in a normal state of mind. It wasn't his nature. Now, though, he kept falling into rages and might easily take leave of his senses. It would not have surprised me if he took a piece of cutlery to carve the larynx out of his tormentor's throat.

"You're dismissed," Vinny told Fitzgerald. "Go cash that check and have some fun. I'll take it from here."

"Oh thank God," Siragusa sighed.

"That's not a bad idea," Fitzgerald said, slipping into his Burlington coat and leather gloves. "I've earned a few cool ones, I'd say." He slapped the priest one more time before exiting.

After the detective's footsteps and other parting sounds faded to oblivion, Vinny grabbed his duffel bag and started rummaging, eventually extracting and flipping open the switchblade. As he moved toward the Father Saragusa, the robed priest fruitlessly began to screaming and convulsing to try to break free of the chair, imagining the worst, that Vinny had gone temporarily insane and was about to commit a homicide of passion. I opened my mouth to yell. Nothing came out. Saragusa broke into prayer, was crying out for divine intervention when the tip of Vinny's switchblade quickly and cleanly slit open the duct tape, first around his ankles and then his wrists. Peeling the tape away, Vinny set the disgraced clergymen free.

We walked a limp Saragusa to the van, as though still in our custody. Vinny swung open the van's back doors and threw the priest inside. He said, "You're going home Father."

Saragusa, pupils still dilated, asked, "In the biblical or temporal sense?"

"Back to the rectory."

The priest exhaled and tumbled onto the mattress. By comparison it felt heavenly. Then he began to wonder how many sins of the flesh had been committed on the Sealy Posturepedic. There were probably splotches of DNA all over it. What a disgusting thought.

Saragusa howled the Stations of the Cross almost the entire drive back to Endicott, praying…

> *Mary, my Mother, you were the first to live the Way of the Cross.*
> *You felt every pain and every humiliation.*
> *You were unafraid of the ridicule heaped upon you by the crowds.*
> *Your eyes were ever on Jesus and His Pain.*
> *Is that the secret of your miraculous strength?*
> *How did your loving heart bear such a burden and such a weight?*
> *As you watched Him stumble and fall, were you tortured*
> *by the memory of all the yesterdays,*
> *His birth, His hidden life and His ministry?*

Vinny's head was splitting. He threatened to turn Saragusa back over to Fitzgerald if he didn't shut his yapper.

When we came to a halt by the rectory at Our Lady of the Immaculate Conception, my brother yanked open the van's back doors. *"Get out."*

The disheveled, bruised figure barely had the energy to make the thirty-foot stroll to his door.

It seemed the Missing Recipe Saga had finally come to an end.

Vinny found himself back at Uncle Nunzio's doorstep, standing in the grip of the relentlessly cold air. He had been rehearsing his soliloquy, ready to disclose all the details in such eloquence that Nunzio would be reticent to interrupt. It was all about the delivery.

The door swung open. The plume of air that escaped the house was rich with fine aromas. The Great Man again had a newspaper folded under his armpit, and a smoldering El Producto protruding from his mouth. It was early. His face was still puffy from the night's slumber. The stare was blank. Vinny handed over a white ten-by-twelve inch envelope.

"This what I think it is?"

Vinny nodded. The end of cigar flamed brilliant red, and a cloud of white smoke came from the corner of the mouth and floated away in slow, distorted motion. Nunzio lifted the envelope's flap, extracted the laminated recipes, gave them a careful examination, stuffed them back in the envelope and nestled them under the same armpit as the morning newspaper.

"These are going to the bank and my safe deposit box."

Vinny opened his mouth to say something, but Nunzio held up a conductor's hand and brought the notion to an instant halt.

"No time for this," he said. "Busy, busy, busy."

How could a man speak so clearly with a large object stuck in his face? The door swung closed. Vinny stood on the stoop for a good long while, unsure what to make of his uncle's curt behavior. He was about to give Nunzio a sanitized version of where the recipes were found, how they had been pilfered, the shocking culprit, and so on. Nunzio would have pummeled

Vinny for the way Father Saragusa had been brutalized, though he apparently wanted to be none the wiser. Or perhaps Father Benito Saragusa had already gone to Nunzio on bended knee to explain this transgression and beg forgiveness. Maybe the priest was trying to get out in front of the situation, tell his own version of events and underplay the severity of his sins. If so, Uncle Nunzio would have seen the priest's battered face and known that something violent had taken place. He would have questioned the priest and probably been told the complete and sordid tale. Nunzio would have been revolted. It would have placed Vinny's future as Mangia House proprietor back in jeopardy, even with the recipes retrieval. Now it became apparent to Vinny that it was an oversight that he did not demand some assurance that Nunzio would be left out of the conversation, that his battered face at Sunday services be explained away as a tumble down the rectory stairs.

Vinny finally stepped off Nunzio's stoop, walked to the Econoline van and drove for the restaurant. He called Father Siragusa's phone at the rectory. The priest answered so weakly one would have guessed he was suffering the flu. Vinny said, "I'm just checking on your welfare. It was a rough night."

Saragusa said nothing. Vinny couldn't even hear breathing. Then Vinny asked the priest if he had called Uncle Nunzio in the past 24 hours. Saragusa huffed just a bit. "So that's your big concern?"

Silence.

Saragusa finally said, "I've had no communication with your uncle for days. Has that satisfied your need to know?" Vinny quietly hung up the phone.

That evening the restaurant was sold out again all night. Vinny was pleased to see several patrons staring up at the fresco and pointing to some of its features. Uncle Nunzio walked in the door near closing time. He walked behind the bar, edged his way past me. I opened my butane lighter and got his cigar smoking again while he poured himself a glass of Primitivo. He carried the serving of wine around the place, clinking glasses with friends and longtime patrons. Eventually he made his way to Vinny and blew two smoke rings.

"You have your restaurant back," he said.

It was then Vinny realized that every muscle in his body had been tensed for many weeks. Even internal organs seemed to relax in one sudden glorious release. Vinny expelled some air.

"For *now*," Nunzio said.

"For now?"

"Everything in life, other than family love, is conditional," Nunzio said. "Watch what you say. Watch what you do. You had better get yourself back in charge of this place. I'll be watching."

"I just wanted to say—"

"Never mind," Nunzio said. He was out the door and on the road in seconds.

Vinny was flabbergasted. The biggest crisis of the Great Man's business life and he didn't even ask who had robbed the safe, or about the potential that copies of the recipes might be in circulation. It was as though he didn't have to ask, as if he already knew. Or maybe he knew nothing at all and preferred ignorance. But that was never Uncle Nunzio's way. Vinny was feeling light-headed and found a seat.

Minutes later he called me away from the bar and made me swear to secrecy everything that had happened. I consented. It was easy. I had no intention of divulging a thing. I was too humiliated by being a participant in the whole sleazy episode. I should have intervened more forcefully; instead, I was completely intimidated by Wes Fitzgerald and his harrowing appetite for violence. I could have called the police, then I feared my brother might be tried, convicted and sent to prison for kidnapping. The kidnapping of a priest would have turned any jury venomous toward the defendant. I could have called on Jablonsky, though I wasn't sure I trusted him either. In any event, the probability was high that he and Fitzgerald would have old-fashioned shootout and somebody would end up dead, probably an innocent bystander like me.

No, I had no interest in letting others know how cowardly I had acted. Anybody would have plainly seen that some act of gallantry was in order.

Vinny demanded that Fitzgerald honor the same vow. The crazed detective said, "All my work is strictly confidential. Besides, I get my rocks off on knowing things other people don't."

Vinny called a mandatory family meeting that evening. We found ourselves sitting around the boardroom table yet again. Everybody's blood pressure was elevated. The barometric pressure in that room was so high my joints were hurting. Everybody was staring at Vinny as he said, "This is an emergency meeting of the Board of Directors of Marciano's Mangia House."

"Yeah, we get that," Maria said. She had the night off and was called to the premises from home, where she and Shekko Lombardi had been watching a pornographic film about erotic happenings behind some colored door.

"The recipes have been found," Vinny announced. "They are now in Uncle Nunzio's safe deposit box at Marine Midland Bank."

The room erupted. Questions flew. Declarations and accusations crossed the room like arrows.

"What do you mean 'found?'" father said. "You mean here, on the property?"

"They were stolen. The case was cracked by that private detective I hired, Wes Fitzgerald."

"Oh, that ugly cuss," said Ginger, a sour expression stamped on her face.

"Who stole them?" Ringo called out from the far end of table.

"I'm not at liberty to say," Vinny said.

Mother had a shocked look on her face. Father said, "Are you kidding me? After all this you're not going to tell us who did this?"

"It was not a family member," Vinny said.

Angie pounded a fist on the table and went into a series of conniptions. "I've been telling you that all along and you've been too thick-headed to listen."

Mother said, "It was one of those damn employees, wasn't it?"

"Our employees are all innocent. Or at least not guilty."

Mother said, "Well then who in blazes took them?"

"I told you, I've been asked to keep that a secret. That's all I can tell you right now." Then Vinny bolted from the room. Then I started getting questioned. Everyone in the room knew Vinny and I had been spending an inordinate amount of time together.

"I have no idea what he's talking about," I said, but nobody believed me. I was one of the world's most transparent liars. I got up and bolted in much the same fashion.

The next evening sergeant detective Clyde Jablonski showed up with Ginger strapped around his hip like a holster for his other weapon. Vinny immediately led him downstairs and into the boardroom to prevent him from saying anything around the crowd that might raise eyebrows.

"Your investigation is over," Vinny told Jablonsky. "Case solved and closed."

"So your sister tells me. Who committed the crime?" The lawman's voice was half-an-octave higher than usual, his vocal chords still frostbitten by the devastating cold outside air.

"Thank you for your service I this matter. It has been very much appreciated."

"Protecting the guilty?"

"It's just one of those things."

"I would like to know that my time was not wasted, nor taxpayer dollars."

"Well aren't you the vanguard of the public trust," Vinny said.

"Am I going to have to investigate the solving of this crime?"

"You just stand down," Vinny snapped.

"I'm told that Fitzgerald solved this one."

Vinny nodded without enthusiasm.

"You handled this whole thing very shabbily," Jablonski said. "I'm starting to think that somehow you were involved, that you had an ulterior motive for creating this big drama."

Vinny riled. "You know, Fitzgerald is right, your nose is way too straight to be a real cop. Unfortunately, there are dire consequences for assaulting a police officer. Otherwise I'd slug you in the face right now and add a crook to that schnoz. Maybe then you'd look a little more authentic."

"You think you could take me?" Jablonsky said, gazing downward at Vinny. Tall men carried with them the conceit of physical superiority. This was an illusion, never mind the detective's martial arts training. Jablonsky had leverage and reach, but there is no substitute for strength and having a lower center of gravity.

"Yeah, I do."

"Maybe one day I'll leave my Glock and badge at home and we can settle the question."

Vinny fell back into the leather chair at the head of the boardroom table, crossed his legs and smiled. "I would look forward to that."

Jablonsky's leather boots and jacket creaked as they left the room.

A night later, Wes Fitzgerald took a seat at the bar. I could see he had just gotten a semi-professional haircut. I smelled sewage, which I associated with evil, every time he came around. This time, though, he was sporting a mood I didn't think was part of his repertoire: joviality. Apparently his bonus check had cleared the bank. He was in a mood to spend. He ordered a shot of Jameson and a Sam Adams draft. I lit his cigarette with my Zippo flip-top butane lighter and considered moving the flame to the side of his head and setting his greasy hair on fire, or adding some additional blistering to his scabrous complexion. He knocked back the shot of Jameson and let out a king-of-the-jungle roar as the whiskey burned his belly. That earned him a searing glance from my wife Sadie, who was sitting five stools down. She made a rare appearance at the restaurant to complain to me about how badly she was treated during a shopping trip earlier that day. She always worked up an appetite with her incessant complaints, so she ordered a veal parmagiana with a side order of angel hair pasta with marinara sauce.

Sadie was bemoaning the poor customer service from both the sales clerk and general manager at Boscov's department store at the Oakdale Mall in Johnson City.

"The general manager?" I said.

"The sales clerk in the ladies clothing department was so rude I told her I wanted to see the manager."

I sighed. "This happens to you over and over again, Sadie. I'm sure you're not being singled out. Maybe it's something about your manner, or maybe your expectations are too high."

My wife's face flushed an angry shade of crimson as she arched a lethal eyebrow toward me. Fitzgerald was starting to take notice.

"I might need to go to confession," Fitzgerald quipped, that diabolical smile spreading across the face.

I held a finger to my lips to *shush* him, concerned he would carry the remark further, maybe breaking into: *Forgive me Father for I have sinned, I use a priest's head as a punching bag two nights ago.*

As soon as I put the finger to lips I knew it was a mistake. Fitzgerald gave me a murderous look. He shoved the empty shot glass across the bar said, "Another one." He was already halfway through his sixteen-ounce Sam Adams. I refilled the shot glass and set it in front of him. He knocked it back immediately and unloaded another high-volume roar.

Sadie fired another seething glance at Fitzgerald. "I hope you have an insurance policy on yourself," she said.

"Listen to Mrs. Secret Shopper down there," Fitzgerald said. He could tell from that big head of red hair and her feisty temperament that Sadie was at least half Irish.

Before Sadie could launch a rejoinder, I interrupted. "Detective Fitzgerald, this is my wife Sadie. Sadie, meet detective Wes Fitzgerald."

"Oh, well, this is Mrs. Marciano, I guess I better watch my P's and Q's," he said, the statement dripping with sarcasm.

I huddled close to Sadie and said, "Don't get into it with him. I don't need either of you to create a scene right now."

"You're pretty girl," Fitzgerald called down the bar. "You should have a nicer disposition."

"Yeah, right, because you're Mr. Congeniality," Sadie said.

I stuck a menu in front of Fitzgerald. "What can I get you?"

"Another Sam Adams."

"How about some spaghetti and meatballs? You really liked them last time."

"Yeah, what the fuck. I am a little hungry."

Sadie started complaining about a headache, a chronic condition in her world. Her head split like a pair of tectonic plates at least a few days a month. Her psychosomatic ailments had been sucking the marrow out of our relationship since we married five years previous.

When my wife finished her plate she pushed it away and said, "Well, I'm bored." Soon, she was slipping off the barstool and leaving the premises. She didn't even kiss me before making a wordless departure. I kept an eye on Fitzgerald make sure he didn't follow Sadie's movements or ID her vehicle. When spaghetti and meatballs arrived Fitzgerald launched a full frontal attack. It was one of the most cruel assaults on an entrée I had ever seen. The bowl was emptied in record time. Fitzgerald took out his detective's notebook and scribbled, then slid it across the bar. I looked. It read, "Have you heard from the priest?"

I shook my head.

"All that pomp and mystery surrounding them and they're really just ordinary schmucks," he said. "Just a lot of pretense, if you ask me." He sucked again at his Sam Adams. "I gotta hand it to your brother, he made good on his word. Of course, what choice did he have? He either paid or I would've stolen that goddamn ceiling painting out of the dining room and held for ransom. That would've been worth at least ten grand."

I changed the subject by asking who he like for this season's Super Bowl.

"Nobody. I'm a Jets fan. I've haven't had anything to cheer about since Weeb Ewbank was coaching and Matt Snell and Emerson Boozer were running the football."

"What about Joe Namath? You didn't mention Broadway Joe."

"The guy with the knees and the pantyhose? You gotta be fuckin' kidding. Don't you know anything about me?"

Two guys at the bar, old enough to remember the '67 Jets, got into a discussion with Fitzgerald. It was a welcome distraction, something to occupy the beast. In time, though, he turned back to me, the corners of his mouth glowing red with the residual pasta sauce. The Joker from a Batman episode came to mind.

"Where's Vinny? I need to talk to him." Then he pinged the shot glass with a fingernail and said, "I'll take it on the road."

"What does that asshole want?" Vinny said when I buzzed is office extension.

"No idea. Maybe your check bounced."

Vinny led Fitzgerald out a side EMERGENCY exit and into the frozen night, using the intolerable weather as an insurance policy the conversation would be a short one. They buried their hands in their coat pockets and hunched their shoulders to preserve their core body temperatures. Vinny still was still not convinced the man was capable of feeling heat, cold or pain.

Fitzgerald opened with: "Why not hire me as security around here? Monthly retainer, with a few set evening hours. You get big crowds. I could keep the peace, keep everything in order."

Vinny figured that Fitzgerald knew deep pockets when he saw them. For weeks Vinny had paid all of the detective's fees and expenses immediately and in cash, so Fitzgerald could cheat on his taxes. Then came the $10,000 bounty for retrieving the filched recipes. Anybody could see the place was awash in money.

Vinny thought to himself that it wouldn't be bad to have a Doberman at his disposal. That's how he thought of Fitzgerald, as is Doberman, even though he wasn't as good-looking as a Doberman. Then again, he didn't need the guy on retainer; one could always call in the vicious dog when needed.

"I can't have you prowling the place. It wouldn't be good for business. Too menacing. I assume you know that about yourself."

It occurred to Vinny that ruffians like Fitzgerald used to help run America's cities during its crude early years when gangland bosses made decisions and sent their henchmen to enforce their edicts. Now guys like him were more like rare animals that had escaped from the zoo. This was about the time Vinny was expecting Fitzgerald to do a 1930's era shakedown, saying something approximating: *You have a nice place here. Be a shame if something happened to it. Probably a good idea to reconsider my offer.* That evening several windows would be busted out, and Fitzgerald would come back around the next day to explain how the incident never would have happened if he was on the payroll and keeping vigil over the Mangia House.

Instead the private eye came back with: "The first time we met, your girlfriend was cheating. At least you thought so. Was that at a complete fabrication or might she be two-timing you? Something you need invested?"

The air was so cold that each time one of them spoke they were puffing like locomotives.

"What girlfriend?" Vinny said.

Fitzgerald raised his eyebrows.

"I don't date women, I fuck them."

The detective smiled at the remark. This time it was in approving smile rather than a harrowing one. "You're a man's man," he said, "that's why I like working for you. You also pay your bills on time and in full. What the hell happened your brothers? One's afraid of dogs, the other one is a basketball fan and has no taste at all for the rough-and-tumble stuff."

Vinny didn't have a reply. During the silences the only sounds were muted shouts from the kitchen and ice flow of the passing Susquehanna.

"Don't suppose a priest will be coming around anymore."

Vinny looked upriver. "I called him, just to check. He's okay. He's sore. He's healing."

"I think he's got a concussion. Maybe two. You should have heard him praying when I forced my way into his pad. He was crying out for Mother Mary like a little boy. All the while I was whipping him like a stepchild."

Vinny kept gazing at the frozen horizon. "Forsaken by the Mother of God," he said to no one in particular, producing eight puffs of vapor with the remark. "I'd say the man's faith has been shaken."

"I could stay on him," Fitzgerald said, "just in case there are some copies."

That only made Vinny think that perhaps Fitzgerald made a copy or two for himself. They might come in handy if the detective's hardscrabble life got any more difficult along the way. With a look and manner like Fitzgerald's there was no telling how much business he was chasing off with first impressions alone.

"Still don't understand how a man dressed like a priest could get all the way to that safe without anybody noticing him in a place this busy," Fitzgerald said. "Never did get a straight answer out of the guy about how he pulled that one off."

"Would do you think happened?"

"Don't know." Two more puffs of vapor appeared and then vanished. "I'm not in the business of not knowing, so I hate to say 'don't know,' but sometimes you just don't know. Further interrogation would be required."

Their evanescent conversation chugged on into the night.

Vinny attended Sunday morning mass. The curiosity was too great. He sat in the back pew of Our Lady of the Immaculate Conception and saw Father Benito Saragusa take the pulpit. Pews were three-quarters full. The priest was still looking woebegone even from this distance. Skin discolorations from the beating were still in evidence. His abasement had been total, and it showed in his movements, his expressions and the chastened tone of his voice.

Candles burned in red votive containers, the stained-glass windows glittered with supernal images, incense perfumed the air with frankincense and myrrh, and then the organ bellowed, bringing the Sunday service to life. The church was so large, so ornate, so immaculate. Saragusa moved slowly into place and addressed the congregation meekly, still recouping his strength from the night he was forcibly descend into hades.

Vinny felt no guilt, sorrow or justification. He felt nothing at all.

"In the name of the Father, the Son, the Holy Ghost," Saragusa began.

Saragusa would go through his ministrations in perfect order, just as they had been ritualized and sanctified by the Vatican centuries ago. The proceedings would move from biblical readings to homily to creed to intercessions. There would be the preparation of the Eucharist and then the symbolic distribution of the body and blood of Christ during Holy Communion.

"A reading from the Holy Gospel according to Luke," Saragusa announced.

*Can a blind man lead a blind man?*
*Will they not both fall into a pit?*
*A disciple is not above his teacher,*
*but every one when he is fully taught will be like his teacher.*

By this point the priest had spotted his prodigal parishioner sitting against the back wall and looked directly into his eyes and said…

*Why do you see the speck that is in your brother's eye,*
*but do not notice the log that is in your own eye?*
*Or how can you say to your brother,*
*"Brother, let me take out the speck that is in your eye,"*
*when you yourself do not see the log that is in your own eye?*
*You hypocrite, first take the log out of your own eye,*
*and then you will see clearly to take out the speck that is in your brother's eye*

His eyes had been fixed on Vinny for several moments, only looking away when my brother started blinking A couple of congregants peeked over their shoulders to see who the pastor was targeting.

The liturgy rolled on. The parishioners chimed in to echo the clergyman's declarations. Then the man in the black vestments and white collar climbed to an elevated position, stationing himself at a separate lectern and microphone, the one reserved for his sermons, and started in, speaking about the wages of sin. The sound system was excellent, his voice crashing through the speakers as his voice gained volume and cadence. He started to rail. Several heads nodded in agreement.

Then his volume quickly fell as he receded back into his everyman role as the imperfect child of God, the sinner, the corrupted. It was not a role he assumed very often. Saragusa believed a priest had to maintain a higher stance in life. Imperfect, yes, but more perfect than thou; elsewise, why would one follow the scrappy little holy man? His eyes grazed Vinny's again and again.

"Separation from God does deplorable things to good people," he cried. "Let us pray."

The gathering recited the Nicene Creed in unison with Saragusa.

*We believe in one holy Catholic and apostolic Church.*
*We acknowledge one baptism for the forgiveness of sins.*
*We look for the resurrection of the dead,*
*and the life of the world to come.*
*Amen.*

Vinny crossed himself out of habit.

The collection basket came around. Vinny dropped a twenty, even though he didn't want to contribute. One had to keep up appearances when a businessman who was perceived as an upstanding member of the community and church.

Just before Father Saragusa called his flock to the altar to partake of the Eucharist, Vinny quietly slipped out of the church.

Seventeen days after the melodrama at the abandoned Binghamton warehouse, Father Benito Saragusa returned to Marciano's Mangia House. It was ninety minutes before opening. He was knocking at a door. I acknowledged his arrival with a slight bow, then made the sign of the cross. He did the same, as though returning a salute.

Vinny was in the kitchen sharpening his cutlery again. His face had the same homicidal expression it always did while sharpening blades. My brother's cheeks tensed when I told him who had come calling.

"He's devoted his life to the Catholic Church," I said. "He's never even been with a woman. Show the man some charity."

Vinny removed his apron and walked to the dining room. There he was in his ever-present black vestments. Vinny kept a cool distance and a chilly expression, slightly angling his face so just one of his two incredulous eyeballs was visible.

"I haven't been able to sleep," Saragusa said. "I wake up during the night with a thudding chest."

Vinny gestured toward a booth and they sat. There was an interval of silence between the two men as they settled and examined one another. More than ever, Saragusa he was looking like a rodent. His shrunken head still had some vague markings of the beating he had taken from Wes Fitzgerald. The starbursts of pain were fresh in his memory.

"I have a trip to Vatican coming up, my annual pilgrimage. I need to clear my conscience before going and having meetings with members of the Catholic hierarchy."

"With the Pope?"

"His lieutenants. The Pontiff is virtually unreachable. One day, I hope. Come with me Vinny. Come to the Vatican. I want to bring you back into the fold. Don't let my transgressions chase you off the path. I couldn't live with myself if my actions caused to you abandon your religion."

"You committed a mortal sin, Father."

"Well, actually, it was a venial sin. Still, you have no idea how many times I've recited the Act of Contrition."

"How *could* you?" Vinny hissed. "Look at the mess you've left me in. You *knew* this was tearing me apart, that my family was in crisis. You *knew* I had falsely accused my own kin. You took my confessions and didn't return those recipes. I could have lost the restaurant. I could call the Vatican about this Father." Vinny saw a glint of fear come to Saragusa's eyes. "What would the local bishop think of this kind of behavior from one his ordained?"

Saragusa place his hands and elbows on the table and leaned forward to speak in a hushed voice. "Look," he said, "I have no other excuse than I needed the money. Everyone thinks the Catholic Church is so rich. My parish's finances are in shambles; we needed a cash infusion. People don't worship the way they used to. Our numbers are dwindling. The collection baskets bring in half what they used to. People have lost their belief. They have trouble conceiving of the supernatural. Meanwhile, we have a large, magnificent church that needs constant maintenance. There is a gardener taking care of the grounds. There is my residence, salary and my Lincoln Continental. Don't get me started on how much it costs to house, clothe and feed the nuns. It all costs. People don't understand the material sacrifices we make, the vows of chastity, poverty and obedience that we take. It's a very restrictive life, an ascetic life. Then I come here a day or two every week and I see you, Vinny, eating, drinking and carousing like Dionysus. You haven't exactly had a heavy cross to bear. I know you've given, Vinny, I'm not saying you haven't shared your good fortune with the Lord. It's just that your contribution has not been commensurate with your ability to give. The church relies most on those like you, people of means, people who have been blessed. To whom much has been given, much will be required. Do I have to resort to Luke 12:48? Do I have to resort to the clichés?

Vinny was turning crimson over the priest's excuses.

"I was seduced. I come in here a few times a week and I see transactions going on all around me. There's a river of money flowing through this place every night. You don't seem to have a real appreciation for this blessing your uncle handed over to you."

Vinny went incandescent and started spluttering at the notion that the full faith, credit and prosperity of the restaurant was completely attributable to Uncle Nunzio and Uncle Nunzio alone, as if it had been a free ride for Vinny. Saragusa held up a hand to deactivate the young man. "I know you've done your part," he said. "My point still stands. You've been blessed. You are swimming in abundance. I didn't think I would do any harm by dipping the bucket in just once."

"*Half a million bucks,*" Vinny growled. "Do you know how many nights that river has to flow for me to make that kind of money?"

"I was foolish. I rationalized that maybe God would understand. I mean, look around this place, Vinny. Nudity galore. I've been after you for years about the temptations. Instead you ignored me, and the bacchanalia kept increasing." His eyes grazed the painting on the wall next to them, depicting of two semi-nude lovers laying in post-coital fatigue. "Then came the capper, the ultimate insult." Saragusa gestured to the ceiling. "The breasts have multiplied, and now there are penises too."

"It's a religious scene, Father, I thought you would approve, you would see the glory in it. There are religion writers at newspapers around the state who have hailed this piece of work; they have drawn comparisons to the Sistine Chapel; my god, Father, the Vatican."

"Do you even pray anymore Vinny?"

"Every morning Father, and it's the same prayer every time: 'Oh God make me good, but not yet.'"

I want you to pray for me. I might be a priest but I'm still a man of imperfections. I meant no harm."

Vinny sniffed.

"I feel God has forgiven me; I feel I have the capacity to forgive myself. I'm asking the same of you. It would be the Christian thing to do. It would be the Catholic thing to do."

"I don't know that I can forgive. It's too soon."

"I'm so ashamed; you must be able to see that."

"Are there copies? Of the recipes?"

"Absolutely not."

"Do you swear to God?"

"Yes, I do."

"Wait here." When he returned Vinny was dusting off a rarely used Bible with a damp paper towel. He set the Word of God on the table and directed Saragusa to place his left hand on top of it and to raise his right.

"Do you swear — with God as your witness and the ultimate Judge of your eternal fate — that you made no other copies of the recipes and that none are in your, or anybody else's, possession?"

Saragusa's eyes were filled with sincerity as he locked on Vinny's eyes and said, "I swear to God, and I swear to you, Vinny. I swear on my mother's grave and I swear on Holy Cross of the Savior. There are no copies."

Vinny's body relaxed. It was the last fear pending. Now he had an answer. Now he felt back in control of his destiny.

Saragusa said: "Now promise me something, that that gorilla you sent after me will never around again. I've come into possession of a firearm." His voice cracked with the disclosure. "Never thought the day would come. I'd rather shoot and kill him then be abducted and tortured again. There's a part of my psyche that is been demolished."

"I didn't know he would do that, Father."

"What does your Uncle Nunizo know?"

"He never asked."

Another magnitude of stress lifted from the priest's body.

"Isn't that curious," Vinny said, closely appraising Saragusa's reaction through a squinted left eye, as though pinching and holding a monocle in place. The priest looked back at Vinny dumbly. "Uncle Nunzio is a man who always wants an explanation of the details. As big a deal as this was, he isn't asking. Isn't that curious?"

Saragusa's hands plead ignorance.

"I'm astounded. It's as if he already knows. Did you say something to him?"

"No."

"Did he say something to you?"

"Absolutely not."

Vinny walked Father Saragusa to the door. It was a slow, lonely walk. "I hope you will start coming to the Mangia House again, as long as it's just to eat. People have missed you, Father. They've been asking. Our customers are comforted by your presence and they enjoy your personality. You have been a fixture here for a long time. I would like to have you back."

Saragusa gave a sad nod. Vinny opened the door and the priest, in all his blackness, disappeared into the white flurry of a snowstorm.

The Christmas holiday came and went without the true spirit of Christmas ever being expressed. We all attended midnight mass on Christmas Eve. New Year's Eve and New Year's Day also came and went with the less-than-usual quotient of drinking and merriment. The spirit of the entire holiday season was muted by scandal and family dysfunction.

The falsely accused gathered around the restaurant's boardroom table one week into the New Year. It was a Marciano family annual tradition, during which we listened to Vinny wax clumsily about the year past and announce what kind of cash disbursement each member the family would receive from the pool of retained earnings the Mangia House had generated. This was always a time of great anticipation, even though certain family members were never satisfied their bonuses. This time was different. Vinny dispensed with the preamble and went straight for the numbers, announcing that each and every one of us would receive a $65,000 bonus check — and that meant even Angie and Maria, who Vinny figured might use the money for evil purposes.

We were all more or less stunned. A lot of money had been spent the previous year to upgrade the physical facilities, let alone pay for Enrico Zepeda's fresco and the grand ball that had been staged for its unveiling. Then there were the many thousands spent on private detective Wes Fitzgerald, which only I was privy to.

"We ended the year exceptionally strong because people have been coming in droves from around the Northeast to see the fresco." Vinny smiled meekly at me. "I expect it will continue generating big crowds."

Maria couldn't help herself. She was smiling broadly. Angie was the exception. She would not be placated and still had a hideous look on her gimlet-eyed face. Vinny was obviously trying to buy his favor back into the family, she surmised, and this was just a form of indulgence. She was having none of it.

Mother Margherita, unfazed by the money she and Father Albie had just received, said: "When are you going to tell us who stole those gosh darn recipes?"

Vinny and I were the only ones who knew, and perhaps Uncle Nunzio. It would stay that way out of respect for Father Saragusa, despite how egregiously he had trespassed on our lives.

The meeting gradually dissipated. Mother and father went home and watched TV. So did Ringo. Angie went out to dinner with Hans Sprink and plotted her defection. Ginger had a round of vigorous sex with sergeant detective Clyde Jablonski, who she was getting ever more deeply involved with. Until the leather-clad Jablonsky had come along, Ginger was operating under the assumption that she was the future Mrs. Brad Pitt. Maria went home and lied to Shekko Lombardi, telling him that the bonus totaled only $25,000 to ensure he would not confiscate the full bonus for his own purposes. The balance would go into Maria's secret bank account. I sent an email to my financial planner to set up a meeting and plan for my future with Sadie.

Vinny headed to the rectory at Our Lady of the Immaculate Conception Church and the residence of Father Benito Saragusa. When he knocked he could hear a sudden rustling behind the door.

"Who is it?" His voice sounded especially nasal.

"Father, it's me, Vinny. Sorry for the surprise visit. I want to give you something."

Saragusa cracked the door and peered past Vinny to see if he had brought along any muscle. Vinny could tell from the little man's posture that he had the side of his foot braced against the bottom of the door to guard against a strong-arm entry. He might have also had a loaded firearm at hand. That concerned Vinny. The nervous and an inexperienced person with a handgun was likely to accidentally shoot somebody, most likely himself.

"It's okay Father. I'm alone. I just came by to hand something off to you." Vinny flashed a white envelope.

The priest cautiously backed away from the door and provided Vinny with just the opening he needed to slip in, and nothing more. Then the door was quickly shut and double dead-bolted.

Saragusa tried to find a less frenetic state of mind as he sat and grimaced at Vinny. The elder man thought being a select member of the priesthood had given him immunity from the bad people in this world, certainly immunity from physical assault. What kind of person would do such a thing to a clergyman? It had been a violation beyond violations. How could a human being come so undone? That man lived in the area. He could be the cat with the mouse and keep coming back and toying with him. Fitzgerald's giant, Buick LeSabre with its gaudy paint job kept rolling through his mind.

Physically, Saragusa he had pretty much recovered. Psychologically, he had decided that he was damaged for life. He would never have another sound night's sleep. His heart would never beat regularly again. Even worse than that, it made Saragusa ask himself the unthinkable: Is there really a God? If there was a God, how could he let something like this happen to *me*, a man of God, one who had devoted his life to the Savior? What happened to grace? He wanted an explanation.

My God, Vinny thought, looking at the diminished figure before him, what have I done? Vinny was experiencing an entirely new emotion. It was called shame.

"I want you to have this." Vinny handed over the envelope.

"The Christmas card you forgot?" Saragusa asked.

Vinny frowned and shook his head.

"Should I open it?"

"Please."

Saragusa tore into the envelope and pulled out a single slip of paper that he immediately recognized as a check. It was tinted green and was made payable to Our Lady of the Immaculate Conception in the amount of $50,000.

Saragusa's eyes bulged. "Vinny ... what is the meaning of this?"

"What you did was almost unforgivable Father, but I still wanted to help. I've been attending the church since I was a little boy, and I know this institution means everything to you. You were right when you told me that I've been blessed. I want to share some of my good fortune."

Saragusa's eyes misted.

"I also want to compensate you for the pain and suffering. If I had not hired that detective I probably never would have caught you. But he also went way out of bounds with you. I know that. I went there too. It was a blind rage. It wasn't very Catholic of me. I hope you can find it in your heart to forgive me Father."

A babel of Catholic incantations started coming out of the priest's mouth. He came to his feet and used the edge of his hand to trace the sign of the cross in the air in front of Vinny's face. He ended with, "May the Lord bless you."

Both men were on their feet now. They hugged.

"I'll let myself out Father." Vinny exited the rectory. Father Benito Saragusa watched after him, waving as Vinny and his Ford Econoline van, that Sodom and Gomorrah on wheels, pulled away.